THE SCANDAL

OF

NATHANIEL THOROLD

A Fact Based Novel

by

John Reed

Published in Great Britain by jrrpublishing

eMail; jrrpublishing@virginmedia.com

Web; www.johnreedbooks.co.uk

e. johnrr@ruskington3753.plus.com

ISBN 978-0-9929117-1-3

Acknowledgements

I would like to thank my wife Lynne for her continued patience during the assembling of this book, particularly during the later stages when I was working to get it print ready.

I am also indebted to the members of the Pudsey Library Writers Group for their help and encouragement in all aspects of my attempts at writing, particularly Roger Barton and Barry Fox.

I must not forget Judi Blackstone who took the trouble to proof read the book and save me many hours of valuable time.

My son Simon designed my website through which I am able to sell this and my previous book about my childhood in Ruskington.

Prologue

I was brought up on a council estate in Lincolnshire and there were frequent rumours in our family which we were always keen to perpetuate. These concerned a long lost ancestor who had fled to Capri and spent the family fortune.

A few years ago whilst I was researching my family history I discovered there was at least a grain of truth in the rumour. I found several references to a Nathaniel Thorold, an ancestor through my mother's side who might just fit the bill.

Although his early life was a mystery, I found plenty of references to his later life which included setting up a very successful business in Naples, an unconventional relationship with a married couple which resulted in a complaint to the Pope saying, 'A *scandal has been caused on the island by the co-habitation of a certain married woman with an heretic English nobleman and that they are continually behaving in a flagrant manner in public causing distress and dismay among the population.*'

He also inherited a large estate at Harmston from a distant cousin and an obituary said he ran through his fortune and deeply in debt went abroad in 1745. Intriguingly the will in which he inherited the estate in 1738 identifies Nathaniel already in Naples so there is a discrepancy with the obituary.

On Capri, he built the most exclusive mansion which was known as the 'Palazzo Inglese' where he lived with his unconventional family for the rest of his life. On his death his 'wife' panicked because she thought there was no will and not being married she was entitled to nothing so she got a local scribe to write one in her favour. Two real wills surfaced and were so complicated that they were being contested in London nearly one hundred years later.

His rise from being a farmer's son who built a reputation as a gambler, spendthrift, and adventurer who escaped the clutches of money lenders by leaving the country, to founding and running a successful business, inheriting the Harmston Estates and being Knighted, was the stuff of legends.

This book is a fictional version of Nathanial's life based around facts gathered from published sources. It covers his life from birth on a farm in the Grantham area of Lincolnshire to his death in October 1764.

John Reed
October 2014

PART 1

The

Reluctant Farmer

Chapter 1
July 1734

The kitchen door burst open and the red faced cowman, dripping water where he stood, yelled, 'For God's sake Nat, the bastards are already at Stamford and there are six of them!'

Terrified, Nathaniel leapt up from his breakfast table and gave urgent orders to prepare his horse and get some supplies packed for a long journey. A journey that was to test his resolve and his ability to overcome some of life's hardships.

As Mo was leaving to get things moving, Nathaniel shouted, 'You are coming with me Mo, so get your horse saddled up as well. Make sure the dogs are locked up, we don't want them following us, and don't hang about!'

'Right boss, I'll get on with it, but if you are in such a bloody hurry then we will have to take George with us. He's not the brightest but he is the best man we have with horses and for safety's sake we need a third man.'

'If you insist, but get on with it.' said Nathaniel, in too much of a panic to argue.

***

He had just had a sleepless night knowing that the debt collectors would be on their way but he had not expected them for a couple of days. His hopes that the recent stormy weather would have delayed their journey North from London to Lincolnshire were in vain. If the heavy mob was only fifteen miles away then he had to get out of here and as far away as possible immediately.

There was absolutely no way he could raise the cash the collectors wanted and he was not prepared to risk a spell in Nottingham debtors prison. He was also aware that the practice of nailing the ear of a debtor to a post, although now discontinued, still happened in some country areas. In short, he was scared stiff and in a state of panic.

***

His last trip to London was all a bit of a blur. He had spent a great deal of time drinking and gambling and he knew he had lost heavily. He had difficulty remembering exactly what he had lost but the stakes were high and he knew that at one point he had put the farm up as collateral to cover his losses. However, he remembered that he had clawed back most of the money, but after that, his memory was a blank. When he awoke in the morning, still in the chair at the gaming table, his pockets were empty and he began to fear the worst. With trembling fingers he unpinned a scruffy piece of paper attached to his waistcoat and with a sinking feeling in the pit of his stomach, read the scrawled message 'Nathaniel Thorold, you have exactly two months to repay your debt or we will be along to escort you to Nottingham debtors prison.'

The two months expired yesterday!

***

The rain had eased and it was turning into what promised to be a beautiful summer morning. The birds were singing, swallows swooped through and round the buildings and swifts screamed as they flew at high speed catching air-borne insects, in what appeared to be a game of chase the leader. However, whilst the general atmosphere was still tranquil, everyone was rushing around like demented ants trying to do the master's bidding. Orders were being shouted, horses were being readied, clothes were being packed and provisions for the long journey were prepared.

Nathaniel had already packed his personal items in a locked box a few days earlier in readiness for such an event. The pair of prized pistols he had bought from his gun maker friend, Richard Pearson, had been checked over and plenty of ammunition was made readily available. He had bought them at a bargain price but had not paid Richard in full, and as he had packed them he wondered why he had not been approached for the remainder, but in truth he couldn't care less.

***

Nathaniel Thorold was a thirty year old Gentleman farmer who had a penchant for the poker tables of London. Over a long period of time he had built up debts which he was finding difficult to settle, and like most gamblers, he always thought his next game would win it all back. As an only son he had been brought up in comparative wealth and as a consequence developed from a lonely, weak child into an arrogant self-centred young man who thought the world revolved around him and him alone. He was also a domineering bore who had a problem seeing any other point of view but his own.

His late father had worried endlessly about his persistent fraternising with the workforce and despaired of him ever developing into a man who could deal successfully with his subordinates. His domineering and arrogant

2

attitude to others was probably born out of an underlying shyness and an overreaction to the inability to gain the respect of his workers.

Practical things never interested Nathaniel, but he had a sharp mind and, apart from his gambling, a razor sharp ability to sort out problems. When his father had died, Nathaniel was only nineteen years old and the estates were left to him even though he had never shown the slightest interest in farming. However, because of his age, and his father's concern for Nathaniel's general attitude, everything was left in the hands of trustees until he reached the age of twenty five.

Nathaniel's father had quickly decided that if Nathaniel was ever going to run the estates successfully after the trustees had handed them over, he needed to widen his administrative skills and learn to take his responsibilities seriously. He concluded that some form of business experience was essential and so arranged for him to go to London to study business with a distant cousin, Samuel Thorold.

***

Mo Clark was Nathaniel's head cowman and drinking partner. He was a couple of years older than Nathaniel and was born in one of the estate cottages. He had worked on the farm from a very early age and had been made head stockman in his early twenties shortly before Nathaniel's father had died. Maurice was a short, powerful, red faced man who could handle himself in a crisis. He had been an invaluable help to Nathaniel on more than one occasion. He had a pronounced limp as a result of an accident involving a fall from a horse when in a race with Nathaniel as a young man. Maurice and Nathaniel had known each other as long as they could remember.

***

'What the hell's going on Mo?' called out John, as Mo came out of the manor house, 'what's the panic about?'

'The boss has blown it this time and he's doing a runner. The collectors are in Stamford and will be here by midday, so he is out of here and taking me with him. I haven't a clue where we are going and I don't think he knows himself.'

'Well, it looks as if it's up to me to keep things going then. It would have been nice if he had told me.' said John.

'You will be OK John, you've done it all before and the boss trusts you. Sorry I can't stop but I must get on, he's going berserk in there.'

***

John Fowler was the farm manager and in charge of the entire workforce. He had been working for the estate since marrying Edith, Mo's eldest sister, and lived on the farm with Edith and their two children. John got on well with Mo but he made it plain that he thought that Mo was too close to Nathaniel and he should not get involved in Nathaniel's spendthrift ways.

Mo lived in a small thatched cottage on the edge of the farm with his mother and other sister, Ivy. His family had lived there for several generations and all the male members had worked on the farm in some capacity or other. The cottage was one of a group of six and although, in accordance with his status as a foreman, it was one of the better ones, it was still very basic. There was one room on the ground floor and an upstairs room built into the roof space, which was accessed by a wooden ladder. Headroom was very limited and a small window provided a minimum of natural light. Beds were bare wooden boards with a straw filled mattress on top, covers were no more than old discarded pieces of woollen cloth sewn together to form blankets to keep out the worst of the cold. A small partition gave a minimum amount of privacy for Mo's mother and sister and Mo had his bed at the other end of the room. The only other item of furniture was a small locally made, rough-hewn chair.

Downstairs the living room had a rough table placed centrally and four three-legged stools which had originally been made for use as milking stools. An open fire was used for heat and cooking. All water had to be drawn from the well behind the manor house.

***

After he had left Nathaniel, Mo rushed round to collect a few essential items for the trip and tell his mother what was going on.

'How long are you going to be away?' asked Ivy, Mo's mother. 'Where do you think you are going?'

'I've no idea where we are going or how long we will be away, just that I have got to get ready very quickly and have no time to hang around talking.'

'Well' said Lill, Mo's sister 'that's typical, he just up sticks and expects you to jump.'

'I've no choice, he's my boss and our landlord and he has always been good to me. Besides, he is a good mate and he relies on me for lots of things. He is in real trouble and if he doesn't go now, we could all be out of a job and a house if these men get their hands on him. He needs time to clear things up and he will not get it by staying here.'

'If you don't know where you are going, promise you will let me know how you are getting on and where you are.'

'Of course I will, Mum. I'll let you know what's going on when I find out myself.'

Sounding full of self-pity, Ivy whined, 'I don't know how we will get by without you to look after us Maurice, we rely on you for everything. There is only Lill and me now your Dad has passed on, and if you leave, it will make things very difficult for us.'

'When are you going?' asked Lill forcibly, interrupting her mother.

'Now' said Mo. 'Don't worry about me, John's staying here and will make sure you are OK.' With that he gave them each a quick kiss and was gone.

'I hope they know what they are doing' said Ivy and promptly burst into tears.

***

'Where are those bloody horses,' shouted Nathaniel and 'where the hell is Mo? I can't stand here all day waiting for a lot of useless incompetents, for God's sake get a move on. You lot, get on with your work and stop cackling like a lot of stupid chickens.'

***

In the kitchen, oblivious to the events out in the yard, Sylvia Butler the cook, cum housekeeper was muttering to herself as she cleared up the half-eaten breakfast, 'Don't these people ever appreciate what a cook does for them? I sometimes wonder if they know we even exist!' and then, as she turned away from the table, 'at least the dogs will enjoy it.'

Sylvia had been employed by the Thorold's since she was a young girl of about fourteen years of age and had never married. She 'lived in' even though she had close relatives in the village. Her work was her life, and she looked after Nathaniel as a son. She was present at Nathaniel's birth and always thereafter regarded his upbringing as part of her responsibilities.

Nathaniel came back into the kitchen and said, 'Sylvia, when those men turn up, send them to see Ephraim Woolaston, he will sort them out.'

'Where are you going in such a rush Nathaniel?' she pleaded, trying to find out what was going on.

'I don't bloody well know, but it will be a long way from here.' he said

5

as he rushed out of the door.

Chapter 2
Early Days to 1718

It was a cold, miserable November morning in the year 1703 where the fog hung low over the farm and the out buildings. It was one of those days when it would probably never lift and the thick hoar frost gave the impression of a layer of snow covering the trees and hedgerows. It was as if the whole countryside was covered with a thick icy blanket in which sounds were muffled and unreal. At this time of year it could stay for several days before things changed.

While the outside farm employees were all busy at their work the household staff were pretending to busy themselves but at the same time waiting in excited anticipation. The Master was prowling around growling at anyone who came near, and his wife was upstairs in the Master's bedroom in the final stages of her third pregnancy. The two previous ones had ended in the child being stillborn so feelings were very tense. Also in the bedroom were Dr. Betts and Miss Joyce the housekeeper, and stationed outside the door was Sylvia Butler the young chambermaid. She was there purely to run messages and do the bidding of the two people inside but at fifteen years old and the eldest of six children she probably had more hands on experience with babies than the other two put together.

The doctor had been in attendance for about two hours now and the situation was beginning to come to a conclusion. 'The missus is in a lot of pain, doctor,' said Miss Joyce, 'can't we do something about it?'

'I am doing all I can Miss Joyce, we must wait and let nature take its course. Just keep her as comfortable as you can and hope it comes soon.' The doctor had replied in a self-assured manner but was inwardly unconvinced. He was beginning to get very worried indeed.

***

Things happened very quickly after that. As Sylvia listened with her ears pressed against the door, she heard the doctor say 'it's a boy' and 'get that girl in here to take the baby, we have serious work to do.'

Sylvia was half way through the door before Miss Joyce called her and passed over the little parcel wrapped in a rough woollen blanket. 'Take the baby and keep him warm by the fire in the kitchen, tell Mr. John it's a boy and he's fine but Mrs. Anne is not too good.'

***

John Thorold and his wife Anne were both in their early thirties and had been married for nearly ten years. John had taken over the farm about five years previously after the death of his father, Eubulous, but just two years later John's Uncle Richard had also died. Having no male heir of his own, Richard had left all his considerable property to his nephew, and John had been propelled from the position of a hardworking, 'hands on' farmer to the owner of an estate of thirteen farms spread around the south of Lincolnshire. John and Anne both wanted a family and John was very keen to have a son to eventually inherit the estate. They were both very apprehensive and desperately hoped that this would be 'third time lucky' and if fortune was on their side, and if they should be blessed with a son, they would name him Nathaniel after John's grandfather.

***

Sylvia was on her way down to the kitchen and saw the Master prowling around in the library so she knocked on the open door and walked in. The library was quite a small room, fitted out with an old oak desk which had two drawers to the left hand side and an old leather swivel chair. There was an oil lamp burning on the desk, providing a boost to the poor light coming through the narrow casement window. The window gave the appearance of being narrower than it actually was because of the heavy draped curtains at either side. Books lined the wall opposite the door and the only other item of furniture was an old leather armchair to the side of the window.

As she entered the room, John turned towards her, his back towards the window and his face in darkness, enquired, 'Yes Sylvia, any news?'

'Mr. John, Sir, this is your little baby boy isn't he beautiful?'

'Thank you Sylvia, he certainly is, but how is Mrs. Anne?' his voice conveying his concern.

'I am not sure sir, but I was told to take the baby and keep him warm. The Doctor and Miss Joyce are still with her.' Sylvia paused, not sure what to do. 'Can I take him down now Sir?' she asked.

'Of course,' he said 'but I must go and see Mrs. Anne.' as he left the library and bounded up the stairs, two at a time, to see his wife.

***

Nathaniel was nearly two years old when his mother died. She had

8

been confined to her bed ever since Nathaniel's birth and except for a couple of hours each day, the young Nathaniel had been cared for by Sylvia Butler the chambermaid.

Sylvia had hardly expected such a promotion from chambermaid in such a short time in employment, but her natural empathy with the young baby was instantly recognised by Miss Joyce and Mr. John. Her duties as chambermaid were not entirely renounced, she still had to carry out a considerable number of her old duties but had to fit them round her baby minding duties. She was very happy in her new role.

As time went on, Sylvia was spending more and more time with Nathaniel. Initially she had given him his morning feed and then taken him to his mother for the rest of the morning but as Mrs. Thorold's health deteriorated, the baby spent less time with his mother.

When Mrs. Anne passed away, Sylvia took over all baby minding duties and only went to see her mother in the village when she was taking the young Nathaniel out in his carriage. She had no desire to go back to live at home with her young siblings and so stayed at the 'Big House' where she was quite comfortable. Sylvia was very friendly with the Clarkes and often spent an hour or so with Ivy and her two children, Lillian and Maurice. As the children grew up, they naturally played together and Nathaniel and Maurice gradually developed a bond which was to last throughout their lives.

***

As Nathaniel was approaching the age of four years, Mr. John's thoughts turned to his young son's education and so he arranged a meeting with the parish vicar to discuss a way forward.

John Thorold was the holder of the Advowson and as such was the patron of the village church and had appointed the Reverend Roger Spratt to the living of Borton in 1699. He was a very conscientious and popular vicar whose dedication to his parishioners was total. He had never married but there was a young widow in the village who interested him, although she had no idea that the vicar harboured such feelings.

'Come in Roger, let us go through to the library.' John led the way, 'Please take a seat. You know why I asked you to come?'

'Yes, and I agree with you, it's time young Nathaniel was taught some basic skills. He will get nowhere if he can't read and write and he will also need to learn the lessons laid down in the good book.' replied the vicar.

'It's not just his formal education I am concerned about,' said John. 'Somehow we have to get him to understand the social differences and responsibilities of life as a gentleman and the different ways of the labouring class. At the moment he is very friendly with Maurice, and although Maurice is a bright and intelligent boy he is, after all, one of the workforce and will never be a gentleman.'

'I can see the problem you have John. Maurice is the only boy of Nathaniel's age within miles and to find a gentleman's son nearby is impossible.'

'I know, however I think we must get him started at school and always emphasise aspects of the other problem where possible. Not having a mother to advise him does not help. I really miss poor Anne, she would have known what to do.'

The discussion was short and amicable and it was decided that Nathaniel's education should be carried out by the vicar and start on the next Monday morning. Nathaniel was to: *'Arrive at the vicarage at ten of the clock each morning from Monday to Saturday and to be collected at twelve thirty prompt in the afternoon.'* It was also noted that, *'He was to be clean and tidy and have with him a slate and a piece of chalk.'* Any contravention of these basic rules and the child would be sent home immediately.

Sylvia was given her instructions and told in no uncertain terms that it was her responsibility and hers alone that Nathaniel attended lessons as explained and that he complied with the rules as agreed by Mr. John with the Rev. Spratt.

***

Sylvia duly delivered Nathaniel to the vicarage front door on the appointed day at the agreed time. It was only a short walk from the Manor house, and next to the village church of St John the Baptist. Sylvia knocked on the door using the large brass lion's head knocker which Nathaniel had wanted to operate. However, he was not tall enough to reach it and Sylvia did not want to lift him and mess up his clothes. After a couple of minutes they could hear footsteps coming down the stairs and into the hall. The heavy door creaked as it opened and the vicar appeared.

'Good morning Miss Butler, thank you for being on time with the boy. Please be here at twelve thirty sharp to collect him,' and to Nathaniel, 'Come in boy, and wipe your feet.' He closed the door with a bang as they both went

10

inside. Nathaniel had not previously had much contact with the vicar and even then it was mostly in the church on a Sunday where he went to the regular service with his father. If his father was away he would go with Sylvia. This was the first time the vicar had said more than a couple of words to him, and he was feeling very nervous and somewhat apprehensive. The vicar, dressed all in black with his thin greyish face and his slightly balding head had a quite frightening effect on the youngster.

'Settle down boy, I won't bite you. Just sit down at the table and keep quiet.'

Nathaniel sat down and because of his small stature could hardly see over the top of the table. The vicar promptly picked a bulky cushion from an armchair, which when placed on the chair, raised Nathaniel enough to see what he was doing.

'That's better' said the vicar. 'Now, there are a few rules which you must obey if you are going to learn anything from me, first, you only speak when you are spoken to but if you want, or need anything you must raise your hand to attract my attention. Next, you pay attention at all times and lateness will never be tolerated. Finally, whenever you speak to me you will call me Sir. If you fail to observe any of these rules you will be punished, and in a severe case your attendance here will be cancelled. Do you understand boy?'

'Yes Sir.' replied a trembling Nathaniel.

Changing the tone of his voice, the vicar replied, 'Good! then Nathaniel, we can now begin to develop your future.'

Although Nathaniel thought it was a very long morning, he was delighted and surprised when he heard the church clock strike twelve-thirty. He had gradually seen the Reverend Spratt in a different light. He was not the ogre he first thought, but had treated him kindly and approached the task of teaching this anxious young boy with the utmost of patience and understanding.

'You can gather your things together now Nathaniel, I have just seen Miss Butler coming up the garden path.' said the vicar as there was a knock on the front door.

'Hello Nathaniel, have you had a nice morning?' asked Sylvia.

Yes thank you miss,' was his gentlemanly answer.

Nathaniel was a very polite, willing and receptive student for the seven years he attended lessons at the vicarage and Reverend Spratt was very pleased with his progress.

After discussions with the vicar, Mr. John decided an approach should be made to the King Charles Free Grammar School in Bourne for Nathaniel to attend as a boarder. The school was administered by the headmaster Mr. Richard Myers who had been appointed by the Lincoln Cathedral Chapter and followed strict religious rules and teachings.

***

A meeting was arranged with the headmaster Mr. Myers, where John explained that at home Nathaniel had only children of the farm workers to play with and this was already becoming a serious problem. Nathaniel was showing signs that he was getting too close to some of the future workforce and, in particular, his language was becoming extremely coarse. 'I am worried that if he doesn't change soon, and gain their respect as well as their friendship, he will never be able to exert his authority when he needs to in the future. I know Borton is near enough for my son to attend on a daily basis, but I think we will only achieve our aims if he attends as a boarder. He will then be able to spend more time with boys of a similar background and social status.'

Mr. Myers explained that the school was very much in tune with Mr. Thorold's objectives. He convinced John that it was a good school and only enrolled students from the type of background that would give Nathaniel all he needed to know about gentlemanly behaviour.

Agreement was reached on the provision of uniform and books, attendance and expected standards of behaviour. Fees to be paid were discussed and agreed and when they would become due. Nathaniel would start at the school on the first day of the January term after his eleventh birthday.

When Nathaniel heard of these plans he was not at all pleased and his main objection was that he would never see his friend Maurice again. His father was not at all happy with Nathaniel's reaction and put it down to childish tantrums. When the decision on his future schooling was made, Nathaniel still had a couple of months to go with his education at the vicarage and his behaviour noticeably worsened from then on.

Over the next couple of weeks Sylvia had detected a significant change in Nathaniel's behaviour. No longer was he the cheerful, talkative young lad she was used to, but he was surly and un-cooperative and regularly refused to get ready for school. She was very worried about this unusual reaction to her efforts and it came to a head one day when she had to threaten to get his father involved before he agreed to go to the vicarage. When she returned at twelve thirty to pick him up, Reverend Spratt took Sylvia aside and said Nathaniel had behaved very badly all morning and he was proposing to go to see Mr. Thorold that very afternoon to discuss his future attendance at lessons. 'If you could find out what is behind it Miss Butler, I would be very grateful, so I will try to see you first if that is alright.' he said.

'I will do my best, vicar, but I can't promise anything.' said Sylvia.

As she was preparing lunch for Nathaniel she was also trying to question him about his attitude when he suddenly burst into tears. Sylvia quickly took him in her arms and hugged him and between his sobs he tearfully said, 'I am not going to live in Bourne away from you and my best friend Mo. My father says I have got to go to live there soon and I don't want to leave here, ever.'

'Don't worry my love, you will be home every weekend and all your friends will still be here.'

'But father says I will be living there at the school.' sobbed the little chap.

'I am sure he did, but you will be going on Monday mornings and come home on Friday afternoons, so it is not like being there all the time. You will also have holidays fairly often when you will not have to be at school at all. That doesn't sound so bad, does it?'

'I suppose not, but I don't really want to go away at all.'

I know, but it will not be as bad as you think and I bet you will make lots of new friends. I am sure that after a while you will begin to like it.' said Sylvia, 'Now eat up your dinner like a good boy and promise you will not be naughty with the Reverend Spratt again. Promise?'

'I promise.' said Nathaniel, rubbing his eyes.

Sylvia answered the knock on the kitchen door and it was the vicar standing there in his black coat and black cleric's hat. 'Good afternoon Miss Butler, have you had an opportunity to talk to the boy?'

'Good afternoon vicar, do come in. Yes I have, and I think I may have got to the bottom of the problem.'

The vicar sat at the large kitchen table and Sylvia explained Nathaniel's apprehension about his imminent move to school at Bourne and the vicar understood his concerns. 'I will talk to the boy's father, but I think it was just a failure to explain clearly what is going to happen. I am sure this can be remedied quickly and hope the boy gets back to his usual cheerful self. Thank you for your help Miss Butler. Could you tell Mr. Thorold that I am here now?'

'If you would just wait in the drawing room, I will tell him and I am sure he will be down in a couple of minutes.'

***

'Good afternoon Roger, I understand the boy has been behaving badly today, have you dealt with him in the usual manner?'

'I gave him some extra lines to write but I think the problem will be easier to sort out than giving him a good thrashing. He is overly concerned about having to go to school at Bourne because he thinks you said he was going to live there permanently. Miss Butler has tried to explain that he will be home at weekends and holidays and he has calmed down somewhat but I think it would be better if you saw the boy and explained it a bit more clearly. He seems to have the impression that you are abandoning him.' he declared.

'Alright I will, but he also needs to understand that a good education is essential to good prospects and it is also a gentleman's duty to ensure he is prepared for his responsibilities. I will talk to him this evening and I am sure you will continue give him a good grounding in the three 'R's. I am pleased with his progress so far Roger, so we must get this current problem sorted out quickly.'

'Don't be too hard on the lad John, he's having to grow up very quickly and he doesn't have a mother like the other boys do. Anyway, good luck with him this evening, he has been a perfect student so far, and we want to keep it that way if we can.'

When John called an upset Nathaniel into the library that evening, he sat him down and stressed that he was not sending him away for ever and cleared up all the doubts he had about never seeing his friend Mo again. At the same time he also pointed out in as simple a way as he could, that as he grew up he would have responsibilities that Mo would never have and he had to start to learn how to handle them like an adult.

After the meeting, although it seemed to have been successful, John had serious doubts whether he had dealt with the problem sufficiently well enough to allay all the young boy's doubts, and he said to himself, rather prophetically as things transpired. 'only time will tell, only time will tell.'

14

***

The first day of Nathaniel's schooling at Bourne started off with a tantrum. The pony and trap were brought round to the front door of the manor and Nathaniel's luggage was brought out and loaded.

Sylvia had ensured that Nathaniel was clean and dressed ready for his new venture and Mr. John just had his boots to put on and then he was ready to take him, and as he picked up his gloves he heard a loud scream from the kitchen, 'I'm not bloody going!' followed by sounds of footsteps running up the stairs.

'Oh, hell,' said John, 'I half expected this,' and then shouted, 'Sylvia, get him down here this minute, any more nonsense like this and he is in for a good thrashing, and he will still go to Bourne.'

Sylvia ran up the stairs after Nathaniel to try to get him to return downstairs. She found him lying on his bed, sobbing and determined he was not going anywhere. 'You heard your father, didn't you? You had better get down there for your own good, you know what will happen if you don't.'

'I am not going and that is that!' shouted the angry young boy.

Persuasion was not working and Sylvia was beginning to get the feeling that she would be in trouble if the lad stayed in his room much longer. By this time, Miss Joyce, the house keeper had entered the discussion and said to Sylvia, 'There's only one thing for it, we will carry him down and let the Master take over from there.' and between them they picked up the writhing lad and marched him down the stairs for the master to sort out.

'Bring him in here.' shouted John from the drawing room, 'stand in front of me, boy.'

Miss Joyce and Sylvia held the struggling Nathaniel in front of his father, who had his horsewhip in his hand.

'Please don't hit me father, please don't. I promise I will do as you say but please don't hit me.' he begged.

'I am a tolerant man but you have exhausted my patience and this is your last chance. We are going to take you to school now and any more behaviour like this will result in the appropriate punishment and you will not like it. Do you understand?' said Mr. John slowly and clearly.

'Yes, father. I understand.'

'Dry your eyes boy, and get into the cart.' and, 'Sylvia, help him and ensure he is alright.'

It was another of those bright and sunny winter mornings when there had been an overnight hoar frost leaving the trees and hedgerows covered with a thick layer of white snow-like rime. Sylvia had wrapped Nathaniel in a blanket to keep him as warm as possible and his father was also well prepared for the cold and had a heavy blanket over his knees. As they set off, Sylvia waved goodbye and continued to wave until the cart disappeared down the lane. As she wiped a few tears from her eyes she turned back to the house and saw Miss Joyce doing the same.

The trip to Bourne passed without a word being spoken between the two passengers. The young lad was careful not to upset his father anymore because of the consequences that he might suffer, and the father was struggling to control his rage. However the poor pony took more than its usual share of the whip and was expected to run faster than it normally would.

***

The school at Bourne consisted of a small building which was nearly one hundred years old, situated in the grounds of the Abbey Churchyard. It could accommodate up to ten pupils at any time and as they came into the yard it seemed as if all the students and their relatives had arrived at the same time. Nathaniel was trying to suppress a fresh outburst of tears when he saw someone he recognised. He remembered the boy from a family gathering at Grantham a couple of years before, but was uncertain who it was. His curiosity overcame his rejection of his father and he asked, 'Father, who is that boy standing near the statue on the grass?'

'That is the son of a friend of your dear late mother, I think his name is Charles Watson and he lives at Thurlby, just the other side of Bourne. He is not a new boy, I think he has been here since last September.'

***

Rev. Myers the headmaster greeted everyone as they arrived and took Nathaniel and two other new boys aside and gave them a very short, welcome talk. He explained that he would tell them more later in the day when they were settled in. They were then introduced to Peter Gardner, an older pupil who was to act as a guide to show them to their room. Peter was a short, fat boy with a flat, pug nose. His eyes were small and close together and his head was topped off with a thick shock of ginger hair. He treated the new pupils with a degree of distain and regarded his task as an inconvenience which he

16

had to put up with. The only words he spoke were, 'Follow me' and 'This is your room.' The new boys were not impressed. The room upstairs in the attic was very small and contained three small wooden beds, each with a straw filled mattress and a rough woollen blanket. There were three wooden chairs and a series of wooden pegs on the wall on which to hang clothing. Walls were a dirty white colour and bare and there was a casement window which overlooked a grassy area in front of the chapel. The top section of the window was cracked and there was a gap at the bottom in which a previous tenant had stuffed some old rags.

When the senior student had left the three young boys stood and stared at the bleak room. None of them had lived in such a place and were not looking forward to staying there overnight, never mind living there for a few years. Nathaniel was the first to speak, 'This is awful, I didn't want to come here in the first place and I certainly don't want to sleep in that flea pit! What do you two think?'

George Montini, a tall thin boy with a rather large nose and protruding ears, replied, 'It's disgusting, my dog Nell has a better kennel than this place, hasn't she Neville?'

'She has, and I think our pigs are better off than us!'

Neville Donnison had attended the same first school as George and they had known each other since they were infants. Neville was a rather short lad with a shock of dark, curly hair. His round face always had a smile and he was also a bit of a prankster.

Both George and Neville came from farming families and lived close to each other in the village of Corby Glen, a few miles west of Bourne. George's father was an Italian who had married a local farmers daughter and settled down working on the family farm.

They agreed with Nathaniel that the room was awful. However, Neville explained that they had already been told that this room was always used for new starters and eventually they would all be moved to better rooms.

'At least I am only here Monday to Friday each week, you poor sods are here until the end of term.' said Nathaniel. 'I don't envy you one bit.'

'Good God, that's rat shit on the floor,' shouted Neville, pointing to the damning evidence, 'I should have brought a trap.' As they all studied the proof on the floor, Nathaniel said, 'I am going home on Friday and I can bring a couple of traps back with me but I don't fancy rats running under my bed until then. What are we going to do for the rest of this week?'

'We are going to see the headmaster later, so we could ask him what to do.' said George, 'he might have a couple of spares locked away.'

To which Neville, ever the cynic said 'I wouldn't get your hopes up, that sour old sod probably breeds them.'

'What about Peter Gardner?' asked George, 'he should know what we could do.'

'We won't get any help from that stuck up, toffee nosed sod either.' muttered Neville.

***

After lunch in the main hall, the three new boys were ushered into the headmaster's study for their promised briefing. The boys stood in front of the headmaster who was standing behind his desk with a large cane held threateningly in his right hand.

'I am the Reverend Myers and I am your headmaster and tutor for as long as you stay here. I expect exemplary behaviour at all times from my students and any deviation will be punished severely.' he said, slamming the cane into his left hand. 'The school has a good name in the town and anyone who causes that name to be doubted will be dismissed from the school immediately and your parents will be informed exactly why. Do you all understand?'

'Yes Mr. Myers,' they answered in unison.

'I am not Mr. Myers to you, you will always call me Sir from this minute on.'

'Yes Sir.' was their immediate response.

The headmaster returned to his theme, 'You will be shown where your lessons will take place and you will be in the correct place at the correct time, lateness is never tolerated. If you have any problems you must be outside my study ten minutes after classes cease and I will deal with you then. Have any of you anything you want to ask me now before I dismiss you?'

Neville, being the bravest of the three spoke up, 'We have rats in our room sir, what can we do?'

'Rats are a common animal in this country and can be found anywhere. I have not heard of them in the school and if there are any I am sure they will do you no harm.'

The boys stood in bemused silence as the headmaster continued, 'If

18

that's all then you are dismissed. Wait in the corridor for Peter Gardner who will show you the classroom and give you any more information you may need' were the headmaster's final words.

'You had better bring your traps Nathaniel. We are going to get no help from him.' said George.

As they waited in the corridor Neville remarked, 'I don't like the look of that cane and I certainly don't want it anywhere near my backside.'

***

Their first night in their new school was a long wakeful one. The draught from the broken window made creepy whining noises and the freezing cold crept through their rough blankets and prevented any chance of a good night's sleep. The possibility of rats scurrying around underneath the beds was constantly on their minds, and the blankets, although pulled tightly over their heads, failed to keep out the noises of the night.

It was still dark when a school prefect came round to give them their morning call and getting out of bed took their minds off the rats. At least they thought they were now in a position to see the rats, but in reality, the single oil burning lamp they had to light the room, created more shadows than light.

***

The first week of school passed in a blur for Nathaniel and he was delighted when Mo turned up at the school with the pony and trap to collect him for his weekend at home. Nathaniel's father had thought it would be a good idea to send Mo to pick up his son as it might help to put him in a good frame of mind for when he arrived home. This plan worked and Nathaniel behaved himself the whole weekend apart from a quiet moan to Sylvia about the state of his living arrangements at the school.

'Where do we keep the rat traps Mo?' asked Nathaniel. 'I need a couple for our room at school.'

'They are hanging up in the cart-shed above the workbench. You haven't got rats at school have you?' asked Mo incredulously. 'I thought it was a fancy toffs school.'

'We have and they are great big ones, I have seen one nearly as big as your cat.' replied Nathaniel, with just a little more exaggeration than was necessary.

'Do you know how to set them?'

'Of course I do, I have set them dozens of times.'

19

'Well, make sure you keep your fingers out of the jaws until you have set them properly.' said Mo.

Nathaniel was taking the traps back to his room to have them handy for Monday morning when his father saw him.

'Where are you taking those traps Nathaniel?' asked John.

'I am taking them back to school to catch the rats that come into our room.'

'Are you saying that there are rats and *you* have to get rid of them yourself?' John asked angrily.

Nathaniel explained to his father what had happened and what the boys had decided to do but his father was not too happy. He threatened to go to see the headmaster until Nathaniel persuaded him not to because it would make things very difficult for all three boys. John agreed not to be hasty and wait for a while, mainly because Nathaniel had not complained once about the school, and also because he was talking positively about going back on Monday. It was a remarkable change in Nathaniel's attitude.

***

Nathaniel's trip back to school early on Monday morning was uneventful and Mo was again in charge. This was to become a regular routine and provided a chance for the two to talk over the last weekend together and plan the next weekend.

'See you on Friday, Nathaniel, and take care with those traps.'

'Don't worry, I will. Cheerio.' replied Nathaniel.

As Mo drove off down the lane, Nathaniel walked over to the side door to his room where he saw George and Neville with a couple of other boys.

'Have you got the traps?' called Neville.

'What traps, boy?' the headmaster asked as he came round the corner from his study. 'I thought I told you that if there are rats, they will do you no harm.'

Neville was again the first one to reply, 'But they keep us awake at night, Sir and we would like to get rid of them.'

'Very well, you may use the traps but I think you are wasting your time. No one has reported sighting rats to me so they are probably only in your imagination.'

'Thank you Sir.' said the three boys in unison.

After the headmaster had gone on his way, the boys went to their room to decide on a suitable place to set their traps. They eventually decided to fasten one to the leg of Nathaniel's bed and the other to Neville's so that there was one near the door and the other near the window. Nathaniel fastened his to his bed first and then set it by forcing the jaws open against the strong spring. It was a task which required concentration because with the jaws held open you then had to force the very strong spring down to where it would click and hold the jaws in the open position. If the trip plate was touched, the spring would be released and the jaws would snap violently shut. Anything trapped in the jaws would be killed instantly. As Mo had said to Nathaniel. 'Make sure you keep your fingers out.'

With both traps set, the boys suddenly realised that there was nothing to attract the rats into the traps.

'What about bait?' asked George. 'They won't go near unless we put some bait on the plate. We are wasting our time if we don't find something to attract them.'

After a discussion on the type of bait to use it was decided that they would bring something from their evening meal depending what is available.

***

That evening the boys sat down to a plate of very fatty boiled bacon and boiled potatoes. To call it bacon was a misrepresentation, it was nearly one hundred per cent fat with a very slim sliver of lean. All three agreed that the rats could have the lot as it was something that they all loathed. Mr. Myers was well aware what the boys were planning and made sure that they ate nearly all the unappetising lump of fat telling them that 'It is good for you and will keep you warm through the winter.' He did, however, let them take a couple of small chunks back to the room to prime the traps.

The traps were carefully set before they went to bed leaving a candle burning on the shelf. None of them went to sleep for quite some time but soon after they had all dropped off, the first trap was triggered with a loud snap. All three jumped up and George took the candle and checked the traps. Neville's trap had been sprung and contained the first dead rat.

'That Myers hasn't a clue, the place is full of vermin and that's not just the rats.' observed Neville, scratching himself.

'So let's get back to bed and see if there is another one tonight. We might have enough for a meal at this rate.'

'It would taste no worse than that crap we had tonight, but at least the rats like it.' said Nathaniel.

After the excitement of catching their first rat, they all went back to bed. They heard the second trap go off about an hour later but none of them got out of bed that time. They set the traps every night after that and for the first week they caught at least one rat every night. After the first week catches diminished until they gave up after about three weeks, but they kept the traps in the room just in case.

***

School continued very quietly for Nathaniel. His reservations about being away from home subsided and he became very friendly with George. He also saw quite a lot of Charles Watson, the boy he had seen on his first day at the school. Charles taught Nathaniel and his two roommates to play poker and they soon became very keen and played regularly. They didn't play for money as none of them had any to spare but instead played for points.

***

At weekends, Nathaniel went home and he would spend hours with Mo riding their horses, both were competent horsemen and would ride over the fields and quite often to neighbouring villages. They would sometimes take a pair of ferrets and a couple of the dogs out with them and see if they could catch a rabbit or two for the pot. After blocking most of the exits to the warren, the ferrets would be put down one of the open holes to flush out any of the resident rabbits. The dogs would then set off and chase the rabbits and occasionally caught one before it disappeared down another hole.

On other occasions they would set snares on known rabbit runs and go back the following morning to see if they had caught anything.

One Saturday Mo asked Nathaniel if he had ever seen the village from the church roof. Nathaniel hadn't so Mo suggested it would be a good idea to go and have a look. They waited in the churchyard until the Reverend Spratt had gone home for lunch and crept quietly into the church to make sure no one was still around. When they were sure it was all clear, Mo said 'This way Nat.' and led the way into the vestry and up some narrow stone steps to a room with several ropes with fancy coloured ends hanging through holes in the roof. 'Don't touch those ropes Nat, you will have the whole village in here to see what is going on.' There was a steep, narrow ladder in the corner leading up to a trapdoor in the roof and Mo started to climb. 'Be careful Nat this is quite steep but we are nearly there.' Mo slid the bolt off and pushed the trapdoor

22

open and climbed through into the bell chamber followed by Nathaniel who was shaking like a leaf. After a bit of probing Mo found out that Nathaniel had lost his footing on the ladder and nearly fallen to the floor. 'You had better go first this time. Just take it easy and I will be right behind you. When you get to the top, slide the bolt open and push the door and then you can step out onto the roof.' and added 'Don't worry, it's not so steep and it's flat at the top. Careful where you put your hands though, this place is covered in pigeon shit.'

Nathaniel set off carefully and was soon at the top enjoying the view. 'It's fantastic,' he said. 'I can see the church at Bourne and I can just make out the spire of Grantham church in the distance.' They spent the next half an hour or so pointing out different places they recognised and then realised that they should start to go down or they would be caught by the vicar returning after lunch.

They made it safely and no one had caught them, however, later that day Nathaniel's father asked, 'Did you enjoy the view from the tower? It's a fantastic view isn't it? You can see for miles from up there, but you must realise, once you are up there, every one down here can also see you.' This was confirmed later as everywhere he went around the village, he was asked if he had enjoyed the view. Even the vicar mentioned it at church on Sunday.

They were both competitive and often staged races with each other. One weekend when Mo was about sixteen years old, the two of them were having a race and Mo's horse was spooked by a bullock. He had just jumped a hedge with ease but unfortunately he landed next to a bullock, sleeping in the sun. The bullock jumped up and the horse stumbled and threw Mo into a ditch. 'My bloody leg's broken!' screamed Mo, 'help me, Nat. Get me out of here.' Nathaniel went straight into panic mode and started to ride off home in a rush. 'Come back you stupid bastard!' shouted Mo. 'Where the hell do you think you are going?'

Nathaniel pulled up, 'Going home to get help, I can't do anything. You need help quickly.'

'Well, get me out of this bloody freezing ditch before you go or I will have drowned or frozen to death before you get back.'

Nathaniel jumped off his horse and tied it to a convenient tree and turned to the task of getting Mo out of the ditch. The ditch was steep sided and about four feet down to the water level. Mo was lying in the water up to his waist and obviously in a lot of pain. It was not going to be an easy task and

Nathaniel had to get into the ditch at some stage. This was something that he was not so keen on doing, and as he gingerly lowered himself down the bank he slipped and fell into the freezing cold water. He got himself back on his feet and put his arms round Mo and tried to lift him but found it impossible. Mo was a great deal heavier, and he realised it was going to be quite a struggle getting him out of the ditch.

'How the hell are you going to get me out?' asked Mo. 'You haven't a clue have you?'

'I don't know.' replied a fearful Nathaniel.

Mo was in considerable pain and fed up with a rescuer who was obviously clueless so he decided it was time to take charge of the situation. 'Now listen to me Nat, get out of the ditch and go to your horse. Get the rope that is attached to the saddle and bring it back here. Got it?'

'Yes Mo.' said Nathaniel, and climbed out of the ditch. 'I'm wet through and its freezing cold.' moaned the rescuer.

'How the hell do you think I feel? I'm still in the ditch and have a broken leg. Get on with it and stop your bloody moaning.'

'Alright, I'm going.'

Nathaniel came back with the rope and Mo told him to tie a loop to fit under his arms. When he had completed this to Mo's satisfaction, his next instruction was to tie the end of the rope to his horse. When Mo was ready he would give the order to gently walk the horse away to pull him slowly out of the ditch. Mo steadied himself as best he could and then gave Nat the signal. As the horse pulled slowly away Mo tried to help by using his good leg as a lever. After about ten minutes, accompanied by screams of pain and mouthfuls of obscenities Mo was finally hauled out of the water onto a dry patch of grass where the bullock had been lying.

Nathaniel unhitched the rope from the horse and tethered his horse back to the tree. He brought a horse blanket and covered Mo and tried to make him comfortable.

'What are you going to do now?' asked Mo.

'Going home to get help.' replied Nathaniel.

'That's three miles, you daft sod, you will be ages. Go to Dick Spurr's cottage in "The Drove", it is less than half the distance. Don't hang around here and don't stop to get yourself dried. My leg is giving me hell!'

Luckily, Dick was at the cottage with his two lads, Les and Alan tending some new born lambs. They got the horse ready, attached a cart and set out following Nathaniel to the scene of the accident. They soon had Mo in the back of the cart and headed off home to the manor. Les rounded up Mo's horse and was dispatched to Bourne to get the doctor.

Mo was taken to his mother's cottage and lifted gently onto the table to await the doctor. He was still in pain and his mother stood by, mopping his brow and giving words of comfort. His sister Lillian was not at all sympathetic, 'What the hell have you been playing at?' she shouted. 'You can't be trusted anywhere. I bet you were with that layabout Nathaniel again, where is he anyway?'

'He's gone to get dried off.' said Dick as John Thorold came into the cottage.

'The doctor is on his way Maurice, we will soon have you fixed up. Nathaniel tells me it was an unfortunate accident and you were very unlucky.' said John. 'and thank you Dick, you and the boys did well today. You can go back and carry on with your work now, everything seems to be under control.'

'Thanks Dick.' said Mo through gritted teeth from the table as the pain continued to cause him concern.

Doctor Betts arrived about an hour after Mo had been laid on the table and immediately diagnosed what everyone already knew, that Mo had a broken bone in his left leg. As a young man, Doctor Betts had been a ship's doctor and had a reputation as a bit of a butcher. As soon as Mo saw him, he shouted, 'Get that bloody butcher out of here, he will have my leg off if you give him half a chance.'

'Calm down Mo, I will make sure the doctor does nothing of the kind. He is quite capable of mending it.' said John.

'You are quite right John, I have no intention of cutting it off. Have you a bottle of rum in the house?' asked the doctor 'I think we will need it to ease the pain.'

'I think so, I will go and check.'

John soon returned with the rum. The doctor had obtained two stout boards from the carpenter and had also produced a thick leather strap from his bag. He was about to fasten the boards either side of Mo's leg. 'This might hurt Maurice get some of that rum down you before I start, and bite hard on the leather' said the doctor as he tried to get the two ends of the break together. Even with a big swig of the rum Mo still cried out as the doctor moved the

25

bones. As the boards were put in place he still needed some more of the rum.

'That's it,' said Doctor Betts, 'don't put any weight on that leg until I come to see you again. Get the carpenter to make you a crutch but don't stand on that leg at all! Mrs. Clark you make sure he behaves and does as he is told. Now get him to his bed and make sure he stays there.'

'Do you understand Maurice and you Mrs. Clark?'

'Yes doctor.' they both replied.

***

It was about six weeks before Mo ventured out of the cottage on his crutch. The carpenter had made a good one that was strong enough to bear the weight of Mo as he hopped along. It had a well-padded cross piece which slotted neatly under his arm and the length had been adjusted to fit. The doctor had been to see Mo the day before and had given his approval but insisted Mo should only stand for short periods. The splints were to be kept in place at least until the doctor's next visit. Mo was still suffering, but the pain had eased considerably.

Nathaniel missed his chats with Mo on the school run and he was driven there and back by whoever was available at the time, sometimes it was one of the farmhands, and sometimes Miss Joyce, if she had to go to the shops in Bourne. He visited Mo at weekends and caught up with the gossip but he felt at a loss as to what to do with no Mo around.

***

About eight months after the accident, Nathaniel's father called him into the study and explained that he thought Nathaniel had learnt just about all he would ever learn at school and had decided that he should leave at Christmas. He would be nearly fifteen years old and it was about time he did some work and got to know how to run a farm and all its employees, after all, he would eventually have the responsibility of running the whole place.

Nathaniel was a bit upset in a way because he would miss his friends at school. Especially George who had even taught him a few words of Italian – swear words mainly. He looked forward to seeing more of Mo, who would be able to ride again by then. Mo's recovery had been slow and it was quite likely that he would be left with a permanent limp.

The last few months at school went very quickly and his best mate, George had already left, so Nathaniel did not feel so bad about leaving. Charles Watson had left a few weeks before George but Neville was staying on as his

26

father had high hopes for him. The only thing Neville could think of was that his father wanted him to enter the church but his response to that was, 'They can stuff that, they will never get me praying for a living!'

The day for leaving arrived and farewells were said and promises to keep in touch were made. Nathaniel packed his meagre belongings and said goodbye to the headmaster. As he walked out of the main entrance, his cart arrived and to his delight he saw it was Mo who was driving.

'That's it then Nat, your brain's topped up for the rest of your life. I bet it's good to be educated isn't it?'

'Just what I expected, sarcasm and a cripple on a cart! How are you doing mate?'

'Fine, jump up and let's get off home.'

'Just don't forget who taught you to read and write, you will thank me one day.'

'I thank you now, just let's get off home, mum's got fatty bacon on the boil. My favourite!'

Chapter 3

Life after school began very slowly for Nathaniel, his father had no real plan of what he was going to give the boy to do. So he just told Nathaniel to follow him around and 'pick things up.' It did not take long to see that this was not working and so, about a week later as they were checking what George Headland was doing with the horses, John said, 'Nathaniel, the most important thing in the working of this farm is the wellbeing of the horses. You know George very well and you know there is no better man with horses than him, so I want you to work with him from now on. I want you to learn everything you possibly can so that you could take over from him if it was ever needed. You will need to be fully aware of what George does when you eventually take over the running of the estate.'

'Yes father, does that mean every day, all day?'

'It certainly does, and when you have finished that, you will move on to learn about the cattle and sheep. There is a lot more to running an estate than walking around pretending you know it all. It takes time to gather all the knowledge you will require to be a successful farmer.' Then turning to George, 'George, I want you to teach Nathaniel everything you know. He is here to work, not watch, so make sure he does everything you tell him to do. I expect him to be with you for several months so he will have no excuses for not doing things correctly. I want you to keep me informed of his progress and any problems tell me straight away. Is that clear George?'

'Yes, Mr. John.' was George's reply.

George was a well-built man in his fifties and had been working with horses since he left school. He was not the brightest man on the farm but was an excellent, conscientious worker. He was also very well-known throughout the area and had lots of contacts who could help in an emergency.

When Nathaniel was about five years old George had taught him to ride on a small pony, and ever since had kept his eye on the young lad's progress as a horseman. He had never married and lodged in the village with one of his sisters, whose husband had died a few years before. His sister Charlotte was the widow that the local vicar, the Reverend Spratt was secretly a bit sweet on. George had been in charge of the horses and their work on the farm for the last ten years or so. It was a very responsible job and with roughly twenty working horses and a staff of thirty labourers a very demanding one.

28

As with many fifteen year olds, Nathaniel's attitude to the job was largely one of disinterest. With the natural impulsiveness of youth thought everything was easy and that he would be able to master it in a week or so. George decided it was time to crack the whip and give him a hard, physical job to do. Nathaniel had never done any physical work at all, so he had no idea what was coming when George told him he was going to learn a bit of ploughing. He had seen the farmhands ploughing plenty of times before and so he thought he would be able to do it quite easily.

George, with some help from Nathaniel, rigged up two horses and attached them to the plough and George set the horses off across the field to cut the first furrow. He explained to Nathaniel all the finer details and then gave him the chance to show what he could do while under supervision. George thought he was doing surprisingly well and asked, 'Do you think you could do it yourself now, Nathaniel?'

'Of course I could, it's dead easy isn't it?' replied the cocky youngster.

'Right then, you can see what we have done so far, just keep the line straight and the plough dug in to the right depth and make sure you control the horses or they will control you. Ready?' Nathaniel nodded in response. 'Off you go then and finish the field.'

'What, the whole bloody field?'

'Of course, it won't do it by itself, will it?'

Nathaniel set the horses moving and dug the plough into the soil but as the horses moved, the plough kept lifting out of the ground. Digging it back in was proving to be very hard work and while he was concentrating on this, the furrow began to wander from the original straight line. Getting the horses back to where he wanted them was also becoming a problem and by the time he was half way through his first cut across the field he was shouting at the horses and swearing at the plough and was yards away from the line that he should have been following.

George arrived to rescue him just as he burst into tears. 'So, it's easy is it Nathaniel? Is that why you are crying?'

'I can't get it right George.' Nat sobbed. 'I can't do it, can I?'

'You can't do it now but you will be able to soon, all the lads took time to learn and they do it from dawn to dusk with hardly a break. Let this be a lesson to you and don't ever assume you can do things without practice and good teaching.'

After work that day Nathaniel sought out Mo and poured his heart out to him that as far as he was concerned there was no way that he wanted to be a farmer, or indeed have anything to do with farming. He had had enough in one day to last him a lifetime.

'You can't say that Nat, the farm will be yours one day and you will need to know what you are doing.'

'I know Mo, but just look at my hands, they are red-raw. That's from just one day.'

'Come on Nat, you are fifteen years old, not a little baby. You have to grow up quickly now that you have finished school. Now, if you don't mind I haven't finished work yet. I have still got to milk the cows.'

***

Nathaniel had a very sleepless night and awoke in the morning determined to try again and not let things get him down. He was also worried that George would have told his father about yesterday's events and that he would be in line for a telling off when he went for his breakfast.

Breakfast passed without comment from his father and so Nathaniel thought with a bit of luck he might get away with it, but he knew that if George had said nothing this time, he would definitely not get away with a repeat performance.

It was a chastened Nathaniel who turned up for work that morning and George never once mentioned the subject again.

***

The next two years were uneventful as far as Nathaniel was concerned. He did all that was required of him and although he worked hard his heart was never in it. His dislike of farming and all that was involved in it was unchanged and he dreaded the prospect of some day in the future having to take over the running of the estates. He often expressed these concerns to Mo who repeatedly said that he should have no worries as he had learnt well in every area that he had worked.

'I know I could do almost anything they want me to do, but I just don't like farm work and I dread having to be involved with it for the rest of my life. It's dirty, smelly and very cold work most of the year.' pleaded Nathaniel. 'You know how I feel and I think I could make a better life for myself doing something different.'

'Have you ever told your father how you feel? He really does deserve to know.'

'No I haven't, it would really upset him and I don't want to do that especially as he has not been very well of late. I feel as if I am sliding slowly into a pit with no chance of ever getting out.'

These conversations with Mo happened frequently and, until now, nothing ever changed. One Saturday evening when Nathaniel had been in a particularly miserable mood, Mo suggested they visit *"The Five Bells"* public house in the village and have a tankard of strong ale to cheer them both up. There were two pubs in the village, the other one being *"The Kings Head"*. Nathaniel had never been in either of the pubs before but he had sampled ale during the harvest celebrations last autumn so he was willing to give it a try.

Both of the village pubs were quite small and *"The Five Bells"* was in Church Lane not far from the vicarage. It was a thatched cottage which also served as the landlord's home. One room was used as the area the customers could relax in and enjoy their ale. The landlord, William Grimes, brought the ale from barrels stored in the back room.

It was a short walk to the pub and Mo said there would be a few of the farm lads there and they could all have a good laugh.

'Well for goodness sake, don't mention my problem to any of them, will you. If it gets out and my father hears about it I will be in real trouble.'

'Of course I won't,' said Mo 'what do you think I am, I've known for a couple of years already and no-one other than me has a clue, so I have obviously kept it quiet so far.'

'Thanks Mo, I should have known better than to ask.' said Nathaniel.

When they arrived it was fairly quiet with only a few drinkers there. Mo got the drinks and sat down with Nathaniel in the window seat with two other local lads both of whom worked with Mo at the farm. One of them suggested they should have a game of dominoes to which they all agreed. The game continued in a friendly fashion until a few more local lads arrived and started to make the occasional sarcastic remark about the boss's son slumming it with the locals. Nat did not rise to the bait but the remarks then began to get personal. Mo told them to back off but this only made things worse. They started to direct their comments at Mo and called him the boss's lacky and accused him of trying to make out that he was one the toffs. When they accused him of having his head up the boss's arse, Mo exploded and leapt off his seat, landed a punch on the ringleader's jaw knocking him to the hard earthen floor and prepared for the next attack, whoever it came from.

All hell broke loose with everyone involved in a mad brawl. There were no sides, just a fight for fight's sake involving all the young men. The old men continued to chat and enjoy their drinks whilst watching the fight spill out into the pub yard. The landlord watched from behind the bar and said to the old men, 'They will be back in a couple of minutes. It's the same every Saturday night.'

When the fight subsided, Nathaniel was wiping his bleeding nose and Mo, grinning all over his face said,

'That was a good one Nat, are you OK?'

'Fine, a bit bloody and bruised but I am alright.'

'The hard work has developed your muscles well. You would not have stood up so well to a fight like that a couple of years ago.'

'Does that happen every Saturday Mo?' asked Nat.

'Every Saturday without fail someone always finds a reason to get one going. It's just a matter of knowing when to jump in.'

'You might have warned me.' said Nat, rubbing his aching jaw.

***

The next morning John asked his son if he had been at *"The Five Bells"* the previous night.

'Why do you ask?' queried Nathaniel, trying to eat some bread while his jaw ached painfully.

'Because I can see you have a black eye and you have skinned your knuckles. You were late home as well and you made a hell of a racket when you finally did arrive. I therefore conclude that you were in the Saturday night fight at *"The Five Bells"*. Am I correct?'

'Yes father you are correct, I was there.'

'Well I don't mind you going there as long as you behave like a gentleman should behave. That means avoiding fights like that whenever you can. I appreciate that you will inevitably get caught up now and again, but don't make a habit of it. And don't get a reputation of being a very good fighter, this will only make you a target for everyone to knock down. You are now at an age where you will be regarded by many as a young adult but some will always see you as an overgrown schoolboy and it is very important that you should behave in a way that shows you in the best possible light. I don't intend to be, or want you to think that I am overbearing in this matter, so I will

32

leave things for you to decide how to present yourself. I will always be here to advise and help you in any way that you would like.

I am also aware that, having seen you carrying out the tasks given to you on the farm that you have worked hard and conscientiously to learn how we do things, but at the same time it is fairly obvious to me that your heart is not totally into farming. So, from today I am going to give you the opportunity to get involved in the running of an estate from the viewpoint of the owner. You will find that it is an absorbing task and will stretch your abilities to the limit, not in a physical way but in the application of your mental competence. I hope that this will go some way towards changing your attitude towards being an owner. I have told all the senior workmen of my intentions and so they are fully aware that you will be working as my assistant. I would advise you very strongly to use the knowledge they have and not to be arrogant in any way. I am sure you will agree that they still know more about the routines on the farm than you probably ever will. When we have finished our breakfast we will make a start by going through some of the estate papers.'

***

Nathaniel was already aware that his father owned a few farms scattered around various villages in the county and had visited some of those which were within a short ride of the manor. He was totally unaware, though, of the extent of his father's property empire. As his father went through the list of holdings, the list getting ever longer, he asked, 'Who is looking after all these properties father, you are not away very often and so you can't run them all?'

'That's perfectly true Nathaniel, in some of them I employ a manager and others are leased out to members of your late mother's family. Where there is a manager, he is paid a salary and where the properties are leased then they pay an agreed rent for the term of the lease. This pile of papers contains all the legal documents covering the properties we are discussing. They are usually kept in a strong box at the chambers of Mr. Ephraim Woolaston in Church Street, Grantham. Any legal work I need to be carried out is dealt with by him. Mr. Woolaston deals with all collections of rents and leases and ensures they are received on the due dates. He also, after deducting his commission, deposits the money in my account and sends me details of all the transactions he carries out. This is a monthly routine which I expect to have delivered to me on the first Monday of each, and every month.

I usually look through these documents once a year and they are

33

delivered here by a lad from the solicitor's office. I try to get them back to Mr. Woolaston within the week. Whilst they are here it is important that they are kept securely in my strong box at all times when they are not in use.'

Nathaniel was extremely interested in this new side of farming and understood the importance of the documents and also the need for their security whilst in their possession. He was fascinated by this insight into his future life, particularly the money side of things. He could already see that the hard graft he had put in so far would help to keep control of the activities on which the income was reliant.

***

When they had finished their breakfast and Sylvia had cleared the table, Mr. John scooped up all the documents and they moved into the library. They both sat down and Mr. John pulled a bundle of papers from the big pile, 'I think we will start with the financial statement for each individual farm to give you an indication how each farm is performing. This of course only applies to the managed farms, the leased farms just pay their rent and so long as they do that on time then it is really none of our business.'

'Holt Hall farm at Frieston is the first one we will go through. This farm is managed by Edward Wood who lives at Holt Hall and as you can see, he is operating a very profitable business running cattle and sheep on some very marshy ground. You will be meeting Edward in the next couple of weeks as I intend to pay him a visit and congratulate him on his fine work.'

This perusal of the papers continued with only a very short break for lunch. Nathaniel's head was spinning by the time his father called a halt at the end of the day.

In all they spent three days locked away in the library and at the end Nathaniel was having great difficulty remembering who was where and what they were doing. He had made a list of all the important documents and was working hard to commit them all to memory.

At breakfast Mr. John said, 'Nathaniel, I want you to saddle up your horse and deliver the box of documents to Mr. Woolaston in person today. You know where his chambers are, don't you?'

'Of course father.'

'Good, it will give you a chance to get to know Mr. Woolaston. You haven't met him before, have you? If you get there early enough he might take you to *"The Angel"* for lunch. He goes there every day and often conducts

34

business meetings there.'

'Right, I will get off as soon as I can. I don't want to miss a good lunch and a jar.'

'Just go carefully Nathaniel, and look after those documents as if your life depended on it. Give my regards to Mr. Woolaston and tell him I will be over to see him soon. I will see you when you get back.'

***

The sign beside the butcher's shop in Church Street, said 'Woolaston, Snipe and Partner' above an arrow which pointed down the untidy, dirt strewn ginnel at the side of the shop. Nathaniel came to a door which had a notice saying, 'W, S. and P. Upstairs'. He entered and clambered over piles of boxes and papers scattered all over the stairs and knocked on a rickety old door on which a splendidly carved plaque indicated that Mr. Ephraim Woolaston was the occupier. Nathaniel knocked tentatively on the door and waited. No-one came and so he tried again and eventually heard some movement inside. It still seemed an age before the door was opened by a small grey faced man who was leaning on a stick.

'Yes, what can I do for you young man?'

'I am Nathaniel Thorold and I am returning some documents from my father for the attention of Mr. Woolaston.'

'Oh yes, he is expecting you sir. Would you take a seat for a few minutes as he is with a client at the moment.' The small grey-faced man hobbled round the back of a tall desk and climbed, with some difficulty, onto a high stool, dipped his quill into a messy ink pot and started to write.

A door behind the clerk opened and a loud voice boomed out, 'It's been nice meeting you George, tell your father I will sort it out, and be in touch shortly.'

'Thank you Mr. Woolaston, I will,' and the young man shook hands with Mr. Woolaston and turned round to leave the room.

'Good lord, it's you George.' exclaimed Nathaniel. 'How the hell are you?'

Ephraim Woolaston, a large, red faced man with a bald head and mutton chop whiskers down to his jaw bone said, 'You, young man must be John Thorold's son, and you two obviously know each other.'

'Yes sir, we were at school together in Bourne.'

George Montini, grinning all over his face, turned to Nat and said, 'We

35

had a great time didn't we? But we haven't seen each other since.'

'Well George I intend to go to my lunch at *"The Angel"* at twelve of the clock and if you are still in town you are both very welcome to join me.'

'I still have some business to conduct in town so I would be delighted to join you. Thank you very much, sir.' and turning to Nat 'I hope to see you too Nat, we have a lot to catch up on.'

George said his goodbyes and was shown out by the old clerk who struggled from his stool and managed to get to the door just after George had departed. As he struggled back to his desk Ephraim boomed, 'You must be Nathaniel. Glad to meet you.' and he held out a sweaty hand and limply shook hands.

'Pleased to meet you too sir. As you can see I have brought the papers my father has been checking over and father is very pleased with the way things are progressing.'

'He should be pleased, they are the best results I have seen for a few years. How is your father, by the way, I haven't seen him for a while and he was not too well the last time? He was having breathing problems as I recall.'

'He is not too bad at the moment but he suffers badly in the winter months. He sends his regards and says he will be along to see you soon.'

The meeting progressed steadily and Mr. Woolaston checked all the documents were correctly in place and any notes that had been made by Mr. John were recorded and action taken where necessary. The old clerk was called in to deal with a few clerical amendments and then told to store the documents in the strong box. As he used both hands to pick up the bundle of papers, his stick, which he had propped against Mr. Woolaston's desk, fell to the floor. Nathaniel quickly picked it up and the clerk, voicing his thanks, struggled out of the room with the bundle tucked under one arm and the stick in the other.

'I think we have done all we can Nathaniel and can now safely adjourn to *"The Angel"* for a good lunch and a pot or two of ale. I am famished, how about you?'

'Yes I am pretty hungry too.' replied Nathaniel.

'You know where I will be Watson. Fetch me if I am needed.' said Ephraim as they left the office.

Nathaniel realised that it was the first time he had heard the clerk's name mentioned.

Chapter 4

Lunch at *"The Angel"* proved an interesting event for the two young lads. With his booming voice and ebullient personality Ephraim – known to all in the room as Effy dominated proceedings. Both lads had decided on ham and eggs for their lunch and Effy chose boiled fatty bacon and boiled cabbage, apparently it was his favourite, and he had it every day.

'Why do so many people love fatty bacon?' asked George.

'God knows,' said Nathaniel, 'It's the most bloody awful thing I have ever tasted. I wouldn't feed it to the pigs.'

'It's a man's food.' said Ephraim. 'You will love it when you get older.'

The lunch over, Ephraim settled into his favourite seat in the bay window with a jar of ale and regaled all and sundry with tales of his exploits as a young, lean, and fit young man. No one believed a word of what he said, but it proved to be a good hour's entertainment, especially for Nat and George, the only two in the room who had not heard all the stories before.

It looked as if Ephraim had settled in for the rest of the afternoon, so after profusely thanking their host, Nathaniel and George made their excuses and left. When they were on their way to collect their horses from the stables they arranged to meet the following Saturday lunchtime at *"The Nags Head"* public house in Bourne. 'We haven't had much of a chance to catch up today have we?' said Nat.

'No chance. Effy doesn't stop does he?' was the reply.

***

By the time Nathaniel had reached the age of eighteen years he had mastered the tasks of administering all their farms and the various people involved, and his father was generally pleased with his progress. Nathaniel was quite obviously capable but he was increasingly getting involved in gambling with some wealthy youths in Bourne and John was very worried where it was leading. He was associating regularly with George Montini who was known to be heavily in debt and whose father had threatened to disown him. He was also still subject to mood swings and periods of petulance when things were not going as he thought they should, something which John thought he should have got over as he had grown older.

Even so, his main concern was about his own health. He had to rely more on Nathaniel but he still did not believe Nathaniel's heart was in farming.

John's breathing problems were getting worse and he had suffered very badly during the last winter. Doctor Betts had told him he was very lucky to get through it, and said the only real solution was to spend the winter somewhere warm in future. Although he was capable of doing most things, he still required supervision, so there was no way John could leave the running of the estates to Nathaniel.

John had to formulate a plan to cover the situation if the worst came to pass and he was worried that it might come sooner than later. He did not think he could survive another winter particularly if it was a bad one. The only solution was to seek the advice of Ephraim Woolaston the next time he went to Grantham.

***

As John struggled up the steps to Ephraim's office he had to stop twice to catch his breath and when Ephraim came out to greet him he was shocked by John's appearance. He looked drawn and his cheeks were pinched and pale. The healthy glow of an outdoor life had completely gone.

'Come in and sit down John.' He was shocked at the difference since they had last met and tried not to mention health or to stare at him. 'I have been giving your problem some thought, John and I think I have the bones of a solution, if you agree.'

'Well, it has worried me for a while now and I need to get it sorted before the onset of winter. If you have a solution I would be eternally grateful.'

Ephraim described his plan to put the whole of the estate in trust for Nathaniel until he reached the age of twenty-five years. The trust should be administered by a group of people who John knew and in whom had total confidence that they would control the affairs honestly, and in the best interest of Nathaniel's future. The age of twenty five years would give Nathaniel time to adjust his ways, and his attitude to business before he actually took over.

'This is a smart way to control what is going on.' said John, 'I like the idea.'

'Right then, the first thing to do is to decide who you want to be trustees, I suggest you nominate three and you must get their agreement before we can proceed.'

'I would like you to be one of the three Ephraim, and I would also like Joseph Godbold and of course, George Heap. All three are honest and trusty gentlemen. Do you agree?'

'Thank you for your trust John, I would certainly like to be one of the three and the other two are perfect for the job.' said Ephraim with a smile on his face. 'If you can get the agreement of Joseph and George I will get started on the formal agreement and the details of the trust. I will bring it out to you for you to check and when it is all agreed and written out we will all have to get together to sign it.'

'That's fine,' replied John. 'Could you send for my chariot now?'

'Of course. Watson, send a boy round to get Mr. Thorold's chariot and don't hang around.'

'Yes sir, Mr. Woolaston. Right away.' Watson struggled off the stool, hobbled to the door and shouted down to the alley and told the yard boy to pass the message.

***

On the way back home, John thought the solution suggested by Ephraim was the best that he could do in the present circumstance. He had serious concerns about Nathaniel, especially his penchant for gambling on horses and poker and what Nathaniel referred to as the good life. Nathaniel was eighteen years old and he should have started to settle down by now. It was very important to give him more time to see sense and see the need for responsible behaviour. He was John's only child and there was no other close relative he could leave his estate to. John was a very worried man who was aware that he had not a great deal longer to live. It was imperative that the problem was sorted now.

John's thoughts went back to when Nathaniel was born and how his poor wife had suffered. He wondered how it would have been with her alive and able to raise Nathaniel and where he had gone wrong. Oh, how he wished Anne was still with him. Despite the bumpy road John closed his eyes and slept fitfully and had to be wakened when they arrived home.

The next morning, John settled down to write letters to Joseph Godbold and George Heap to explain his predicament and to ask for their help. If they agreed with his request to be trustees then would they contact Ephraim at Grantham to let him know?

Speed was of the essence. He sealed the letters and sent for George Headland the head horseman.

'George I want you to deliver these letters this morning, one is to Mr. Godbold and is marked with a cross, and the other is to Mr. Heap and is

39

marked with a circle. They also have their names written on the packet so that if you forget which is which you can let them pick their own. You know where they both live don't you, George?'

'Yes Mr. John, Sir.'

'Good, then off you go and don't give them to anyone else. If you can't find them bring them back to me.'

***

A couple of weeks later a messenger arrived from Grantham to say Mr. Woolaston would be arriving the next day with all the documents for Mr. John to go through and agree.

He arrived as arranged, and the two of them spent the morning going through the documents and checked that they were as agreed, and ready for signing. Everything was approved and Ephraim said he would get the other two trustees to come to his office at a time agreeable to John and they would all sign and witness the agreement.

After Ephraim had departed, Nathaniel asked his father what had been going on and so John told him what he had arranged and why he had done it. Nathaniel was not at all happy and flew into a rage which frightened John so much he almost collapsed. He told Nathaniel to leave the room and sat down heavily in his chair. He held his head in his hands and said to himself, 'Thank God, I have done it just in time, we must get it signed quickly. At least Nathaniel thinks it is already signed, if he thought otherwise I think he would have killed me to stop it.'

'Another seven bloody years before I get my money, who the hell does he think he is? It's my bloody inheritance, my right!' screamed Nathaniel in his room. 'The bastard doesn't trust me to do anything these days.' Then he flung himself on his bed and burst into tears.

Although he was in considerable pain, John made the journey to Grantham to sign the papers with the trustees. He explained Nathaniel's reaction to the news of the arrangements and said 'I think you gentlemen will have a difficult task when I am gone. I fear he may get worse rather than better and I dread to think what will happen to the estate when he reaches twenty-five years old. If he continues his gambling he will lose the whole lot but at least you should be able to keep things going until then.'

He was very tired when he arrived home and there were several of the workers congregated in the Yard, some were talking quietly in small groups while several were crying and wiping their eyes. Sylvia greeted him tearfully as he alighted from his chariot and informed him that Jack Green had died half an hour ago, whilst milking. Jack had been head cowman for as long as John could remember but was in no fit state to do much about it that day other than offer his condolences to Jack's family. In the morning he would have to appoint a replacement.

***

Over breakfast the next morning, Nathaniel was very quiet, as he had been ever since he had heard his father's plans. 'Who do you think should replace Jack, Nathaniel? My opinion is that there is only one person who could do the job successfully. Have you any suggestions?'

'It can only be Mo.' replied Nat, 'but I don't suppose you will want him, will you?'

'Why wouldn't I want Maurice? As far as I am concerned he is the man for the job and it seems that you agree. I think I will have a word with him after breakfast and tell him the good news.'

'He will be delighted father, I wish you could be so sure about your only son. How do you think I feel when you kick me in the teeth like you did?'

'You know why I feel like I do Nathaniel, I have explained to you time and time again what you need to do. You know I am a sick man and have not long to live and, of course, the future of the estate concerns me deeply. Someone will need to take on the responsibility of running the whole of my estate and even though you know what is required, you have yet to prove to me that you are committed to the task. At the moment I do not think you are ready and you also have a serious social problem. You know what it is and if you can't control your gambling and your temper, I see no real reason to give you my trust. I have subsidised your habit for long enough and it has got to stop before it's too late. What I am doing is giving you an extra few years to come to your senses, and even if you can't see it now I hope you will in the very near future. The trustees are all very capable and fair gentlemen and they will help you, provided that you are willing to help yourself. The way you reacted to what I told you yesterday reinforced my opinion that you still have quite a way to go before you are ready to take over.

Furthermore, the money is not yours, it is money to enable the estate to operate efficiently and thrive. It has been my responsibility to use the money left to me by my father in the best interests of the estate and to ensure we can continue in business. It is not there to subsidise one selfish person's gambling habits. We can only help all our workers to stay in work if we are successful. Until you understand and are completely dedicated to that task you are not ready for the job. Do you understand?'

'Yes father, but *you* don't understand. I am not a heavy gambler and I win as much as I lose so it's not fair to say I have a problem. I only gamble at weekends and once in a while I have a race with someone who thinks he can ride better than me. You can ask William Grimes at *"The Five Bells"* and he will tell you that what I say is true.'

'You can say what you like Nathaniel but remember, I know all the landlords for miles around here and I always know by the next day which pub you have been in. I know all the fights you have had and they usually happen when you are losing at poker. I know when Maurice has come to your rescue and I always know when you get drunk. Just don't try to say I don't understand. I know your reputation and just think yourself very lucky I have not completely deserted you. This is your last chance to redeem yourself just stop making excuses and grow up! Now go and get on with your work and ask Maurice to come and see me please.'

Nathaniel went out into the yard and crossed over to the barn, muttering to himself and cursing his bastard of a father. Mo came out of the cowshed just as Nathaniel was heading towards him and as Mo said, 'Good morning Nat.' Nathaniel lashed out with his foot at a wheelbarrow as he passed it.

'What in hell's name is up with you this morning Nat?'

'Father wants to see you in the library now.' was all Nathaniel said.

'What for?'

'You will find out when you see him.'

Mo was a bit worried because of Nathaniel's attitude and so went directly to the house where Sylvia took him through to the library.

'What's it all about Sylv?'

'I haven't a clue Mo, perhaps you had better go in.'

The library door was open and Mr. John saw Maurice arrive and beckoned him in.

'Maurice, you know about the sad event that occurred yesterday and you realise that we need someone to be in charge of Jack's men. Well, both Nathaniel and I think you are the right man for the task and I would like you to take over immediately from where Jack left off. I have been impressed by the way you work and although you are still a young man I know you will do a good job. Are you happy with that, and have you any questions?'

'Thank you very much Mr. John, Sir. I won't let you down. Does anyone else know yet?'

'Not yet, but I will inform everyone during the morning.'

'I haven't any other questions but what the hell is up with Nat?'

'I think you had better ask him.' said John.

***

Nathaniel was in a vile mood all day and every time Mo went to say something he just walked away. Eventually Nathaniel told Mo he was going to "The Five Bells" later that evening and did Mo want to come.

'Not unless you are in a better mood, what the hell's going on?'

'I'm sorry, it's not your fault Mo. I'm pleased for you, I really am. If you come and have a jar I will tell you tonight. I have to get it off my chest or I will go mad and there is no one else I can talk to. Promise you will come.'

'OK, but I might be late as I have a lot to do today.'

As Mo was going about his new job and talking to his men, he was repeatedly asked about Nathaniel who was storming around the farm swearing and kicking anything that got in his way. He was in a foul temper and efforts were made to keep well out of his way as he did not have a good word for anyone. Rumours were rife, and speculation had it that he was going to be disinherited. The whole workforce knew of Mr. John's displeasure at Nathaniel's behaviour and they also knew that Mr. John had been involved in discussions with Mr. Woolaston who had also been at the farm all yesterday morning. This visit was seen as the catalyst to the present situation.

That evening Nathaniel arrived at "The Five Bells" quite early and there were only a few of the older regulars sitting in their usual seats or playing dominoes at one of the long wooden tables. Nathaniel said nothing to anyone. He was on his third refill when Mo came through the door and espied him, sitting on his own and bent over his ale. 'Good evening Will, what sort of mood is he in? 'asked Mo, pointing to Nathaniel.

'I haven't a clue, but he's certainly not talking to anyone, so tread carefully.'

'I have been treading carefully all bloody day and I am getting sick of it. If he doesn't open up quickly I'm not stopping, I've got better things to do than sit down with a miserable sod all night.'

'I don't blame you.' said Will, serving Mo his ale. 'Good luck.'

Mo crossed the room and sat next to Nathaniel, 'Hello Nat, what have you got to say for yourself? You have been in a shit mood all day and an apology would not be out of order.'

'I know and I am really sorry, I shouldn't have behaved like that but father had a real go at me today. I have never seen him so angry and it was not very nice.'

'It's not the first time he has given you a going over, you should be used to it by now and I would have thought it would have bounced off like it usually does. Anyway, you never take any notice of him do you?'

'I have never had one like today, it was horrendous. Get me another pot of ale and I will tell you all about it.'

Mo called William and ordered another ale for Nathaniel and when he brought it over he said to Will, 'I think it's going to be a long night.'

'Well just watch your mate, he's had a few already.'

***

'Right Nat, let's hear it, right from the beginning.'

Nathaniel told Maurice everything that his father had said and during the telling, consumed a few more jars of ale. He started to get a bit excited when he got to the explanation of the agreement his father had drawn up and Mo calmed him down but said, 'You can surely see why he is worried can't you? He's been telling you for over two years and you have completely ignored him. What did you expect him to do?'

'I thought I would get everything when he passed on, not have to wait for at least seven years.'

'He has not passed on yet, and you may have to wait another ten years if his health improves.'

'Yes but the money is mine when he goes he has no right to put it in trust. It's wrong.' Nathaniel whined.

'I am sure he told you the money is not yours, so I suggest you start doing what he wants before it's too late. The trustees will have the final decision when you inherit. They will be obliged to do the best for the future of the estate.'

'I can't do a bloody thing around here without him finding out about it. He has spies everywhere and there's one over there.' He pointed to the

44

landlord William and shouted, 'That nosey bastard reports back to him every time I come in here. Bloody Judas!' He leapt off his seat and before Mo could intervene, he had hold of William by the throat and was trying to strangle him. Mo, with some help from some of the other lads managed to force Nathaniel off and after a few seconds William managed to point to the door and with difficulty said, in a croaking voice, 'Get out of here, and never ever come back in this Inn whilst I am the landlord!

'That was the most stupid thing you could ever have done,' shouted Mo. 'what the hell got into you, have you gone mad? Everyone within miles will know what you have done and they won't need William to tell them. You stupid bastard! It will be me in front of your father tomorrow and I could do without all that crap.'

Mo escorted Nathaniel home and before he left he told him, 'Stop behaving like a spoilt child Nat, you are just proving to your father that he was correct in his opinion of you. If you don't start to behave sensibly, he could easily decide to cut you out of his will altogether and what would you do then?'

'He can't do that, there is nobody else to leave it to, I am his only child.'

'You just try his patience anymore and see what happens, but don't come crying to me when it's too late. Now, get off to bed and get your excuses ready before you see your father at breakfast.'

***

John had not had a good night. He was still having difficulty breathing and was feeling tired when he got up that morning. He thought it might help if he had a short walk around the field to get some fresh air before he went for breakfast. As he walked, he spoke to a few of the workers and it was not long before he heard of Nathaniel's performance of the previous night. By the time he sat down to eat he was fuming with rage and had almost decided to call on Ephraim and change his will completely.

He had nearly finished his breakfast when Nathaniel entered the room. 'Don't sit down Nathaniel. If you want breakfast, you will eat it in the kitchen. I will see you this afternoon to tell you what I intend to do with you when I have made up my mind. Now go away and stay away until I call you.'

'But father I......'

'You heard what I said, now go!'

As Nathaniel left the room he heard his father coughing loudly and gasping for breath.

Nathaniel sat in silence in the kitchen as Sylvia prepared a breakfast for him. 'Why do you do it Nathaniel?' she asked, 'you are bright lad, what do you think behaving like a spoilt child is going to do for your future, nobody will take you seriously and you will always be treated like a schoolboy. None of the workers will ever look up to you when you take over from your father if you carry on like this.'

Nathaniel said nothing but thought, 'If I ever take over, fat chance now.'

Mo kept well out of Nathaniel's way all that day. He had plenty of work to do and listening to Nat would only be a distraction he didn't need. He knew Nat was capable of running the farm successfully but it was up to him to change his ways and start taking things seriously. If only he would listen to his father and act on it, the whole atmosphere would change dramatically. He said to himself, 'He must be on his last warning by now. If he doesn't change he will be disowned!'

***

'Sylvia, would you find Nathaniel for me please, and ask him to come to my study now?' asked John.

Sylvia went into the yard and asked a few of the men if they knew where Nathaniel was and no one seemed to have seen him since morning. Eventually, someone said they had recently seen him go into the barn so she went into the gloomy interior and tried to adjust her eyes to the semi-darkness. She called his name a couple of times and got no answer. She was about to leave when she heard a small shuffling sound and Nathaniel appeared from behind an old cart which was loaded with hay.

'What on earth are you doing there Nathaniel? You look terrible. How long have you been in there? Why were you hiding?' Sylvia fired her questions at him in quick succession. 'You had better get inside and get yourself cleaned up, your father is waiting for you in his study and you can't see him looking like that.'

'I have been thinking.' was all he said as he crossed the yard and went into the house. He felt it was as if he was on his way to his own execution.

When he had tidied himself up he went down, and with his heart beating fast and hard, knocked on the study door. His father called him in and

46

told him to sit down, pointing to the chair the other side of the desk.

***

'Nathaniel, we both know why you are here and I am not listening to any more of your excuses so I want you to listen to me for the last time. Your behaviour last night was disgraceful and will not be tolerated by me or indeed anyone in the village. My first reaction was to remove your name from my will immediately, however, even though I still am inclined towards that action, I have decided to give you one final chance and by that I do mean final, there will be no more let offs. First, your allowance will be stopped for one month starting today. Second, your behaviour will be on trial for the next six months and any misdemeanours during that time will result in you being written out of my will with immediate effect. Finally, the first thing you will do is to go down to *"The Five Bells"* and apologise to William Grimes and beg his forgiveness. You will also offer to work for him for a week without pay or complaint.' John paused, but before Nathaniel could respond he said, 'I don't want to hear what you have to say and you had better believe what I have said. If you don't start to behave like a gentleman and earn the respect of everyone in the village, you are finished. I mean every word of it so go now and get started at *"The Five Bells"*. Please close the door on the way out.'

***

Although the whole thing had been discussed and arranged with Nathaniel's father, William Grimes was not at all pleased when Nathaniel turned up to tender his apology. His neck still carried the marks of last night's attack and he was still in a degree of pain. He was in no way going to make it easy for Nathaniel, nor was he going to lift the ban on drinking he had imposed. 'What does sorry mean to you Nathaniel? I have heard it from you so many times in the past I don't think you have any idea what it means or how to show sorrow. As for your working for me, I accept, but just do not think you will get an easy ride. You will work from seven in the morning until dusk, starting tomorrow. You will not be fed by me so bring your own food if you want any, and you will definitely not be touching any of my ale. I will think about your apology overnight and then decide whether to accept it or not. Now go home and don't be late in the morning.'

That night Nathaniel spent long hours on his bed thinking over the day's events. He had never seen his father so angry and he realised that it was his last chance. His behaviour in the pub was inexcusable and seeing the marks on Williams's neck ·had finally made him understand that he could not go through life thinking of himself to the detriment of everyone else. He understood, at last, that he could have killed the man. His best friend Mo had agreed with what his father and others had said so he must be doing something wrong. He vowed to do as his father wanted and to try to behave in a more responsible way. He had finally understood that if he carried on in the same old way he would be left without a penny and all that that would mean. His future was in his own hands he vowed that he would make a start tomorrow at *"The Five Bells"*.

***

John was still in his study after his meeting with Nathaniel. He was still suffering quite badly with his breathing and the confrontation with his son had not improved matters, but more seriously, he was worried that he would not have the strength to carry out his ultimate threat if things did not improve. He also thought it would be useful to prepare an alternate will that would only require signing if needed. If he did that, then the action could be taken very quickly with minimum trouble and so he decided to contact Ephraim in the morning.

There was a knock on the study door and Sylvia put head around and asked, 'Are you free to see the vicar Mr. John?'

John wasn't expecting a visit but he replied that he was and asked Sylvia to show him in.

'Come in Roger and take a seat. What can I do for you?'

As Roger sat down he noticed that John was looking very old and tired. He seemed to have aged since he last saw him, only a few days ago, and thought it best not to mention his health.

'Well, there are two things really, I was extremely disturbed to hear of the fracas in *"The Five Bells"* last night and of Nathaniel's involvement. It worries me deeply that he seems to be going off the straight and narrow in an alarming way and I don't think he knows how to control his actions. He could have killed William and we all know what the result of that would have been.'

'I agree entirely with what you say Roger, I have dealt with him this afternoon as best I can.' said John who then went on to explain his actions and what he proposed to do if no improvement was forthcoming.

'I am pleased.' replied the vicar, 'now for my news. I have recently made the acquaintance of a widow in the village and we are now seeing each other formally. I am sure you have heard the rumours.'

'No I haven't heard anything, who is the lucky lady?'

'It is Charlotte Headland, George Headland's sister.'

'Congratulation Roger, she is a lovely lady. Let's have a glass of rum to celebrate, I needed cheering up!'

'I would love one, John, thank you,' and deciding the time was right to broach the subject of John's health, continued, 'but I haven't asked you how you are feeling lately. We are all concerned about your health of late. Have you seen signs of any improvement?'

'Not really, I have difficulty getting a good night's sleep and feel very tired most of the time. I find it hard to concentrate on anything for long and this business with Nathaniel is really getting me down.'

They both relaxed over the glass of rum and talked in general about happenings in the village. Eventually Roger said it was time he went home and John thanked him for coming and said, 'It's been lovely seeing you this afternoon, we have put the world to rights again. I feel much better now than when you arrived and I am delighted for you and Charlotte. It's wonderful news.'

***

Nathaniel was at *"The Five Bells"* before seven the next morning determined to do as he was told and show willing. He had made up his mind that if he was going to get back in his father's – and Mr. Grimes' – good books, then he had to comply with all instructions without question. This was going to be hard and he realised it was going to be a very difficult week.

Nat's first task was to clean out the stables at the back of the pub. He made sure the job was done properly and the place was spotless before he told Mr. Grimes he had finished. He was then put straight on to cleaning out the pig sties. Other than half an hour break for lunch his work was continuous. By the time he went home he was absolutely exhausted and Mr. Grimes had not made any comment on the standard of his work. This upset Nathaniel, but he was not surprised and he certainly was not going to let it show.

The work at *"The Five Bells"* continued at the same rate for the rest of his punishment and Mr. Grimes had still made no comment, either good or bad. When Nat finished feeding the pigs for the last time and cleaned up afterwards he went to tell the landlord that he had finished and was told to wait outside the back door and he would be out to check his work in a couple of minutes.

When William came out he had a pot of ale in his hand and said, 'You have done a really good job Nathaniel, I didn't think you had it in you. Here drink this but just remember the ban on entry to the pub still stands so don't bother coming round and trying it on.'

'Thank you Mr. Grimes, you will never get any more trouble from me and I am extremely sorry about what happened last week.'

The landlord had kept Nathaniel's father fully informed of progress during the week and John was very pleased by what he heard but he still had very serious doubts as to the future.

***

The next six months were a long hard slog for Nathaniel. He was determined to keep his behaviour and actions under control and comply with his father's guidelines. He now fully understood the error of his ways, and even though he had lapses, he made sure they were only minor and that other people were never involved. He also found that if he wanted to let off steam, a good gallop on his horse would help to clear his head. Mostly he went on his own and other times with Mo. Mo was still a very good friend who was always willing to listen to his occasional outburst and Nathaniel knew it would go no further. Mo was always at hand to offer advice or help and Nathaniel relied on him to help keep on track.

"The Five Bells" pub was still out of bounds and after promising the landlord of *"The Kings Head"* that he would behave at all times, Nathaniel was allowed in. His future visits there were dependent on strict rules whilst on the premises, one of which he was never to be involved in a fight. Any contravention would result in a lifetime ban and as he didn't want to go all the way to Bourne for a drink, he had to behave. The first Saturday night at *"The Kings Head"* resulted in Nat being goaded by some of the lads to try to get him involved, but, helped by Mo he resisted the temptation and kept well clear of the inevitable fracas. This did prove difficult, but, over time it was accepted that he would not get involved and apart from having to suffer the occasional name calling, he managed to keep out of trouble.

During the few months of warmer weather, John's health improved and with Nathaniel seemingly back on track John was a much happier man. He was hoping Nathaniel could continue his improvement and would not have to implement the new will he had drafted with Ephraim's help. He had taught

50

Nathaniel nearly all the tasks he could, and was pleased when his son had negotiated new leases on two of the farms without any help from anyone. Ephraim Woolaston had reported that he could not have done it better himself and said that Nathaniel's attitude was spot on. John had high hopes but still had serious worries that there would be a relapse. John thought to himself, not for the first time, 'Only time will tell, only time will tell.'

***

Winter was fast approaching and it was time for John to decide on what action he was going to take about Nathaniel now that his six month warning was due to expire. There was no doubt that his son's behaviour had been exactly as had been asked of him, but doubts still lingered in his mind, 'was it permanent or will he revert to type as soon as I lift the threat.' It was a difficult decision but it had to be made. John was also aware that his health problems were likely to return as winter came and if it was as bad as last year, he might not survive.

No matter which decision he made, Nathaniel could not take over the estate until he reached the age of twenty-five years, so John would see Nathaniel in the morning and tell him that he had survived his six month warning period.

***

At breakfast the next morning, Nathaniel was the first to arrive soon to be followed by his father. They exchanged the usual pleasantries and talked generally about the day's work to be done. When Nathaniel had finished he excused himself and started to get up from the table to leave and his father said, 'Sit down for a minute Nathaniel, I have something to discuss with you.' Nathaniel sat down again and John continued 'It is almost six months since we discussed your attitude at length and I am pleased to say you look as if you have taken my suggestions to heart. Everyone has seen a great difference in the way you approach your work and particularly your general behaviour to others in the village. I can only say I am delighted to remove the threat I made and I hope that you will not revert to your old ways again. I know that you still have some work to do to restore any credibility you may have had with William Grimes at "The Five Bells", but I am sure you will manage that eventually. Well done Nathaniel.'

'Thank you father, I have tried my best and I now realise how important and responsible my position is, especially when I eventually take

51

over. I just wish you had not imposed the trustees on me until I am twenty-five.'

'Although you are doing very well at the moment you must remember that you are only eighteen years old. I was nearly twenty eight when I took over and it was very difficult for me and I had no one to guide me at all. If I died now you would be struggling in several areas of the job. You would be on your own and at the mercy of some very experienced people who would take advantage of your age and lack of experience. That is the very last thing I would like to happen. The trustees will be on hand to give you help and valuable advice which would be otherwise unavailable to you. Do you understand what I mean?'

'Yes, I think so, I am very pleased you are not striking me from your will but I worry that the trustees might interfere and try to run the place.'

'That is not their job, they are appointed solely to make sure things are run in a proper business-like manner and help you in the best way they can. You know them all, and I am sure you agree they are all honest hard working men'

'Yes, and I like them all too, so that is a good start.'

***

By the middle of November the winter had set in and the damp freezing fogs were settling on the flat landscape. It was impossible to avoid the cold, even on the occasional bright sunny day the temperature remained below freezing. The ground was rock hard and the rivers and ditches were frozen solid. The cattle they had kept to overwinter were brought inside and fed on hay and turnips that had been kept for that purpose. Most of the stock had been slaughtered or sold at the markets so as to ensure the small amount of fodder available would be adequate for the remaining stock. It was important that these beasts survived the winter and were able to breed in the New Year. They always prayed that the winter would not be too long or too severe.

***

Every autumn a couple of pigs were killed and the meat kept for the master and his friends. Very rarely would any of the farm workers be given any for their own use and meat was considered a luxury that was beyond their reach. However some of them were usually given a small plate of the pigs 'fry,' which consisted of liver, kidney and other parts which could not be preserved for later consumption.

The killing of the animals and preparation of the meat fell to Mo and his team and on a good dry day the selected animal would be put in a small pen on its own, and while one of the men held a bucket under the pig's neck, the man with the knife slit the pig's throat. As much as possible of the ensuing flow of blood was caught in the bucket. When the pig had fallen and died it was hoisted by its back legs and with its legs separate, hung from a high beam and the remaining blood drained into the bucket. Its stomach was then slit open and its internal organs pulled out into a large wooden bath or tub. Meanwhile plenty of water had been boiled and using sharp blades dipped in the hot water all the hairs were scraped off the carcase. The bath of entrails and the bucket of blood were taken into the kitchen in the master's house and the fry was separated and divided into equal portions to share out. The blood was kept ready for making black pudding. The intestines were cut into three feet lengths and given to the younger children to be cleaned ready for use as sausage skins. This was a very dirty and painstaking job where all the contents had to be squeezed out. They were then carefully turned inside out and cleaned properly great care being taken not to tear the delicate structure. Once the lengths were as clean as they could get them, they were put in a tub of brine and soaked overnight to sterilise them.

Meanwhile, preparations were being made for salting the meat in order to ensure it stayed edible for as long as possible. It meant scraping a large number of blocks of salt into a large shallow wooden tub until there was enough to cover all the joints of pork that were to be preserved. It was a job that was hated by all the workers and they all tried to be doing something else at the time this needed to be done. Consequently it usually ended up with the youngest workers and children getting the sore, salt encrusted hands so detested by everyone, but it was essential that this task was completed before the carcase was cut into joints. This would take place when it had hung for a few hours, the blood had drained out and all the hairs had been scraped off.

For salting, the carcase was cut in six big joints, two front legs, two back legs and two whole sides. These were placed in the tub and the salt thoroughly rubbed into the joints. It had to be well covered before they left it to do its work. Any smaller bits of meat, which had been cut off were taken to the kitchen to be turned into sausages, pork pies and brawn. When the main joints had spent sufficient time in the salt they were taken out and hung up, usually in the kitchen or another dry place to dry out. When fully cured, meat was cut off as required.

Nathaniel had never really liked farming and the whole operation of killing large animals repulsed him. Whenever this was to take place he made an excuse to visit one of the other farms or had business to attend to in Grantham. Today was no exception and he had gone to discuss farm rents with Ephraim Woolaston.

***

There was no break from the cold and John was beginning to suffer quite badly. His cough was getting worse by the day and he was unable to do the few physical tasks he liked to do. He spent more time indoors in front of the fire and rarely ventured outside.

Nathaniel was approaching his nineteenth birthday and was dealing with more and more of the tasks his father used to handle and was growing in confidence. His attitude and application to the job was obvious but his father would still not rescind the agreement that involved trustees being appointed.

John still had a nagging feeling in the back of his mind that there was a chance of Nathaniel reverting to his old ways. It was less than a year since he had imposed the threat to Nathaniel's future and the boy was still very young. As he had said many, many times, 'Only time will tell, only time will tell.'

***

With the onset of winter the work on the farm went into a different mode. Where they could break the surface of the fields, George Headland had his men out with the horses turning over the land to allow the frost to break up the earth. It was a hard job, the days were short so there were few breaks and the horses had to be groomed and fed when they were brought back. Working in the dark with only an oil lamp for illumination was not easy.

Mo had his men feeding and milking the cows and keeping the sheds clean, any spare time the men had, they were out in the fields cleaning out ditches or 'plashing' the hedges. There must be no gaps where the cattle or sheep could escape when they were back in the fields next year. Farming was very labour intensive and a backbreaking job at the best of times and on a cold, freezing winter's day it was very uncomfortable.

Nathaniel, although working extremely hard and doing all that was expected of him, still did not have his heart in the job. He had decided that farming was not for him but he couldn't think of anything else he would like to do. He considered it frustrating that he should be tied to the farm but on the

54

other hand knew that if he went elsewhere then his money would dry up and he would never get it back. He had often discussed it with Mo who always pointed out the advantages that would come his way eventually. 'Still', he thought, 'Someday I will be able to make up my own mind. I have just got to wait until I am twenty-five.'

**

As the New Year arrived, John was thinking, 'Just a few more months and the weather should start to improve, and so might my health.' He knew in his heart of hearts that he was only trying to fool himself, and in reality, he was deteriorating quickly. The last time he went outside the house was over a month ago and that was for the funeral service of Miss Joyce, the old cook and housekeeper.

Mr. John decided to send for Ephraim Woolaston and go through all the necessary papers and to get them in order. He knew he would not last through the winter. He also made arrangements to see the other two trustees later the same day as he was seeing Ephraim. They could stay and have dinner with him and all four enjoy a final evening get-together. The meeting was arranged for the last week in January and when the work was complete they all sat down and enjoyed a glass of rum and talked of old times. Although John was looking extremely poorly, the atmosphere was relaxed and there was a great deal of laughter. Afterwards they all enjoyed a hearty meal of ham and eggs cooked by Sylvia, the newly appointed cook and housekeeper.

When the guests said their farewells they all knew that it was the last time they would see their friend. It was bitterly cold as John stood in the doorway watching them get in their carriages. It was a crisp, clear, frosty night and the moon was shining brightly as John watched them disappear down the lane for what he knew, was the last time. He closed the door behind him and struggled up the stairs to his bed coughing as he went.

On the first day of February, Sylvia took John's breakfast to his room and placed it on his bedside table where he liked it, Dawn was breaking as she went to open the curtains and said, 'Good morning Mr. John.' There was not much light in the room yet, and so she went downstairs to get the wood and kindling to light his fire. When she came back into the bedroom she noticed that John had not moved and his breakfast was still untouched. She went over to the bed and spoke to him again and when he did not reply she realised he was not breathing. He had passed away peacefully during the night.

Chapter 5

Early 1722

It gradually dawned on Nathaniel that his father had gone and would never return. Never would he be able to talk to him or ask his help or advice. What his father had tried so hard to tell him started to mean something now that all the bravado and false confidence of youth had disappeared. He suddenly understood one of the reasons his father had appointed trustees, it was because he was not yet ready to run the estate on his own and Nathaniel was thankful that knowledgeable people were now at hand to help should he need to call on them.

***

At his father's funeral, Nathaniel, whilst in conversation with Ephraim Woolaston, had suggested arranging a meeting between himself and the three trustees at Ephraim's chambers in Grantham. Ephraim agreed and said, 'Of course, it is important that we get things sorted out fairly quickly. I also need to read the will, so we will do it at the same time. I suggest that one week from today, at nine o'clock in the morning should be convenient. Would that be alright with you?'

'Yes that will be fine.'

'Good, then I will confirm that with the other two before I leave.'

***

Nathaniel was up early on the day of the meeting and was quite nervous and apprehensive about what the outcome would be. He had no idea what the will would say but he already knew that most of any inheritance would be delayed until he was twenty-five. He was the first to arrive at Ephraim's chambers and was greeted by Watson who was still struggling to move with any trace of speed.

A voice bellowed from the inner room, 'Come in Nathaniel,' and as Nathaniel entered his room, 'take a seat, the others should be here soon, I saw George Heap in town earlier. How are you getting along at Borton now that you are in charge?'

'Things seem to be settling down quite well, thank you. It has been quite an upsetting period, particularly for the household staff, but Sylvia is well in control and keeps them occupied. The farm side of things has carried on with little sign of disruption'

56

Joseph Godbold and George Heap arrived together about ten minutes later and Watson once again clambered off his high stool with difficulty and tried to get to the door before the visitors closed it. He did not quite make it and hobbled back to his stool and had the usual struggle to climb back in his seat.

'Watson,' boomed Ephraim. 'Get me the Thorold papers.'

'Yes Sir, right away.' said Watson and once more dismounted his high stool, hobbled over to the pile of papers on the steps and started to rummage through them. No sooner had he started when Ephraim once again bellowed.

'Watson, it's alright, I've found them, they are here on my desk.'

Watson tidied up the papers as best he could and with a look of complete resignation, started out on his painful journey back to his desk.

**

'Welcome gentlemen, it's nice to see you all again. Don't look so worried Nathaniel, it will all become clear very soon.'

'I can't help it Mr. Woolaston, it is my future that's at stake here. I am sure anyone would be nervous in my position.'

'Probably so, but let's get on with it and put you out of your misery.'

Nathaniel tried to relax as Ephraim took the ribbon off the will with a flourish, rolled open the package and in an exaggerated manner, flattened out the paper with the palm of his hand. He cleared his throat loudly and started to read the document:

'In the name of God, Amen, I, John Thorold of Borton in the County of Lincoln being somewhat unfit in body but of good and perfect remembrance thanks be to Almighty God, do ordain, make and publish this to be my last will and testament written all with mine own hand and manner. Following such, I commend my soul into the hands of Almighty God, the father, son and Holy Ghost hoping to be saved of God's most mercy and favour towards me. For the only merit death and passion of Jesus Christ my only perfect saviour through faith in his blood and my body I desire to have it brought to the earth and buried decently without all pomp next to my beloved wife Anne. Also I do revoke, repeal and frustrate all former wills and testaments made by me before this twelfth day of November in the year of our Lord God One Thousand Seven Hundred and Twenty One.'

Ephraim droned on for what seemed an age and there had been no mention of Nathaniel, who remained just as nervous as when he arrived in the chambers, and now he was beginning to get a bit worried. Some of the senior workmen had been left a small cash sum and the poor of the village had been provided for, but still no mention for him. What the hell was going on? He glanced to either side at George and Joseph to see their reactions and Joseph was fast asleep.

'Obviously he's not expecting to benefit from a bequest. Still, he will benefit from being appointed as an executor and that will provide him with a few pounds.' thought Nathaniel sarcastically.

'...and for my only son Nathaniel,' intoned Ephraim 'I leave all my property, farms, tenements and hereditaments, both freehold and leasehold. All my personal belongings currently in my Manor House at Borton and all my deposits in the Bank of England in London. The aforesaid bequest will not be available to my son Nathaniel until he attains the age of twenty five years. Until then the estates will be administered by the appointed trustees, Ephraim Woolaston, Joseph Godbold and George Heap.' Ephraim paused for effect and took a sip of water, before continuing, I am fully aware that Nathaniel's heart is not currently in farming and so he needs to get things clear in his mind as to what he is interested in. I have therefore, provided Nathaniel with, under the control of the trustees, enough funds for him to go on a tour of Europe to see if this will help him make a decision upon his future direction in life. I expect him to start this tour in the immediate future and to be away for no more than one year. I have also arranged for him on his return, to spend six months in London with my cousin, Samuel Thorold who is very successful in the ironmongery business. This should give Nathaniel a good grounding in modern business practices.'

Ephraim carried on for quite some time but Nathaniel did not take in what was being said. His thoughts were wandering at leisure, through exotic countries of Europe, no farm to worry about for a whole year. He said to himself, 'Thank you father, thank you. London as well, it couldn't be better.'

Ephraim continued his flat, monotonous utterance....

'......In witness thereof I have put my hand and soul unto this my last will and testament and published to be my last will this Twelfth day of November anno domini One Thousand Seven Hundred and Twenty One by me John Thorold in the presence of them whose names hereunder be written.'

Ephraim then read out the names of the witnesses, rolled up the will carefully and deliberately, tapped the end of the roll to straighten it and said, 'That completes the reading of the will of John Thorold, late of Borton, your father. Have you any questions you would like to ask now Nathaniel, or would you like to go through any part of it again while we are all here?'

'Yes there is one question. When I go abroad for the year, am I expected to go alone or will I have a guide to show me the best places to go?'

'Your father has produced an outline route for your tour which includes a list of places he would expect you to visit and what to see in each place. There is a contact for you in each of the countries and they will supply you with local guides who can also speak English. He does not expect you to be alone at any time. All the contacts you will visit are all well respected gentlemen and are knowledgeable in the requirements of the English traveller. There is also provision enough for a companion to accompany you throughout. These details will be given to you by the trustees at a more appropriate time. Do not worry, you will have a great adventure.'

'Thank you, but what is going to happen to the estate from now on?'

'We will all get together a week from today at Borton and discuss the whole business of the estate and decide on a suitable time for your tour to commence. Are we all agreed on a week from today at Borton?'

All agreed and farewells were exchanged and as George and Joseph departed Ephraim said loudly, 'Watson, put these papers away where we can find them in a hurry.'

'Yes Sir,' said Watson changing direction as he staggered back towards his stool after having closed the door for the two departing gentlemen.

'Well Nathaniel, you have an awful lot to digest. If you have any questions or worries please contact me immediately.'

'Yes I will, and thank you very much. My head is spinning already and I expect I will have a great many questions for you over the next few days.

***

The next few weeks flew by and a great number of important decisions had to be made regarding both the estate and Nathaniel's trip to the continent. The most important thing that concerned Nathaniel was getting the financial arrangements in place and in particular, his monthly allowance. The first thing he discovered was that the trip was to be financed separately from his normal monthly allowance and the trustees said they would not change the current arrangements. He was to stay on his present allowance until he set off for his tour and then that would stop as he changed to the allowance for the tour, which as the trustees pointed out, was very generous.

The sum his father had set aside for the trip included provision for Nathaniel to take a man as his personal help. Nathaniel desperately wanted

Mo to accompany him but, as the trustees strongly stressed, Mo was much too important to the farm to let him go away for a year. Ephraim pointed out, once again, the trustees were there to ensure the estate was to run in a business-like manner and to send one of the key men away for a year was at best stupid, and at worst catastrophic. Nathaniel carried on with his argument but to no avail, the trustees were refusing to change their minds and as Ephraim finally pointed out, they had the authority and also held the purse strings. The trustees categorically refused to pay for Mo to leave his job for the trip and when Nathaniel had found someone he thought would be suitable, they would have to give their approval before they would release any funds. This was to be Nathaniel's first confrontation with the trustees and one he had no chance of winning.

Before the end of the first meeting Nathaniel was fuming. He had expected that the trustees would do as *he* wished, but in reality, they had done what they thought was best and had considered the wellbeing of the estates first. Failing to get an increase in his monthly allowance was absolutely devastating to Nathaniel. He was convinced that as the new man in charge he should have been given a generous increase but the other three did not agree. He considered that he had been ignored on the issue of his personal help for the trip and his authority had been undermined on his quest for an increase in his allowance. He quickly understood that he was not the new man in charge, but that these three old bigots were running the show and he was very angry. Was this really what his father wanted?

Nathaniel stormed out of the meeting and lashed out at anything or anyone who was silly enough to get in his way. He left the other three before the meeting was over and Ephraim said. 'It looks as if John was right, we have a big task on our hands, God knows where he has gone.'

'Well at least he will be out of the way for a year, so let's hope he sets off fairly soon.' replied Joseph.

***

In the house, Sylvia, who had dodged into the pantry when she heard him coming, said to herself, 'Here we go again! It looks as if he doesn't want to go to school again and this time there is no master to calm him down.'

***

Nathaniel saddled his horse, mounted and galloped away shouting and urging the horse to go faster. He headed away from the farm and across

60

the fields towards Bourne, just trying to relieve the anger and frustration that had built up inside him. He soon realised that he had made a fool of himself but he could not bring himself to return to the meeting and he would never forgive his father for imposing these three doddering old fogeys on him. It was just not fair, 'I am the rightful heir and the money should be mine now, not dependent on those old fools.' he shouted as he hit the horse harder and galloped faster over the open fields. He had no idea where he was heading and suddenly realised the light was fading and it would soon be dark. He was beginning to feel the cold already, 'I suppose I had better head for home or I will be stuck out here in the cold and catch my death.' As he turned for home he eased back on the reins and the horse steadied to a respectable trot. 'I don't know what I am going to say to old Ephraim when I get home.' he thought. 'I bet he won't be too pleased.'

***

'Oh, there you are,' said Sylvia as Nat came in from the stables. 'I thought you might be cold by the time you arrived home so I have prepared some hot soup to warm you through.'

'Thank you Sylvia, that is very kind of you but I think I could do with a tot of rum first.'

Sylvia went to the library where the rum was kept and when she came back she asked, 'what on earth was all that about Nathaniel? Your guests left shortly after you went out and Mr. Woolaston said he would like to see you at his chambers tomorrow morning at nine o'clock. All three of them were so angry, they didn't even say goodbye.'

Nathaniel ignored her attempt to find out the reasons for his departure from the house but told her that he would see Mr. Woolaston as requested. He was not looking forward to the meeting but it had to be done. He had made a bloody fool of himself and he knew it and tomorrow would be the time to make an effort to retrieve his dignity and respect. He was not optimistic. Later that evening Nathaniel decided to go round to *"The Kings Head"* for a quiet drink before retiring and as he crossed the yard he met Mo who was at the wood store getting some fuel for the fire. 'Like to come to *"The Kings Head"* for a quick one Mo? I could do with a bit of company after this afternoon.'

'Just let me take this wood indoors and I will be with you, but if you think you can behave like you did this afternoon you can think again. The whole farm saw the mood you were in and I am not putting up with it. I've

61

had a bellyful of your moans over the last few months and you certainly upset those gentlemen today. They were in a foul mood when they left.' replied Mo.

'Thanks for that short vote of confidence. I will start walking and you can catch me up. See you soon.'

Nat was in *"The Kings Head"* and buying the ale when Mo came in. There was a small circular table with two chairs in the corner just inside the door and Mo sat down and waited for Nathaniel. I hope to goodness we are not going to get one of his 'nobody loves me' sessions, thought Mo, I have had enough of them to last a lifetime.

'Right Nat, what happened this afternoon?' said Mo, 'Get it off your chest and then we can have the quiet drink you promised.'

Nathaniel told Mo in great detail what had been said at the meeting in the afternoon and why he had been upset about a couple of things. He said the trustees had been arrogant and overbearing and said that they thought that they were in charge. 'I was really upset when they said I could not take you on my tour and argued a little with them but they would not change their minds. I am sorry Mo, but I would have loved you to come.'

'Well, you have no need to worry about me on that score because there is no way I would have gone with you. I don't want to go to foreign parts and I am very happy to stay where I am, thank you.' said Mo. 'As for not giving you more money, are you really surprised they refused because I am not, and I bet you shouted and stamped your feet before storming out in a huff, didn't you?'

'I did, but I was upset and disappointed with what they had said.'

'...and I bet you blamed everyone but yourself. Am I right?'

'Yes you are, I even blamed my father.'

'Well Nat, you have only confirmed why your father brought in the trustees. He told you many times to grow up, and so did I. Behaving like a schoolboy only confirmed what the trustees already expected and you played right into their hands. Now, let us forget it and enjoy our drink, and don't for the Lords sake, get drunk tonight.'

Nathaniel took his friends advice for once, stayed sober and had an early night. He lay awake for quite some time pondering on how he was going to deal with tomorrow's meeting and fell asleep before he had come to any conclusion. At breakfast he asked Sylvia if Ephraim had indicated who would be at the meeting. Would it just be Ephraim and himself or would the other two be there as well but she did not know. He thought he could do with a good, stiff rum but decided that it probably would not help matters. He knew he was going to have to grovel as he had never grovelled before and would have to keep a very clear head for the meeting.

***

When Watson opened the door Nathaniel smiled and asked quietly, 'What is the mood like in there, Watson?' Watson raised his eyebrows, pursed his lips and sucked in a deep gulp of air, but said nothing.

'It's that bad is it? Well, wish me luck.'

Watson knocked on the office door and when Ephraim bellowed 'Come in.'

Nathaniel, his heart pounding and hands trembling, and fingers crossed, went in. Joseph Godbold was sitting on Ephraim's left and George Heap on his right. 'Sit down Thorold.' said Ephraim, pointing to an upright chair on the opposite side of the desk. 'I think you have something to say to us, haven't you?'

Nathaniel knew this was the time to begin his act of contrition, and began, 'I humbly apologise to each of you, both as individuals and as a group for my stupid actions yesterday. I am thoroughly ashamed of what I did, it was inexcusable. I had no justification for the way I behaved, it was the action of a spoilt child and was infantile in the extreme. I understand that you three honourable gentlemen were only doing what was required of you for the benefit of the estate and I responded as if you were out to steal my inheritance, which of course, I know full well that is not the case. I therefore beg your forgiveness and trust you will allow me to prove that I am a responsible, though still inexperienced young man. I assure you that the behaviour you witnessed yesterday will never be repeated and I understand that your decisions made at the meeting will stand. Please forgive me.'

'Thank you Nathaniel,' said Ephraim, in an unusually quiet manner, 'would you please wait in the outer office whilst we discuss your statement.'

Nathaniel waited outside as requested, and Watson, seated on his high stool clicked his teeth, raised his eyebrows and muttered softly, 'You will be lucky sir, if they don't cut your tongue out. I have never seen the boss so angry.'

Thank you for those few words of comfort Watson. That's all I need.'

***

In the inner chamber the trustees had already decided that their hands

63

were tied in how they could react to Nathaniel's behaviour. Their job was to administer the estate as best they could with the objective of handing it over to Nathaniel at the agreed age of twenty-five, and trying at the same time, to ensure he was capable of running things himself by the time he reached that age. At the moment it looked to be an impossible task and Joseph said, 'I think it will be best for all concerned that we get him off on his tour as soon as is possible. Just get him out of the way for a year and see what that does for him.' The other two nodded in agreement.

'We have got to find a suitable companion for him very quickly,' mused George, 'Any ideas?'

'I think when we refused him his choice of Maurice, we also gave him the option of finding someone suitable himself, and if that's the case we ought to ask him if he has any suggestions.' remarked Ephraim.

The other two nodded in agreement and Joseph expressed the opinion that anyone Nathaniel thought suitable would likely be one of his heavy drinking pals.

'I think we should give him one month to find someone we all agree is sufficiently responsible and if he fails, then we decide who it shall be. He might not like it but we have to get this scheme moving.' said George.

They all agreed and Ephraim suggested they call Nathaniel back in to tell him of their decision, but George said why not let him stew a bit longer. 'He certainly grovelled enough but I do not believe he has the ability to change his attitude. How many times has he apologised like that to his father, after all that's the reason we have been appointed as trustees.'

'A good idea, we will give him another few minutes but I have booked a table at *"The Angel"* for lunch so we better not wait too long.' said Ephraim, tidying some papers on his desk.

***

Nathaniel was trying to appear calm as he waited in the outer office but was failing miserably. He had tried taking deep breaths but it made no difference, his heart was still thumping madly and even when he tried to watch a spider devour a fly it had caught in its web, he could not concentrate. The sound of Watson's quill scratching across the paper was getting on his nerves but he dare not comment. In the end he asked Watson if he had any idea why they were taking so long and immediately realised that of course, Watson had no more idea of what was going on than he had himself. Watson shrugged his shoulders, raised his eyebrows and carried on with his scratching.

'Watson,' roared the voice from the inner office and Watson struggled off his stool, using his stick, hobbled across the room and knocked on the door.

'Come in.'

Watson struggled with the door knob and stumbled as he entered.

'Tell Mr. Thorold we will see him now.' boomed Ephraim.

'Yes Sir.' said Watson.

'Mr. Woola.....' but Nathaniel was already in the room before Watson could finish his sentence.

'Sit down Nathaniel.'

Nathaniel sat down and said nothing.

Ephraim began. 'We have listened to your apology and have grudgingly accepted it, although we all think it should have happened yesterday. The tenor of your statement indicates that you understand why you needed to make it and we hope that what you say is honest and well meant. We hope you will have no cause to repeat the actions that necessitated it. Such behaviour, as you fully understand, is totally unacceptable in any business situation.'

He continued, 'A large part of yesterday's discussion centred on a suitable companion for your trip to foreign parts and we indicated that you were free to select someone reliable who you would be happy to spend a year with. We, of course, would need to approve of the person you select and would have the final say with any appointment. We therefore are giving you one month from tomorrow to inform us of any such person and if you fail to find someone we will appoint someone for you. We appreciate that it would be better for you if you can find someone that you will get along with, but we must get things moving very soon. Do you understand, Nathaniel?'

'Yes, Mr. Woolaston.'

'There is one more thing before we finish. The matter of your allowance is closed and will not be discussed again until you return from your trip.'

'I understand.' replied Nathaniel as he thought to himself, 'I have got off lightly this time, it could have been far worse.'

'Very good, then we will see you again one month from tomorrow. If you find a suitable candidate, then we will see you earlier.' said Ephraim.

Chapter 6

On his way home, Nathaniel was deep in thought, had he come out on top or had the old fogeys won? By the time he arrived back at the manor house he had decided that his performance yesterday had produced absolutely nothing. Mo would not be coming with him on his trip and his tantrums regarding his allowance had been a waste of time, and after all that he had to go grovelling to the trustees and pleading with them for their forgiveness. I must bite my tongue in the future and think things through before I react; there is no way I am going to get caught out like that again.

His thoughts strayed to next Saturday, he had arranged to meet George Montini, his old school friend, in Bourne and they were going to the races. There was an annual Spring fair in Bourne where the local farmers would get together and organise races amongst themselves. Mostly the races were over open countryside and used natural features such as hedges and ditches as obstacles. Various courses were laid out and involved riders with varying degrees of ability. Neither George nor Nathaniel had entered this time, Nathaniel because his horse had only just recovered from a fall in which it had damaged a rear leg and George because he couldn't be bothered.

They had arranged to meet at *"The Nags Head"* Inn for lunch and a couple of ales before moving off to the races. George was already there when Nat arrived and was sitting by the side of a big log fire enjoying the warm glow and swigging his first pot of ale. 'Over here Nathaniel.' called George. 'Molly, get Nathaniel a pot of ale and bring it over.'

Nathaniel sat down and Molly arrived very quickly with a big pot of foaming ale. 'There you are my dear, do you two gentlemen want anything to eat?'

'Well I am starving,' said George, 'How about you?' Nathaniel, with his mouth full of ale, nodded his head in agreement. 'What have you got today Molly?'

'We have some nice strong cheese with homemade crusty bread and some lovely fatty bacon with boiled potatoes.' said Molly. 'What do you fancy?'

Both Nathaniel and George answered simultaneously, 'Cheese please.' and when Molly had gone to the kitchen both laughed and Nathaniel said, 'we could take some of that fatty bacon and load up a few rat traps, I am sure they would love it!'

After their lunch they mounted their horses and went to the field where the races were to take place. The field and surrounding area was extremely busy with groups of people chatting to friends they had not seen for ages and gentlemen in their carriages competing for the best vantage points. Safe areas had been set aside for non-competitors to tie up their horses for a fee and another area for the bookmakers. There were stalls which were selling all kinds of household equipment and others selling farm and garden produce.

Probably the busiest stall was one where the stall holder stood on a wooden box, expounding the virtues of his wonder cure. It would cure every type of ailment that country folk were ever likely to suffer and he held the large congregation of gullible spectators in his thrall. There were magicians, clowns, acrobats, tumblers and beggars everywhere you looked. Pickpockets were also reported to be around and warnings were given as people entered the field.

After Nathaniel and George had secured their horses and paid the fee to the attendant, they strolled around the entertainment area for a while, the racing was not due to start for another hour or so, and usually these events were late starting. They chatted to several people they knew and then Nathaniel spotted Neville Donnison looking very pleased with himself as he wandered past the butcher's stall. He was deep in conversation with a very pretty girl who was holding tightly to his arm.

'Hey look, George. There's Neville with a very attractive young lady. Let's go and have a word with him.'

'Didn't you know, that's my sister, Grace? Neville has been stepping out with her for a few months now.'

'Why didn't you tell me George, she's a beauty and I didn't even know you had a sister.' and as they approached their friend, Nathaniel called out, 'Hi Neville, I haven't seen you for ages, who is the beautiful lady?'

'Oh, hello Nathaniel, how are you? Can I introduce Miss Grace Montini, she is George's sister.'

'I am pleased to make your acquaintance Miss Montini. Your brother and I were at school together with Neville.'

'It is nice to meet you at last Nathaniel, I have heard a lot about you.'

'Nothing too bad, I hope.'

Grace, turning to George said, 'Have you seen Toni today George? He said he would be here this afternoon, so he will be around somewhere.'

'I haven't seen him as yet but I expect we will bump into him sometime.' said George.

'Who is Toni?' asked Nathaniel.

'He is my eldest brother.'

As they said their farewells to Neville and Grace, Nathaniel said, 'First you introduce me to a sister I knew nothing about, now you tell me you have a brother, you are full of surprises.'

'I have three brothers and two sisters, Toni is the eldest. He will be thirty in a couple of months. Then there is Samuel, William and Charlotte. You have already met Grace.'

'and I always thought you were an only child. What else haven't you told me?'

George laughed as they walked on and said that he had not thought it important and anyway, Neville knew all his family so the topic never arose.

***

The races were due to start at any time and Nathaniel suggested that if they were going to place any bets then they should make their way to the bookies' area otherwise they would miss their chance of a good win.

'If you are true to form Nathaniel, you will lose all your money before the last race.'

'I broke even at that meeting we went to in Sleaford so you know full well that I don't lose every time. Just sometimes! and another thing, you are a bigger gambler than I ever will be.'

They placed their bets with the first bookmaker they saw and wandered off to find a good point to see the race. It was easier said than done as the fields were so flat and the crowds were so deep. They found it impossible to get close to the track, so they gave up and went for a drink until the winner was announced. The result was not what they wanted, neither of them had won anything so they had another drink to give themselves time to sort out the next winner.

Their money went the same way in the second race and when George said his father was riding in race three, Nathaniel straight away said that was where he would put his money. George said Nat was a bigger idiot than he had thought. No way was he going to back his father.

While George was still deciding what to back, a smartly dressed

68

gentleman strode up to them and said, 'Wasting your money again, George.'

George looked up and said, 'Hello Toni, Toni this is my friend Nathaniel. Nathaniel, this is my brother Toni who I told you about earlier.'

'Good afternoon, Nathaniel, nice to make your acquaintance.'

'It's nice to meet you too, Toni. I understand there are still a few of your family I haven't met as yet. I have just put some money on your father in the next race so I hope he does well.'

'Wasted your money I would have thought.' replied Toni.

George explained that although his brother was always called Toni, it was short for Antonio after his Italian grandfather.

They all had another pot of ale as the next race progressed and waited for the result to filter through. When it was called out Nathaniel was delighted, George's father had won and he had a good sum to collect for a change. A few minutes later Georges father came in for a drink and introduced himself as Paulo. The conversation turned to how Paulo had come to live and marry in England and how he would like his sons to go to his old country and see his relatives sometime in the future. Toni could speak fairly good Italian but he would improve by talking regularly to native Italians. He thought Toni should go fairly soon whilst he was still single and young enough to enjoy the trip.

Paulo and Toni said their farewells and went off to see the horses while Nathaniel and George sorted out the next winner.

'What does Toni do?' asked Nathaniel.

'He is a teacher at the school attached to the church at Corby Glen where we live.'

'A bright lad, is he?

'Oh, yes. He is very knowledgeable in lots of things. As well as Italian, he can speak French and Spanish.'

'Come on George, we had better sort our horses out for the next race or we will miss it.'

After the last race they checked their winnings, in Nathaniel's case it was a loss but George had broken even, and then went to get their horses. They decided that it would be a good idea to call in at *"The Nags Head"* and down a quick drink before they said their goodbyes. *"The Nags Head"* was very busy but they managed to get a seat as two people were just leaving. Molly soon came over and took their order for ale and asked if they wanted anything to eat.

'There is still some boiled bacon and potatoes left if you are hungry.' she said.

The lads politely refused, George made his usual gagging noise and pulled a funny face to show his disgust.

The main reason Nathaniel had suggested calling in *"The Nags Head"* was that he wanted to sound George out regarding his brother Toni. From what he had heard during the afternoon it appeared that Toni had all the attributes required for a companion on a trip to the continent. He could speak three languages, he was intelligent and he was holding down a responsible job. He was also about thirty years old which he thought the trustees would see as a distinct advantage.

Nathaniel began to tell George about his problems over the last few weeks but said he was really looking forward to his trip abroad, if only to get away from the farm for a while. Working in London also looked promising but the main problem at the moment was finding a suitable travelling companion. He explained that he had been given a month to find someone and if he couldn't, the trustees would find someone.

'I will come with you Nathaniel, I would really enjoy it.'

'.. and I would love it to be you, George. We would have a great time but the trustees would regard you as a drinking mate and they want a companion with a responsible attitude. Someone like Toni who is a bit older and has proved to be reliable.'

'Well, why don't you ask him, I bet he would jump at the chance. He is always saying he would love to have a look around the cultural sights of Europe.'

'Do you really think he would be interested? asked Nathaniel.

'I know he would. Why don't you come over tomorrow after church and have some lunch with us and you can discuss it with him?'

'I will, thank you very much. I hope you are right, I have been frantic thinking about who to ask ever since they refused to let me take Mo.'

'That's settled then. We will see you tomorrow for lunch. You know where we live don't you?'

'I know you live at Corby Glen, but not whereabouts in the village.'

George gave him directions to his house and they finished their ale and went on their different ways.

***

Nathaniel was in high spirits as he made his way home to Borton and was looking forward to meeting Toni the next day and seeing what he thought of his proposal. The signs were promising as Toni's father had already expressed the notion that he wanted Toni to go to Italy and George had confirmed that Toni wanted to go. The bait that should clinch the deal was that all expenses would be funded by Nathaniel's father's bequest and Toni would have to pay nothing. Nathaniel's high spirits were somewhat dampened when he thought of Ephraim and his cohorts and was concerned that they might not approve. After all, they had disagreed with most of what Nathaniel had said.

***

Mo had just finished milking when he heard someone singing a jolly tune and then the sound of horses hooves on the cobbles in the yard. He went out of the cow shed to see who the visitor was and to his surprise he saw Nathaniel grinning from ear to ear.

'What on earth has got into you Nat, are you drunk again?' asked a very perplexed Mo.

'No I am not, I have just lost money at the races but I think I have found a substitute for you on my trip to foreign climes. I don't think even old Ephraim will refuse this one.'

Nathaniel dismounted and handed the horse over to one of the stable hands and then proceeded to tell Mo about Toni Montini.

'You are not taking that gambler with you, are you? You will be in trouble before you get to Dover.'

'No, that's the wrong one, Toni is the eldest brother and he is a teacher at the village church school in Corby Glen. I think I should be safe with him.'

'Thank goodness for that, it sounds as if he is an upright young man. Not like his young brother, he has a reputation for miles around and will gamble on anything that moves. I am going round *"The Kings Head"* when I finish here Nat, are you coming?'

'No thanks Mo, I need a clear head in the morning I am going to Corby Glen for lunch and I have to convince Toni that he wants to come with me.'

'Good luck then, I will see you when I see you.'

***

Nathaniel slept soundly for a change and awoke feeling refreshed and optimistic about the outcome of his visit to Corby Glen. Sylvia prepared him a big breakfast of ham and eggs which he ate with relish. It was a long time since she had seen him eat so well and he was in a much better frame of mind than usual. She thought he might have met a young lady, after all he was dressed in his Sunday best and was not going to be home for lunch. She was going to ask him where he was going but she didn't want to spoil the mood.

It was a beautiful Spring morning when he set off. The sky was clear and bright with a few wispy, fluffy white clouds floating gently on a light westerly breeze. Birds were in full song, males trying to convince females that it was time to get together, each trying to outdo their rivals.

Nathaniel's optimistic mood had carried on from last night and he was certain that with a good argument he would convince Toni that he could not afford to refuse such a generous offer. He had allowed himself plenty of time to get to Corby Glen and rode at a leisurely pace occasionally stopping to chat to people he knew. When he got to Bourne he had plenty of time to spare and so he called in at "The Nags Head" and had a pot of ale. Refreshed, he carried on, and once in Corby Glen he followed George's directions and found the house quite easily. The family had just arrived home from church and they welcomed Nathaniel effusively and noisily and he was initially confronted with a blast of questions and a plethora of idle chatter. This quickly settled down as the girls went to their rooms and Mr. and Mrs. Montini excused themselves.

George apologised for the noise but said it was not unusual with a family of eight all talking at once. He also said that he had mentioned Nathaniel's proposal to Toni and he was very interested in hearing what he had to say. 'Toni has just had to go and see the parents of one of his pupils but will be back for lunch and you will be able to talk to him after we have eaten. Father is also keen to hear what you have to say.'

***

After a very enjoyable lunch of roast pork, boiled potatoes, cabbage and a rich brown gravy, Paulo suggested that Nathaniel, Antonio and himself should adjourn to the library to discuss Nathaniel's proposal. George, however, was not very happy to be excluded from the meeting and expressed his displeasure quite strongly. He was very politely but firmly told by Paulo that, although he was a good friend of Nathaniel, the proposal had nothing at all to do with him.

When they were all sitting comfortably, Paulo was the first to speak, 'Well Nathaniel, from what I have already heard, which I must say is only a

72

very sketchy outline of your plans, you sound to have a very interesting proposition for Antonio to consider.'

Nathaniel then explained as fully as he could what his father had decreed in his will and how and why the trustees were in control of events. The need for a companion was explained and Nathaniel told them of his anxiety to appoint someone he knew rather than have the trustees make a decision which could result in him having to spend up to a year living with someone who he could not get along with. 'I fear that more than anything,' said Nathaniel 'just imagine what it would be like, not just for me but for the other person as well. It could ruin the whole trip.'

'I totally understand, but you don't know Antonio very well do you?'

'No but at least I do know him, and there is still plenty of time to get better acquainted before we go. We will also be able to plan the whole event before we go and any problems that may occur could be sorted out before we actually depart.'

'How will the trip be financed?' queried Toni.

'Everything, including the companion's expenses are covered in the fund set up by my father, so there will be no extra money required from you.'

'That sounds good.' said Toni with a smile on his face, 'The whole idea sounds to be just made for me, doesn't it father?'

'I agree, I think it could be the making of you Antonio. What is the next step, Nathaniel?' asked Paulo.

'Well, as I explained earlier I have to inform the trustees of my preference and they will, of course have to approve it but I don't see any problems at all. I don't think they are likely to find anyone more suitable so if you agree, I will inform Mr. Woolaston tomorrow morning and we will arrange a suitable time for a meeting.'

'Not old Effy Woolaston! You won't have any trouble there, he is a very good friend of mine and you know him too, don't you Antonio?'

'Yes father I do, he bought me lunch at *"The Angel"* the last time I was in Grantham.'

'It's agreed then, you make the arrangements for the meeting and we will go ahead subject to approval. Thank you Nathaniel it has been very nice talking to you. Would you care to stay for afternoon tea, I am sure the ladies would like it?'

'No thank you, sir. I had better get on my way.'

'Good morning sir.' said Watson, shuffling off his high stool and heading slowly towards Ephraim's office. 'I will just check to see if Mr. Woolaston can see you now, I know he has another appointment in ten minutes.' He tapped on the door of the inner office, opened it and said, 'Mr. Thorold is here sir, could you see him now?'

'Come in Nathaniel,' boomed Ephraim from the inner office. 'I can only spare you a few minutes so what brings you here at such short notice?'

'I think I have a solution to the problem of my companion for the trip through Europe.'

'Oh yes, and who do you propose should be the lucky person?'

'I think you know him, it is Antonio Montini from Corby Glen.'

'Not that gambling layabout. You don't seriously expect us to approve him do you? We could never trust him with your father's money and I don't understand why you thought we ever would. Haven't you learnt anything?'

'No not him, that's George. Antonio is George's eldest brother, he is the schoolteacher at Corby Glen and is nearly thirty years old. He also speaks French and Italian so I think he would be ideal for the job.'

'Of course, I am sorry. I jumped to the conclusion that you were referring to your mate George. I know Toni is an upright and honest individual and I like him very much. He is not at all like George and I didn't realise you knew him.'

Nathaniel told Ephraim of his visit to the Montini's house the previous day and that both Antonio and his father were very interested in the proposition and had given permission to approach the trustees to put Antonio's name forward.

'Well done Nathaniel, I think you have done yourself proud this time. My personal opinion is that he is perfect for the post and I will contact Joseph and George to get their approval. I am sure that they will be fully in agreement with me and express their consent. If that is so I will contact you in the next couple of days to set up a meeting for us all at your house. We will go through everything with Antonio and hopefully get his agreement.'

'Thank you Mr. Woolaston, I think we have the right man. Now all we need to do is convince him.'

Watson slowly lowered himself from his stool and, stick in hand, hobbled towards the door to open it for Nathaniel. Ephraim escorted Nathaniel out of his office and said goodbye.

'Thank you Watson,' as he approached the door, and, 'Goodbye Mr. Woolaston'

Watson made his way slowly and painfully back to his desk, clambered back up into his seat, picked up his quill and dipped it into the ink, when, as Nathaniel was going down the stairs.....

'Watson, bring me the Thorold will.' boomed the voice from the inner office.

Nathaniel collected his horse and set off home a very happy man.

***

A few days later, a smart young man arrived at the manor house on horseback and asked to see Mr. Nathaniel Thorold. One of the yard hands took the horse's head and held it while the gentleman dismounted.

'I will take your horse sir, and if you care to knock on the door over there someone will inform the master.'

Sylvia answered the knock on the door and asked, 'Good morning sir, who shall I say is calling?'

'I am William Montini and I have a package which I am obliged to deliver it to Mr. Thorold personally.'

'Very good sir, if you will follow me I will inform Mr. Thorold that you are here.' Sylvia showed him into the library and said, 'If you would just take a seat I will tell him immediately.'

William sat in the leather armchair and made himself comfortable and did not have long to wait.

'William, how nice to see you again. What brings you to this part of the county?'

'It's nice to see you again Nathaniel, I am on my way to see a cousin of mine at Sleaford and Toni asked me to bring you this package and to make sure I handed it to you personally.'

'I expect old Ephraim has been in touch with him and it concerns my proposition. Anyway, did he say he was expecting a reply immediately?'

'No he didn't mention it at all, just make sure you received it safely.'

'Good, then you will stay for lunch won't you?'

'That's kind of you, I would love to. It will make a nice break in my journey.'

Nathaniel called Sylvia and told her Mr. Montini would be staying for lunch and she should inform the yardman to look after his horse.

After lunch and William had gone on his way, Nathaniel opened the package and read the letter. Toni had heard from Ephraim and had sent him a reply saying he agreed to a meeting with Nathaniel and the trustees and that he was thrilled about the prospect of a prolonged trip. He also said he had not entirely believed Nathaniel initially but now he was fully committed. He had of course, quite a few things to deal with before he could leave. The most important was getting a date so that he could give sufficient notice to the church who employed him as a teacher.

The very next day another messenger arrived, this time from Ephraim at Grantham saying he had received confirmation from Antonio that he wished to be involved as a companion on the trip and would like to meet all concerned to discuss matters further as soon as possible. If he was accepted, Antonio had said that he thought he could be available from August onwards. He was committed to his teaching post until at least mid-July. Ephraim also provisionally suggested a meeting be held at Nathaniel's house on the third day of May at ten o'clock in the morning to formally approve of Antonio's appointment and to produce a plan to get the venture moving.

***

The third day of May proved to be the most miserable day for several weeks. After what had proved to be a glorious start to spring with day after day of continuous sunshine, the rains had come with a vengeance. The heavens were black with thick storm clouds and the dry sun-baked fields and byways were turned into rivers of thick, clammy mud and deep, rutted puddles which made any form of travel, either by carriage or on horseback extremely difficult. There was no relief from the constant downpour all morning and the first of the four to arrive was Antonio. He had travelled from Corby Glen on his horse and had arrived nearly an hour late. He was full of apologies for being late for the meeting but felt much better when he was told that he was the first to arrive. He had managed to put his horse in the stables and had taken off all his outer soaking wet clothes and put them to dry before the other three arrived in their carriage.

Ephraim, Joseph and George had faired only slightly better. The journey had been very difficult and their coach was continually sliding sideways and slipping into the deep water-filled ruts. The carriage had become stuck in the mud on several occasions but usually the coachman and his

76

assistant had managed to free the vehicle and get moving again. However, on just one occasion they had to get out and help to free it from the clinging, sodden, mire and Ephraim had arrived at Borton in a foul mood with his best pair of boots nearly ruined by the mud.

Nathaniel sat them all in front of the drawing room fire and managed to calm them down with a good sized glass of rum each. Shortly afterwards, at his suggestion, Sylvia brought in an early lunch consisting of a big platter of home-made bread, butter, and strong cheese with pickled onions. There were also two big flagons of ale to wash it all down.

When they were all relaxed, and dried out as best they could, they all adjourned to the dining room where the business was to be conducted around the large dining table. Ephraim took charge and Antonio was quickly endorsed as Nathaniel's companion for the forthcoming trip. Everyone knew him and were completely satisfied with his selection.

On completion of the first part of business Ephraim extracted a package from his bundle of papers. On the package was written, 'Nathaniel Thorold, Grand Tour. Not to be opened until the trip is ready to be planned.' and it was signed, 'John Thorold.'

Ephraim proceeded in his usual theatrical manner, emphasising every movement and making it last to create, what he thought must be seen as a dramatic task. 'For goodness sake, get a move on Effy,' snorted Joseph, 'or it will be midnight before you get it open!'

Chapter 7

June -August 1722

Nathaniel and Toni were both very excited by the prospect of their trip and could not believe the scope they had been given in the package unveiled by Ephraim at the meeting two weeks ago. Although they did not have to visit all the places named, they had been given the names and addresses of contacts in Bruges, Calais, and Paris for the first stage of the tour. Plans were then in place for them to move on to Italy via Switzerland and further contacts were named in Berne, Milan, Genoa, Livorno and Rome. All the contacts had been briefed by Nathaniel's father on what the two tourists would like to see. The named contacts would assist them on their travels by acting as agents in the provision of suitable accommodation, travel arrangements and introductions to other useful people who could help to ease their passage and gain access to important cultural sites and exhibitions.

It was suggested that the return journey should be through Spain and into Portugal but it was left for Nathaniel and Toni to decide what they would like to do and where they would like to visit. They could then return through France or return to England by sea depending on the time they had left, but they should be back within a year of their departure.

***

Nathaniel had recently made a visit to Holt Hall farm at Frieston to talk to Edward Wood, the manager. Whilst discussing the business of the farm, they also talked about Nathaniel's future trip and how the plans were progressing. They discussed the logistics involved and Edward asked, 'How are you going to cross the North Sea, have you arranged that part of the journey yet?'

'No, not yet, we have to decide on the most convenient route for us, but I think we would prefer to go from a handy port in eastern England. We know it will mean a longer sea passage with a shorter overland start but I think we would prefer that rather than going all the way to Dover or the south coast.'

'Well then, while you are here, I think I should introduce you to Max Hoboer, a friend of mine. He's the agent for a Dutch trading company and is based in Boston. He books cargo and passengers on boats crossing the North Sea all the time, so if you wish, we could go to see him tomorrow, I am sure he could help.'

'That would be very helpful indeed, Edward. I appreciate your offer very much.'

'I have some business in Boston anyway, so we can kill two birds with one stone. We could invite Max to lunch and you could see if he might be of help to you.' said Edward. 'Max is very good company and I am sure you will enjoy meeting him even if you don't do any business with him.'

***

Nathaniel and Edward rode the three miles into Boston under a cloudless, clear blue sky and when they arrived at the agent's office in a back street behind The Haven, Max was out on business. Edward had some other people to see, so Nathaniel arranged to meet him at noon for lunch in *"The Anchor"* hotel on the harbour front. 'You can't miss it,' said Edward, 'when you smell the fish you are nearly there.'

Meanwhile Nathaniel enjoyed a pleasant stroll through the busy side streets taking in the atmosphere. Long before he arrived at The Haven, he could detect the strong smell emanating from the fishing boats assembled side by side as they unloaded the morning's catch. He saw *"The Anchor"* hotel just a few yards along the wharf and bought himself a pot of ale and watched the world go by as he drank. He had just refilled his pot when Edward arrived with a tall, but rather stout middle aged man whose florid face was adorned with a large, carrot coloured, grey flecked beard. When he took off his tricorn hat his head proved to be completely lacking in hair apart from a narrow fringe just above his ears. 'Nathaniel, allow me to introduce Max Hoboer, the man I brought you to see.'

'Good morning Max, how nice to see you,' said Nathaniel. 'I am hoping you will be able to help me in the very near future.'

'It's nice to meet you Nathaniel. Edward has told me roughly what you require and I am sure I will be able to make suitable arrangements for you and your companion.' replied Max, in what Nathaniel thought was a strong French accent.

The three of them settled down for a quiet lunch which proved to be anything but quiet. The crew of a Swedish brig which had recently docked and unloaded its cargo of timber, decided it was a good day to dispose of their hard earned wages and chose *"The Anchor"* as the right place to do it. Singing sea shanties and dancing to the music was, although very distracting, just noisy but it soon turned to minor arguments and then a full scale brawl ensued. A

79

few of the quieter members of the crew left before things deteriorated, but a hard core of about six seamen remained and all of them joined in. Meanwhile the landlord was trying to get the fighting mob outside but was failing miserably, and gratefully accepted Max's offer of help.

'Max must be bloody mad.' said Nathaniel to Edward, 'he will get himself killed.'

'Just you watch, my money is on Max.' replied Edward. 'I haven't seen him beaten yet.'

While the landlord was shouting at the sailors and getting no response, Max grabbed the largest of them by his vest, pulled him closer and sunk his knee into the sailor's groin. The effect was immediate, the sailor screamed and sunk to his knees clutching the damaged part of his anatomy.

'One down, five to go.' said Edward gleefully, and as he spoke, Max head-butted a second sailor who fell in a heap, writhing on the sawdust strewn floor. 'Two down, four to go.'

Two of the remaining four decided that they would be better off out of it and left quickly by the front door, but the final two thought they could deal with the red bearded maniac and stayed to finish the show. They approached from the front and Max had his back to the wall between two tables. The first one took a swing but Max moved quickly to the side and caught the assailant's elbow, swung him bodily round and drove him hard, head first into his companion's chest. Both tumbled into a heap on the floor gasping for breath. The landlord and Max took one each, and lifting them off their feet, flung them out onto the street to cool off.

The response from the clientele was an immediate round of applause, and from the landlord, free drinks for Max and his friends.

'What did I tell you Nathaniel, always put your money on Max. I have never seen him beaten yet and I have never seen him leave an inn without having a fight at some stage. We always get free beer. What a man!'

'I enjoyed that,' said Max as he sat down and promptly downed his ale. 'It's nice to have a bit of exercise now and again, and help a friend at the same time.'

Nathaniel was impressed, and in an aside, said to Edward, 'I am glad he does not live at Borton or half our workers would be absent with broken bones.'

***

80

'Now Nathaniel, what is it that you want to see me so urgently about? I am sure we will not be disturbed again so we could get down to business now if you wish.' said Max.

Nathaniel explained the situation as best he could and said no decisions had been made so far. However, he realised the need for fixing a date for the trip to the continent, and also, a convenient port of departure was equally important. He emphasised that this discussion was the first he had had on the subject and that he thought that Boston would probably be the most appropriate port to use. 'So Max, how do you think you could help me?'

'Well Nathaniel, you have certainly come to the right person to arrange a passage starting here in Boston. I deal with cargo and passengers travelling to all destinations on the continent on a daily basis. Any boat that departs from here, without cargo or passengers arranged by me, is a rarity indeed. I expect to have several brigs departing throughout the month of August to ports from Bergen in the North to Lisbon in the South. Just tell me which port you want to go to and I will give you plenty of notice of suitable departures.'

'I think we would prefer to head for a port in The Low Countries. Father has provided us with a contact in Bruges, so if we can make use of him we will be able to use his local knowledge while we are there. He will also be able to assist us in our onward plans.'

'That should not be a problem. There are regular sailings each week to that part of the continent which offer the standard of accommodation you would require. I am sure I could get you a good price with the right captain. The Swedish Brigs are modern, well crewed and are always competitively priced. You have seen some of them earlier this morning. I will need to know what you are taking with you in the way of luggage and belongings as cargo space is always at a premium and that is where the ships make their money. They are, after all, cargo carriers and passengers are generally carried as an afterthought.

Also it is quite important to know that your choice of transport is not going to carry dried fish or a similar cargo. However, if you sail from some of the southern ports, a few of the ships tend to be designed for the exclusive transport of passengers. If that suits you better, then I could arrange it for you but it will certainly prove to be more expensive and of course, a long trip by road before you set sail.'

Costs for the passage were discussed and agreed and Max explained that once Nathaniel had given him a date to work to, he could start things moving. Nathaniel said that if Max could work to a departure for sometime in the second week in August for a boat going to The Low Countries, that would suit his purpose. Max said that Nathaniel and his companion ought to be in the Boston area for a few days before the agreed week so that he could embark at short notice. 'These boats don't have a strict timetable and rely on a full load of cargo being available and loaded. They are, of course, totally dependent on the tides and the state of the sea but August is not generally a month that has a lot of delays.' said Max. It was also agreed that Max would send a message to Nathaniel if there was not going to be a suitable sailing during the agreed week

'Max, is it possible that you can inform our contact in Bruges of our intentions prior to our arrival so that he can make suitable arrangements?' asked Nathaniel.

'Part of the job old chum,' said Max, 'I do it all the time, I send a message with the captain of the ship that leaves the week before yours and he makes sure it is delivered promptly on arrival. Just give me your contact's details and I will see that he is informed.'

'Thanks Max, that is wonderful. The man's name is Jacques le Clerque, and his chambers are at Rue de la Cloche, Bruges.'

'As good as done, Nathaniel. Now, if you have no more to ask then I must be off, I have a boat to meet later this afternoon and I have to make sure a very good client is treated with the utmost respect. I will contact you to keep you informed but you can rest assured that you will be going to The Low Countries during the second week in August. Good bye Nathaniel. Have a safe journey home and I will see you in August.' He shook hands with both of them and departed.

'What a splendid fellow.' said Nathaniel.

'I know,' agreed Edward, 'you won't meet many like him.'

Edward invited Nathaniel and Toni stay at Holt Manor for a few days before they embarked and Nathaniel gratefully accepted. This would make sure they were on hand to take advantage of any change of sailing times which may occur at short notice.

***

It had been a hectic two weeks for them both, Toni had handed in his resignation and would be available to travel after the end of July. This was in line with Nathaniel's arrangements with Max that the second week in August would be ideal.

Nathaniel had spent a great deal of time going around the farms and briefing the managers on events and how things were to be dealt with while he was away. He had also discussed at length, how the trustees would manage the estate. This concerned him a great deal, but the thought of an extended holiday outweighed any worries that he might have over the running of the estate.

They had decided that they need only plan the short trip to Holt Manor at Frieston and a short stay with Edward. They would contact Max as soon as they arrived and then await his instructions. Nathaniel explained that Max would inform Mr. Le Clerque when and where they would arrive in The Low Countries and hopefully he would be waiting for them when they got there. They would rely on Mr. Le Clerque for their activities during their stay in The Low Countries and would seek his assistance in the planning of the next leg to Paris. What they were to do was entirely dependent on the recommendations of Mr. Le Clerque.

Nathaniel suddenly realised that the whole thing relied on Max informing Mr. Le Clerque of their arrival. If he failed then they were going to experience difficulties from the moment they arrived. 'What the hell are we going to do if Max doesn't inform Mr. Le Clerque?' he exclaimed, 'we are going to be in deep trouble.'

'Not really,' said Toni, 'I can speak French fluently and half the Belgians speak French so you have no need to worry. Just stay close to me.' he jested.

***

They arranged a short meeting with Ephraim to finalise a few minor details and explain what was planned so far. Ephraim was pleased with what he heard and gave his approval on behalf of the trustees and wished them well on their travels. He emphasised how important it was that Nathaniel should keep the trustees aware of their movements as often as possible. This was for their own benefit as Ephraim would need to supply funds to them via agents in the places they were staying.

After the meeting they both went into Grantham to make some final purchases. Nathaniel decided that he could use a new travelling trunk for all his belongings as the one his father had used, the one he had intended to use, was starting to look as if it would fall to pieces. Nathaniel reasoned that it was so old it would never stand the handling of ships' crews, and after all the initials on the lid of the trunk were his great grandfathers', so it was time a new one was introduced to the family.

Toni decided he had everything he needed, and anyway, he pointed out that once they had found a base they would always be able to purchase what they wanted wherever they were. 'We are going to some of the largest towns and cities in Europe, I think they will have more choice than good old Grantham, don't you?' he asked.

'I suppose you are right, but I need the trunk for the journey.' replied Nathaniel

***

The beginning of the first week in August was taken up with last minute packing and on the Thursday, soon after dawn, Toni arrived at Borton Manor on his horse accompanied by a cart loaded with a heavy trunk. His trunk was unloaded by a couple of yard lads and loaded onto a cart with Nathaniel's new, equally heavy trunk.

While two horses were being hitched to the cart, Toni and Nathaniel enjoyed a plate of bread and cheese washed down with a jug of ale. Sylvia was fussing around like an old hen and checking that Nathaniel had everything that he would need and was packed safely in his trunk. 'Are you sure you have packed everything Nathaniel?' she asked again, as she had been asking all morning. 'I will just go to your room and check that you have not left anything.' Sylvia was going to miss Nathaniel terribly and she was very concerned about what she would do while he was away.

There was a knock on the kitchen door and Mo poked his nose around and said, 'Hi Sylvia, will you tell the boss that the cart is loaded and ready. George has saddled up the boss's horse and it is hitched near the front door. Mr. Montini's cart has just departed for home and we are ready to go.'

Sylvia passed on Mo's message as Nathaniel came down the stairs.

'Thank you Sylvia, we are ready now.' said Nathaniel picking up his hat and cape. He didn't think he would need his cape today but he preferred to have it handy just in case it was required.

Nathaniel and Antonio went outside and the horses were ready at the door as he expected. Mo was in charge of the cart with the luggage and Jack, one of the yard lads was going with him as his assistant. A small group of household staff were assembled outside ready to say their farewells and Sylvia

84

was at the front sniffling and trying unsuccessfully not to shed a few tears. The staff were aware that just because the master was away for the next year, they were not going to have a holiday. The whole house was going to be cleaned and refurbished from top to bottom and they were going to have to do it.

Before mounting his horse, Nathaniel briefly said goodbye to the staff and told them he would miss them all. Sylvia by this time was in floods of tears and so Nathaniel gave her a hug. This only made her worse and she rushed back into the house and stayed there until she heard the horses going down the drive. She then went back to the door and, still crying, waved goodbye until the travellers had disappeared from sight.

***

'That's it Nathaniel, we are on our way and it looks as if it will be a dry day for once.'

'I hope you are right, these roads can be treacherous if we have a heavy rainstorm. There are quite a few fords to cross and some are frequently impassable. I think we should look on the bright side and hope that things go as planned. I must admit, it is lovely to be on our way after all the events of the last six months or so.'

'At least we should be able to relax now and look forward to our adventure.' replied Toni as he watched the cart swaying and rocking in front of them as it made its steady way out of Borton and on towards the wide, flat expanse of the fenlands of Lincolnshire.

'If the weather stays fine we should make steady progress and reach Frieston by nightfall. If we encounter any problems then we can always stay the night at a suitable hostelry. There are several on our route and with a bit of luck we should be at Sutterton in time for lunch. Old Ted Stacey and his wife Maud at "The Thatched Cottage Inn" always provide good, tasty fare. I always stop there if I am in the area at the right time of day.' said Nathaniel.

'Well we managed an early start this morning so we should be alright.'

The cart and the two following horses passed through a few small villages scattered thinly along the track, each village marked by a church spire and a windmill rising like sentinels out of the flat, open countryside. At this time of the year, every available person was employed in the fields gathering the harvest. Men with scythes were cutting the standing crops of mainly oats and barley but with some wheat as well. Others, both men and women were twisting some of the straw into rough ropes and tying the cut crop into sheaves. The sheaves were then stood on end with the grain at the top and leant against each other in rows to let the grain dry. Everywhere was a hive of activity and thoughts of rain were banished from their minds. Rain now could prove disastrous for everyone.

They continued to make good time and Mo was managing to avoid the deeper ruts and holes in the ground. Even so, every time they hit a deep rut, Jack was caught unawares and lurched sideways nearly falling off the smooth wooden seat at the front of the cart. 'If you are that tired Jack, I think you should sit in the back with the trunks so that you don't fall off and end up under a wheel. I don't want your mother getting on at me just because you managed to get killed under a cart wheel.'

'Thanks Mr. Clark but I will try to stay awake from now on.' replied Jack.

**

'What village is that over to the left?' Toni asked Nat.

'That's Gosberton, we are making good progress and we will soon see the spire of the church of St.Mary the Virgin at Sutterton up ahead. We will rest there and have something to eat. I am sure Ted and Maud will have something tasty for us.'

'I am ready for a bite to eat and I could down a pot of ale in quick time so a stop would be very welcome. We seem to have done extremely well for time so far, despite being with the cart. When we get a bit closer we will ride on ahead and prepare someone to feed and water the cart horses when they arrive.'

It was not long before the church spire at Sutterton came into view and Nathaniel told Mo that Toni and himself were going on ahead to *"The Thatched Cottage Inn"*. 'I will get them prepared to deal with your horses and get some food ready for the two of you. How are you Jack, are you managing to keep awake?'

'Yes thank you, sir.'

'I bet you have never been this far from home, have you?'

'No sir, never.'

'Well you have still a few more miles to go and you will be away all night, which will be new as well, won't it?

'Yes sir, it will.'

**

86

Nathaniel and Toni came around the corner by the churchyard and saw Ted, the landlord of *"The Thatched Cottage"*, sitting outside on a bench in the sun. He was relaxing with a pot of ale and a pipe of tobacco. 'Good morning landlord,' said Nathaniel, 'I see you are enjoying the sunshine this lovely morning.'

'Good morning Mr. Thorold, nice to see you again so soon. Yes it is a bit quiet at the moment, most of the regulars are in the fields busy working on the harvest. We won't be seeing much of them until after the harvest is safely in.'

'Toni, this is Ted Stacey the landlord of this delightful hostelry,' and to Ted, 'my companion is Mr. Antonio Montini and I am sure you will look after him in your usual capable manner.'

'Nice to meet you Mr. Montini, Sir. You are most welcome at *"The Thatched Cottage Inn"*

'Where is Maud today Ted, have you given her the day off?' asked Nathaniel.

'No she is in the kitchen, complaining about the heat. If you two gentlemen fasten your horses to the rail, I will get them fed and watered for you. You can sit here at an outside table, but if you prefer you can go inside where it is cooler.'

They both decided that it would be better inside as they had been in the sun all morning and as Ted was showing them through the door, Nathaniel told him that Mo would be arriving soon with Jack, and they had two horses which required feeding and watering as, of course, would Mo and Jack.

'Don't worry sir, I will make sure they get all they need.'

They sat down at a large table near to the empty fireplace next to which was a large stack of logs waiting for a turn in the weather. The small bow window to their right looked out onto the edge of the orchard where the apples were just turning from green to a delicate reddish hue. The plums were already being picked as soon as they were ripe in order to prevent the wasps stealing the best of the crop. A gentle, cool, breeze wafted lazily through the slightly open window carrying with it the sounds of insects and birdsong from the garden. A bumble bee was buzzing noisily at the window trying his best to escape through the glass and a couple of flies scurried to and fro in a completely random manner seeming to have no idea of where they should go or what they should do.

Toni had shut his eyes and was completely relaxed and Nathaniel was snoring gently when Ted banged two pots of ale on the table. 'Here you are gentlemen, get these down you, I bet you are thirsty after your long trip. What would you like to eat?'

'Thank you Ted. What have you available today?'

'We have my favourite today, some lovely fatty bacon and boiled potatoes, or there is roast beef, roast potatoes and cabbage if you prefer.'

'Definitely roast beef!' exclaimed Nathaniel.

'The same for me too.' said Toni and then asked, 'why does everyone think that fatty bacon is enjoyable? I think it is nauseating.'

'So do I, but at least we get a choice, at school it was take it or leave it and it was usually served up at least twice a week.'

'Yes I know, and George told me you used it as bait in the rat traps.'

'We did, and it was very successful too. The rats loved it.'

***

They enjoyed a leisurely lunch and then, having ensured that Mo and Jack had also eaten and were refreshed and ready to go they set off on the journey to Frieston. They made good progress until they reached Boston where the streets were crowded, very busy and extremely noisy. It took an age to negotiate the narrow streets where houses and businesses were crammed closely together and they also had to fight their way through several flocks of sheep being driven through town to new pastures to the west. Once clear of the town, they had no more problems and arrived at Holt Manor just before sunset.

The trunks were unloaded and taken into the manor house. All four horses were stabled for the night, Mo and Jack were accommodated in the loft above the stable and Nathaniel and Toni were shown their rooms in the manor.

***

Mo and Jack were up early next morning preparing for the journey home. Rain clouds hung heavily over the low, marshy landscape and although it had not started to rain, Mo said, 'Jack, I think we are in for a muddy trip home so we had better get going while it's still dry. Have you got everything packed and secure?'

'Yes Mr. Clark, I am ready to go.' was the short reply.

'I will just go and see the boss to check if there is anything we need to know and tell him that we are all set to go.' and walked off towards the Hall.

'Come in Mo,' called Nathaniel. He was sitting in the kitchen with Toni and Edward just finishing off breakfast. 'You ready to go then Mo?' he asked.

'Yes boss, we are all ready now and hope to get well on the way before the rains come. Are there any last minute instructions?'

'Just one thing, Mo. We will probably be here for anything up to a week before we sail and will need to keep our horses until then. Mr. Wood will contact you when we have gone so that you can send a couple of lads to collect them. You can contact Mr. Montini's father when his horse is back at Borton.'

'I'll see to it boss.'

'Good bye then Mo and have a safe journey home.'

'Thanks Nat, you have a good time too and I will see you in about a year's time.'

***

Nathaniel and Toni finished their breakfast and thought the best thing to do was to go to Boston and see the shipping agent, Max Hoboer. Edward was going to be busy at the farm and as there was no real need for him to go with them, and could find their own way to Max's office. If he was not there they knew it would not take long to find him. They had all day to themselves and so they were in no particular rush to get things done, after all, the boats set their own timetable and they may be sailing the next day or the next week. It was out of their control but when they found Max they would have a better idea of when things would happen.

The horses were brought round to the main door and Nathaniel and Toni mounted and set off. They had prepared for wet weather and had brought their heavy capes with them just in case. The journey to Boston was uneventful and fortunately the rain stayed away although the skies remained heavy and threatening all morning.

Boston was its usual busy, bustling self, especially around the Haven. The voices of many different nationalities could be heard as the sailors mixed and did business with the local inhabitants.

When they finally found Max's office, they had a very difficult job to get in. There were about a dozen foreign sailors packed into his outer office, all shouting and making threatening gestures. It looked as if Max was in the inner office with an equally threatening number of sailors. 'I think we will come back later and maybe it will have been resolved by then.' said Nathaniel.

'Do you think he needs help, it all looks a bit dangerous, don't you

89

think?' asked Toni with a hint of concern in his voice.

'Believe me, Max is the only person I would not worry about in that situation, I have seen him in action and he doesn't need help, I can assure you. We will come back after we have had a cup of coffee, I saw a coffee shop in Beck Street next to the "Black Bull Inn" we could try there.'

'I didn't know coffee shops had reached these parts already, I know they are very popular down in London because my father went to one there recently and said he enjoyed the atmosphere. It was more refined than a public house.'

'I didn't know either, but I have heard they are nice places to relax so I thought we could give it a try.'

They made their exit from Max's office and retraced their route until they saw the "Black Bull Inn" and the coffee shop just nearby. They entered the coffee shop through a small door and went in to what looked, on first impression, like any normal public bar in any inn. However, the atmosphere was more subdued and most of the clientele were either businessmen or local gentlemen. They were generally seated in small groups drinking either coffee or tea, smoking their pipes and talking in muted tones. Nathaniel pointed out an empty table and as they sat down a young man came to take their order. They ordered two coffees and declined anything to eat. 'This is all very comfortable,' said Toni, 'much better than a noisy pub bar. It looks as if it is a good place to discuss business in reasonable privacy.'

'Yes it does, and it is obviously used as a meeting place by business people.'

'The young man said that they serve food, but it looks as if it is only light snacks rather than full meals so it is not a place you would come for your lunch.'

The waiter brought the coffee and they spent a comfortable hour or so talking and passing the time of the day with a couple of local traders who told them what to do and where to go in Boston. They also mentioned the places and areas to keep well away from. As they were about to leave Max Hoboer came in and came over to their table, 'Hello Nathaniel, nice to see you again, I didn't know you were in town today.'

Nathaniel introduced Toni and told Max that they had called at his office earlier but decided to call back when it was quieter. 'We thought you were a bit busy and would prefer us to come back later.'

'Oh that, I was just allocating cargo for later in the week and three ships wanted the two loads I had to offer. It's always like that, you can never please everyone.'

'We thought you were going to have a fight on your hands.' said Toni as Max ordered more coffee.

'It's the way I prefer things to happen. If there are more boats than cargo, the price I have to pay comes down as they compete for the job.' Max surmised. 'Anyway, I assume you are now staying at Holt Hall with Edward until I can arrange your passage.'

'Yes we are, we arrived yesterday evening and decided, in spite of the weather, that we would let you know that we were here and check that you have things in hand.' said Nathaniel, 'I assume you will be able to get us away sometime next week as arranged.'

Max took a sip of his coffee and replied, 'I have two loads waiting at the moment, one is to go to Amsterdam and the other is destined for Ostend. I am expecting two Swedish brigs to dock sometime in the next couple of days and they will almost certainly take the loads so you will probably have a choice of where you go. When they dock, they will have to unload and then load up the new cargo so they will both be in port for a couple of days, that will give you ample time to see the captains and decide which one suits your needs.'

'The Ostend one seems perfect but there is still the matter of informing Monsieur Le Clerque of our arrival. How can you get a note to him so that he can await our arrival?'

'That's no problem, I have a brig loading at the moment which will sail for Zeebruge on the morning tide. This afternoon, I will give the captain a note which he will arrange to be forwarded to Bruges when he docks. Mr. Le Clerque should get it in ample time for him to meet you.'

'That's good news, I hope he will be there but we can always wait for him if he encounters any problems. I think we have done what we set out to do so I think it is time for some lunch. Would you like to join us at *"The Anchor"*, Max?'

'Not today, thank you Nat. I have some urgent business to attend to out at Sibsey so I must be on my way.'

'Right Max, so I will expect to hear from you when the two Swedish boats arrive.'

Max promised he would inform them, said his goodbyes and left. As

Nathaniel and Toni left the coffee shop the sun broke through and by the time they reached the Haven the rigging on the boats in the harbour was steaming as the heat of the sun dried off the recent heavy shower.

Settled down comfortably in *"The Anchor"* with their pots of ale, they both declined the offer of fatty bacon for lunch and chose ham and fried potatoes instead.

It was a beautiful evening by the time they arrived back at Holt Hall and Edward's cook offered to prepare them a meal but they decided to wait for Edward to come home from supervising the harvest. They nevertheless, accepted an offer of a flagon of beer and sat outside in the evening sun to drink it. The peace and quiet was only interrupted by the song of blackbirds singing to each other from their perches in the high thorn hedges.

***

Two days later a message was delivered to Holt Hall for the attention of Mr. Nathaniel Thorold. Nathaniel opened it and Max, in a very short note, said that the two boats would start unloading this afternoon and would Nathaniel and his companion care to meet him at his office after lunch.

Nathaniel, in an even shorter note, said yes he would be there.

***

Nathaniel and Toni had an early lunch at Holt Hall and set off to Boston and reached Max's office just as he was returning from his lunch.

'That was good timing Nathaniel, if you would just let me sort out a couple of things, I will be with you in no time.' True to his word, Max was soon back with them and they set off to the Haven.

'Gentlemen, both boats are docked, and the *"Ulrika Eleonora"* is going to take the Amsterdam cargo and the *"Greve Sparre,"* which is a brand new brig, is going to Ostend. I think it is certain you will chose to take the *"Greve Sparre"* as that will take you exactly where you wanted to go. It will be carrying a mixed cargo so there will be no foul smells and the master, Jonas Von Emden, is a likeably fellow who enjoys having company on his many trips. I have not spoken to the master of the *"Ulrika Eleonora"* as yet as I thought the *"Greve Sparre"* would suit you best. We can always talk to him later if you want to.'

The Haven was, as usual, bustling with life with ships loading and unloading their cargoes. Sailors were busy on the dockside mending and patching sails and local traders were trying to sell their goods to the ships before they sailed. As they walked along the wharf, dodging carts filled with goods and men carrying heavy loads to and from the ships they soon recognised the *"Greve Sparre,"* it stood out as the cleanest, tidiest and smartest ship in the harbour and was obviously a new ship.

Max led them up the gangway and speaking in Swedish asked the first sailor he met, 'Can I speak to the captain please?' The sailor went away and almost immediately the master appeared. Speaking English he said, 'Welcome Max, I hope you are well. Are these two gentlemen you mentioned?

Max introduced Nathaniel and Toni and confirmed that indeed they were the two passengers and that they were keen to see what sort of accommodation was available. The master took them below decks to see the passenger's cabins and Toni was not very impressed. 'There is not much room is there Nathaniel? I don't think I could sleep in there for long. What do you think?'

'I know the cabins are very small but I don't really think you will get much more room than that on board any ship in the harbour. Space for passengers on any cargo ship is very limited. At least this is very clean and tidy but I suppose we could look at the *"Ulreka Eleona."* What do you think Max?'

'Don't forget that the *"Ulreka Eleona"* is going to Amsterdam and that is a very long way from Ostend where your contact is,' said Max 'and it will take you at least three days to cover that distance by road. If you want to get away this week you don't have much choice do you?'

'It is just that it seems small to me but I suppose it should be adequate.' said Toni. 'I was just surprised at how small a space it is.'

'How long will it take to get there, Captain?' asked Nathaniel.

'We should be no more than three days, but of course it very much depends on the tides and the weather.'

'Well Toni, it's going to where we want to go, it's going at the right time and we only have to put up with small accommodation for a few nights. If we wait for another ship it probably will be more cramped than this one, so I think we should accept what's on offer and get on our way.' stressed Nathaniel.

'You are right, Nathaniel,' said Max. 'and the accommodation on this brig is better than any I have seen anywhere else. Take my word for it Toni, you will not get any better.'

'Right then, this one it is, and I am sure it will be satisfactory.' agreed Toni reluctantly.

'What is the next step, Max. Do we send our luggage down first?'

'Yes, you should send your heavy trunks down tomorrow morning so that they can be loaded in the hold. Bring anything you need for the trip with you when you are ready to embark. The *"Greve Sparre"* will be sailing on the high tide tomorrow evening, so you will need to be here by, at the latest, six o'clock.'

Captain Von Emden said he was looking forward to having the two travellers as passengers and was sure that they would enjoy the trip. It would be a short journey and he said, 'The weather looks set fair and we are not expecting any storms, so we must just hope it stays that way.'

Nathaniel, Toni and Max said their farewells and as they walked away from the *"Greve Sparre"* towards Max's office they skirted a group of sailors unloading barrels of salted fish from a weathered brig and Max pointed to it saying, 'That's the *"Ulrika Eleona."* Would you like to go and have a look at the passenger accommodation Toni, whilst we are passing?'

'No thanks Max, I think I have smelled enough already. I don't think I could stand that pong for two days or more.'

'I don't think you would have liked the accommodation, either.' retorted Max

***

Nathaniel and Toni arose early the next morning and spent some time making sure they had packed their belongings in the correct place, those items needed on the voyage in handy baggage and everything else stored neatly and tidily in their trunks. When the trunks were packed they were secured with leather straps and padlocks. They were then collected by two of Edward's men, taken down to the yard and loaded on to a cart for transporting to the docks.

Before the carter set off, Nathaniel wrote a short note to Ephraim Woolaston informing him of what had been happening and when they were due to sail for Ostend. Plans were running smoothly and he would send a letter in a couple of weeks updating him on their progress. He also wrote a note to Mo telling him to arrange the collection of the two horses from Holt Hall when it was convenient.

The letters were given to the carter and he was told to hand them to Max Hoboer who would arrange for them to be forwarded to Grantham at the earliest opportunity. He was also given instructions to make sure the trunks were delivered to, and loaded on board the *"Greve Sparre"* presently tied up in

94

the Haven dock at Boston.

**

'I am beginning to feel that it is really going to happen.' said Nathaniel to Toni, 'I hope you are looking forward to it as much as I am.'

'I really am,' was the reply, 'I never expected to be going on such a journey so soon. I have always dreamed of a visit to Italy to see my grandparents but I always doubted that I would get the opportunity, and now it is actually happening. Thank you so much for choosing me to accompany you Nathaniel. It is wonderful and I am so grateful.'

'It is my pleasure Toni, I am extremely pleased you could come. I could have ended up with someone imposed on me by the terrible three.'

**

Having sent off the trunks and the letters, Nathaniel and Toni realised they had not yet eaten so, having made sure that they were not too late they settled down for a good meal of eggs and bacon and fresh bread and butter. Edward came in just as they started to eat and apologised for being late, apparently one of the cowmen was ill and he had helped out with the milking. This meant an early start getting the cows in from the fields and breakfast was always taken after milking was complete.

'Have you managed to get everything ready for the off?' queried Edward. 'I bet you are both quite excited aren't you?'

'Yes we are. We have just been saying how we have been looking forward to going and now it's almost time to say goodbye.' replied Nathaniel. 'You have been a magnificent host, Edward. We can't thank you enough. Staying here for these few days has made our preparations so much easier and introducing us to Max has been a blessing.'

'It has been a pleasure having you both here, I have enjoyed your company and it is nice to have someone to talk to in the evenings. It can get a bit lonely out here in the fens on your own. It's not so bad in the Summer, but the dark nights of Winter seem to last forever. Still, that's enough about me. What are you two going to do for the rest of the day?

'We have not planned anything at all, but your carriage is going to pick us up at four o'clock this afternoon. We have to be ready by then.'

'I am going to visit a friend in Saltfleetby this morning, I am thinking of buying a new mare to replace old Doris and he has a two year old for sale. I am afraid Doris is a bit past it now and she won't be able to work for another

95

year. You can come with me for the ride if you wish.'

'That's kind of you Edward. It's a lovely day today and I am sure Toni would like the ride. I know I would. There is plenty of time to get back here before four.'

'It will be a relaxing day for us,' said Toni. 'We are all packed and ready to go so let's enjoy our final day.'

***

At four o'clock that afternoon Edward's carriage was outside the front entrance to the Hall, baggage was already loaded and all was ready for the short journey to the Haven. Inside the Hall Edward was rushing around, checking that nothing was forgotten and asked, 'Are you sure you have packed everything Nathaniel?'

'Of course I am sure Edward. Do you know that you sound just like Sylvia? But at least you haven't been to check my room as she did!'

'The carriage is ready at the door Nathaniel, so I think you had better get going. You really don't want to miss the boat do you?'

'You are right Edward, so thanks again for everything and I will see you when we get back.'

The usual parting pleasantries were exchanged and the carriage set off with Nathaniel very relaxed but Toni was still concerned that the onboard accommodation was very cramped. He was also very apprehensive about the weather conditions and the possibility of being seasick. He had never been to sea but had heard horrific tales of people suffering for day after day for long journeys and he had convinced himself that he was going to be one of those. It was still a lovely calm, bright summer's day but Toni, still concerned about the sea being rough, said, 'The wind is getting up a bit don't you think, Nathaniel? I hope it won't be too rough at sea.'

'There is not a breath of wind out there at the moment Toni. Just calm down and think of where we are going to be in a few days' time.' said Nathaniel, realising that he could have a problem with Toni if he worked himself into a panic. 'It will be as calm as a millpond if things stay as they are. You have nothing to worry about.'

'How do you know, you haven't been to sea before have you?'

'No I haven't, but thousands of people go every day without any problems so why worry before you know what it is like? When we get to the Haven we will call in at *"The Anchor"* and you can have a couple of rums to

96

settle you down, it's all in the mind you know.'

'I know, but I just can't help it.' whined Toni.

The trip from Frieston was uneventful but things got very busy as they approached Boston and after a lengthy struggle through the crowds in the town they arrived at the Haven. It was bustling with activity, and the dockside where the *"Greve Sparre"* was berthed was awash with barrels, crates, packing cases and a vast assortment of cargo, all in the process of being loaded. The ship's crew were stowing the cargo carefully in the various holds as fast as it was brought on board. Great care was taken to pack it in and secure it safely to prevent it moving in the event of bad weather.

'I hope our trunks are here somewhere.' said Toni, casting an eye over the cargo to see if he could identify his own trunk.

'I hope they are already on board and stowed away carefully,' said Nathaniel. 'after all, they have been here since early morning.'

Nathaniel engaged a porter to take their luggage on board and he and Toni followed, always trying to avoid the rushing workmen carrying the cargo from the dockside onto the brig. They were met by Jonas the ship's master who told them that the ship would be sailing at seven thirty and they should be on board by seven o'clock and no later. The gangway would be removed at five minutes past seven and anyone not on board by then would not be sailing with the ship. 'We have to catch the high tide or wait another twelve hours and that will not happen for anyone.' he said. 'We wait for no-one and don't forget, if you have any problems whatsoever, please discuss them with me and I will try to sort them out for you.'

'My friend Toni has one, can you convince him that the sea is quite calm at the moment and is likely to remain so for the whole of the voyage?' pleaded Nathaniel, 'he is absolutely sure that he will be sick as soon as we leave harbour.'

'Sea sickness is something that does not affect everyone so Toni, if this is your first ever trip to sea you don't know if you will suffer or not. I doubt if anyone would be sick in weather conditions such as we have at the moment so I suspect you will be perfectly alright. Just forget about it and relax.' said Jonas. 'I would go over to *"The Anchor"* and have a rum or two to relax a bit if I were you.' Then to a crew member, 'Olaf, would you please show these gentlemen to their accommodation.' and with that he left to check that the cargo loading was going satisfactorily.

They were then shown to their berths, which were next to each other, by one of the crew. 'When we have sorted out our things we will go to "*The Anchor*", said Nathaniel. 'we have got to calm you down quickly.'

Toni was still concerned about the limited amount of space in his berth and what with the continuing worry about seasickness, he was working himself into quite a state.

Nathaniel had soon got things sorted for the trip and went next door to see Toni who was still trying to find space for all his belongings. 'For goodness sake Toni, stuff it in anywhere, you are not here for ever, it's only three days at the most. Let's get moving and get to "*The Anchor*" before the ship sails. You have got to get some relaxing medicine in you pretty quickly, anyway, I am famished and could eat a horse.'

'Well I must say I am quite hungry myself, but I do wish I had a bit more space for my things.'

'We can always ask the captain if there is any free storage space when we sail, but let us get over to "*The Anchor*" now, no more ifs and buts.'

Chapter 8

1722 – 1723

The day after Nathaniel and Toni had sailed, Ephraim Woolaston received the message informing the trustees of the details of the trip to Ostend. He was inwardly relieved that Nathaniel had finally started his year away and would no longer have to worry about what was happening on the estates as a result of the young man's actions.

'Watson!' boomed Ephraim.

Watson struggled from his high stool and hobbled into Ephraim's office. 'Yes, Mr. Woolaston, sir? he said in a questioning tone.

'Send a message to Mr. Godbold and Mr. Heap and ask them to be here for a trustees meeting on Monday morning at ten o'clock sharp. Also, tell them Mr. Thorold and Mr. Montini have now left the country.'

'Yes sir, of course.' replied Watson in his usual subservient tone and slowly made his way back to his stool. As each day went by he was finding it more and more difficult to get around the office and there were times when the pain in his legs was unbearable. He was slightly more mobile when he could use his stick, but when he had to put it down to enable him carry bundles of documents he had started to stumble and sometimes dropped things. Ephraim did not appear to have noticed that he was having trouble and Watson was frightened of losing his job, and more importantly, his income. He was getting increasingly worried about his future and was very worried what Mr. Woolaston would say when he realised how bad things were getting. After the usual struggle to climb onto his high stool, he dipped his quill into the ink and started to draft the letters to the two trustees.

***

On arrival at Woolaston's Chambers on Monday, before he climbed onto his stool, Watson collected all the Thorold papers he could find and gathered them close to hand near his desk. As he struggled onto his seat he thought to himself, 'At least I have saved myself a good deal of walking around later in the morning.' He was just congratulating himself when there was a knock at the outer door and was starting to get down to see who was there at that early hour, when, 'Watson! See who that is, and tell them we are not open for business until nine o'clock.'

'Yes, Mr. Woolaston, sir.' was the reply as Watson struggled across the office to unlock the door.

'Good morning Watson, is he in yet?' asked Joseph Godbold. 'I know I am early but I was in town early this morning so I thought I would call in for a chat.'

'He is, Mr. Godbold, I will see if he is free but I think he is busy at the moment.'

'Tell him if it is not convenient, I will call back later, as I have a few other things to attend to.'

Watson asked Joseph to take a seat while he checked to see if Mr. Woolaston was available. Ephraim came out of his room to apologise and said that as he was very busy at the moment and he would see him at ten o'clock as arranged. As Ephraim was going back into his room he turned and said, 'Lock that door again Watson, I don't want any more interruptions.'

Just before ten o'clock, Ephraim shouted from his room. 'You can unlock the door now Watson. When Mr. Godbold and Mr. Heap arrive, show them straight in, and then I don't want any interruptions until after we have finished. I expect it will take the remainder of the morning.'

'Very good, Mr. Woolaston sir.'

The two trustees arrived together, a point much appreciated by Watson, and they were shown into the inner room where they were greeted by a beaming Ephraim. 'Welcome to the first trustees meeting of the Thorold estates without the presence of Nathaniel Thorold. I trust it will be an amicable event with minimal disagreement, and if that is the case it will be the first time ever.'

***

Ephraim opened the meeting, 'Welcome gentlemen, we have some fairly basic decisions to make today but I don't think the business of running the estate will be as onerous as we at first thought. The first group of about half of the farms are leased out to members of the extended Thorold family and these will require no more work than I currently do. That is, ensuring that rents are paid in full and on time twice every year. The second group are the managed farms, they are the ones owned latterly by the late John Thorold and controlled by him. However all the documentation and accounts came to me first for checking before John saw them, so as you can see, I deal with some of the details already. Both these groups have experienced farm managers controlling activities, so the day to day operations should not require much

100

input from us. The third and final part is the estate at Borton. John, of course, lived at Borton and ran the farm himself so there is no manager employed at this site. Nathaniel is away for the next year or so and when he returns he will be going to London for at least six months. We are going to have to sort out some sort of control very quickly and as we are busy with our own work, we can't be at Borton full time. There are no people at Borton capable of managing the whole estate even though the men who are in charge of some of the areas are good at their jobs, but I would say that is as far as it goes. Have either of you two gentlemen any suggestions as to how we can sort this problem out?'

'I can see the problem,' said George. 'I can also see why John was very worried about the future of the estate. It was bad enough when Nathaniel was here, but if he was incapable of managing, I don't see any of the current employees will have the necessary skills.'

'That's true, but we don't need someone to run the estate at the moment, we are here to do that. We need a capable farm manager to control things at Borton.' observed Joseph 'and finding a suitable candidate should be our first task.'

'Personally I don't think we can risk leaving it to see how it goes and I agree with Joseph and that we should start searching for an experienced farm manager as soon as possible. I do not think any of us could spare enough time from our own daily routines to give the supervision that is required,' replied George.

'It will not be easy, all the good men will be employed already. If we can't find a suitable candidate before then, the Grantham annual hiring fair will take place in about six weeks' time. It's due on 29th September. The trouble is that those who turn up at Michaelmas are usually the labourers and other unskilled workers. Those who have the experience we require and turn up at the fair will probably be the dregs or those with other problems.' argued Joseph. 'Whatever we decide, we will have to be heavily involved at Borton for some time yet and I think it will take at least a couple of months to recruit a good manager. Even so I still think we must try to attract someone to manage the farm and ease the load on us.'

They discussed the various problems and options for some time and the decision was finally made to try to find a suitable man with the necessary experience to take the job. The job would have to be a on a temporary basis until Nathaniel was available to take over. This could create a problem and even so, they all realised that they would have to be quite heavily involved until an appointment was made. They were also aware that if this took too long, that they would reach a point where it would be a waste of funds to employ someone as Nathaniel would be back soon from his sojourn on the continent.

They agreed that they would all pass the word around to all their contacts to see if they could identify possible candidates. Between the three of them they thought that if there was a suitable person available they would soon find out.

***

The *"Greve Sparre"* had slowly negotiated the passage out into the open sea and, although he was convinced that he would feel poorly, Toni still had not felt at all seasick. Nathaniel had spent the time with Toni on the upper deck, initially watching Boston slowly disappear and the shipping thinning out. Now that they were clear of land Nathaniel said he was feeling very hungry and was Toni ready for something to eat. Toni said he was, although he was worried that he might be sick. 'For goodness sake, stop worrying Toni, you haven't been sick and you don't feel sick and you won't be sick. The sea is as calm as a mill pond and it will probably stay the same for the whole trip.'

Although it was quite late, they asked Jonas if they could have something to eat, and shortly after, the ships cook had quickly produced a tasty fish stew and some crusty bread. 'I enjoyed that,' said Toni. 'If the food keeps to that standard I will be a very happy man.'

'I am pleased you liked it,' said Jonas, 'we have a very good cook and he produces some excellent food from a limited amount of ingredients.'

After their meal Nathaniel thought he would take a walk on the upper deck, 'Would you care to join me Toni? It's such a lovely evening and a bit of fresh air before we retire would be very pleasant.' hoping he was not going to hear more of Toni's seasick worries. At the same time he thought 'If he can keep fish stew down, there is absolutely nothing wrong with his stomach.'

'Sleep well gentlemen' said Jonas, 'I am going to get some sleep while it is quiet. You have to grab it while you can, you never know what will happen next in this job. I'll see you both at breakfast.'

'Goodnight Captain, we will see you in the morning. Come on Toni, let's have a stroll before bed.' It was a clear, moonless night with only a few ships lights to be seen on the water but the sky was lit by millions of twinkling stars, a display that could only be seen on such a night as this. Toni had forgotten his seasickness phobia and was happy just looking at the stars and listening to the gentle sound of the water lapping around the ships bows and the sound of a warm, light breeze easing its way through the rigging. 'It's so peaceful Nathaniel, but I am very tired and I am ready for my bed.'

'Yes. So am I, I think I will turn in now.' With that, he said a cursory goodnight and went below to his berth.

***

Nathaniel arrived at breakfast after Toni and Jonas. Toni was in the middle of an extended grumble about being unable to sleep in such conditions. It was too noisy, there was a continuous creaking of timbers and the noise of the water lapping against the ship's side was simply unbearable. People were running around all night in heavy boots on the deck above his berth and, in addition, he had no idea how anyone was expected to get to sleep while the ship was moving about like a horse violently trying to eject a rider.

'Good morning Nathaniel, did you sleep well? asked Jonas.

'I did. I had a wonderful night and feel totally refreshed.' replied Nathaniel. 'Now, what's for breakfast I am famished.'

'Your friend Toni here, had a lousy night, he has not had a wink of sleep all night.'

'That's funny, he was snoring so loudly before I got into bed that I thought he was going to keep me awake.'

'Didn't the noise of the sailors in their heavy boots thumping around on the deck above annoy you?'

'I never heard them at all.'

Jonas interrupted and said to Toni, 'I must defend my crew Toni. All my sailors have soft canvas shoes for working in the rigging but most of them work all day barefooted, so I am not sure that you would have suffered noise from them.'

'How is your stomach this morning Toni?' asked Nathaniel, trying to change the subject.

'It's fine, thank you. I think you were correct when you said I was worrying too much.'

'I am sure you were, and I think you are worrying too much about your accommodation. If you could relax, and remember with a bit of luck you could be ashore in a couple of days enjoying a proper bed. It's not as if you

103

have to put up with it for a couple of months.'

'I know I am being stupid Nathaniel, but it's so different to living on a quiet village farm where there is hardly any noise at all. Here, there is noise all the time, it never stops. I suppose I would get used to it eventually, but thankfully, as you said, it's not a long trip.'

'Just try to forget about it Toni and enjoy your breakfast and we will go on deck to get some fresh air and see what is going on.'

'Just be careful while you are on deck.' said Jonas, 'When the crew are busy with the sails they have to move very quickly and ropes and sails can do serious damage to anyone who gets in the way.'

'Everything seems so complicated up on deck and I am pleased the crew know what they are doing. If you have time before we reach Ostend, it would be very interesting if you could explain to us how you operate all the sails and how you use the different sails for different tasks, Jonas. It is a great deal different to farm work.'

'I am sure I could manage that and I would be delighted to explain it all to you. How about after lunch? It should be fairly quiet then.'

'That would be lovely,' said Nathaniel. 'don't you agree Toni?'

'Yes it will, I look forward to seeing how they do things.'

***

After a good lunch, Jonas escorted the two travellers onto the upper deck and started to tell them about their transport. The *"Greve Sparre"* was a Snow Brig built in Malmo nearly three years ago and Jonas von Emden had been the captain ever since its first trip. He said he hoped to remain in charge for many more years. 'She is a lovely ship, the best I have ever worked in and I am very happy to be in command for as long as the owners will employ me. Since we first went to sea we have traded out of Stockholm to the south as far as Lisbon. Most of the trips, however, are between Sweden, England and northern France but we have to go where the business wants us to go. Sometimes we might go from Sweden to Boston and then pick up a cargo which takes us straight back to Sweden or another time, like now, we are on our way to Ostend. We have to see what is available there and see where our next cargo takes us.'

'How are you employed?' asked Toni, 'Are you on a trip by trip basis or for a set time?'

'Oh, purely on a trip by trip basis. As I have explained, when we set out we have no idea when we will be back in our home port so a time bound contract is impossible. Every time we go back to Stockholm I can leave or stay. It is up to me, and of course the owners, whether or not I get the next trip. I always try to follow their instructions as closely as possible and so far they have always been pleased with my work and have asked me to do another trip. Let's hope that they continue to be satisfied with me.'

'What about the crew, is it the same for them?'

'I decide who will crew the ship. They also work trip by trip but you try to keep the best. You get a reputation as a captain and a good reputation attracts the good crews. If you are known as a bad captain, whatever the reason you will have trouble getting a decent crew and you are likely to end up with the riff raff.'

'Your crew seem happy enough.' commented Nathaniel.

'Yes they are, I am lucky that they have nearly all been with me since the first trip. There have been a few changes but they were usually for domestic reasons. As you would expect, people like a change now and again and sailors, particularly their wives, are no different.'

'Do you get any trouble from your crew when you dock after a long spell at sea?' asked Toni.

'We get the usual problems with drink in most ports. They all go to have some fun and inevitably some of them end up in a fight, quite often fighting each other but mainly it's a fight with another ship's crew.'

'I was nearly involved in a fight in Boston a few weeks ago,' said Nathaniel, 'but my friend Max Hoboer sorted it all out very quickly. I think a Swedish crew was involved in that one at *"The Anchor."*

'All my crew know Max and if he is anywhere near, it would be very silly to get involved in a fracas, as he would soon break it up in his own ruthless manner.'

***

It was another clear and bright but frosty January morning and Ephraim had convened a meeting of the trustees of the Thorold estates. All three members were there and before they got down to business, Ephraim and George had to endure a long elucidation of all the ailments that Joseph had suffered over the last month or so and how, in particular, the cold weather was playing havoc with his rheumatism. 'We are all very sorry to hear of your problems Joseph, but we have some work to complete here before you can go

105

back to your sick bed.' said Ephraim sarcastically. 'You are not the only one suffering, my bloody toothache is giving me hell, and while we are at it, have you anything you want to get off your chest before we start George?' he continued in a peevish tone.

'Nothing at all,' said George, 'I am feeling perfectly well.'

'Thank The Lord for that, so let's get on with the business then.' Ephraim said, with a contemptuous smirk directed towards Joseph.

Ephraim opened the meeting, 'I have had a few short letters from Nathaniel, each one reminding me to arrange for more funds sent out to him. He is obviously enjoying himself and they have already visited Ostend, Bruges and Lille and were in Paris when he last wrote. They were about to head off on the long trip to Barcelona. Apparently they have decided to go down the west coast of France to Bordeaux and then follow the coast road into Spain. They then hope to get to Barcelona visiting San Sebastian, Pamplona and Zaragoza on the way. If all goes well they hope to get there by Christmas. Antonio is proving to be a great help and his ability to speak both French and Italian fluently has already managed to extricate them from a few difficult situations. It looks as if they are keen to eventually get all the way to Naples where Antonio's grandparents live. We all know that Nathaniel's father wanted to widen Nathaniel's knowledge of the art and treasures of the region but I get the impression that he is not the slightest bit interested in such things. The tone of his brief letters give me the feeling that they are doing very little in the way of cultural activities and quite a lot of socialising in the bars and coffee houses of wherever they are visiting. Unfortunately we are not in a position where we can do anything about it other than cutting off his supply of funds and I suggest this would be an absolute waste of time.'

'Why do you think it would be a waste of time Ephraim?' queried Joseph, hoping his outburst regarding his ailments had been forgotten.

'If I wrote to him and said that he would get no more funds if he failed to do as required, then he would just tell us what we wanted to hear. We have no way of checking what he is really doing at all. He can tell us what he wants and we are none the wiser. As I said, it would be a waste of time, surely you can see that?' said Ephraim, continuing his sarcastic manner with Joseph.

'I suppose you are right.' replied Joseph passively.

'I agree,' said George, 'he seems to be the same Nathaniel that his father was so worried about, and I am at a loss to see how we can change his ways. If he carries on in the same manner then there is very little chance of him ever running a successful business.'

'It is a very delicate situation, we have seen sparks of interest from him in the past but we could be trying to rescue a lost cause.'

'When have we ever seen sparks of interest from him, Joseph? I don't remember any. You must have been dreaming.' replied Ephraim, his toothache still having an effect on his attitude.

'Don't you remember the way he negotiated the new tenancy agreements soon after John died? I think you said he carried them out in a very professional and business-like way.' retorted Joseph, keen to fight back against Ephraim's belligerence.

Ephraim promptly changed the subject by reminding the meeting that their prime responsibility was to run the estate professionally and maintain its profitability. The second was to give Nathaniel every opportunity to develop the skills to be able to take over when he reached the age of twenty-five years. To help in the second objective John had specified the foreign trip which Nathaniel was currently enjoying, and on his return, a period of time to be spent in London with a distant cousin, Samuel Thorold, developing business skills in Samuel's successful ironmongery business.

Joseph was feeling a little more confident now and asked, 'When are you going to contact Samuel Thorold, Ephraim?'

'I have already contacted him by letter and received his reply last week. Unfortunately he received my note too late to see us on his last visit, although it was on the very sad occasion of his brother George's funeral at Harmston and he probably would not have had time to see us. His brother Sir George, who was Lord Mayor of London a couple of years previously, had died in the last few days of October last year and Samuel has inherited the Knighthood and all the estates at Harmston. He is now known as Sir Samuel Thorold of Harmston in the County of Lincoln, so we are now dealing with a knight of the realm. Sir Samuel says he will let us know the date of his next visit to Lincolnshire when he will be delighted to meet us to discuss Nathaniel's stay in London. I think Nathaniel is in for a bit of a surprise, Sir Samuel appears to be a very fastidious man.'

'I didn't realise that John had such illustrious relatives,' said Joseph. 'He certainly kept quiet about them! It looks as if there will be no more fights in pubs for Nathaniel then. What do you think George?' smiled Joseph.

'I think Nathaniel will have some very serious decisions to make if he is going to stay the course. It might just prove London could be the making of him.' was the reply.

'Or not.' murmured Ephraim, his hand pressing on his painful tooth.

Ephraim, obviously in pain, was eager to end proceedings as soon as possible so that he could get a painkiller, preferably in the form of a good stiff rum, so he suggested they remove to *"The Angel"* and conclude their business over lunch. 'Do you think you could manage to get there without help Joseph?' he asked sarcastically. 'I could get Watson to give you a hand if you need one.'

***

As he walked through the door of *"The Angel"*, Ephraim ordered a large glass of rum from the potman, 'and don't hang about Tom!' he said, still holding his cheek. As he settled himself at his favourite table. he asked the other two what they wanted to drink.

Tom came with Ephraim's rum and took the orders from George and Joseph, by which time Ephraim had finished his rum and so he ordered another. 'If this doesn't get any better I will have to get Jack Burr to pull the bloody thing out.'

'Jack Burr?' queried Joseph 'he's a blacksmith, he will have no idea what to do. Why don't you see Fred Vickers the barber, he is quite skilled at that sort of thing?'

'Jack did my last one and he didn't charge me for it and he had it out in no time.' snapped Ephraim. 'Anyway it's my bloody tooth.'

'Quite right, Ephraim, it's your bloody tooth.' said George who realised Ephraim must be in considerable pain as it was unlike him to swear so much in public.

'What are we going to do regarding the position of manager at Borton?' asked George. 'We haven't had much luck so far and there does not seem to be any suitable candidates around at the moment. The hiring fair was a waste of time, as we suspected it might be.'

Ephraim, still pressing his hand hard on his aching cheek, pointed out that Nathaniel had already been away for five months of the proposed twelve. 'During that time they have completed a successful harvest which we all know is the busiest time of the farming year. As the farm has carried on without any noticeable serious problems, do we need to continue with this fruitless search?'

They all agreed with Ephraim and they would discontinue the search but if a suitable candidate presented himself in the near future they would reconsider their decision. George thought it was the right thing to do but privately thought Ephraim would have not been so hasty to reach this conclusion if he had been in his usual ebullient mood. The pain he was suffering was obvious to all and was clearly influencing his behaviour.

***

Tom came back with the drinks and asked if they were staying for lunch and George and Joseph decided that they would both have Ham, Eggs and Boiled Potatoes but Ephraim had decided he had had enough for today and brought the meeting to a close by declaring, 'This rum could do with being a lot stronger, it's not eased the pain at all. I am going to see Jack Burr now and I will let you both know as soon as I can when the next meeting will be.' and still pressing his hand to his cheek, pushed his chair back from the table, stood up, left *"The Angel"* and headed off to the blacksmith's forge.

'As far as I understand, we have decided to make no decisions today and the next meeting will be arranged later.' said George.

'That's about it. Old Ephraim is in a lot of pain and I think he will get worse before he gets better. Jack Burr is excellent with a rasp around the mouths of horses but I would hate to think he was about to remove one of my molars.'

Tom brought the lunch and as they started to eat, Joseph dipped a slice of ham into one of his eggs and murmured, 'Poor Ephraim.'

George smiled contentedly and replied, 'Poor old Ephraim.'

George and Joseph cleaned their plates, leant back in their chairs and relaxed as Tom came to ask them if they had finished and would they like another drink. They decided that they would stay where it was nice and warm in front of the big open fire and have a couple of pots of ale before they left for home.

'What do you think of John having such noble relatives, George? That was a bit of a surprise to me, I hadn't a clue, had you?'

'No, I had no idea at all, I thought he was just a hard working farmer with a bit of property elsewhere which he had inherited. He had once mentioned he had a distant cousin who had a bit of land and also had a thriving business down in London so I was aware that there was a bit of money in the family, but a Lord Mayor of London, no less. That was a bit of a shock.'

'Well John was not short of a penny or two so it appears that the family owns a fair chunk of the county and that Hall at Harmston must belong to them. It's a great big place, and I saw it when I went to Lincoln last year. The one who died, George, the Lord Mayor must have built it as it is only a couple of years old.'

'If they are only distant relations, I would think the chances of Nathaniel ever getting his spendthrift little hands on any valuable inheritance are very slim.'

'I agree, there must be lots of family in line before Nathaniel. Can you imagine him in charge of a big London business? It doesn't bear thinking about, does it?'

'I wonder if Ephraim knew?' pondered George.

'Probably, he does keep things close to his chest sometimes.'

'I know I would not change places with him at this moment. He must be stark raving mad to go to Jack's to get a tooth pulled.'

'I definitely agree with you on that.' said Joseph. 'However, I think it's time for me to be on my way or it will be dark before I get home.'

When they left *"The Angel"*, the sky had clouded over and the first signs of snow were drifting gently from a leaden sky and people were scurrying to and fro, trying to get to their destination before the snows gained strength. 'It's home for me.' said George, 'I don't want to get caught in Grantham if it gets any worse.'

'Nor me, the beds at *"The Angel"* are nowhere near as comfortable as the one at home.' replied Joseph.

Having said their goodbyes, they parted and went their separate ways, both feeling very satisfied and pleased with themselves. After all, they had concluded an important and what could have been a very stressful meeting in a very relaxed manner. No more thought was given to Ephraim and his aching tooth.

Chapter 9

It was the middle of February and the ground was still covered in a layer of snow as it had been for the last three weeks. Fodder for the few remaining cattle was getting used up very quickly and most of the farm hands were out in the low lying field near the frozen beck. They had the backbreaking task of clearing the snow and trying to lift all the turnips they could. Most of the turnip crop had been lifted and stored in 'graves' before the hard winter had set in. These 'graves' comprised a large heap of turnips covered in a thick layer of straw and then covered again with a layer of earth. The 'grave' would be opened and turnips taken out as needed and re-sealed when enough had been removed for immediate use. This method of storage was also used for potatoes and other root crops and was normally sufficient to tide the farm over for the winter. This winter however, stored turnips had nearly run out and the part of the crop which had not been lifted was still in the frozen ground and was urgently needed. Although it would prove to be very difficult and uncomfortable, it had to be lifted.

When they had cleared a patch of snow the workers had to dig the turnips out of the frozen ground, knock the worst of the soil off and then load them into a horse drawn cart and get them into a shed to cut them up for feed. After a short while in the field, workers could no longer feel their fingers and the biting cold chilled them to the bones. Chapped fingers were common and often turned septic as a result of being ingrained with dirt.

John Fowler, a mild mannered man was very worried regarding the state of the farm animals and was driving the men as hard as he could in the freezing conditions so that the beasts might be fed. They still had a reasonable supply of hay left but they needed something to supplement it and this was all that was available. It was a desperate situation to be in and the future of the farm demanded that some breeding cattle survived until the spring to regenerate the herd. George Holland, the stable man said he knew someone who had a good supply of turnips but as yet nothing had come of it.

Mo, who was directly in charge of the cattle, had laid off the two milkmaids for the winter period as this was the usual practice. The one fulltime girl who lived on the farm and was retained for the winter, was not getting much milk out of the hungry cows. Things were getting desperate and Mo suggested to John that they should inform Mr. Woolaston of the present state of affairs.

'If we don't tell him what is going on and if we start to lose any of the herd, we will be the ones to get into deep trouble. With a bit of luck, he might know where we can get enough supplies to tide us over.'

'You are right Mo, I will get things started here first thing tomorrow and then get off to Grantham. Will you look out for me while I am away, just make sure they don't slack off?' said John.

***

Sylvia had been taking her new responsibilities very seriously since she had taken over from Miss Joyce, just over a year ago. She had settled into her additional responsibilities very quickly, even though she hadn't had any family living in since Nathaniel had set off to foreign lands last August. She had made sure the household staff had set about giving the house a good spring clean, with the instructions that it must be finished and ready for when Mr. Nathaniel returned from his foreign trip. He was not expected to return until July or August and she was well on course for having the house ready by then. The top two floors were almost complete and there was just the ground floor to do. Doing one room at a time, they had cleared each room of all its furniture, and had the chimneys swept before washing the walls and windows and scrubbing the floors. The floors, doors and the rest of the woodwork had been given a coat of polish while all the linen had been washed and ironed and any repairs made where required. The furniture had been replaced and covered with sheets and the linen placed in dry cupboards until it was needed.

Cleaning the ground floor was going to be more labour intensive as there was a great deal more lifting to do, particularly in the Master's office where the desk was very heavy. Sylvia would have to ask John Fowler to provide a couple of strong men to help move things around but she did not see this as a problem.

Sylvia was applying herself to the main task with great passion, she desperately wanted to impress Nathaniel when he eventually arrived back home, and she wanted to take her mind off the fact that when he was away from home, she worried for him. It was as if he was her own son and he was out of her reach, all the time he was away, she felt desperately lonely and missed looking after him all the time. Nathaniel was in his late teens but she still regarded him as a child.

***

112

There was a knock on the kitchen door and before Sylvia could get to open it, there was a blast of icy cold air and Mo came in and asked if she was busy.

'No, come in Maurice and shut the door behind you, you look frozen stiff.'

'It's bloody cold out there.' replied Mo, repeatedly swinging his arms across his chest and smacking them as far around his back as possible. 'It's bloody difficult to keep warm for any length of time. I just wish it would give us a break, but I suspect that this weather could go on for another month yet.'

'Sit yourself down in front of the fire, I will get you a bowl of hot soup. It's a bit thin but it will warm you up.' said Sylvia. 'What did you come to see me for anyway?'

Mo explained that there were eight men and women who had been in the field all day and would have to go home in a couple of hours' time to cold homes and no chance of hot food to warm them up. 'They are nearly dead on their feet,' explained Mo. 'is there any chance of getting something like this?' he said, indicating the soup, 'so that at least they can get something warm in their stomachs.'

'I will do what I can, but all I have is a few cabbage leaves and some potatoes. If you take them to the barn and let me know when they are coming I will have something ready.'

'Thanks Sylvia, you are an angel.' Mo handed back the empty bowl, gave her a peck on the cheek and left, slamming the door behind him.

***

The frozen workers had all gathered in the barn and were gradually warming through and enjoying their soup. Sylvia had also brought a couple of loaves of bread which she had baked in the morning and shared them around to eat with their soup.

'Thank you so much Sylvia, you can see what a difference that has made, they are nearly on starvation rations this time of year and anything like this is a banquet to them.'

'That's alright Maurice, they deserve it. I know I wouldn't want their job in this weather. By the way, have you heard from Nathaniel at all?'

'Not a word since the day he left. I know Mr. Woolaston has, but I think he was just asking for more money. I saw Mr. Montini from Corby Glen when I was at Bourne market a couple of weeks ago and he said he had heard

113

from his son a couple of times. By all accounts, they are having a good time.'

'I would have thought he might have been interested in progress at the farm but he has never shown a lot of interest has he?' pondered Sylvia.

'I just hope he hasn't been hitting the ale again.' said Mo. 'If he has, he could be in trouble when he gets back home. Mr. Woolaston has spies everywhere and he won't miss something like that.'

'I just wish he would just let us know where he is and what he is doing.' Sylvia sighed wistfully.

***

It was the last few days of February and Nathaniel and Antonio had just arrived on the outskirts of Barcelona. They were tired and weary and just about fed up with their travels. The long, slow, trek across the remote plains of northern Spain had dampened their previous enthusiasm for foreign travel. The plan was to be in Barcelona by Christmas but they had finally arrived two months behind schedule. They had managed to get lost twice, and on one occasion, due to Toni's inability to master the Spanish dialect used in the area, had followed vague instructions only to end up in the evening back where they had started from in the morning. Soon after leaving Pamplona, Nathaniel had been taken ill with a fever and had been confined to bed for ten days in the remote small town of Jaca, miles from the route which they had planned. Barcelona was a welcome sight and they decided to find lodgings and stay for a couple of weeks to revise their plans for the remainder of the trip.

The *"Taverna Nouvel"* on the Carretera de Balboa had comfortable rooms to rent and so they booked a room each, initially for two weeks with the option of extending their stay if required. 'I think the first thing to do is to write to old Ephraim and get some more funds. We are not desperate as yet but it will be a few weeks before we get a reply.' said Nathaniel.

'A good idea, we don't want to run out do we? If we are staying for a while, do you think we should sell the horses?'

'I think so, they have done a good job since we bought them in San Sebastian and we won't need them here. We can always buy more when we move on.'

'I am sure the landlord Seve will know where to go to sell them, but I expect he will want a cut.'

'He certainly will, but I am still a bit worried about your ability to deal with this local version of the Spanish language, after all, Spanish is not your best subject, is it?

'Don't worry Nathaniel, I will soon pick it up, I am already more confident than I was when we first encountered it.'

Once they had settled in to their rooms and unpacked their belongings they decided to go for a stroll in the late afternoon sunshine to get their bearings. After a short stroll they entered the busy port area and eventually found an empty table outside a taverna. They sat down and ordered a carafe of local red wine and when the waiter brought it, they sat back with the intention of relaxing and watching the world go by. They had only been there a few minutes before a scruffy young boy asked for money. By the time the third one had arrived the waiter advised them to go round the back and sit on the patio where it would be quiet. Here they found comfortable seats under a vine covered pergola and settled down with their wine. 'It's nice to be able to relax isn't it?' said Toni.

'It certainly is, it's been a rough trip and I don't want to go through that again.' replied Nathaniel, leaning back in his chair and stretching out his legs. 'I will write to Ephraim this evening before I forget, we don't want to be on the streets begging like those boys, do we?'

'Well, that's the most important thing at the moment and I think we should stay here until we get a reply. That will give us plenty of time to explore the area and get some advice on planning the next leg of our trip.' observed Toni.

'Yes I agree, and I think we should try to sell all four horses tomorrow, we don't want to be paying out for stabling if we are going to get rid of them, do we?'

After an agreeable hour, they decided to go back to their lodgings in time for the evening meal. Seve, told them of a customer who was looking to buy some horses for his place of work and interested in making a purchase. Once the meal was over, Nathaniel and Toni were introduced to the prospective purchaser. After thoroughly inspecting the horses and a long period of intense haggling, a deal was finally struck for all four horses.

'You did well there Toni, we got a bit more than we paid for them. Well done!'

'Yes, I was pleased with my Spanish this time. The proceeds will keep us going for most of our stay here.' replied a very satisfied Toni.

***

After a couple of weeks enjoying a leisurely life seeing the sights and getting to know their way around the bustling streets of this vibrant city, their minds turned to planning the next stretch of their journey. They sought the advice of several local businessmen who had travelled extensively as part of their work and wherever possible talked to people who had made journeys into France and Italy. Nathaniel and Toni had thought it would be best to work their way along the coastal route and avoid, where possible the mountain tracks on their way to Italy and finally to Naples. Their main concern was not with the route, but the fact that they were quite a way behind their original schedule. They had intended, rather optimistically, to have reached Genoa by now but they were still in Barcelona roughly three months behind their planned timetable. The information they had gleaned from their recent contacts indicated that even if they stayed on the coastal route, they would find that certain parts would prove quite hazardous. The stretch soon after entering France either side of Cap Cerbere, between Barcelona and Perpignan was extremely difficult. The objective of reaching Naples, which was over one thousand miles away, to see Toni's relatives was seemingly impossible, considering that they had to get home in August.

'What options are still left to us, Nathaniel?' Toni asked. 'The chances of seeing my family look to be bleak after all we have been through.'

'The first option would be to turn round and head for home, but I think you will agree, that is a nonstarter.' replied Nathaniel. 'I think we should sit down and look at the facts.'

'The first thing we must do is stay in Barcelona until we hear from Mr. Woolaston, we must get the money sorted out before we can do anything.' replied Toni. 'It also seems certain we will not get to Naples and back home in the time allowed.'

'To be honest Toni, I would love to get to Naples but as it is out of the question, we could do a tour of southern Spain and up through Portugal before heading home. We might be able to do something like that in the time allowed. Even if it meant not getting home until September it would not matter too much and we will still have to rely on the vagaries of ship's movements.'

'I don't know what to think,' said Toni, 'I am desperately disappointed that we will not be going to Naples and I think we should have a word with a few more people and see if we still have any other options. We still have a couple of more weeks before we have to make up our minds because we won't

116

hear from Mr. Woolaston before then.'

***

That evening, just after they had finished their meal, Seve, joined them over a drink and politely asked if they wished to extend their stay, as they had only reserved their rooms until the following morning. Nathaniel apologised for not mentioning it before, and explained that he had forgotten all about it but yes, they would like to stay for at the least, another two weeks and possibly longer. Their future travel was discussed and it was explained that where they would be going was, at the moment, uncertain.

'We were heading for Naples where I have a number of relatives but it will take too long to get there as we have to be home in England during August.' explained Toni.

'If you really want to get to Naples, why don't you go by ferry? asked Seve.

'What ferry?' asked Nathaniel, glancing with a look of doubt at Toni.

'The Barcelona to Naples ferry of course. It sails every Monday and Friday and takes no time at all.'

'We didn't even think of a direct ferry, did we Toni? It sounds as if it is exactly what we need, so thank you for telling us. We will look into it first thing tomorrow morning.'

'You know I am not keen on boats, Nathaniel, so I don't know if I want to.' said a worried Toni.

'Don't you be stupid Toni, you were perfectly alright the last time we were at sea and if we don't go to Naples by sea, we will not be going at all. Do you really want to see your relatives or not?' responded Nathaniel, with a real trace of anger in his voice.

'Of course I want to see them, but you know that I worry about boats.'

'Well, any more of that nonsense and we will be turning round and going home. Do you understand?'

'Yes Nathaniel.' was Toni's weak response.

'Well, *you* want to go to Naples, *I* want to go to Naples, and the only chance of going to Naples is by ferry so that is what we are going to do.' decided Nathaniel. 'I will write to Mr. Woolaston tonight and tell him that as soon as we get his remittance, we are going to Naples by ferry. We can be contacted at your grandfather's address and if he hasn't already got it, he can get it from your father.'

117

Chapter 10

Ephraim had called a meeting of the trustees for the first week in May and welcomed George and Joseph to his office himself.

'Where is Watson?' asked George as they sat down. 'are you on your own today Ephraim?'

'Yes I am, I have been on my own for over a week now, the silly old fool slipped on the snow at the front door and has damaged his leg. I don't know if he will ever come back either. It is very inconsiderate of him and I would have thought he could have made a bit of an effort to get to work, after all, he is sitting down most of the time when he is here. If he doesn't get back soon I will have to get rid of him and employ someone who can at least get to work.'

'It is very inconvenient for you Ephraim, I don't know how you manage things on your own.' Joseph sympathised.

'I know, I missed lunch at *"The Angel"* yesterday. I had so much to catch up on.' whined Ephraim. 'We had better get down to business or I will end up missing lunch again.'

Ephraim sorted through a pile of papers and pulled out the letter from Nathaniel, which had been written just over a month ago on his arrival in Barcelona. Ephraim explained that there was the usual request for more funds and related the problems they had encountered on the way. 'They are trying to decide what to do next and will let me know as soon as they make a decision and they are staying where they are until the funds they requested arrive. They should have received them by now as I took the package to the carrier the day after I received the letter.'

'There is not much chance of them reaching Naples if they are still in Barcelona is there?' commented Joseph. 'It is a very long way to get there and then make the long journey all the way back home by the middle of August.'

'There's no chance,' agreed George, 'I wonder what bright idea they will come up with this time.'

'It's as I said last time, they can do what they like and tell us anything they want to and we will be none the wiser. Now I think we should get on with the other business. As regards the farm at Borton, after a bit of a struggle, we managed to get some more fodder and feed for the animals. It took a week or

118

so and we had to go as far as Ruskington, the other side of Sleaford to get it. Unfortunately one of the five cows died before the first load arrived and it was a close call for two of the remaining four. It was a good thing John Fowler and Maurice Clark had the sense to come and let us know the situation before it was too late.' Ephraim reported.

'I think the men at Borton have done a very good job in the circumstances and I am sure we can forget about any recruitment of a farm manager now. These men have proved their worth and guided the farm through one of the worst winters for years.' said Joseph.

'I agree, and we should not forget Miss Butler, she has really sorted out the house over the last few months and she has proved to be good support to the farm workers.' replied George.

Ephraim extracted another letter from his pile of papers, 'This is a letter I received from Sir Samuel Thorold last week and he says he will be visiting Harmston in early July. He expects to be up here for at least three weeks and he will contact us soon as he has sorted out his priorities. He says he definitely will see us this time as he is keen to get Nathaniel involved on a new business project he would like to start.'

'There's an optimist if I ever saw one,' laughed George. 'Nathaniel organising a new project, I look forward to seeing that one!'

There was a loud knock on the outer door and then the door slammed shut and a large man entered the office, 'Mr. Ephraim Woolaston?' he asked.

'Yes, that's me, who the hell are you?'

'I am a carrier, sir and I have a package for you, marked urgent.'

'Thank you very much, my man.' He took the package and gave the carrier his fee, ushered him out of the office and closed the door. 'It looks as if it is another short note from Nathaniel,' he said as he slit it open and unfolded it to see what it said. 'They haven't received the last parcel I sent but as soon as they receive it, they are going directly to Naples by boat. He explains it will cost less than buying horses and they should be there in four or five days. They can be contacted at Antonio's grandfather's residence in Naples. As this was written over three weeks ago, I suspect that they are probably in Naples by now.'

'Do you have the address in Naples, Ephraim?' asked George.

'No, but I can get it from Antonio's father the next time I see him.'

***

The package was delivered to the *"Taverna Nouvel"* two days before the end of April and they promptly went down to the shipping agents office to secure their accommodation on the next available ferry. They were a little disappointed that the next ferry on Friday morning was fully booked but there plenty of space on the next one due to depart on Monday morning at eight o'clock.' With a bit of luck, you will be seeing your relations before the end of next week Toni. How does that sound?' asked Nathaniel, grinning from ear to ear.

'It's brilliant, I can hardly believe it. Just a few days ago it seemed that we would never make it and now we are almost there.' gushed Toni, delighted at the prospect of seeing his extended family, most of them for the first time. 'I will send a message to my grandfather on the Friday ferry and you can be sure there will be a welcome party waiting to greet us when we arrive.'

'I really am looking forward to that Toni, I have heard a great deal about Italian hospitality. It's great to be on the move again, we have had a good time here but I think we are both ready for a change and Naples sounds just the place for me. How about you Toni?' Nathaniel asked, knowing full well what the answer would be.

'I have been waiting years to get to Italy and now it is within touching distance so I think we should get back to the Taverna and start gathering our possessions together ready for the journey, don't you?'

'I do, and we have a lot of accounts to settle before Monday so we can't waste any time.' replied Nathaniel.

***

The few days to departure passed quickly and they were soon on their way. It was a beautiful clear morning and the sun sparkled on the calm, azure Mediterranean Sea. A light breeze filled the sails and the ferry made steady progress while the few passengers relaxed in small groups as they enjoyed the atmosphere and settled in to life at sea.

'Not felt sick yet, Toni?' enquired Nathaniel, rather sarcastically.

'Not yet, I don't think I could be sick in such lovely conditions.' was the reply.

'I have told you before, it's all in the mind. You have crossed from Boston to Ostend and now you are at sea again and still have not suffered so I should forget about it if I were you.'

'You are right of course and I will do my best, I promise. Isn't it a beautiful day, though?'

***

The weather stayed warm with a light cooling breeze for the whole of the ferry trip and as they approached Naples most of the passengers were on deck and corralled into safe areas clear of the seamen working the sails. Vesuvius, with its gently smoking crater, dominated the background as the city and its larger buildings gradually came into view. Toni was beside himself with excitement at the prospect of meeting all of his relations and Nathaniel smiled as he said, 'For goodness sake, Toni, calm down or you will be having a seizure if you carry on like this.'

'I can't help it Nathaniel, I have a large family to see. I met my uncle Luigi a few years ago when he came to England to see my father, but he is the only one I have ever seen.' replied Toni.

As the ferry entered the harbour and gradually approached the wharf, a sizeable crowd were discernible on the dock awaiting the ferry's arrival. The closer the ferry got, the more the faces of individuals became recognisable and Toni thought he could see his uncle in every face on the dockside. It wasn't until a group of about twenty people of all ages from small children to an old gentleman started shouting, '*Benvenuto in Italia Antonio*' that they realised this was their welcoming party.

Toni was overcome with emotion and promptly burst into tears while Nathaniel tried to blink away a few tears without anyone noticing that he was also affected. The contrast between the quiet and calm of the steady progress of the ferry and the volume of noise on the wharf was deafening. Nathaniel could hardly believe that such a small group of people could generate so much noise and as everyone in the group was talking or shouting at the same time, it was impossible to understand what anyone was saying, even if you understood the Italian language.

***

Once the gangway was in place and secured, passengers were allowed to go ashore but Toni and Nathaniel had to wait a while before they managed to get ashore and meet the welcoming party.

Introductions took ages and after being introduced to each relative by his uncle Luigi, Toni introduced Nathaniel. After what seemed an age, introductions were complete and Nathaniel still hadn't a clue who anyone was, even Toni could only remember a few of them.

121

When their belongings had all been gathered together on the jetty, they were loaded onto a cart and the whole party set of in various types of horse drawn transport to meet Grandfather Antonio at his house for the prearranged family gathering.

'How far have we to go to your grandfather's house?'

'It's not far out of town so we should not be too long.' replied a still very excited Toni.

***

The trustees had all arrived early for the meeting in Ephraim's office waiting excitedly in anticipation of meeting a real knight of the realm. Sir Samuel Thorold had contacted Ephraim and said he would come to see them at ten o'clock in the morning on the first Tuesday of July. He also stressed that he would not be able to stay longer than one hour as he was having lunch afterwards with a very good friend at Belvoir Castle.

'Do you think he will be on time?' pondered Joseph. 'The roads will be a bit muddy after all that rain last night.'

'Of course he will, he will have made allowance for the conditions and will have set off early.' said Ephraim in a patronizing, haughty manner. 'Watson, get off your idle backside and keep a watch through the window. I want to know the minute he arrives.'

Watson struggled off his stool and with more of a limp since his accident, struggled to the widow with the aid of his stick. 'What does this gentleman look like, Mr. Woolaston, Sir?' he asked.

'He will look like a gentleman, you silly fool. How do you think I know what he looks like, I have never seen him before?'

'Steady on Ephraim,' interrupted George 'you were a bit hard on him. He is doing the best he can and is still having trouble with his damaged leg.'

'All the time I pay him a wage, he will do as I say and I beg you to mind your own business George, it's nothing to do with you.'

'Have you heard any more from Nathaniel?' interjected Joseph in an effort to change the subject. 'I wonder if he has managed to reach Naples by now?'

Watson, peering through the grime and dust covered window turned and called, 'Mr. Woolaston, sir.'

'Shut up Watson, and keep looking.' was the blunt answer.

'But there is a fancy coach approaching Sir, it might be him. There is a coachman and another man at the back of the coach.'

'Why didn't you say so the first time, you stupid man, Joseph, George, come on let's go down and welcome him to our humble office.'

***

When they arrived outside the office building, a footman was opening the door of the coach and a tall, distinguished gentleman alighted. 'Good morning gentlemen,' he said 'I am Sir Samuel Thorold and trust that I find you all in good health on this somewhat grey day.' He was dressed in a very fashionable plain blue coat, embroidered along the edges and pockets. He had a plain waistcoat which was in lighter shade of blue and his shirt was frilled at the cuffs. Around his neck he wore a knotted, lace cravat and he sported a tricorn hat on top of a good head of dark curly hair. His breeches were of a cream coloured woollen material and were buttoned below the knee and in his hand he carried a cane with a silver handle in the shape of a ram's head.

'Good morning Sir Samuel, welcome to Grantham. I am Ephraim Woolaston and these are my colleagues, Joseph Godbold and George Heap. If you would care to follow me, we will go upstairs to my chambers.' They all went upstairs and were met by Watson who was struggling to stay on his feet for more than a few minutes and looked as if he was in considerable pain.

'Your man looks to be in some distress, Woolaston. Should he be at work?'

'He has just come back to work after an accident so he is still struggling a bit, Sir Samuel.' said Ephraim.

'He looks as if he could do with some more rest if I am not mistaken, he looks half dead to me. Anyhow, I think we ought to get down to business, as you know I have an appointment at Belvoir Castle this afternoon and I don't want to be late. What do you know of Nathaniel's current whereabouts, have you heard from him recently?'

'The last correspondence we received was from Barcelona and he was preparing to catch a ferry to Naples. By my calculations they should have arrived in Naples during the first week of May but we have heard nothing since the last note from Barcelona.'

'As I understand the situation, Nathaniel is due back home in August and if he is still in Naples then he will never be back by then. Do you have an address in Naples where you can contact him?'

'I have,' replied Ephraim. 'His companion, Antonio Montini has family in Naples and I have obtained the address of his grandfather and I can send correspondence there.'

The discussion then centred on how Nathaniel could possibly get back to England by mid-August and the general consensus was that it was impossible. Sir Samuel thought he had a possible solution and went on to explain that as part of his business in London, which he had inherited from his brother Sir George, he imported a considerable amount of goods such as marble, both uncut and carved items, ceramics and decorated tiles from Italy. In order to maximise his profits he was the part owner of two trading vessels which regularly carried cargo to and from Italy and Spain. One of these vessels, the *"Marston Maid"* sailed from London to Italy two weeks ago carrying a cargo of pottery and domestic kitchen utensils to Spain and Italy. It was then due to pick up a full cargo of assorted marble from Livorno in mid-August and call in at Lisbon on the way back to collect decorated floor tiles. 'I suggest that you should send a letter to Nathaniel informing him that he should make his way to Livorno early in August and wait for the *"Marston Maid"*. She is under the command of Captain Wilson and Nathaniel should report to him on his arrival, and as part of his development he is to sign on as crew and work his passage home. His companion, Antonio should have the choice of either staying in Italy or coming back as a paying passenger, it will be entirely up to him.'

'That sounds like a brilliant solution to me, Sir Samuel.' said Ephraim.

'It is,' agreed Joseph, 'but Nathaniel won't like it one bit.'

'It is not a matter of whether he likes it or not, he knew he should be back by mid-August and he would never have made it. As it is, it will be September before he gets home and the bit of hard work he will have to do will test his stamina and dedication.' emphasised Sir Samuel.

All three trustees were nodding their agreement and Ephraim said that he would get the letter off to Nathaniel that very day.

'Well Woolaston, I think that is about everything but before I go I will write some instructions for Captain Wilson which you can forward with the letter to Nathaniel. He can deliver it to the captain when he meets him.' He then asked Ephraim if he could have a sheet of paper and wrote out his instructions, sanded the ink, folded and sealed the paper and gave it to Ephraim. 'That's it! Thank you all for your help and co-operation. It has been nice meeting you at last and I now look forward to hearing what Captain

124

Wilson will have to say regarding young Nathaniel's reactions to something he definitely will not like. Goodbye gentlemen, I must get on my way now or I will be late for my next appointment and then I will be in real trouble.' With that, he picked up his stick, put on his hat, left the office and went down the stairs to his waiting coach.

***

'I pity Nathaniel when he goes to London for his period with Sir Samuel.' smirked George.

'He won't know what has hit him,' replied Joseph. 'The crafty old bugger is using the trip home to really sort him out and Nathaniel will have no idea that he is being observed and reported on for the whole trip.'

'Do you think Antonio will come back with him?' asked Ephraim. 'I can't see Nathaniel working while Antonio is taking it easy as a passenger. It's bound to cause friction isn't it?'

'I tell you what.' said George, 'Sir Samuel is a shrewd operator, he will have Nathaniel weighed up in no time and heaven help if he doesn't do what is required.'

'I think John was the shrewd one, setting up the scheme in the first place.' was Ephraim's analysis.

***

'The convoy of carriages and riders on horseback took quite a while longer than Nathaniel had anticipated. By the time they had gone through the centre of Naples they spent a further hour on dry, dusty country roads passing through small villages and isolated homesteads. They approached Grandfather Antonio's villa along a long straight road through olive groves situated on the lower slopes of the gently steaming Mount Vesuvius.

Grandfather Antonio, a short, rotund old gentleman with a red cravat tied around his neck and wearing a dark blue beret was waiting for them while sitting on a bench at the front gate. There were two of his dogs sitting at his feet and as the cavalcade approached, the dogs leapt to their feet and barked their welcome as only excited dogs can do and Antonio, with the aid of a stick, eased himself to his feet to welcome his visitors. 'Benvenuto alla mia casa, benveuto alla mia casa.' he repeated, 'Entri e distenda I miei amici' he called out and guided the bustling throng of relatives through the gates and into the courtyard of his beautiful home.

125

After another long introductory session with dozens of ·excitable relatives, Nathaniel and Toni were shown to their rooms and had a chance to wash and freshen up before going down to join the family for a meal. Everyone was taken onto the patio where a sumptuous feast was spread out on heavily laden tables. Nathaniel was ushered to a seat between two Italian ladies but Toni explained to them, that as he did not understand the language it would help if Nathaniel could sit next to him.

'Thanks Toni.' said Nathaniel, 'I don't know what I would have done on my own but at least you can translate for me.'

'I know what you mean, but when you have been here for a few days, I am sure you will start to pick up a few words.'

'I hope so, but they talk so loudly don't they? I thought your family at Corby Glen were noisy but these are even louder!' exclaimed Nathaniel.

The festivities went on well into the evening and gradually the guests thinned out as they departed for their own homes. Grandfather Antonio had gone to his bed hours ago and by now only a few remained. Nathaniel was reunited with Toni after a while, having spent the time meeting relatives who talked incessantly in a language he did not understand. 'I tried to stay with you Toni but somehow we split and I could not get back to you. My head is spinning and I haven't a clue who I have met or what they are talking about. We must stay together until I can start to understand the basics of your language.'

***

The next couple of weeks were spent visiting the homes of the various members of the Montini family in the wider Naples area and generally enjoying their hospitality. Little thought was paid to visiting museums or sites of historic interest and the two travellers were very busy enjoying themselves. Towards the end of June some decisions had to be made regarding their journey back home and it became obvious that there was no way of getting home by mid-August by an overland route so they decided to seek a boat trip all the way home. They soon found they had quite a choice of boats available but Toni desperately wanted to see his cousin Fabio who lived and worked in Livorno.

This was initially a bit of a problem as Livorno was a town many miles to the North of Naples and Nathaniel argued that there was no chance of getting there and getting home by mid-August. Toni brought all his relatives in

126

to the discussion and together they convinced Nathaniel that it was possible as there were plenty of boats plying their trade out of Livorno. They also argued that as it was still only the middle of June, if they set of in the next couple of days they would have plenty of time. The final factor that swayed Nathaniel's scepticism was that cousin Fabio was a shipping agent, the probability was that there was an excellent chance of a better deal for the passage than they would get in Naples. They decided that the quickest way to get to Livorno was by boat and so it was duly booked for two days' time.

'Nathaniel, when did you last write to Mr. Woolaston? I can't remember you writing since we arrived in Naples.' asked Toni.

'You are right, I haven't written since we left Barcelona and he will be fuming by now. I have not had cause to ask for more funds so it had completely slipped my mind. Your relatives have been so generous and their hospitality has been fantastic so we have hardly spent anything since we arrived here. I think I will wait until we are in Livorno and then let him know the details of the boat we will be going home on.'

'Well, for goodness sake make sure you let him know as soon as possible. You don't want to be in his bad books the minute you get home, do you?'

'I certainly don't, how is your packing coming on Toni? I have started mine but it won't take long to finish it off.'

'Oh, I have almost finished now. It will be ready to put on the cart first thing in the morning.'

The cart was due to collect all the baggage at seven o'clock in the morning for delivery to the docks to load on to the Livorno ferry. Nathaniel and Toni were setting out a bit later with several of Toni's relatives who wished to see them off on their journey. As they relaxed over a glass of Antonio's red wine, Toni asked, 'Have you enjoyed your stay in Naples Nathaniel?'

'It has been fantastic, the people are so friendly, and the food has been excellent and there is always plenty of it. I know I am going to miss it when we get on the boat for home.'

'It's not over yet, cousin Fabio has a reputation as a wonderful and generous host so we can expect the hospitality to continue until we finally set off for home.'

***

Their arrival at Livorno was a repeat of the one at Naples although the crowd was not quite so numerous. Fabio met them on the dockside and after giving Toni a bear hug and an extravagant welcome in Italian, turned to Nathaniel, and much to his delight, spoke to him in fairly passable English. After the greetings were over they departed for Fabio's villa which was situated about an hour's ride out of town and on the way, Toni explained their plans regarding booking a passage to England, if possible before the end of July. 'No problem at all.' said Fabio in his broken English, 'there should be at least one cargo departing before then. I know the *"Juliet Star"* is due in any time and she will almost certainly take one of the cargoes that is waiting to go to England. I am not sure whether it will take the one for Liverpool or the one for London but either should be suitable for your requirements. If you come into work with me tomorrow we can get you fixed up and then you relax here until you sail.'

The visit to the docks with Fabio proved very fruitful and they found that the *"Juliet Star"*, although it had not arrived yet, should be departing for England around the first of August so they booked their passage there and then. There was also a boat that was leaving that very afternoon so Nathaniel sat down in Fabio's office and wrote a letter to Ephraim Woolaston informing him of the current situation.

'That should please old Ephraim,' Nathaniel said to Toni, 'at least he will know we are intending to come home eventually.'

'It could be quite interesting if we get home before he gets this letter, after all, we don't know where either of the boats will be calling on their way, do we?' replied Toni.

'Well, we had better take it down to the captain before he sets sail this afternoon or we will definitely be home before he hears from us.' concluded Nathaniel.

Chapter 11

August 1723

Near the end of August, both Joseph Godbold and George Heap received a message from Ephraim Woolaston to attend a meeting 'At my office in Grantham at ten o'clock tomorrow morning, and don't be late, this is urgent.' Both of them were at a loss to think of what was so urgent. It was obviously something to do with Nathaniel and as far as they were concerned, everything to do with him was sorted out and under control.

Joseph and George bumped into each other in town on their way to the meeting and George said as soon as they met, 'What the hell is going on Joseph, it must be serious for old Ephraim to panic like this.'

'I have no idea unless Nathaniel has met some strumpet and decided to stay in foreign parts for ever. I thought we had more or less got him fixed up in London for the next few months.' was Joseph's considered opinion.

'I expect we will find out soon enough.' said George as they climbed the stairs to Ephraim's office. Watson was waiting at the outer office door and let the two gentlemen in, ushered them into Ephraim's office and closed the door behind them.

'Good morning Ephraim,' said George. 'Watson is looking a bit more agile since we last saw him.'

Ephraim exploded, 'Forget Watson, we have more important things to talk about than the hired help' and he slammed a letter, which was obviously from Nathaniel, onto the desk. 'What do you make of this?'

Joseph, who was nearest to Ephraim, picked it up and read it out aloud:

'Dear Mr. Woolaston,

It is some time since I wrote a letter to you but as I have not yet run out of funds I perceived it unnecessary to bother you. I have, until yesterday, been in Naples staying as the guest of various members of Antonio's extended family. Yesterday we arrived in Livorno to stay a short while with Antonio's cousin Fabio, and to reserve a passage home from here on any convenient sailing. This very morning we have secured a passage on a trader called the "Juliet Star" under the command of Captain James Briggs, whose destination at the moment is uncertain. However it will arrive at either London or Liverpool. It is due to depart Livorno on or about the first day in August so we should be home towards the end of August or early in September.

I am writing this letter in the dock office in Livorno so that I can give it to the Captain of a ship leaving later today - which incidentally has no spare accommodation – so that you may be aware of our future movements.

Kindest regards,

Nathaniel Thorold

Post Script, Neither Antonio nor I want to leave such a warm and pleasant country.'

***

'So that's what this meeting is all about is it? He obviously has not received our last letter giving instructions what to do, so I suppose he is well on his way home by now.' observed George, 'I suppose he could walk through the door at any time.'

Joseph nodded his head in agreement, 'I don't see that it is much of a problem, at least he is doing what he was told to do in the first place by trying to get back home about this time of the year.'

'What about Sir Samuel?' raged Ephraim 'what are we going to tell him?'

Joseph cast a quizzical look at Ephraim, 'I don't understand your problem, just tell him the truth he will understand perfectly.'

'But he has gone to all the trouble of making arrangements for the trip home and now it has all been wasted.'

'Sir Samuel only made the arrangements because he thought Nathaniel would never do it himself and now that he has, Sir Samuel should be very pleased with the lad.' commented George. 'but I think we should get a message off to Sir Samuel immediately.'

Ephraim gradually calmed down and realised that he could not change the situation whatever he did, so he wrote a quick note and dispatched it off to London by the evening carrier. 'I hope Sir Samuel is in London and not up at Harmston or Nathaniel will certainly be here first.'

***

At about the same time as Ephraim was raging over Nathaniel's last letter, the "*Juliet Star* had just weathered a heavy storm off the coast of Northern France and was tacking through the dangerous waters of the English Channel. They were still negotiating the remains of a storm which had almost blown itself out overnight. Toni had suffered badly from seasickness and had taken to his bunk even before the storm had caught up with them and was still

130

nowhere to be seen. The strong South Westerly wind had helped them make good time and they would soon be able to turn into the more sheltered waters of the Thames estuary. Nathaniel had not seen Toni for the last three days and decided to go and raise him from his bunk. As he entered Toni's cabin the strong smell of vomit was overwhelming and Nathaniel covered his nose with his handkerchief. 'Come on Toni,' he said as he gagged in the oppressive atmosphere, 'it's time you got yourself up and had something to eat. You must be famished.'

There was a groaning noise from under the bed cover and in a miserable, sorry for himself voice, the response was. 'Clear off and leave me alone.'

Nathaniel refused to go away and attempted to pull Toni's bed cover off and was shocked at what he saw. The sun-bronzed Toni had all but disappeared and in his place was a pallid, ashen-faced, ghostlike creature. To make matters worse, his head was on a pillow which was covered in smelly, stinking, dried vomit. Nathaniel recoiled at the sight of his companion who told him in very impolite terms, to go away and leave him alone.

Nathaniel was at a loss as to what to do and at the first opportunity, which was over lunch, told the captain what he had found. Captain Briggs, was a tall, very astute seaman who had many years of experience dealing with crew problems and regarded this as part of his job. He dealt with such things on a regular basis as part of his daily life at sea and observed that the ship would be anchoring later in the evening to wait for the next tide to take them up the Thames. This would provide the perfect opportunity to get a couple of crew members to get Toni out of bed and get him cleaned up. 'Don't worry about your friend, they will not hurt him but I know he will do as he is told when he sees who I send.'

The "Juliet Star" anchored off Gravesend later in the evening and about an hour afterwards, as Nathaniel and the captain were sitting down to supper, Toni appeared, still looking pasty faced but very clean and tidy. 'I am very sorry Nathaniel but I felt so ill and I feel such a fool. I don't even know what day it is and I am very hungry.'

'How did you manage to get out of bed? When I saw you, you were refusing to move and you looked terrible.'

'A couple of crew members came and told me to get up and when I said I was staying where I was they just dragged me out and cleaned me down with cold sea water. I dried myself and got dressed and while I was doing that they stripped my bed and made it up again with clean bedding.'

'Well you certainly look better, now get some supper down you and you will feel much better.'

Toni sat down and tried to make up his mind whether or not he wanted to eat. He had eaten nothing for nearly three full days and although he was very hungry he was still frightened that he would not be able to keep it down. After some thought he said 'I thought I smelled fresh baked bread as I was getting dressed so I think a chunk of bread and a piece of cheese would be enough for the time being.'

Captain Briggs leant back in his chair, rubbed his stomach and pointing to the remains on the table said 'You are very lucky Toni, a barge came alongside as we anchored and brought some badly needed, fresh provisions so I hope you enjoy your meal. We certainly enjoyed ours, didn't we Nathaniel?'

'We certainly did James, I think it was the first time I have had roast pork and plenty of good meaty gravy for over a year.'

'Well, I think I will stick to bread and cheese.' replied Toni, 'I don't think I could tackle a roast meal at the moment.'

Captain Briggs sent for Toni's bread and cheese and while they were waiting, Toni, who had been in his bunk for days asked, 'Where are we now, James? I know we have anchored but I haven't a clue where we are. All I could see outside was a shoreline obscured by a sea mist. There was the odd set of sails gliding slowly by, but nothing to give me a clue.'

'We are off Gravesend waiting for a suitable tide on which we can navigate safely up the river to London. I know the river extremely well but the ship's owners, and the insurers, always insist we pick up a Thames pilot for the last few miles. One of them will come on board soon after we sail in the morning.'

'What time will we sail tomorrow? asked Nathaniel.

'As the tide starts to flow we will raise the anchor and should be under way by about four o'clock.'

'So we will be in London some time tomorrow, that's wonderful. We should be home the day after.'

'Don't rush things Toni, we have to organise transport for our trunks and get ourselves fixed up too. It could take a few days before everything is sorted out. We should try and enjoy a few days in town while we have the chance, after all we are still on holiday until we get home.'

***

Sir Samuel read the message from Ephraim Woolaston and considered what action he should take. He did not want Nathaniel and his friend wandering the streets of London when they arrived and he guessed, correctly, that Nathaniel would want to stay a few days and enjoy himself before travelling north. Sir Samuel wanted Nathaniel's introduction to London and the people of importance, to be controlled and under his guidance. He wanted it to happen when Nathaniel came to learn some business skills later in the year and not by a random binge trip round the public houses and other dives of London after a long trip away from home.

First he had to find out if the *"Juliet Star"* was coming to London or going elsewhere and so he wrote a short note to find out if he had need to be concerned. He despatched one of the clerks to the harbourmaster's office to check what was known of the ship's movements and instructed the clerk, if necessary, to wait for an answer before returning immediately to the office.

Within the hour, the clerk had returned with a note which stated that the *"Juliet Star"* had been sighted that very morning sailing in the outer reaches of the Thames and would probably have to anchor overnight. It was due to arrive in London tomorrow, either late in the morning or early afternoon.

'We will have to get ourselves organised Adnitt.' said Sir Samuel. Jonathan Adnitt was Sir Samuel's business manager and right hand man. 'I want you to meet this ship and bring the two travellers to my house in Ormond Street and they can stay with me. I also want a cart to collect their baggage as soon as it is unloaded and again, have it brought to my house.'

'Certainly sir, I will get on to it straight away.'

'I will have them stay overnight with me and I would like you to arrange for two of my horses to be made available to transport them to Lincolnshire immediately after they have breakfasted. A cart with two men will also be needed to follow them and deliver their heavy luggage to their homes as well.'

'Very good Sir Samuel, will there be anything else?'

'Not at the moment Jonathan, I will let you know if I think of anything more. I think we have everything covered for the moment, I just don't want them loose around town and I want them sent on their way home as soon as is

133

possible. I don't know what sort of chap Antonio is, but I know Nathaniel's reputation is a bit suspect. I certainly don't want any wild behaviour reflecting on my good name before he comes under my control.'

Jonathan left the office to attend to his duties and Sir Samuel sat down and penned a short note to Ephraim Woolaston informing him of what he had learnt and the actions he had taken to control the situation. He also informed him that he would be visiting Lincolnshire during the third week in October and would call in to discuss Nathaniel's future at a date and time which he would confirm later.

***

Nathaniel awoke in the morning to a steady rumbling noise and a lot of shouting on the deck above his berth. It puzzled him for a few seconds as he did not really know where he was before he remembered, and then he realised that it must be the crew hauling in the anchor ready for the short trip to the docks in London. Toni was also awake and was feeling very hungry. The small portion of bread and cheese the night before had proved enough at the time but was insufficient to last the whole night so he got out of bed and went to search out something to keep him going.

His first port of call on his mission was the cooking area on the aft upper deck, where he found the ship's cook and his two assistants preparing a mountain of food. One of the assistants was cutting thick chunks from a side of salted streaky bacon and passing the slices to the cook. The cook had a large pan on the cooking range, which consisted of a metal box on a metal base which held the fire. This was designed to keep the fire in a controlled area safely away from the wooden structure of the boat. A metal grill was placed over the fire to enable the cook to rest his frying pan and fry the bacon safely. The other assistant was cutting up big loaves of bread into inch thick slices.

'Good morning chef, what time do the crew have breakfast?' asked Toni.

'They don't stop for breakfast when we are in a river, sir. All hands must be at their posts in case of an emergency. They have to be ready for anything.'

A puzzled Toni asked, 'Why are you cooking all that bacon then if they can't eat it?'

'Well sir, once the anchor is hauled in and we are on the move, we will distribute this lot among the crew and give each one a chunk of bread and a

134

couple of bits of bacon which they can eat while staying at their posts. You look hungry sir, would you like a chunk?'

'Oh, yes please, I am absolutely famished.'

Toni sat down on a bollard and ate his unexpected meal as if he had not eaten for months. He had forgotten how much he disliked fatty bacon, and when challenged by Nathaniel, who had just arrived, he justified his actions by saying, 'This is not boiled fatty bacon, it has been fried and actually tastes delicious. Anyway, there is a bit more lean meat in this than the stuff usually served up in public houses.'

'I just hope for your sake that we don't have another storm before we get to the docks or you will regret eating all that fatty stuff.' was Nathaniel's sarcastic reply. 'I think I will try some anyway.'

While they continued their snack, they reminisced about their adventures over the last year. 'I don't really think we achieved the objectives set out by your father, do you?' asked Toni. 'I think he wanted you to get to understand the various cultures we would encounter and see some of the art treasures that are to be seen, particularly in Italy.'

'I thought he was a bit vague in what he said, and anyway, we had a brilliant time didn't we?'

'We did, and it was fantastic seeing all my relations. I have lots to tell the family when I get home and I would love to go out there again.'

'I think you had better take the long overland trip if you ever go back Toni. You would not want an experience like the last few days again, would you?'

'Certainly not.' was Toni's curt reply.

As they reminisced their thoughts turned to the future and life back in Lincolnshire. Nathaniel rubbed his hands together in anticipation and said, 'Let's forget about that for a while, we still have a couple of days to enjoy in London. It is supposed to be a wonderful place for young men like us with a bit of money in our pockets and we can at least let our hair down while we are here.'

'Have you been here before Nathaniel?'

'No, have you?'

'I came once with my father when I was about ten years old. I thought it was very noisy and dirty with hundreds of people milling around shouting all the time. I didn't like it at all, and was glad to get home again.' was Toni's

135

opinion.

'I suppose you want to go straight home then, do you?'

'You are in charge Nathaniel. I suppose it may have changed and I might love it.'

'Well we can't go straight home as we will have to spend at least one night here to get our transport organised. We can get booked into a decent hostelry, have a night out and then see what we think before we make up our minds.'

***

As they sailed further up the river, there was more and more to see. First the occasional boat sailing past on its way out to sea, then small traders and fishermen and gradually a whole variety of small craft scurrying to and fro between the shore and boats at anchor.

The Thames river pilot was now on board and the ship's captain followed a safe route to the docks under the advice of the pilot. As they neared the docks, the river traffic became very congested and it was difficult for the uninitiated like Nathaniel and Toni to see where they were going, but eventually they saw men on the dockside putting out fenders made of coiled and wound rope. These large pillow-like objects were put out to act as a buffer to stop the boat being damaged as it came alongside.

Seamen on the boat were equipped with coils of light lines attached to heavier ropes and as they neared the dock, the small lines were thrown to be caught by those on shore. These lines were hauled in by the dock workers until they brought the heavier ropes with them. These were tied to bollards to secure the boat. When this was complete and the boat secure, a gangway was lowered from the boat to the shore and tied securely to the boat to allow traffic and goods to flow.

Nathaniel and Toni had watched the whole procedure, making sure that they kept well out of the way of the very busy crew members. Quite a few people were on the dock to welcome the boat but Nathaniel concluded that the majority would be traders, keen to find out what had just arrived.

'I don't think *he* is a trader.' said Toni, pointing at a very smartly dressed gentleman just alighting from a horse drawn carriage.'

'Probably the boat's owner.' answered Nathaniel in an offhand manner. 'Whoever he is, his clothes are worth a king's ransom.'

'They certainly are, but don't you think we ought to collect our

136

belongings and say farewell to James?'

'Yes but we should wait until he settles down a bit. He will be extremely busy for a while yet.'

As they started to go and gather their possessions, Toni said, 'Nathaniel, that well-dressed gentleman just coming up the gangway. I am sure he keeps pointing at us!'

'It won't be us he's pointing at, he is probably the boat's owner, checking the boat for storm damage. Come on, let's get packed ready to go.'

***

As they were busy putting the last few items in their bags ready to go, there was a knock on Nathaniel's cabin door. He answered it and found a seaman stood outside with his hat in his hand who said, 'Compliments of the Captain Sir, would you and your companion please go to his cabin immediately?'

'Thank you, will you please tell him we will be along presently. I will just collect Mr. Montini.'

Nathaniel went to Toni's cabin, banged on the door, opened it and said, 'I don't know what he wants but James has asked us to go to his cabin now. It seems a bit strange because he knows we would call on him before we left.'

'Probably he has been called ashore now and does not want to miss us. You were probably right about that gentleman, he could have been the owner and he wants to discuss business with James.' replied Toni.

'Well he must have a reason, just leave that and let's go and see what he wants.' Nathaniel knocked on the captain's cabin door and was let in by the captain's cabin boy who closed the door behind them and stayed outside.

As they entered the cabin they were confronted by Captain Briggs, and standing to his side and in the shadows was the well-dressed gentleman they had seen earlier. James welcomed them, 'Come in gentlemen, I would like to introduce Mr. Jonathan Adnitt.' and to Sir Samuel's representative, 'Mr. Adnitt, this is Nathaniel Thorold and his companion, Antonio Montini, they have travelled as paying passengers with us in the "*Juliet Star*" from Livorno in Italy.'

'Good afternoon gentlemen, I am delighted to meet you both. You will no doubt be wondering who I am and what on earth I am doing meeting you as you arrive from your long trip. You both know my name but you will not

137

know that I am representing Sir Samuel Thorold, in fact I am his business manager in London. I…..'

He broke off his introduction as Nathaniel interrupted by asking, '*Sir* Samuel, when did that happen?'

'Sir Samuel's brother Sir George passed away in October last year not long after you had departed on your journey and obviously you were not informed of the unfortunate event. Sir Samuel, as he is now known, inherited the title on his late brother's death.'

'I am very sorry to hear it.' replied Nathaniel, 'but I don't think I ever met him.'

'Probably not, but you are aware that your late father arranged for you to spend some time in London learning some business skills. Sir Samuel is very keen to meet you and get to know you in order to plan where to fit you into his business. After all, he has not seen you since you were an infant.'

'Will I get the chance to see him before I leave London for home?' asked Nathaniel.

'You certainly will. I have been directed by Sir Samuel to invite you and Mr. Montini to accompany me, in my carriage to Sir Samuel's house in Ormond Street where he would be delighted for you to stay until your departure for Lincolnshire.'

'We would be delighted Mr. Adnitt.' said Nathaniel through gritted teeth. He could see his plans for a night in the city hotspots disappearing fast, as he looked at Antonio and tried to hide his dismay.

'I am really looking forward to meeting Sir Samuel.' said Antonio. 'It is very kind of him.'

'Good, then if you will collect your hand luggage we will be off. There is no need to worry about the remainder of your possessions, they will be collected as soon as they are out of the hold and brought direct to you at Ormond Street.'

Mr. Adnitt had some business to conclude with Captain Briggs and so Nathaniel and Toni went to finish their packing. Nathaniel slammed his bag on the deck and kicked at it in the petulant manner he regularly adopted as a young boy. 'That has just ruined our plans for our stay in the big city,' he raged. 'Toni, I am really upset, but that shrewd old sod has sewn up all the loose ends and is going to keep his eye on us for the rest of our stay. Our chance of a bit of a break in London has just been blown out of the window.'

Toni wagged his finger at his friend, 'Well don't you behave like a spoiled brat in front of either him or his right hand man, or you will be in it up to your neck and you won't be able to blame anyone else but yourself.'

'I know, but he has completely ruined a good night out.'

'Forget it, he knows your reputation and he is not going to let you ruin his, whatever you say. He has an awful lot to lose in that respect. In business an unblemished reputation is essential, and he sees you as a possible threat to his good name. Let's get packed, say thank you to James for his kindness and hospitality and then get on our way to Ormond Street, you never know, you may be pleasantly surprised.'

The carriage ride through the streets of London was eye opening to Nathaniel, and although Antonio had been there many years before, it had the same effect on him. He still did not like the noise, the crowds and the general rush of activity even though they were sheltered within the confines of the coach from the worst of the crowds. He vowed he would never come to London again, even if it meant staying as a teacher in Corby Glen for the rest of his life. Nathaniel, on the other hand, longed to get out and mingle with the people and have a drink in a boisterous, crowded pub or coffee house.

'Mr. Adnitt, I know that he is a very successful businessman, but what does Sir Samuel do?' asked Nathaniel.

'Over the years Sir Samuel has built up a very successful ironmongery business and not only is he currently the Grand Master of the Worshipful Guild of Ironmongers of London, but he is also part owner of two boats which trade between the Mediterranean and England and is very active in importing and exporting a wide variety of goods. He is also an Alderman of the City of London and is greatly respected for his contribution to work for the underprivileged and the poor of this great City.'

'He sounds as if he is a very busy man. What did his brother, Sir George do?'

'They were partners in the same business but Sir George, being the elder, was the senior partner. Sir George was elected the Lord Mayor of London a couple of years ago.'

'That must have been a great honour for the family. Lord Mayor of London, eh?'

As they continued to chat the coach rumbled on through the noisy, smelly streets until gradually the streets became less busy and the houses and buildings less crammed together. Eventually they entered a wide, tree lined street where the houses were all large, detached, widely spaced apart and set in their own well cultivated and cared for gardens, which were obviously tended by experienced and specialised gardeners. 'Gosh, there must be some very wealthy people live around here,' exclaimed Nathaniel. 'I have never seen so many large houses all in the same street. Where are we Mr. Adnitt?'

'This is Ormond Street and Sir Samuel Thorold lives at the next house on the right.' replied Jonathan as the coach turned into a short drive, and came to a halt in front of a series of steps leading up to the main entrance. 'I am sure you will appreciate that this house is built on the proceeds of years of hard work and a well-tuned business brain. No one gets to live in a house such as this without a great deal of dedication to the job.'

'I am deeply impressed.' said a stunned Nathaniel while Antonio sat silently in the coach staring open mouthed at the house. The coach door was opened by a footman and Jonathan Adnitt climbed out followed by Nathaniel and Antonio and as they walked up the steps to the front door a tall, elegant middle aged lady appeared and Jonathan said, 'Good evening, Lady Thorold may I introduce Mr. Nathaniel Thorold and Mr. Antonio Montini. They have just arrived from an extended stay in Italy.'

'Good evening gentlemen, how very nice to see you. I hope you have had an uneventful trip, I know how violent the oceans can be at times. Please do come in, Sir Samuel will be home within the hour.' She led her visitors into the large entrance hall and explained that dinner would be served in about two hours and the gong would be sounded to let them know when to come down. 'We will gather for a pre-dinner drink in the ante room, which is just through that door over there.' she said, pointing to a door off to the left of the main hall. 'Sir Samuel will be home and is looking forward very much to meeting you both.' She turned to Jonathan and said, 'I trust you will be staying for dinner, Jonathan.'

'Yes I will, Sir Samuel has asked me to be here for dinner and stay overnight as he wishes me to be present when he discusses Nathaniel's proposed stay with us in the near future.'

'Well I suppose you are all feeling weary so I will see you later on. You will be shown to your rooms now and if there is anything at all that you require, just ring the bell and someone will come to your assistance.'

***

Nathaniel and Antonio were shown up the sweeping, double sided staircase by the butler and they were followed by two servants carrying their hand baggage. Jonathan had obviously been there before and knew where he was going, and went off in a different direction when they reached the top of the stairs. Antonio was the first to be given a room and Nathaniel was shown into the adjacent one. The butler informed each of the travellers of the important details they should know and where everything was situated while the servants unpacked the baggage and stored it in the appropriate cupboards.

When all was complete Nathaniel and Antonio were left on their own to peruse their surroundings. 'This is incredible,' said Nathaniel out loud to himself, 'I have never seen anything like it in my life.' The room was huge and opulently furnished in the style commonly in use by the aristocracy in France. The bed was a huge four poster and was fitted with expensive drapes which, when pulled together would create a completely private expanse. There was a chaise longue covered in fine, embroidered materials and two matching chairs, and the drapes on the large, floor to ceiling windows were of material that was in keeping with the general décor. The room was at the rear of the house and looked out over the large lawn and manicured borders and there were two large horse chestnut trees near the boundary wall at the bottom of the garden. Nathaniel could not control his excitement and quickly went and knocked on Antonio's door.

'Can I come in Toni? It's Nathaniel.'

'Come in,' was the quick response.

Chapter 12

1723 – 1724

It was late evening and dusk was quickly approaching when Nathaniel and Antonio arrived at Borton, Sylvia could not restrain herself and rushed towards Nathaniel, flung her arms around his neck and gave him a big hug before bursting into tears. 'I am so pleased to see you,' she sobbed. 'I have missed you so much, it's been such a long time.'

Ephraim Woolaston had told the staff that the Master was expected home in the next few days so their arrival was not a complete surprise. The house had received a final clean and tidy and beds were made and ready for use. 'It's lovely to be home at last and everything seems to be as I remember it. You are looking really well Sylvia. You must tell me what has been going on when I have settled back in. By the way, Mr. Montini will be staying overnight so will you make sure the guest room is made ready.'

'It is all ready and aired, sir. Mr. Woolaston said he thought Mr. Montini might stay if you arrived late.'

'Good, then I think we could both do with drink and a good tidy up, don't you Toni?'

'Yes I could do with getting rid of these dusty clothes and putting on something clean and a good pot of cool ale would be most welcome.'

***

As the two travellers settled down with their ale, Nathaniel pondered his future and said, 'Do you realise, Toni, I still have five years before I can really say this is mine. I am not looking forward to it at all. Woolaston and his lackeys will be calling the shots and I will have to grin and bear it. Not a nice thought is it?'

'You will be in London for at least six months, won't you? That will break it up a bit, surely.'

'Probably so, but I am not as keen as I was before meeting Sir Samuel and that arrogant sod, Jonathan.'

Their conversation continued spasmodically for a while until Sylvia knocked on the door and asked if there was anything else they needed. 'No thank you Sylvia, we were just thinking of going to bed as we have had a long day.'

Sylvia said goodnight and Nathaniel said to Toni, 'I have got to see Woolaston in the morning and I am not looking forward to that, one little bit.'

'Well I am going to bed now, I will see you at breakfast before I set off home. I hope they have kept my job for me as they promised.'

'You should be alright Toni, your father has a great deal of influence in the village and they only took on a temporary teacher for your absence, didn't they?'

'I sincerely hope so.' he said as he arose from his chair. 'Goodnight Nathaniel, see you in the morning.'

Nathaniel continued to think about his future and gradually became more and more depressed until eventually sleep came over him, and he slept fitfully in the chair until Sylvia woke him for breakfast.

***

Nathaniel managed to see Antonio off soon after breakfast and arranged for Sir Samuel's horse to be brought back later in the day. 'We have had a good time this last year Toni, and you have been a great companion. I hope to see you again soon.'

'Thank you for inviting me along. It would have been years before I could have visited my relatives in Italy and I am eternally grateful for the opportunity you gave me.'

'Well, have a safe journey home and I will see you soon. Oh, by the way, will you tell George I will be in *"The Nags Head"* a week on Saturday evening and would love to see him if he can manage it?'

'Of course I will, so cheerio and be good.'

As soon as Antonio had left, Nathaniel did a quick tour of the farm and spoke to Mo and John Fowler. They discussed the bad weather they had experienced and explained that they had lost one cow and nearly lost two more. Only two of the remaining four had produced calves successfully, but by a piece of good luck, one of them had produced twins. All the horses had survived and with the onset of a mild spring, all the fields had been properly cultivated and the harvest was now nearly complete. Plenty of hay had been stored for the next winter and only one field of barley remained to be harvested and that was taking place at this very moment.

'Well done lads,' said Nathaniel. 'I will go round everywhere when I get back from Grantham. I have got to see Ephraim Woolaston this morning.' As he started to head off back to the house he winced visibly and held his hand to his head.

'Are you alright, boss?' asked Mo.

'Just a bit of a headache Mo, I think it was the travelling that caused it. Oh, by the way, I nearly forgot. There will be a cart arriving sometime later today or early tomorrow with all our heavy baggage, the horses will need stabling overnight and the two lads will need looking after. Mr. Montini's horse and the two in the yard will have to go back to London with the cart.'

'Where is Mr. Montini's horse?' John asked.

'He has taken it to Corby Glen, but it will be brought back later today.'

'We will see to it sir, and we will sort the lads out.' replied John.

***

143

'You look terrible Nathaniel.' was Sylvia's brief comment as he returned to the house. 'What on earth were you doing sleeping in the chair all night? I had made a lovely comfortable bed up ready for you and you stayed down here. Mr. Montini managed to get to his bed alright, so what was wrong with you? Or shouldn't I ask.'

'Don't ask Sylvia but could you make me a cup of strong coffee before I go to suffer an hour with that Woolaston fellow over at Grantham?'

'Well you need to sort yourself out before you see him, or you will be off to the worst possible start.' she said as she stomped off to the kitchen.

Nathaniel had two cups of coffee before leaving but while he was drinking, Sylvia kept up a monologue about the happenings over the last year. Nathaniel did not take much of it in as he stared with glazed eyes into the middle distance until he had suffered enough and shouted, 'For goodness sake Sylvia, go back to the kitchen, you can tell me later when this headache is gone.'

Sylvia stormed out of the room, slammed the door shut and burst into tears. Nathaniel's return was not supposed to be like this.

***

Watson welcomed Nathaniel at the outer office door and asked him if he would mind waiting for five minutes as Mr. Woolaston was still with another client. 'Would you like a cup of coffee while you are waiting, Mr. Thorold?'

'No thank you Watson, not at the moment.' he replied. 'Are you getting around any better now.'

'It's still difficult, sir, but I manage the best I can. Mr. Woolaston is good to me though and helps when he can.'

'Watson!' Ephraim boomed from his office. Watson struggled off his high stool and hobbled into Ephraim's den. 'Show Mr. Wood out Watson, and ask Mr. Thorold to come in please.'

Nathaniel went in as Mr. Wood came out, 'How are you Ephraim?' enquired Nathaniel. 'I can't believe it's over a year since I saw you last. Nothing seems to have changed.'

'Well things certainly have changed, we are all a year older and poor old Joseph has taken to his bed for the last two months but fortunately George is still fit and active. As for me, I won't bore you with all my problems or we will be here until midnight.'

'I am sorry to hear about Joseph, he was always so active and lively. Is he going to get better?'

'We don't really know, but George can't attend today either so it should be a short meeting for a change.'

'Well Nathaniel, before you tell me all about your trip, I have had a letter from Sir Samuel to say that he would like you to join his business early next year, no firm dates yet, but he will be here for a meeting towards the end of

October when everything will be finalised. Now, tell me all about your adventures and then I will bring you up to date regarding the estate business.'

Nathaniel spent the next hour making Ephraim aware of all the things he thought he wanted to hear and glossing over points that he thought best kept to himself. There were very few interruptions from the wily old lawyer and then only when he wanted clarification did he say anything. When Nathaniel had finished by describing his very short stay in London did Ephraim lean back in his chair, scratch his head and look Nathaniel directly in the eyes and say, 'So you didn't do what your father wanted you to do, did you?'

Nathaniel was rattled by Ephraim's comment and spluttered, 'I beg your pardon, what do you mean?'

'I understood your father would have liked you to investigate the culture of France and Italy and in particular, toured and seen the cultural antiquities of those countries. From what you have just told me you have spent the majority of your time visiting cafes and pubs and generally doing nothing which would have enhanced your development as a well-grounded member of society.'

'I don't think that is a fair assessment Ephraim, after all I was very poorly for quite some time.'

'Three weeks or so is not a long time in a year and anyway you could have gone to Rome while you were in Italy. You had plenty of time and Rome is on the road from Naples to Livorno. No more excuses Nathaniel, what is done is done, so now you need to know what has gone on regarding the estate.'

Ephraim covered the progress of the estate in both financial and personnel matters and in particular how the very bad winter had played havoc with the supply of fodder which had been put aside for winter feed for the livestock. He also praised the quick actions of Maurice Clark and John Fowler regarding cattle feed. 'If they had not reacted quickly and told me immediately they realised what was happening, then we would have lost all the breeding cows. As it is, we did lose one but luckily one of the survivors had twins which helped a lot.'

'Yes, Maurice and John told me this morning. Did they have any outside help to run the farm while I was away?'

'No they didn't. We tried to get a temporary manager but failed miserably, but those two were doing so well that in the end we did not bother.'

'That's very comforting to hear, I was a bit worried that they might get a little overwhelmed by the size of the task but they have proved they are capable of taking charge, at least on the day to day running of the farm. I assume you and the other two trustees kept a tight rein on the finances?'

'Of course we did, that's what we are here for. We were also there for

145

advice and assistance when required, as you have seen. We do take our responsibilities seriously, you know.'

'I know you do. I wasn't trying to criticise, I just want to know the current state of affairs.'

Ephraim started to gather up his pile of documents, 'Well Nathaniel, I think we have covered all we need to do today so I won't keep you any longer. You can get off home and catch up with all the events that have happened while you have been away, but I would like you to come back next Tuesday so that we can spend some time going over last year's accounts.'

'That's alright with me but there is one thing I would like to know before I go and that is, when is my allowance going to be reviewed?'

'We are going to discuss that at our meeting in October and in case you think you are in for a big rise, don't get too excited. You are going to have to prove you are worth whatever you might get.'

**

Nathaniel went slowly down the stairs from Ephraim's office feeling as if the whole of the world hated him and he was not at all cheered up by the fact that, as he stepped outside, the heavens opened and he was soaked through, even before he got to the stables to collect his horse. The journey home was no better and he wondered why he had bothered to leave Livorno. 'Given the chance, I could have made some money out there, and the weather is far better.' he thought to himself. This state of self-pity stayed with him until soon after he arrived home when Mo came round for a chat and asked him if he would like to go for a drink later on. 'I would like to hear all about your trip and I can bring you up to date with events here.'

'I was going to suggest the same thing, we need to get up to date on everything and the sooner we do it, the better. Anyway, I could do with a drink. It's over a year since I sampled good English beer, the continental stuff is rubbish. They always drink wine and it doesn't quench your thirst.'

'Shall we try *"The Five Bells"* and see if old William Grimes will let you in? I think we should be able to convince him that you are a reformed man.'

'Right, give me a shout when you are ready. I have to have a word with Sylvia now or she will sulk for a week.'

Most of the workforce were in the fields finishing the last of the harvest so things were quiet around the farm, and now that the rain had stopped and the sun was shining, Mo had decided to milk the cows in the field. This was common practice and saved the effort of rounding them up and bringing them into their milking stalls, providing them with fodder, and then returning them to the field afterwards. As he headed off with the milkmaids to the low pasture he turned and called to Nathaniel. 'See you tonight, and don't be late.'

The cows were all feeding on the last of the late summer grass and soon

146

decisions would have to be made on which cows were to be kept for breeding purposes and brought in for the winter. After the last winter, Mo was pleased that he didn't have to make the final decision this time.

Nathaniel found Sylvia in the kitchen preparing his evening meal and sat down in the high backed rocking chair near the fire. 'I am sorry I was in a bit of a mood this morning Sylvia, but I had a crushing headache as soon as I awoke.'

'We all know why, don't we?' she snorted. 'At least you could have tried to be a bit more sociable. You ought to be ashamed of yourself, haven't you learnt anything while you have been away?'

'I am ashamed of myself Sylvia and I should never have taken it out on you. I can see that you have worked really hard while I have been away and the house is spotless. You should be proud of yourself and you are perfectly correct to point out my offensive behaviour. Will you ever forgive me?'

'Only if you promise to start to behave like the gentleman your father wished you were.' she replied. 'You are not a young schoolboy now, you know.'

'I promise. Now are you going to tell me all the local gossip and then show me what you have been busy doing while I was away?'

Sylvia made Nathaniel a coffee and sat down and brought him up to date. Most of what had happened had been local village gossip but the main interest was centred on the village vicar. The Reverend Roger Spratt had frequently been seen walking out with George Headland's sister Charlotte, and there were very strong rumours that they were going to be married in the near future.

'Has George said anything at all?' asked Nathaniel.

'No he has kept very quiet and refuses to be drawn on the subject.'

'Well I am very pleased to hear it, they make an agreeable couple and George does right to keep quiet and not fuel the local gossip machine. It does not surprise me though, as there was a bit of a rumour going around before I went away, but I thought that's all it was.'

***

As they closed the door of *"The Five Bells"* behind them and entered the bar, William Grimes, who was serving ale to a couple of locals, turned around, pointed to Nathaniel and said in a loud aggressive voice, 'Who the hell let him in here? he's barred.'

'Come on William, surely he's served his time by now.' pleaded Mo. 'it's well over a year since you barred him.'

'I know that, but how do I know I can trust him, he nearly killed me last time.'

'I think he has grown up a bit since then and he has a lot to lose by

147

behaving like an idiot again. Can't you give him another chance?'

'Well, what have you got to say on the matter Nathaniel, have you learnt how to control your violent temper at long last?'

'Yes William, I will never do such a stupid thing again, ever,' he said, emphasising the *ever*.

'Well, against my better judgement, the ban is lifted but any more nonsense, however minor, you will be out and this time it will be forever. Do you understand?'

'Thank you William,' said Nathaniel as they sat at a table in the window, 'there will be no more trouble from me.'

Nathaniel savoured his first pot of ale, taking his time to enjoy the bitter taste and the smooth texture he had missed so much during his long trip. There was no doubt, William Grimes made some of the best ale in the area.

'You looked as if you enjoyed that Nat,' said Mo. 'are you ready for another?'

The two of them swapped yarns for about an hour when John Fowler came in. 'I am glad you came in John, it will save me trying to catch you tomorrow. I know you are very busy with the last of the harvest.'

***

Nathaniel settled into a routine and busied himself around the farm for the next few days getting up to date on as many aspects as he could. Tuesday came round very quickly and he arrived at Ephraim's chambers with an overpowering feeling of unease. Ephraim had been very curt with him last week and he was not looking forward to another confrontation with him. He was also interested to see if either or both of the other two trustees were going to be there. 'It could get nasty if they are all there.' he thought.

'Come in Nathaniel, sit yourself down. Would you like a cup of coffee?' he asked with a broad grin on his round, ruddy face.

'I would love one please Ephraim.' Nathaniel replied, at the same time thinking, 'What the hell is going on here?'

Instructions were rattled off by Ephraim, 'Make two cups of coffee Watson, bring me all the Thorold papers from that pile at the top of the stairs and I don't want any interruptions for the rest of this morning!' and then to his visitor, 'We will be on our own again Nathaniel, so we should get through the business a lot quicker than we would with the other two present.'

Watson brought the papers first, and then went off to make the coffee. Ephraim sorted the pile of documents into three and said, 'Well Nathaniel, I have talked with George and Joseph and we are pleased to tell you that, contrary to what I told you at the last meeting, we are going to increase your monthly allowance from the first day of November. It may not be as much as you would wish but we all think it is a reasonable sum in your current

148

situation.' he said loftily, as he pushed a slip of paper over the table for Nathaniel to read.

Nathaniel studied it carefully and desperately not wanting another clash, said. 'Well it's not as much as I would have liked, but at least it is more than I expected.'

'Good. There will, of course, be provision for any unexpected emergencies and these will be considered by the trustees on an individual basis as they arise. Where possible these must be presented for approval before the spending takes place, do you understand?'

'Yes, I understand, so long as you are happy that prior warning will sometimes be difficult to achieve.'

'Of course I understand, we are not ogres you know.' said Ephraim, rather testily.

Nathaniel detected Ephraim's change of tone and thought he must be a bit liverish this morning so he vowed to keep his temper under control for the rest of the meeting. He just said, 'I think you are being very fair Ephraim. I am happy with your proposals, thank you.'

'Good. Then if you have no objections, let us get on with the business we are here for.'

***

Ephraim shuffled the documents on his desk and pulled out a sheet of paper which was apparently from Sir Samuel. 'You are fully aware of your impending trip to London to work in Sir Samuel's business aren't you? Well I have had this note to say he will be calling here during the second week in October. He plans to discuss and agree objectives, and to work out a plan of action. It appears you are going to be allocated a management training position in Sir Samuel's expanding shipping division. This looks as if it is an excellent opportunity for you to be in at the start of a very lucrative business. An opportunity not generally available to everyone and one I hope you will take full advantage of. I know you have met Sir Samuel and his business manager, Jonathan Adnitt and are aware that Mr. Adnitt will be in control of all aspects of your training. That's about all I can tell you at the moment but full details of your stay will become clearer when Sir Samuel calls in to see us next month. Have you any questions on what I have told you so far?'

'No Ephraim, that's roughly what they told me when I was recently in London, it could be a very interesting stay.' he said, but thought it was best to say nothing of his apprehension about the whole stay and that he thought Jonathan Adnitt was an arrogant sod.

'Alright, then let's get on with the estate business. If we look at the leased farms first, everything is running as it should and all dues have been paid up to date and on time so we should be able to safely move on to the managed farms without any worries.'

'When were all the leases last renewed?' interrupted Nathaniel.

'Well I seem to remember that you negotiated the renewal of the lease of one of the farms just after your father died didn't you?

'I did, it was the farm at Spittlegate.'

'You did a damn good job of it too, if I remember.'

'Thank you Ephraim, I just wondered if there were any of the others that need looking at while we were going through the records.'

'No not at the moment, but there will be one or two to sort out next year.'

'Alright, what has happened with the managed farms while I have been away?'

'The results have been a bit of a mixed bag really and all but one have at least turned in a profit. Edward Wood at Holt Farm has again produced the best results, he somehow manages to squeeze out a good profit every year even when the weather is against him.'

'Which farm is the one costing us money?'

'It was Delph Farm at Fishtoft, managed by John Smith, but in their defence they had massive problems with the new drainage system and it broke down and more than half of the low lying land was underwater for weeks on end. It was the first time it had made a loss since your father took it over. John Smith has been there for nearly ten years and has never made a loss before'

'That was a bit of bad luck then, so let's hope it is all sorted out before the next set of figures are due. How often do we review salaries of the farm managers and do we take into consideration the results they achieve?'

'We usually review salaries early in the New Year and yes we do take into consideration how they perform individually.'

As they discussed each farm in detail, Nathaniel became more involved and made several constructive suggestions which impressed Ephraim greatly. He was extremely surprised at Nathaniel's interest in the business and the way he was approaching the meeting. He thought, 'If he keeps this up, he could very likely make the grade. George and Joseph will not believe me when I tell them.'

They had finished most of the business they had planned and Nathaniel asked Ephraim, 'Do you think I should visit some of the farms before the meeting with Sir Samuel?'

'Yes I do, I think you should try to visit them all. You haven't been round to them for over a year and even then you didn't get to see them all. It would be very useful for all of us if you could prepare a report on your findings and see if everything is as you would like it. If you don't go soon, you will be off to London and it will be another six months before you can get things in perspective. Yes, you get off as soon as you can and I look forward to

150

seeing your report when you return. It would be gratifying if you had the report prepared for our next meeting.

'That sounds fine by me, I will enjoy going around them all. I haven't been to the Saltfleetby farms at all so that part will be new to me.'

'Well Nathaniel unless you have anything else to ask I think we should retire to *"The Angel"* for lunch. We could discuss anything else that you might think of then.' He startled Nathaniel when he suddenly boomed, 'Watson!' and after what seemed an age, Watson hobbled in to the office and Ephraim said. 'We are going to *"The Angel"*, so lock up if you go out and I will be back later.'

'Yes Sir.' said Watson and slowly tottered back to his desk.

***

When Ephraim had settled down at his favourite table in the front room of *"The Angel"* and greeted all the regular customers in his usual loud, thunderous voice, he ordered his regular pot of ale and one for Nathaniel. After passing the time of day with several of the other diners, he turned to Nathaniel and said, 'I was delighted with your contributions to the meeting this morning, and may I say, quite surprised at the interest you displayed. You seem to me to have turned something of a corner since we last met.'

'I don't know about that,' countered Nathaniel 'I have always been interested in the running of the business and its financial aspects, it's the actual farm work, and particularly dealing with people I can't get on with. I just hope my work in London will prove useful in that side of things.'

'Well we can discuss that particular aspect with Sir Samuel when we have the opportunity. I also think it would be useful for you to attend the regular meetings of the trustees. I will discuss the situation with George and Joseph and see how they feel but I think it is essential that you should attend and contribute. After all, it will be yours and yours alone sooner than you think.'

'Thank you Ephraim I would love that, I want to be involved wherever possible.'

They finished their lunch and prepared to leave when Ephraim said, 'I just want to say again, thank you for your interest and involvement in the meeting this morning. It was a pleasure to work with you and I look forward to your input in the future. I am sure you will understand when I say that George and Joseph will not believe me when I tell them how things went.'

'Yes I understand, and thank you for your kind comments.'

'Well off you go and I look forward to the results of your visits to the farms.'

As he rode home, Nathaniel contemplated on what had happened and what Ephraim had said, and in general, he was very pleased with the outcome. Much to his surprise, he had found the whole day interesting and left him

151

wanting to be more involved in the day to day administration of the estate. 'I rather enjoyed it and no one got even remotely upset.' he said to himself as he left Grantham with the sun going down in a glorious blaze of orange and red over to his right. 'A very successful day all round.'

***

Nathaniel was planning to start his tour of the farms a couple of days later and had worked out the best way to get around them all whilst not spending too much time away from Borton. In total there were thirteen farms to visit and only nine were managed. These were the ones on which Nathaniel would have to spend some time. The remaining four were leased and all these were relatively local to Borton and would require only a cursory visit to re-acquaint himself with the tenants and to sort out any problems they may be concerned with. He decided two days would be ample to cover these four and he would be home each evening.

Of the nine managed properties, three were local and he planned to allow himself a leisurely day each for them, again coming home each evening. The remaining six would take up the most time as three of them were in the Boston area and the other three were quite a few miles north. After some deliberation, Nathaniel decided that if he went to Frieston on a Monday he could stay overnight and deal with the farms at Fistoft and Butterwick on the Tuesday. If he was amenable to the suggestion, he would stay with Edward Wood on the Monday and Tuesday nights and head off for Saltfleetby on Wednesday.

All three farms in the Saltfleetby area were comparatively small and he should be able to complete one on Wednesday, deal with the other two on Thursday and set off for home on Friday. If all this worked as planned he should complete all thirteen visits within a two week period and have his notes written up before Sir Samuel arrived on the scene.

Well satisfied with his plan, he wrote to all the farms and telling them when he proposed to visit and what he proposed to discuss with them. He also asked them to identify any problems before hand so that they could be sorted out in the limited time he had available. He also asked Edward Wood at Holt Hall Farm and Michael Stitch, the manager at Church Side Farm, Saltfleetby All Saints, if they would be able to accommodate him on the stated nights.

A few days later he received notes that both managers were very happy to have him stay for a couple of nights – or more if he should so need them.

***

His visits to the local leased farms were more like a tour of his mother's family, Uncle James Alcock at Topside Farm, Morton, cousin Richard Alcock, James's son at Westgate Farm, Spittlegate and Uncle Arthur Kaye at Hillside Farm, Hough on the Hill. The only non-related lease holder was John Williams

152

at Mill Field Farm, Laughton. All the visits were completed on Monday and Tuesday as planned and Nathaniel found no real problems to worry about although all of them told of how difficult the last winter had been and expressed their delight at getting through unscathed. John Williams had enquired if Nathaniel had any spare land in his area as he said he could do with building up his milking herd.

Visits to the local managed farms also went well and any minor problems were soon sorted out. James Parks at the Headlands Farm, Manthorpe was a middle aged man who had taken over just four years ago and was making improvements wherever he could. This dedication to detail was evident in the financial results and they had shown an improvement each year.

Robert Anderson was a relatively new manager and had the smallest farm on Nathaniel's estate, North Road Farm, Grantham. Robert, still in his early thirties was a go ahead, keen young manager who asked to be considered for management of a larger farm if one should ever become available. His results were very good and he appeared to get on well with his workforce. Nathaniel promised to discuss it with the trustees if one became available before he finally took over.

On Friday, Nathaniel went to Odder Lane Farm at Gonerby where Edwin James had been the manager for about twelve years. Edwin was in his late fifties and had been running the farm with ease since he had arrived. His health had always been a bit of a problem and had restricted his movement and so he was quite satisfied with the size of the farm. The lease had six more years to run but Edwin told Nathaniel that he might wish to terminate the lease in three or four years' time if at all possible. Nathaniel understood Edwin's concerns and said he would discuss the matter with the trustees at the next meeting. 'I am sure there will be no problems Edwin, you have done a good job here for a long time.'

'Thanks Nathaniel, I would appreciate that.'

***

Monday morning saw Nathaniel on his way to Frieston where he was going to see Edward Wood. He stopped at Sutterton and had a light lunch of bread and cheese and chat with Ted Stacey before continuing on his way. Edward met him on his arrival and they got straight down to business, Edward's good results were noted and they discussed how his approach to running the farm was always more profitable and was it possible to apply his methods to the other farms on the estate. 'I think it is very much to do with the richness of the soil in this area.' said Edward 'most of the farms round here make good money while those on the more marshy soil close by, struggle.'

'You are probably right, Harold Reed at Butterwick does fairly well but John Smith at Fishtoft has flooding problems and has had a poor year.'

153

'I know, I saw Harold a couple of weeks ago and he said John had just about got his drainage sorted out and is hoping for a return to profits this year.'

'Well, I will be seeing them both tomorrow so I will get to see if there are any underlying problems.'

'Shall we have a look around now and you will be able to see what goes on here? I am sure you would like to stretch your legs after your long ride.'

***

When they returned to the Hall, they sat on a bench in the shelter of the garden wall and enjoyed the late Autumn sun. As they enjoyed a pot of ale before dinner they talked about Nathaniel's trip and Nathaniel asked what was Max Hoboer doing these days.

'You will find out soon enough Nathaniel, I have invited him over for dinner tonight and I suspect he will be here very soon. He is nearly always early.'

'That's great; I look forward to meeting him again. He's a hell of a character and really good company.'

'He's still the same, he will never change.'

A few minutes later Max arrived in a pony and trap and after handing over the rig to one of the stable lads, bounded up to Edward, shook his hand and then turning to Nathaniel, promptly embraced him in a breath-sapping bear hug. As Nathaniel was getting his breath back, he said, with a wide grin on his face, 'Good to see you again Nathaniel, you are looking very well, how the hell are you?'

'I'm fine, how about you, you still look fighting fit? But I see you still haven't had a shave yet.'

'No, and I am not going to. No one would recognise me if I was ever brave enough to shave it off.'

A pot of ale was provided for Max as he joined them on the bench and the conversation continued in a lively manner until they were called in for dinner.

***

After visiting Fishtoft and Butterwick the next day, Nathaniel stayed another night with Edward and they continued their discussions on estate business and Nathaniel was not at all surprised when Edward expressed the desire to buy his own farm one day and said, 'Well, when you do decide that you are moving, I hope you will give us plenty of warning.'

'Of course I will, but it might be years before I can afford to set up on my own. I can't see it happening in the near future.'

Later that night Nathaniel was thinking over the day's events and thought, 'Robert Anderson at Grantham might be a lucky lad sometime soon. I can already see two possibilities that might suit him, firstly, we could amalgamate the Grantham and Gonerby farms under the control of one man. Secondly if Robert was still at Grantham when Edward left, Robert could take over Holt Hall farm. This is something I could discuss with the trustees at the next meeting, but let's see what else crops up during the next two days at Saltfleetby. All three are new to me so anything could happen. Already I am puzzled as to why no one has brought up these topics before. Doesn't anyone talk to the managers at all?'

Nathaniel said goodbye to Edward and set off early to Saltfleetby. There were three farms to visit all within a five mile radius, one each in Saltfleetby All Saints, Saltfleetby St. Clement and Saltfleetby St. Peter. Nathaniel had arranged to stay with Michael Stitch at Saltfleetby All Saints for two nights and arrived there in plenty of time for lunch.

He spent the remainder of the day with Michael who he found to be jovial, extremely knowledgeable and a man who it was a pleasure to be with. Probably in his late forties and vastly experienced in the management of the farm he had worked at since starting as a young boy. He had been raised on the farm and had started work learning to deal with horses. As he had developed and vacancies arose he had become a general foreman and eventually taken over as manager about fifteen years ago. As Nathaniel visited the other two farms he discovered that Michael was the man that both Robert Stephens and Samuel Groves went to for advice and help when needed.

As he talked to Michael on the second night, Nathaniel asked 'Do you spend much time with Samuel and Robert? In some ways, they seem to regard you as their boss.'

'I suppose I do spend a fair bit of time with them, probably more so with Samuel than Robert. They are still both learning the job, particularly the handling of people side. Both are relatively new to the job as you know, but Robert is picking things up very quickly and he doesn't call on me as often as he used to. I sometimes have doubts about Samuel though, he is often asking me questions that he has asked me not long before. It might be a confidence thing as he has only been doing the job for a couple of years.'

'I had similar thoughts when I talked to him today. He gave the impression that he was trying to tell me what he thought I wanted to hear, instead of giving me a straight answer.'

'I agree, he does that with me sometimes, but as I said before it is a lack of confidence when talking to people who he thinks are somewhat superior to himself. When you get down to facts, he knows what he is doing and he is achieving satisfactory results.'

'That's true Michael. I think we will just have to keep an eye on him and hope he can gain in confidence as he spends more time in the job.'

155

'I am certain we won't have any real problems with him Nathaniel and you can be sure I will keep my eyes on him.'

'Thank you Michael, it's much appreciated and thank you for your hospitality, I have enjoyed my stay with you but I must get to bed and get some sleep. I intend to be off early tomorrow, it's a long way to Borton.'

'It's been nice meeting you Nathaniel, its years since we had a visit from your father and I hope to see you more often.' was Michael's telling reply.

***

Towards the end of October, Nathaniel received a message from Ephraim telling him that the meeting with Sir Samuel was arranged for 'next Tuesday at ten of the clock' and 'I suggest you are here by nine thirty so that we can discuss any topics of mutual importance.'

Nathaniel had gathered all the relevant points of his visits to all the farms and prepared a brief outline to present to the meeting. His problem was that he could not understand what the estate business had to do with Sir Samuel, and why did Ephraim want it all ready for his visit. Nathaniel thought that Sir Samuel was at the meeting to discuss his visit to London and what he would be expected to do when he was there.

Nathaniel was not a late riser in the mornings as he liked to be seen around the farm before he had his breakfast but at dinner on the Monday evening he said to Sylvia, 'Make sure I am up as usual in the morning Sylvia, I want to be on my way by nine o'clock in the morning. Don't let me lie in!'

Sylvia need not have worried, Nathaniel was up and fussing around gathering his papers and the all-important report, checking his clothes were just right and generally getting in the way as Sylvia prepared his breakfast. 'For goodness sake, Nathaniel, calm down and relax. Can you tell me why you have asked for your horse to be ready at the front door at half past eight?'

'I don't want to be late, it's a very important meeting and I must be there on time.'

'I know, but half past eight, it's ridiculous!' she said as she put his breakfast on the table. 'You don't want to be kicking your heels in Grantham, waiting for Mr. Woolaston to turn up, do you?'

'Alright Sylvia, I know I am being silly but I would rather be early than late and I have to make sure I have everything I need with me, don't I?'

Sylvia thought it was better to let him get on with it in his own way so she just wished him, 'Good luck,' and left the room.

Nathaniel finished his breakfast and went through all his papers once more before going outside and having a cursory check around the farm. He had a quick chat with both Mo and John and went back to collect everything he required. When he went out again to get his horse, Sylvia saw him and said, 'It is still not half past eight Nathaniel, and your horse will not be there yet. Why don't you calm down and let me make you a cup of coffee?'

'No thanks,' he snapped, and then, 'I am sorry Sylvia, I just can't seem to relax.'

***

Nathaniel arrived at Ephraim's office just as the old gentleman was entering the back door. 'Good morning Nathaniel, you are nice and early so we can get on with it before Sir Samuel arrives. How did all your estate visits go?'

'I had a good couple of weeks and met everyone I had planned to see.'

'Good, we will talk when Watson has produced some coffee.'

At the top of the stairs, before he entered the office, Ephraim bawled, 'Watson, two coffees in my office.'

As they sat down Ephraim asked, 'Have you brought your report Nathaniel?'

'Yes, it took a bit of doing but here you are.' he said passing the report to Ephraim. 'I hope you can read my writing.'

'It looks thorough to me, if you give me a few minutes, I will go through it quickly before we discuss it.'

Watson brought the coffees and Nathaniel sat quietly and had finished his when Ephraim eventually said, 'I like it, you seem to have discovered a few very important bits of information and made a couple of well observed suggestions.'

'Thank you Ephraim, but I must say, I was quite surprised that no one had visited some of the farms for several years. I appreciate my father was not at all well for some time so things had slipped a bit, but I think someone, me, should visit at least once a year from now on.'

'You are right, but remember, all the farm managers come here every year with their annual figures so don't be too hard on your father. He saw them all every year so he did get the chance to get up to date with events.'

'Yes, but I am sure I would not have found out some of the things in my report if I had relied on a once a year visit from them. Also, if I remember correctly, I am sure Michael Stitch said that he usually brought the reports from all three Saltfleetby farms.'

'That's true. I agree wholeheartedly that you should visit at least once a year. What do you think about doing it and collecting the reports at the same time?'

'That's a good idea, it will save nine managers traipsing all over the county just to deliver reports. I will put it in my diary'

***

Their discussions were interrupted when Watson, who had been stationed near the window, called through the half open door, 'Sir Samuel's carriage has just turned the corner, Sir.'

'Well get down there and show him in, and be quick about it.'

157

Muttering to himself, Watson hobbled to the door just as Sir Samuel arrived at the top of the stairs. 'Good morning Sir Samuel, please come in.' he said. 'Mr. Woolaston and Mr. Thorold are in the office, please go through.'

No sooner had Sir Samuel started towards the office, Ephraim burst through the door and, beaming all over his large, round face, bowed with a flourish and said in what was a subdued voice for him, 'Welcome to our humble office Sir Samuel, I hope you have had a pleasant journey.'

'Good morning Woolaston, good morning Nathaniel. Yes I have had a very pleasant journey, it's such a lovely crisp, clear morning and is a pleasure to be away from the hurly burly of London for a while.' Turning to Nathaniel, he asked 'How did your visits to all the farms go Nathaniel, did you make any interesting observations?'

Nathaniel told him all that he had discovered and they discussed his observations in detail. Sir Samuel then turned to Ephraim and said, 'Did you get Nathaniel to write a report as I suggested Woolaston?'

'Indeed I did Sir Samuel, and in my humble opinion it is a very detailed and comprehensive report with some interesting conclusions and recommendations. I have it here if you wish to have a look.'

Sir Samuel took the report and all was quiet for about ten minutes while he read it. Eventually he put it back on the desk and thought for a few moments before saying, ' I understand from Mr. Woolaston that you expressed concern that you had certain difficulties dealing with people who you can't get along with, is that correct?'

'Yes Sir, it is.'

'Well it appears that you must have the ability to get along with most people or you would never have achieved a comprehensive report such as this.' he said, picking up the report. 'This shows me that you have the basic skills required and we can develop them when you are with me in London. The report also tells me that your knowledge of the requirements of running a business are already well developed and probably need only minor improvements. Well done, Nathaniel, I am very pleased with what you have done here.'

'Thank you Sir Samuel, I am pleased that you like it.'

'I am extremely happy with your efforts since you came home from your trip and as I know Mr. Woolaston is too. What I propose to do is to get you down to London around the end of January and want you to attach yourself to our import, export side of affairs. As you know, we have been involved in that aspect of business for some time but we have identified an increase of activity where large profits can be made if we can get more involved. We have shares in three vessels currently operating between London and the continent and we think it is possible that we could increase our involvement substantially. You have the ability to write concise reports and have shown that you can analyse situations. What we also need is someone who can carry the analysis further and generate new ideas for profitable business. How do you feel about that?'

'That's quite a challenge Sir, but I like the sound of it. I suppose when I have grasped the basic running of the export business, things will start to follow.'

'We will certainly give you a grounding in the business and would not expect you to bring results immediately, but an uncluttered mind can be a very useful tool where ideas are concerned. Do you think Nathaniel can handle it Woolaston?'

'Yes Sir, I do. I would have had my doubts six months ago, but I am sure he will be an asset to your business. I am also sure he will grasp the splendid opportunity you are giving him to gain valuable skills for his future as owner of the Borton estate.'

'Nathaniel, I know we told you that you would have lodgings with Richard Lawson in Dock Lane but that is now no longer the case. As yet we have not found a suitable place for you but it will be arranged before you come down. I will be in contact with both Mr. Woolaston and yourself in early January to give final details of when we will expect you, and where you will be accommodated. If that is satisfactory, I will be on my way, and I look forward to seeing you in January.'

After Sir Samuel had departed, Ephraim and Nathaniel decided it was time they went to *"The Angel"* for something to eat and a relaxing drink, 'I think we deserve it.' said Ephraim, 'it's been a busy morning, I think you will agree.'

***

The next couple of months flew by and in the first week of January, Nathaniel received a note from Ephraim and with it, a package from Sir Samuel. Ephraim's note informed him of a meeting next Tuesday morning and, as usual, he hoped Nathaniel would not be late. The package from Sir Samuel was much more interesting and as he eagerly opened it, he thought, 'where is he sending me this time, I hope it sounds better than Dock Lane.'

The letter and information supplied was written by Jonathan Adnitt and informed Nathaniel that he would have temporary lodgings in Fleet Road with a Mr. Michael Stevens. Michael was the supervisor of the Thorold Brothers' shipping office in Wapping where Nathaniel would be based. He would work directly for Michael who would be responsible for his training and progress in the company.

Nathaniel was expected to report to Mr. Stevens on the morning of the last Monday in January and he would also be seen by Mr. Adnitt and given more detailed instructions about his responsibilities and what would be expected of him.

The meeting at Grantham was a very short one with all three trustees and Nathaniel attending. Joseph and George emphasised the need for Nathaniel to behave responsibly and, 'Don't, under any circumstances, lose your temper. One showing of your volatile side will result in your immediate return to Borton.' stressed Joseph. 'We know you can keep your rages under control when you want to, so please, we beg of you, take advantage of this wonderful chance you have been given.'

'I agree. You are indeed a very lucky man.' said George, nodding his head vigorously.

'Don't worry, I am sure I will never repeat any of my more well-known tantrums,' said Nathaniel. 'I know this is a chance in a lifetime and I have no intention of messing it up.'

Ephraim started to gather his papers together and said, 'Sir Samuel was very impressed with the report you wrote for the last meeting and thinks you could be an asset to his shipping business. He is fully aware of all your past indiscretions and, although he hasn't said so to me, he will certainly be watching your behaviour closely. Finally, all I have to say now Nathaniel, on behalf of all three of us, is, good luck, work hard and don't let yourself down. It's up to you and no one else'

'Thank you all very much, I won't let anyone down.'

***

Nathaniel had spent the last two months making sure that everything on the farm was working as it should and that everyone knew what they should be doing when he was away. He knew that there would be little interference from the trustees if he managed to stay on top of things while he could. Ephraim had made it perfectly clear that he was available to help when needed but would not otherwise get involved. He was also aware that he would have to get his personal items sorted and ready for his London trip and arrange for his heavier belongings to be transported down to his new address. He had already started to collect things together and put them in a pile ready to be transferred to his new travelling trunk. Sylvia told him several times that all the clothes would have to be washed and pressed before they were packed into the trunk but Nathaniel insisted that they were ready for whatever was required. He did not want to go to London unprepared.

As he was moving to London in January, Nathaniel decided to send his heavy trunk a week before he was going himself. The roads were always in a terrible state with deep ruts and holes at every turn but in January they could be far worse than normal. Progress was likely to be very slow and so a week's head start seemed appropriate. Two of the lads would take the trunk on the farm cart and deliver it to Thorold's office at Thames Wharf and from there someone would escort them to Michael Stevens' residence in Fleet Road.

Nathaniel himself planned to take his horse and so hopefully make much better progress than the cart.

At the beginning of January Nathaniel noticed that Sylvia was beginning to show concern about his wellbeing and safety on the trip down to London. 'Are you sure you will be safe? What if you fall off your horse? Don't you think someone should go with you? Where will you stay overnight? Do you know the way?' were just some of the questions she was continually asking as she fussed over his preparations.

'For goodness sake, Sylvia, I will be alright. Just don't fuss so much you are starting to drive me mad!'

'I am sorry Nathaniel, but I do really worry about you. I can't help it.'

'Well I couldn't manage all this packing without your help Sylvia, you are really appreciated, but please don't worry, I will be alright.'

'I know, but it's not a nice time of the year to be travelling such a long way and anything could happen. You will be careful won't you?'

'Of course I will, and I will be back in no time at all. Then you will wish I was back in London wouldn't you?'

***

Nathaniel, Mo and John Fowler discussed the best way to get himself, his trunk and his other baggage to London safely. The possibility of being robbed was ever present and the main London road was recognised as being particularly dangerous for a lone rider, and so the decision was taken that George Headland and the yard boy Jack would set out with the cart on the Monday before Nathaniel was due to start his job and Mo would go with Nathaniel early on the Friday morning. They would also take a spare horse to carry their baggage and they thought they would get there easily by Monday. Mo would accompany the cart on its return, and also bring the horses back to Borton.

The cart was despatched as planned with George Headland in charge, and Jack the yard lad was his companion and assistant. George had been fully briefed as to where and when he had to be in London and was keen to get on his way when Mo came up to check that he had not forgotten anything. 'Everything looks alright George, have you got the weapon?'

'Yes, it's under my seat at the ready.'

'Good,' said Mo. 'don't hesitate to use it if you have to, it's not an ornament.'

Nathaniel's father had always insisted that when travelling any distance with goods in the cart, they should always be prepared for the worst and should be armed if at all possible. George had the farm blunderbuss under the seat as he had been instructed.

'Is everything ready to go?' Nathaniel asked Mo as he joined the farewell

161

party. 'I can't think of anything else that I should have packed.'

'Everything that was put in the porch is on the cart so they are ready for the off.'

'Have you got everything you need George, and are you happy that you know where you are going?' asked Nathaniel.

'Don't worry Sir, it's a bit late to start panicking now, isn't it?'

'Well good luck and be careful.'

'I will, Sir.'

'Off you go then, I will probably see you on the road somewhere.'

As the cart was driven out of the gate, Nathaniel turned to Mo and asked, 'I forgot to check but have they got the blunderbuss?'

'They have, and George knows how to use it.'

***

For the next week, as she had been in the previous three weeks, Sylvia was in a state of frantic agitation. The trunk and boxes that had been dispatched on the cart had been packed, unpacked and packed again several times as she repeatedly checked the contents. She was determined that everything Nathaniel had, was clean and presentable for his arrival in London but now the main bulk of the luggage was on its way, she focused her attention on the limited amount of belongings Nathaniel was able to carry on his horse.

As she fussed around, cleaning and pressing his clothes, Nathaniel was repeatedly telling her, 'Whatever I wear, Sylvia, it will be filthy before I have gone twenty miles, so don't bother so much. The chances are that I will be wet through and plastered with mud within an hour of leaving home.'

'Yes, but I don't want you leaving home looking scruffy. What do you think people will say?'

Despite Nathaniel's repeated assertions, they were soon forgotten, and as he came down to breakfast the very next morning she was at it again. 'Good morning Nathaniel,' she smiled and as she visibly checked him over, 'Please don't wear that today Nathaniel, you need it clean for your trip.'

Nathaniel was by now getting very irritated by the constant nagging, and had gradually realised that he was consciously trying to avoid Sylvia as departure day neared. Despite his irritation, he managed to hold his tongue and muttered, 'Thank the Lord I am not married to her, I am sure I would have committed murder by now. I hope I can keep calm for the next two days' and then, with a large degree of fractiousness in his voice. 'I am dressed like this because I have a meeting with Mr. Woolaston and the trustees this morning, and I will not be wandering around the farm dressed up in my best clothes when I get back either.'

Sylvia quickly picked up Nathaniel's mood and as she turned away from him she wiped a tear from her eye hoping he had not noticed that she was upset. 'I am sorry Nathaniel, but I always want you to look your best when you

162

are away from the house and I feel I am responsible for making sure you are presentable.' She turned towards him and it was obvious she had shed a tear, 'I am going to miss you dreadfully when you go away, you have only just come back and now you are off again. It's not fair.'

'Please don't cry, Sylvia. I thought you would enjoy it when I was away, after all you will have a lot less work to do.'

Chapter 13

January to June 1724

The first day of the journey to London proved to be uneventful, marred only by the occasional flurry of snow, which, although uncomfortable, did not delay them at all. Between snow showers, they were mostly bathed in the pale, watery, winter sunshine and could steer easily around the biggest potholes in the very churned up road. The fields either side of the road were dead and devoid of any sign of human activity, the only sign of life being in the small villages they passed through.

'Where are we stopping for the night?' asked Mo. 'I am looking forward to getting warm again. My backside and legs are warm enough up against the horse's flanks, but waist up I have no feeling left at all. A nice blazing fire would be a welcome sight.'

'I should think we will be in Huntingdon in about half an hour hopefully before it gets too dark. *"The Bridge Inn"* is alright and they serve good food and a nice jar of ale. I stopped there with Toni Montini on my way from London a few months back.'

'That sounds good Nat. The sooner the better I think.'

They rode in silence for quite some time until, when they passed through the small sleepy village of Great Stukely, Nathaniel said, 'I think this is the last village before Huntingdon, I recognise the little old church. We should be in the warm before long.'

'That's if they have any rooms left for us,' was Mo's ironic comment.

***

There were more travellers along the road as they approached the small town of Huntingdon, most of them heading out of the town, probably going home from the Friday market where they had been selling their produce. Soon they could see the small, solid tower of All Saints church which was bathed in the pale rays of the setting sun standing as a beacon to the weary travellers. By the time they reached the town it would be almost dark.

At the Inn, they were pleased to find that there was accommodation available and when they were shown to their rooms, they were delighted to find that they had blazing log fires burning in the hearths.

'Warm water is on its way gentlemen for you to clean up, and when you are ready, come down and we will get you a nice hot meal,' said Nell, the maid who had escorted them upstairs. 'It is a bit busy down there at the moment so there is no need for you to rush. It will soon quieten down and you will easily get a table.'

'Thank you Nell, we will bear that in mind.' said Nathaniel.

Nearly an hour later, Nathaniel and Mo went downstairs feeling refreshed and a good deal warmer. They also found that Nell had been correct with her prediction and the bar area was nearly empty. They chose a table not far from the fireplace, not near enough to be uncomfortably hot but far enough away to be relaxed and warm. 'Now all we need is a couple of pots and a big jug of ale to wash the dust from our throats before we have something to eat,' said Mo, stretching himself in his chair. 'It's not been too bad a journey, so far has it?'

'Apart from the cold, we have been very lucky. No beggars to speak of, no vandals to fend off and the weather has been kind. I hope it is the same tomorrow, and if it is, we should get within striking distance by nightfall leaving us with a short ride on Sunday.'

Nell brought a great big jug of ale and two pots and placed them on the table. 'When would you gentlemen like to eat?' she asked, 'It's roast pork tonight,' she said, 'with potatoes, parsnips, cabbage and gravy'

'About half an hour alright Mo?' asked Nathaniel, rubbing his hands together. 'Sounds good to me,'

'Yes, that's fine for me,' replied Mo. 'I'm looking forward to it.'

***

They speculated about tomorrow's journey and tried to frighten each other by telling lurid tales of highwaymen and other assorted ruffians. By the time the food arrived, they had finished the jug of ale and ordered another one to help wash the meal down. As Nathaniel wiped the remaining gravy from his plate with the last piece of bread he said, 'I enjoyed that Mo, and by the look of your empty plate, you did too.'

'Best meal I've had all day,' was Mo's prompt reply as he sat gently rubbing his stomach 'but I couldn't eat any more. How about you?'

As they continued their banter, the landlord introduced himself, 'Good evening gentlemen, I am Joseph Corby, landlord of this Inn, I hope you enjoyed your meal and that you find your accommodation satisfactory?' and after confirmation that they had, he said to Nathaniel, 'I believe, Sir, I have seen you before. Have you by chance stayed here in the past?'

After inviting Joseph to sit down with them, Nathaniel explained that he had called in a few months ago and he was highly satisfied with his stay, and as he was heading for London it seemed an ideal place to stay once more.

'Just be very careful tomorrow, we have some visitors staying today who were accosted by a couple of brigands on their way here. Fortunately, as they were armed and vigilant, they managed to chase them off before any harm was done. It is rare that this sort of thing occurred during the hours of daylight but it does happen once in a while.'

'Thanks for the warning, Joseph. At least we have a blunderbuss each so we have some form of defence.' said Nathaniel.

165

'We must remember to have them loaded and ready before we set off,' replied Mo, 'and we treat everyone we meet with a certain amount of suspicion.'

'The other odd thing about today was that it was suspected that one of them was a woman, so you will have to be extremely alert and don't make assumptions.' said Joseph.

***

After a good breakfast of ham and eggs they packed their bags and had the horses brought from the stables. They made sure everything was packed carefully and securely attached to the horses, particular attention was paid to the weapons and they were placed so that they were quickly and easily accessible.

'Are we ready Mo?'

'As ready as we will ever be.'

'Let's go then.'

Dawn was just breaking as they set off and streaks of pink and deeper reddish browns were lighting the eastern sky. There was a chill in the air and signs of last night's frost were all around. A blackbird was singing loudly and cheerfully in the tall, unkempt, hawthorn hedge at the side of the inn.

'It feels almost as if spring has arrived,' said Nathaniel as he mounted his horse.

'That blackbird thinks it already has by the sound of things,' replied his companion.

They had not been on the road for long before the sun appeared over the flat fields, and all the reds in the sky gradually disappeared to be replaced by a brighter, watery, yellowish light which also vanished quickly behind a deep, dark ominous cloud which promised to bring them rain before long.

'I hope that's not rain coming our way already,' Mo said. 'We can certainly do without that, as early as this.'

'Well it might keep the ruffians off the road,' was Nathaniel's curt reply.

After their night at *"The Bridge Inn"* and their early start, they were both still feeling quite tired and so they travelled in near total silence for a couple of hours until they thought they could do with a strong cup of coffee. A short stop at a village inn satisfied their needs and suitably refreshed, they soon returned to the saddle and continued on their way. 'It looks as if the rain is not heading our way after all,' said Mo. 'We might just be lucky again.'

As they continued, Nathaniel pointed ahead to what looked like a small gathering of people. 'What's going on up there?' he asked.

'Probably a preacher or funeral or something,' was Mo's reply.

As they drew nearer, they saw that the crowd were pushing and prodding a very dishevelled man in the centre of the melee. They appeared to be in a very excited state, shouting and waving their arms in the air as they gradually made their way down a small lane off the main road. 'It could be anything,' said Nathaniel, 'just let's be careful, and keep your weapon ready in case of trouble.'

'You there!' called Mo to a couple of stragglers still crossing the main road, 'what's going on?'

'Well Sir, they say he got drunk last night and then he killed his wife when she refused to cook him his supper.'

'What are they doing with him now?'

'They are taking him to town to see the magistrate, if they don't kill him first, Sir.'

Nathaniel turned to Mo, 'Let's get on our way Mo. We don't want to get involved with that lot, do we?'

'No we don't. I don't fancy his chances, do you?' replied Mo.

***

Progress had been steady all day, and other than the crowd they had encountered, nothing untoward had happened. In the late afternoon they were travelling through a very desolate, thickly wooded area and decided that if they came across a decent inn they would stop for the night. They didn't want to travel after dark and so they said they would stop at the next inn and see if it was suitable. They had travelled for a couple more miles with still no sign of habitation when the trees thinned out and they entered a small hamlet of a few small houses and row of cottages which had a distinct air of neglect. There was no inn or church, but as they entered the short main street, there was a carved stone sunk into the side of the road which said Ware, five miles.

'I remember coming through Ware with Antonio,' said Nathaniel, 'it's quite a pleasant little town and there are several decent looking inns. We should be able to get there before dark, shouldn't we?'

'Let's press on then, this is a bit of a dump, isn't it?

They entered the small country town of Ware at dusk and managed to secure suitable rooms at the *"Old Bulls Head"*, a small inn in the centre of the main street. Stabling was adequate and the horses were fed and watered and bedded down in warm, dry boxes for the night. Instructions were given to have them ready for seven o'clock in the morning.

Satisfied that the horses were well looked after, Nathaniel and Mo cleaned up and suitably refreshed, they enjoyed a pleasant, relaxing evening with a good meal and a couple of jugs of ale. 'We haven't come across George Headland, yet,' said Mo, 'I thought we would have caught up with them by now, wouldn't you?'

'They must have made pretty good time, but I suspect they are not in London just yet. They are probably timing themselves to arrive on Monday so they are not hanging around when they get there.'

167

'That's true, George hates crowds so we will probably catch him up sometime tomorrow.'

***

'Morning Mo, feeling fit and ready to go?'

'I will be when I have had something to eat,' replied Mo heading for the breakfast table.

'It should be a leisurely trip today and we should have plenty of time to find rooms near to the shipping office where I am due to meet Michael Stevens. If we don't bump into George before then, we will see him at the office sometime in the morning,' said Nathaniel as he sat down.

'How long do you think it will take today?' asked Mo.

'I think we should be there by early afternoon if the roads are not too busy. There will certainly be a lot more activity as we get nearer to London so it might slow us down a bit.'

***

Nathaniel's prediction proved to be correct, and as they approached London, the road became much busier. People on foot carrying all manner of goods, carts jostling for space with the carters shouting at their animals and each other as they tried to manoeuvre through the crowds. Even so, by mid-afternoon they had managed to find, and settled into a small comfortable inn just off Fleet Road where Nathaniel was going to take lodgings with Michael Stevens. Nathaniel said it must be somewhere near the office at Thames Wharf, because he did not think that Michael would be living very far from his work.

'Let's go for a stroll and see if we can find where the office is situated,' suggested Mo.

'A good idea. It will give us a chance to stretch our legs, but I think we should go now or it will be dark soon and we will never find it.'

After having obtained directions from the innkeeper, they headed off and were very soon in the docks area and even though it was a Sunday, there was still a great deal of activity on the wharf. Not entirely sure where they were, they asked a passing gentleman if this was Thames Wharf. 'No,' he replied, 'it's the next one along, once you have crossed that small bridge you can see over there, you are on Thames Wharf.'

'Thank you for your help,' said Nathaniel, and they continued on their way.

There was a lazy, cold wind blowing off the dull, brown, oily river and wisps of mist were drifting between the boats tied to the wharf. Dusk was approaching as they searched along the dilapidated buildings on the dockside and Mo stated his opinion that, 'It's rough around here Nat, I wouldn't fancy working here. The place stinks worse than a pig sty in a hot summer!'

There were lots of little alleys running at right angles to the main dockside and, having checked the whole length of the dock front buildings,

168

Nathaniel and Mo started to investigate the side alleys until Mo said, 'This looks like it,' and pointed to a roughly painted sign that said *"Thorold and Thorold, Shipping Agents."* Its dirty, white letters were painted on a flaking black background and the sign was nailed to a rickety wooden door. It was hanging loose at an angle and attached to the door by just one remaining nail. The whole impression was one of neglect.

Nathaniel was not at all impressed and thought, 'What the hell am I going to do in a place like this?'

***

Back at the inn the discussion inevitably revolved around the state of Nathaniel's future place of work and the fact that he did not look forward to his immediate future one bit. He was seriously considering going back home in the morning and forgetting all about it but Mo convinced him that he should at least stay and find out exactly what he was expected to do. 'After all, you might not be working in the docks at all, you might have an office in the commercial area near Sir Samuel's own office or that other bloke you were telling me about, Jonathan something or other.'

'I am definitely going home if I have to work with him!' was Nathaniel's curt reply.

'I wonder where George is,' remarked Mo.

'I hope he is somewhere close by, he is supposed to be at that dump on Thames Wharf in the morning. Someone will then go with him to Michael Stevens' residence to show him where to take the trunks and baggage.' .

'If George is going to head for home once he has dropped the load, I think I ought to go with him don't you?'

'Yes, that's right, and you will need to take the spare horse with you. I will be keeping my horse down here for the time being.'

'Just in case you want to do a runner,' joked Mo.

Laughing, Nathaniel replied, 'If I do, I will probably catch you up before you get to Ware.'

***

They had just finished their evening meal and were relaxing with a jug of ale when a young man, probably in his mid-twenties, followed the landlord into the bar. The landlord headed over to Nathaniel and said, 'Mr. Thorold, this is Michael Stevens, he asked if he could have a word with you.'

'Of course he can, I am very pleased to meet you Michael. I am Nathaniel and this is my travelling companion, Maurice Clarke. Please, sit down,' and to the landlord, 'Would you bring Mr. Stevens a mug please?'

Michael was a tall man of muscular build, his dark hair was short and curly and he sported a goatee beard and a moustache which had ends that pointed skywards. He was fashionably dressed in clothes that Nathaniel thought would never be seen in and around Grantham. Nathaniel told Michael that they had been down to Thames Wharf, 'and to put it bluntly Michael, that office of yours is a bit of a dump, and that's being kind to it,' he said.

'I think you may have seen our old office, we moved to a brand new place at the end of last year. It's just around the corner from the old one and is very comfortable indeed.'

'Well that's a relief. I bet you were pleased to move weren't you?'

'I certainly was, we had been there for years but Jonathan would not move until the right place became available. There were plenty of other places we could have moved to over the last few years but none of them were much of an improvement. When we finally moved, it was like moving into heaven. You will love it.'

'I am sure I will, it sounds very nice.'

'I heard this evening that your luggage cart arrived in town this afternoon and is staying at a tavern overnight about two miles from here. I had a message that they will be at our office before nine o'clock in the morning and I have sent them details of our new address.'

'That's good news, George is a reliable, sensible man but you never know what can happen on the roads these days, do you?'

The conversation continued for some time and Nathaniel warmed to Michael's easy, relaxed manner and thought they would work really well together. The talk turned to living arrangements and Nathaniel asked how he would fit into the Stevens' household.

'Oh, I haven't got a household,' said Michael. 'I live in a block of gentlemen's apartments. There are six separate apartments in the building, five are occupied and you have been allocated the only vacant one. It is a good size, but it is on the top floor so it is a good job you are a fit young man. Anyway I am sure you will like it. Sir Samuel bought the building about three years ago and completely refurbished it mainly for use of staff members. Five of us, including you, are single men and four of us are employed by Sir Samuel, the other two are businessmen who have recently moved to London. One of them is looking for a permanent place to move his family into, so if you are not happy with your room, there should be a chance for you to move sometime in the future.'

'That sounds good to me Michael, I am looking forward to tomorrow.'

'I am sure you will settle in easily, they are nice group of men and we all get on well with each other.'

'Will I have access to stables for my horse?' asked Nathaniel.

'There is stabling next door to the apartments and you will have to book your horse in. Mine is booked on a monthly basis and it is looked after very well. I only exercise my horse when I am not working as the office is within walking distance. Don't worry about it, I will show you around all the places you need to know tomorrow. You might even decide you don't need your horse in London after all, once you get to know your way around,' explained Michael.

'Thanks Michael, that sounds exactly what I will need and with your help, I am sure I will soon settle in.'

'Well, I must be off now, I will pick you both up at eight thirty in the morning. We will walk round and I will show you all the important places as we go.'

'Hang on Michael, I will have to take my horse and the spare one so that I can team up with George for the journey home.'

'Of course you will Mo, I'd forgotten about that. It won't be a problem though, I will walk round with Nathaniel and you can follow us. It's not far and it will save you having to come back here again. You can leave your horse here until you can arrange more permanent stabling, Nathaniel. We should be able to sort that out sometime tomorrow.'

'Thanks Michael, sounds good to me, and we look forward to seeing you in the morning.' After Michael had gone, Mo went round to the stables and gave instructions to ensure his horse and the spare were saddled up and ready for a half past eight start. He also explained that Mr. Thorold would not be requiring his horse until later in the day.

When he returned to the bar he found that Nathaniel had already gone to bed so he relaxed for a while and finished the remainder of the jug of ale before retiring himself.

***

When Nathaniel came down for breakfast, Mo was already finishing his final cup of coffee and checking his baggage. 'You're on the ball Mo, couldn't you sleep?'

'I slept like a log, but all hell broke loose outside of my bedroom about two hours ago. It sounded as if half of the population of London were going to the docks and the other half were shouting at them to make less noise. I will be glad to get home and out of this mad house, I don't envy you at all.'

'I must admit, I think it will take me some time to get used to the hustle and bustle of big city life. It's so different to life back home, isn't it? Have you checked the horses yet?'

'No, it's still a bit early for them yet. I have seen the stable lads in the yard so I am sure they will be here on time.'

Just before eight thirty, the horses were brought to the side door and Mo went out to secure his baggage and as he was completing his final checks, he felt a hand on his shoulder, 'Morning Mo, all ready to go?' asked a jovial Michael, 'It looks as if you are going to have a cold journey today, there is a bitter east wind blowing and it could even bring some snow.'

'Why are you so bloody cheerful Michael, have you been on the brandy already?'

'I wish I had, it might have warmed me up a bit. Is Nathaniel up and about yet?'

'Yes, he is in the breakfast room, just go through. I'll be with you in a minute, I've just about finished here.'

'Morning Michael, nice to see you again,' said Nathaniel as he was getting up from the table. 'I am just going to have a word with the landlord before we set off. If it is alright with him, I am leaving all my belongings here until later today. I don't feel like carting this lot all over town. It's alright with you isn't it?'

'No bother, it will be safe here and we will be picking it up this afternoon anyway.'

They set off for Thorold's office and went through some rather rundown back streets and in no time at all they emerged from a dirty side street into a busy, tree lined thoroughfare which was a total contrast to the dock area. Among the gentlemen's carriages, Mo, from his vantage point on the back of his horse was the first to speak, 'I can see George and Jack parked up the street, they seem to be waiting for someone.'

'They are waiting for us, they are outside our office,' replied Michael. 'I wonder how long they have been here?'

George and Jack had not been waiting very long and after Michael had checked that someone was available to guide them to Nathaniel's apartment, they were eager to get going. Nathaniel checked all the baggage was still as it had been loaded and confirmed that it would all be placed in his apartment and after wishing them a safe journey, bade them farewell.

Their guide sat next to George on the cart and Jack was relegated to sit with the luggage for the short journey to the apartment. Mo followed the cart on his horse with the spare horse in tow.

***

Michael took Nathaniel into the shipping office and introduced him to the members of staff who worked there and then he was taken to an old oak table in the corner next to a window. 'This is yours Nathaniel for the duration of your stay with us. I will introduce you to Simon who will be your assistant, he is currently supervising a loading down at the docks. That's his table over there,' he said pointing at a table covered with papers and a lot of small boxes and parcels. 'You will not see Jonathan Adnitt today but he will want to talk to you tomorrow when he is back. That's his room over there.'

'What's it like working for him?' asked Nathaniel expecting to hear the worst.

'He's a very good boss and very fair but he expects all his staff to do everything expected of them. He stands no nonsense from anyone.'

'In the short period I was with him I had the impression he was arrogant and a bit self-important so it's nice to hear I may be wrong.'

172

'Just do as he tells you and you will get on fine, but he also listens to any sensible ideas you may have, so don't be afraid to tell him of anything you think he should know. He won't bite your head off.'

They spent the remainder of the morning discussing general business and in particular, Thorold's involvement in shipping goods around the country and overseas.

Michael took Nathaniel to a coffee house for a quick lunch and then they went on to the stables where they managed to book in Nathaniel's horse for a month and the option of renewal if required. They then had to return to the inn to collect the horse and all Nathaniel's belongings and go back to the stables. When the horse had been settled in to Nathaniel's satisfaction it was late afternoon. The temperature was heading down rapidly, and small flakes of thin snow were blowing around on the cold easterly wind as they headed to the apartment building. 'I wish I had put the baggage on the cart this morning, its heavier than I thought,' moaned Nathaniel. 'How far have we to go?'

'We are here already, I told you last night the stables were just around the corner.'

'Thank goodness for that, I hate the cold, especially when it is dark and miserable.'

'All we have to do now is get this lot up to the third floor, do you think you will manage it?' asked Michael with a grin on his face.

'I am sorry Michael, I shouldn't moan so much, and thank you for your help.'

'Here we are,' said Michael as he opened the door on the left at the top of the stairs, 'welcome to your new home.'

The room was spacious and covered half of the top floor of the building. It was sparsely, but adequately furnished and in front of a window was a table and four chairs. Two high-backed chairs, one of which was a rocker, were placed either side of a blazing log fire, and more logs were stacked at the side ready for use. A narrow bed was placed by the wall behind the door and a small chest with a large bowl and jug on top was at the foot of the bed. The floorboards were bare, with the exception of a small pegged rug placed in front of the fire.

'This is very nice, I am really impressed,' and as he walked over to the window which overlooked a small back yard, he exclaimed, 'my goodness, that's the new St Paul's Cathedral in the distance isn't it.'

'Yes it is, it was declared open about twelve years ago but they are still putting the final touches to it as the statues on the roof are not all in place yet. When you see it on a bright sunny day you will be absolutely astounded, it is so beautiful. You must go and visit it when you get the chance, the interior is just as impressive as the exterior.'

'I certainly will, I have seen many fine buildings in Europe but that is as good as anything I saw over there.'

'I am pleased you like your accommodation Nathaniel, all the residents like it here.'

Nathaniel moved from the window and asked, 'Who lit the fire and warmed the place up?'

'That's Bernard Smith. Bernard and his wife Brenda are housekeeper and cook. They live in the basement and do all the cooking and cleaning for the residents. We always eat at half past six in the evening in the dining area on the ground floor. If you intend to eat out at any time or if you wish to invite a guest to eat here then you must inform Bernard or Brenda before you leave for work in the morning. They will bring you hot water in the jug for you to wash and they clean your room and make your bed every day while you are out at work. Their basic wage is paid by the company but we each contribute to the cost of food and any extras we may have had. Bernard will tell you what you owe each week and Jonathan Adnitt checks regularly with Bernard to ensure that everyone is paid up to date. If you fall behind with your payments and Jonathan finds out, heaven help you.'

'What about the rent for the room, or does the company provide it rent free?'

'You have got to be joking. The rent for the room is taken by the company direct from your wage packet.'

'I suppose that would be asking a bit too much but it sounds very well organised and it's a very comfortable room. I am beginning to feel at home already.'

'Well this company looks after its staff very well and providing you behave in a civilised manner and never do anything to bring the company into disrepute, you will be fine.' Michael explained. 'I will leave you to get settled in now, and I will call for you at about six fifteen for dinner. It will be a good chance for me to introduce you to your fellow residents and of course, Bernard and Brenda.'

'Thanks Michael, I look forward to it.'

***

When Michael and Nathaniel arrived, the dining room was empty but no sooner had they crossed the threshold, a round, smiling, rosy cheeked face appeared round a door at the far corner. 'Good evening Bernard, this is Mr. Thorold who, as you know will be with us for a few months.' No sooner had the introductions been made when a short, rotund lady with an equally happy looking face and dressed in a smock and a bonnet came in. '…. and this, Nathaniel, is Brenda. Don't you ever upset her, she's the best cook in town and we want to keep her happy and here!'

'Oh, you are a wag Mr. Stevens. I am not going anywhere,' and then, 'it's nice to meet you Mr. Thorold and I hope you will be happy here.'

***

Over the next half hour, Nathaniel met three of the four remaining residents, all of whom were single men, Andrew Lawson, who was the Manager in the General Ironmongery Warehouse, Gerald Pickworth, Sir Samuel's Office Manager, and Richard Pearson who was a Gun Maker and had his works in the city. Roger Gough, the only other resident was a married man and was employed as a Legal Secretary for a large Chambers in the centre of London. Apparently he was out looking for a permanent home for his family to move into.

The evening went smoothly for Nathaniel and he thought he would fit in quite well. All the others were keen to help Nathaniel to get to know the places to go and promised to take him 'out on the town' on Saturday evening after dinner.

***

As soon as he arrived at the office the next morning, Nathaniel was called in to Jonathan's office for a quick briefing.

'Please sit down, Nathaniel. Have you settled in to your apartment?'

'Yes thank you Sir, it is very comfortable and everyone is very friendly. Michael has been a great help and has introduced me to all my fellow residents.'

'Good. First, forget the Sir and from now on call me Jonathan. We are quite relaxed in the office, but outside and in our other premises, I would prefer it if you would call me Sir. Now I suppose you would like to know what we have planned for you?'

'Indeed I would, Jonathan,' he said, reflecting on his derogatory first opinion of his new boss.

'Well, like lots of other companies, we have a big problem with shrinkage, in other words, stock is disappearing and causing us concern. We have our ideas where it might be going and have tried to sort it out, but so far we have failed. What we need is a new face with a completely open mind to check out all our controls and see if they can clear it up. We have tried more than once over the last eighteen months and have failed totally. You, Nathaniel are that new face. You have the complete run of the company and all senior people have been told to co-operate fully. They think you are here to learn all our stock control systems so you have the opportunity to investigate thoroughly under the guise of learning the ropes. How do you feel about that, do you think you can crack it?'

'It sounds a hell of a job,' replied Nathaniel. 'Where do you suggest I start?'

'I have prepared a list of all the people who will be of use to you but I suggest the best person to see initially is Gerald Pickworth whom I believe you met last night. I have spoken to Gerald and he is expecting you when we have finished our meeting. I am going there myself so I will take you over and you can get started. Just remember Nathaniel, the only people who are aware of your real purpose here is you, Sir Samuel and myself. No one else has a clue, so please try to keep it that way. Any pilfering or crooked dealing could involve anyone you meet, and the last thing we want is to warn them off!'

As the chariot swayed and jostled its way through the crowded, noisy streets, Nathaniel found it very difficult to hear what Jonathan was saying as he proudly pointed out various interesting places on the way. St Paul's Cathedral came into view and as they approached the beautiful new building they turned into a side street and entered an enclosed yard through large iron gates. A uniformed man checked the carriage and on seeing Jonathan, waved them in.

'We're here Nathaniel. This is the headquarters of the Thorold empire.'

'It's enormous,' gasped Nathaniel as he admired the large house set in well-tended gardens. 'Is this all offices? It looks more like someone's private mansion to me.'

'Yes, it's all offices but some domestic and security staff live in the apartments just inside the gate. It's a lot to take in but you will soon find your way around. First, let me take you to see Gerald and then you can get to work. The sooner you start, the sooner you finish.'

***

They found Gerald at a large table covered with piles of papers and apparently trying to sort them all out into their correct boxes. 'Good morning Nathaniel, welcome to the house of chaos. How are you this morning?'

'I'm fine Gerald, you look as if you need some help.'

'I've been telling Jonathan that for months but I think he is going a bit deaf.'

'I think I had better leave now,' said Jonathan. 'I'll see you both later.'

Jonathan left them to sort things out and went off in search of Sir Samuel. Gerald asked Nathaniel how much of the business he knew.

'Virtually nothing,' was the immediate response, 'but I have to learn all the control systems used in the company, from purchasing through to despatch.'

'Not much then,' joked Gerald, 'we should get through that by the end of the day.'

'As long as that? I had hoped to be on the way home by lunch time.' grinned Nathaniel.

***

'I think we should approach this systematically and start at the beginning.' said Gerald. 'The first and one of the most important things to know is that we have three warehouses in London and every supplier we deal with is allocated the warehouse to which he must send any goods we order from him. When we place an order we indicate on the order form the warehouse to which the order should be delivered. It is always the same and has been agreed with the supplier when the first order is placed.

These papers on this table have all been messed up somewhere in the process and I am trying to get them in some semblance of order so that I can follow the goods through from purchase to sale. If the system is working correctly then we should know how much stock we have in each of the warehouses. Unfortunately, when we have carried out checks in the past it would seem to indicate that items are disappearing somewhere along the way. What we will do now is make a start by going through every sheet of paper and place it in one of three piles, one for each warehouse. Are you happy with that?'

'Yes, no problem. Can everyone who handles the sheets read and write Gerald?'

'All of those with responsibilities for stock control can, but they often hand the papers to someone else and of course, there is no guarantee that *they* can.'

It did not take long to sort out the papers into their correct piles and Nathaniel made notes as he went along to make sure he had recorded things he thought were relevant to his clandestine task. He told Gerald that he always forgot things if he failed to write them down and Gerald didn't ask.

'What's next Gerald?'

'We will have to sort the documents for the progress of each order through the warehouse and on to the customer. What I suggest we do is take one warehouse each and extract the order forms and delivery forms for each order and check that what we received is what we ordered. Gerald had sorted his pile well before Nathaniel, and went on to do the same for the third pile.

When this was complete Gerald took Nathaniel to a nearby coffee house for lunch and when they managed to get a table and sit down in the busy, crowded room, Nathaniel asked, 'Do you have to go through that routine very often, it seems a bit of a chore to me.'

'No it's something I don't normally deal with but I have been saving it up especially for you as I thought it was a good way of introducing you to the process.'

'It certainly helps to see what should happen, but I suspect there is a great deal more for me to get the hang of before I really know what goes on.'

'There certainly is, but you have plenty of time and I am sure you will pick it up quite quickly.'

'What are the main problems you come across with regards to stock control?'

'I think there are three things which cause us problems, the first is that people, no matter how well trained, regularly fail to fill in records correctly. The second is that they fail to ensure that the documents follow the goods at the right time and the third is the one you have already identified, most people in the warehouses can't read or write.'

'Why do you think these things happen?'

'I am not sure, it could be just simple forgetfulness or it could be pressure of work. We are sometimes pressed very hard to meet deadlines.'

The discussion carried on throughout lunch and by the time they were ready to return to the office, Nathaniel had gleaned a lot more information to enable him to identify problem areas. He also realised his questioning must be carefully carried out or it was quite likely that someone would suspect his motives and become suspicious.

Returning to the office, they had to fight their way through the crowds lost in admiration of the magnificent new St Paul's Cathedral. Bathed in the late winter sunshine, the dome shimmered like a well-polished jewel and it was obvious that Wren's design met with the approval of the local population.

'It is outstanding, isn't it? I must go and have a good look around when I get a bit of spare time.'

'You won't get much spare time working for this company Nathaniel.'

As they neared the office, Nathaniel asked, 'What have you got lined up for this afternoon Gerald?'

'Well we can't look at the warehouse stock control system, but we can check sales orders and delivery notes and get them into some sort of order.'

***

The rest of the day was spent sorting and checking deliveries against orders and Nathaniel was building up quite a few possibilities of where things could have gone missing. They had not yet completed sorting one of the warehouses so it looked as if it was going to be a long job As he made notes he realised it was possible that some of his ideas had already been taken care of. He had to check everything before he was in a position to make recommendations.

'Well Nathaniel, I think it is about time to go home, are you ready?'

'I am, is it far from here? I am hopeless at direction and I came with Jonathan direct from the shipping office so have no idea where we are.'

'I think we should walk tonight. It usually takes me about twenty minutes and I think the walk will blow the cobwebs away and help you get your bearings.'

'That's fine by me.'

As they set off, Gerald explained that if he was feeling a bit tired or it was raining he would hire a sedan chair to transport him home. They were in plentiful supply and were always eager for business and, of course you were kept out of the way of all the ruffians on the streets.

'That sounds good to me, I have never been in one before. They don't have them for hire in Grantham. Some of the very wealthy have their own private ones, but that's about it.'

'Well once you are happy and know your way around, we can hire one each.'

***

The next week or so passed very quickly and Nathaniel began to settle into the day to day routine of the office. They eventually finished the paper sorting and Gerald explained quite a few of the associated office procedures that impacted on the systems he was learning, before arranging for him to visit one of the warehouses for an extended period.

On his second Friday afternoon, Jonathan had arranged a meeting with Nathaniel to discuss his progress. Nathaniel went through his findings so far, and stressed that although his knowledge at the moment was limited, there were a few changes that he would probably recommend when the time was right.

'So far so good Nathaniel. I know you are going to look at the warehouse systems on Monday and I have arranged for you to widen the scope of your investigation to include all warehouse systems of operation and not just the control of goods side. This will involve you working on the shop floor under the guidance of Andrew Lawson, the manager at our Thames Wharf Warehouse You have met Andrew at your apartment and no doubt you will become firm friends but as I have stressed often over the past few days, you must maintain strict silence on your actual role. Widening your role might give Andrew the impression that you are being trained to take over his job especially as you are a Thorold family member so be aware that this may cause friction between you. If it becomes a problem, tell me immediately and I will sort it out.'

'I will be as discrete as I can,' said Nathaniel, as the door opened and Sir Samuel in all his finery entered the room.

'Good afternoon Jonathan, good afternoon Nathaniel, I trust you have settled into your accommodation satisfactorily.' He sat down and said, 'I am sorry Nathaniel, but I must talk to Jonathan in private,' and turning to Jonathan, 'Is your business finished?'

'It is,' replied Jonathan. 'Thank you Nathaniel, and remember, be discrete.'

***

'How is he doing, Jonathan?'

'He is doing very well. He has a few good ideas for improvement already and I have widened the scope of his investigation to get a better view

179

of what is actually going on. We know what is supposed to happen but what really happens is something quite different.'

'That's nice to hear, but what about the shrinkage?'

'It's much too early for him to know as yet and that is why I have given him more time to get to the bottom of it.'

'Do you think he will have any problems mixing with the workforce?'

'I don't think so, he was brought up on the farm where all his playmates were workers' children and his best friend is Maurice, the son of a labourer. He seems at home with all classes and that could work to our advantage in the long run.'

'If he keeps it up, then we might be on to a winner. Well done Jonathan.'

***

After a couple of months working in the warehouse he had a much better idea of what went on and how the systems worked. He made copious notes of what he had learnt, always making sure that Andrew only saw the edited version which identified the way things should happen. Having a copy which indicated his thoughts, ideas and future recommendations meant he had to prepare it back in his room. His relationship with Andrew was very relaxed and they often went out on a Saturday evening for a drink and a game of cards. Nathaniel revived his love of poker and occasionally the residents would play in the evening at the apartments where stakes were strictly controlled. Roger and Gerald never joined in but Richard Pearson would play every night if he had the chance.

***

While helping to unload a wagon-load of packing cases, Nathaniel was called over by Andrew, 'The boss is in the office demanding to talk to you and he seems in a bit of a mood,' he said. 'I shouldn't hang around if I was you, he wants to see you now!'

Nathaniel hurried over to the office which was not much more than a small cupboard in a corner under some wooden stairs. 'What the hell have I done wrong this time.' he thought. 'This reminds me of my father's way of doing things.'

'Come in Nathaniel,' said Jonathan 'if you can get in. It's a bit cramped in here but I don't want the whole warehouse to hear what I have to say.'

Jonathan sat on the edge of the table and Nathaniel eased himself into the only remaining space and nervously managed to close the rickety door behind him. There were no windows in the office and the only light now that the door was closed came from a small candle flickering in a glass jar on the shelf above the table.

'Nathaniel we have a big problem which I would like you to investigate. A large delivery of crates containing pottery is missing. Our warehouse at Wapping delivered a large consignment of crates to be loaded yesterday and then we received another order for ten crates. According to our control system we should have thirty crates in the warehouse but the manager says we have none. He says he has never received them. Gerald has all the papers saying that we have received the full amount, so something is wrong somewhere. I want you to go and see Gerald, get hold of the notes and see what you can find. We can't afford to lose this amount of stuff.'

'Have you any paperwork with you Jonathan, if I knew what the load consisted of, I could check this warehouse now?'

'No I am sorry, I am afraid you will have to see Gerald.'

'OK then, I will get cleaned up and get over there as soon as I can.'

'Good man! I hope you can sort it quickly, we have to get that order off tomorrow if possible.'

***

Gerald had the papers ready for Nathaniel when he arrived and they confirmed that a delivery had been made to the Wapping warehouse as it should have been. However, the date was not clear and the receiving signature was no more than a cross, so was no help in identifying who actually accepted the goods.

'I had better get over there and see what is going on straight away. Who is the manager at Wapping?'

'That's John Williams, he is a good steady chap and has been with the company since he was a boy. He must be in his fifties by now and has always been solid and reliable.'

'And who is at the Empire Warehouse?'

'Derek Jones, he is younger and has not been with us so long. About three years I think. We have had a couple of very minor problems with him but nothing serious. His documentation is usually in order.'

'I had better get off then. I will go to Wapping first and then on to Empire if I need to. I don't remember seeing this stock at Thames Wharf while I have been there, but of course I could be wrong.'

Nathaniel introduced himself to John Williams at Wapping and John was quite happy to show him all the stock records. He was convinced that the goods had never arrived in his warehouse and pointed out strongly that if the delivery note was not signed by him it would have been signed by his assistant who could write his own name clearly. 'You can check all my forms and you will find they are all signed correctly. I never let anyone else sign for anything.'

After confirming that John had physically checked the stock, Nathaniel could do no more and set off to Empire Warehouse to meet Derek Jones. After taking a couple of wrong turnings, he eventually found the warehouse tucked away in a rubbish strewn, narrow back street where he had a distinctly uncomfortable feeling that he was being watched. The door to the warehouse was locked and after banging on it with his cane, a small slot slid open revealing a pair of inquisitive dark brown eyes. 'Who is it and what do you want?' demanded the mystery man behind the door.

'I am Nathaniel Thorold and I would like to see Mr. Jones now, if you please.'

At the mention of the name Thorold, the door was opened wide and he was ushered in by a small, wizened old man who walked with the aid of a stick. 'Of course Sir, do come in. I will take you to see him immediately. I will just lock the door first if you don't mind.'

Nathaniel was pleased to get off the street and into the warehouse. Even though it was not very welcoming at least it felt a bit safer, but he was sure he would need an escort through the nearby streets if he left after dark.

As he was guided to the office, Nathaniel took the opportunity to make a cursory check of the warehouse layout and thought at first sight that things seemed a bit haphazard. 'Anyway I will soon find out,' he thought.

'Mr. Jones, this is Mr. Thorold and he asked to see you,' said the little old man to a short stocky man who Nathaniel guessed was in his mid-thirties.

'Good afternoon Mr. Thorold, I am Derek Jones, the Manager of Empire Warehouse. How can I help you?'

Nathaniel explained who he was and what he was doing and stressed that he was working for the company as a trainee and had no executive power over anyone who worked there. 'I have inherited my father's estate and I am in London to learn management skills to help me run my own business. I have been asked to try and sort out a problem of missing goods.'

'That's fine Mr. Thorold, I will help you all I can. Just ask and I will try to answer.'

'Thank you Derek, I appreciate that, but please call me Nathaniel.'

***

'First of all Derek, can you tell me who accepts stock in from the suppliers?'

'Usually it is me or one of the senior warehousemen if I am not around.'

'And what is the next step?'

'Well, whoever signs for the goods, adds the delivery to the warehouse stock sheet and the copy of the delivery sheet is put in my in tray. The stock sheet also records where the goods are stored in the warehouse. The delivery notes are sent on to Gerald Pickworth at head office.'

'That's alright. Can all the people who sign for goods read and write?'

'All three senior warehousemen are able to understand delivery notes and fill in stock sheets, but I have to keep a close eye on them sometimes.'

'Do you ever get goods delivered that should have gone to Thames Wharf or the Wapping Warehouse?'

'I don't think we have ever had that happen in the three years I have been here.'

182

'What would you do if you did?'

'I would refuse to accept it and send it to where it should have gone in the first place, as we are supposed to do.'

'Are your warehousemen aware of that?'

'Of course,' was Derek's defensive reply as he was wondering where the conversation was going. 'Would you like a coffee Nathaniel, I should have asked you before?'

'I would love one please, and while I am waiting, could I have a look at your stock sheets?'

'They are all over there.' said Derek pointing to a tray piled high with papers. 'Help yourself. If you don't mind I will get on with some work while you browse through them.'

For the next hour Nathaniel checked piles of stock sheets and made copious notes as he ploughed through them. 'I don't know how the hell he finds anything in here,' he thought to himself. 'This place needs a thorough going over.'

When he had completed his check of all the stock sheets he had found no sign of any crates of pottery anywhere and was still thinking of what to do next when Derek came back.

'How is it going Nathaniel, have you finished yet?'

'Well I have found no signs of any crates of pottery here so I will have to go back and report to Jonathan Adnitt. They seem to have vanished into thin air.'

***

Jonathan asked Nathaniel to sit down while he finished a letter and sent for two coffees. By the time they arrived, he had finished his letter. 'What can I do for you Nathaniel? I take it that it is to do with the missing goods?'

'It is. I have just come from Empire Warehouse and the stock control system is a shambles. Delivery notes seem to be accepted by anyone and the manager does not have a grip on who does what. There is no record of the missing goods in the warehouse and I am told that nothing has ever been accepted that should have been delivered to one or the other warehouses.'

'Well what is the problem then?

'I just don't believe it. Whoever accepted that delivery could not read or write as is evident on the delivery note. If that was the case, how would he have known to which warehouse it was supposed to go? If he did not know what it said on the note, then he would not have been able to fill in the stock sheet. He almost certainly would be aware that the delivery note should be placed in the tray in the manager's office. The note could have been sent on to Gerald assuming that it had already been entered on the stock sheets and if that is the case then all these crates could be sitting in Empire and no one the wiser.'

'So what are you are saying?'

'There are numerous delivery notes that have been signed with a cross but I did not see any that were destined elsewhere. Nevertheless, I would like a stock take at Empire Warehouse as soon as possible. It is the only way we are going to sort this out. Heaven knows what we are likely to find.'

'What about Thames Wharf, and Wapping warehouses, are you happy with them?'

'They seem alright to me, but we might have to go back to them if we find nothing at Empire.'

'I agree Nathaniel, I will get it organised but you will not be involved.'

'Thank you Jonathan. It will be interesting to see what turns up.'

'You seem to have settled in very well Nathaniel, do you miss the country life at all?'

'Not really, it does get a bit hectic in the city but I am getting used to it.'

'What about girlfriends, surely there is someone you miss? I bet a young man like you will have a girl friend or two in tow.'

'No, there is no one at the moment, so it is not a problem.'

'Well there are plenty of lovely young ladies in London so I expect you will find a companion before long.'

***

That night over dinner Andrew told Nathaniel he would be late in work tomorrow, 'I have been summoned to see the big man first thing in the morning so would you keep your eyes open for me till I get there?'

'Of course I will. Not due for a bollocking are you?'

'I don't think so but you never know. Probably they want me to give them an excuse to get rid of you. Is there anything you would like to put forward in mitigation before the axe falls?'

'I don't think so,' Nathaniel replied as they both laughed and continued their meal.

Andrew didn't turn up at the warehouse all day and Nathaniel suspected that he had been called away to help with a full stock take at Empire Warehouse. That night at dinner Andrew was tight lipped about where he had been but also informed Nathaniel that he would be away again in the morning but should be back by early afternoon. 'So it wasn't a bollocking then?' joked Nathaniel.

'No it was just another one of Jonathan's sudden experimental work projects, which are always top secret. You realise of course that I can say nothing at the moment. Maybe it will come out later, but not from me.'

'Enough said. Richard and Michael fancy a game of poker after dinner, are you up for it?'

'Of course.'

***

Andrew turned up at the warehouse in mid-afternoon and to Nathaniel's' surprise was quite talkative about why he had been away. 'I could do with a good cup of strong coffee and I suppose you are interested in where I have been then?' he said.

'I can't deny that I hadn't thought what the problem was, so what have you been doing?'

'Well, when I arrived at Jonathan's office, John Williams from the Wapping Warehouse was already there. We were ushered into Jonathan's chariot and he took us to the Empire Warehouse. On the way he told us that he thought there might be a problem and we were to carry out a thorough stock check. There was no sign of Derek all the time we were there so we didn't know what had happened. You know Jonathan well enough, he plays things close to his chest.'

'Go on, tell me more. What did you find?'

'For a start, we found that load of crates that should have been at Wapping you were looking for yesterday.'

'Who told you about that? I didn't.'

'John Williams did, you checked his place out before you went to Empire. Everyone said you were sniffing round looking for missing goods.'

'Did you find anything else?'

'We did, the whole place was out of control. We found goods that we thought had been stolen in the past that should have been at one or other of the warehouses. The whole stock control system was in such a mess that we had to rewrite most of it.'

'If Derek isn't there, who is in charge now?'

'I have no idea, I expect they will be putting a supervisor in charge until they find a suitable replacement, assuming they will give Derek the push – if they haven't already.'

'What did Jonathan say when you told him?'

'He blew his top and told John and myself to be at his office first thing tomorrow when he had thought things through.'

'Well he has cleared up the missing goods problem so he should be pleased about that.'

'Yes, but there are still a lot of items that seem to be missing so it looks as if we still have problems to sort out.'

***

John and Andrew met at Jonathan's office and Gerald was already there.

'Thank you gentlemen for the hard work you have put in over the last couple of days, it is much appreciated. As you may have already guessed, Derek is no longer with us and we have a vacancy which needs to be filled

185

rather urgently. In addition to that, we need to assess our procedures to ensure this never happens again.'

'I agree that the procedures may need some tightening in places, but they are working satisfactorily in John's warehouse and in mine.' said Andrew.

'You are right Andrew, but let's look at what has happened at Empire and see if, and where we could improve things,' replied Jonathan.

After some discussion, occasionally somewhat heated, agreement was reached on what should be done to improve formal systems, most of which was already being done in two of the warehouses. 'That's very interesting,' said Jonathan, 'you must have been a very good teacher Andrew, or Nathaniel is a good student. In his notes regarding his investigation into the losses, he has arrived at virtually identical ways of controlling stock as we have. How is he getting on with the jobs you have allocated to him, Andrew?'

'He is shaping up very well, and is proving to be both keen and quick to learn. He gets on well with everyone and will help out with anything you throw at him. He has been a great help to me and I will miss him when he moves on.'

'Well that's a glowing report if ever I heard one. Are you thinking what I am thinking Gerald?'

'Quite probably Jonathan. A possible stop gap at Empire?'

'What do you think Andrew, is he up to it yet?'

'As far as I know there is no one else available half as good as he is. We would probably have to keep tabs on him for a while but I can't see any insurmountable problems. John and I could help out if needed.'

'It would give us breathing space to enable us to get someone permanent. Nathaniel will be with us for another three to four months so he would fit in nicely. What is your view John, could he do it?'

'I have only seen him working very briefly Jonathan, but I was extremely impressed with his knowledge and investigative skills. I am sure he is as good as we will get at short notice and as a stop gap he would be perfect.'

'That's it then, we all seem to be in agreement so I will see him first thing tomorrow. Gerald, would you ask him to be in my office first thing and I don't want him finding out before I see him. Understood?'

They all nodded their understanding, they knew what would happen if word got out!

That evening over dinner, Nathaniel tried to find out what had been said at the meeting but Andrew and Gerald were having none of it. 'Gerald has already told you that Jonathan wants to see you in the morning and that is all you need to know. You are fully aware that when Jonathan instructs you to stay quiet, then you stay quiet, so let that be that.'

Chapter 14

'Do you fancy a ride out to the country on Saturday, Nathaniel?' asked Gerald. 'My horse could do with some exercise and I could do with some company.'

'I would love to. I haven't been out for a few weeks and my horse was always used every day before I came to London.'

'Why don't we all go? We could make a day of it.'

'I have a couple of new pistols that could do with testing so we could all have a go if we can find somewhere quiet,' said Richard. 'I need to see how they handle and it would be interesting to see what you chaps think. You said you wanted a pair of pistols, Nathaniel so you can try them out and if you like them you can have them at a bargain price.'

By the time they had made their plans for the weekend, Nathaniel had forgotten all about today's events and his forthcoming meeting with Jonathan.

***

That evening, Jonathan had a brief meeting with Sir Samuel to inform him of events and report on Nathaniel's general progress. He also mentioned that Nathaniel did not have a girlfriend back at Borton.

'That's good,' said Sir Samuel. 'At least we don't have to worry about him wanting to rush off home every weekend. Come to think of it, he has never ever mentioned a girl to me, do you think he has ever been with one?'

'I very much doubt it. He will know all about animals and their behaviour but I suspect he is innocent as regards women.'

'Well I think we should educate him before it's too late. Have you any suggestions Jonathan?'

'That young gunsmith, Richard Pearson, who lives at the apartments, will know plenty of young ladies who are willing to provide a service. I am sure he could fix something for us.'

'Good, then will you have a quiet word with him and see what he suggests. Remember, Nathaniel must not get any hint of what we are proposing and I suggest we get it over with fairly soon.'

'I will have a word with Richard Pearson in the morning and of course make sure nothing gets to Nathaniel.'

***

Nathaniel was up bright and early to ensure he was on time for his meeting with Jonathan, being fully aware of what would happen if he was late. They arrived at the same time as each other and Jonathan ushered Nathaniel into the office and told him to sit down and he would be back in five minutes.

'He seems in a reasonably good mood so I can't have done much wrong,' he thought, 'so what can he want me to do now?'

'Thank you for your efforts earlier, as you will know by now, things have changed rapidly in the last two days.'

'I am afraid I don't know what has gone on at all in the last couple of days, not since I heard that Derek had gone.'

'You mean Andrew and Gerald haven't told you about yesterday's meeting?'

'No, they said it was more than their jobs worth and promptly changed the subject.'

'That's very interesting, so you have absolutely no idea why you are here?'

'None at all unless you want more done on the operating systems.'

'Well I think I had better start at the beginning and tell you where we are and why you could be involved. You identified that the systems as operated at Empire are an absolute shambles and this was backed up by Andrew and John. The systems themselves are running satisfactorily in Wapping and Thames Wharf so it has been agreed that with a few minor changes they will stay. However, things were found to be far worse than you thought, so bad that we had to let Derek go. There was no evidence that Derek was involved in any fraud or theft, it was just that he didn't possess the skills to manage the job. A new manager has to be appointed as soon as possible but we expect that to take some time. The work has to carry on, and rather than expecting Andrew and John to cover, it would be sensible to appoint a suitable temporary manager and we were unanimous that the right person for the job is you. How do you feel about that, do you think you could cope?'

'Gosh, that's a surprise! I am sure I could manage if Andrew and John were willing to back me up if I ever need help.'

'They have already agreed to that and it was their idea that you should get the job. They are both very impressed by your hard work and ability to learn quickly. Sir Samuel is happy with our choice and is delighted with your work so far. He will, no doubt, want a word with you before long.'

'Thank you Jonathan, I am thrilled to be chosen for the job and I will do my very best to make a success of it.'

'Well, before you get too excited, there is still a problem with missing goods at Empire and so that will be an area where we would like you to get a grip. Andrew and John have produced an up to date list of stock and, as it is such a big task, they have volunteered to help you to bring the records up to date. They will be at Empire this afternoon to make a start. Meanwhile, I suggest you get over there now and put everyone in the picture. It's up to you how you do it, but I suggest you make sure that they know that you are in charge and you will stand no nonsense.'

'I will, don't worry.'

'Good luck Nathaniel, get the basics right now and then you can start to sort out any rotten eggs later.'

***

On the Sunday morning after Sir Samuel and Jonathan's discussion regarding his love life, Nathaniel came down for his breakfast to be greeted with cheers and whistles from his fellow residents.

'Had a good night Nathaniel?'

'Did you get any sleep?'

'Did you learn anything?' were a few of the comments accompanied by raucous laughter and stamping of feet, but when one of the wags shouted, 'First time is always the best!'

Nathaniel held up his hand, called for quiet and said, 'It was a very nice experience thank you, but as for the first time, you must be joking. What do you think I did in Naples during those long Summer evenings, sit on my arse? I would also like to thank you all for your generosity and in particular whoever paid the bill. Finally I would like to tell you it was a lovely surprise and that she was good value for money, but she wasn't really my type!'

***

Once Andrew and John had helped sort out the stock sheets, Nathaniel had a chance to sort out his warehouse staff and find out what they could do. He had ten men working in the warehouse and four wagon drivers. The wagon drivers were also responsible for the nine horses which were stabled in the untidy, cluttered yard behind the warehouse. There were also a variety of carts and wagons which were used for different loads. A large delivery would require the largest wagon which would be pulled by a team of three horses and smaller loads used an appropriate cart. The yard was enclosed by a large rickety wooden gate which Jack, the garrulous, opinionated senior wagon driver, informed Nathaniel, was shut and bolted securely when the warehouse was closed or when a wagon was in the yard, loaded and ready for an early morning delivery.

'Why don't I believe him?' thought Nathaniel, 'I don't believe anyone could make that gate secure in its present state and any low life could be in and out of here with whatever he wanted and no one would be any the wiser. That's going on my list for further investigation.'

Of the ten warehousemen, only Thomas the supervisor, could read and write but Nathaniel soon identified that even Thomas had no clue as to what a stock control system was. 'I always took the papers to Mr. Jones and he dealt with them.' was his explanation.

'Who signs for the goods when they arrive in the warehouse, Thomas?'

'That's the person who unloads the goods, sometimes me, other times a warehouseman.'

'Even if they can't read or write?'

189

'They all have their own mark so we knew who has unloaded each wagon.'

'Can they count?'

'Yes, some of them can.'

'Alright Thomas, I think that will be all for now. Thank you for your help.'

As Thomas went on his way, Nathaniel muttered to himself, 'This is going to be a very long job, probably longer than I have got.'

One of the agreed alterations to the paper work was to insist that the supplier, in addition to putting the warehouse name on the delivery note, would include the relevant warehouse number. This had to be large enough to be seen instantly so that any warehouseman would be able to see it had arrived at the correct place. Empire was designated number "2" and Nathaniel, after much coaching made sure his entire workforce could recognise a number two, he had even painted a large '2' near the warehouse door so that if in doubt, they could check. They were instructed to check with Nathaniel or Thomas if there was any doubt and not to unload until they were absolutely certain the goods were at the correct warehouse. Once the system had been running for a few weeks and all the suppliers had got the message, it settled down and seemed to be working satisfactorily

Just as Nathaniel thought everything was under control, he was carrying spot checks on goods against the stock sheets and found a discrepancy of four crates of domestic crockery. The stock sheets had indicated there were one hundred crates in the warehouse two days ago and an order for sixty crates was dispatched yesterday. Nathaniel's quick check only found only thirty-six crates in stock. The order had been loaded onto two wagons and delivered to the docks, and the papers, when checked, showed that thirty crates were loaded on each wagon and thirty crates were loaded from each into the hold of the boat.

Nathaniel interviewed everyone involved and they all indicated that what was recorded was accurate. The wagons were loaded in the morning so there was no question of the goods disappearing overnight from the still insecure back yard. The only hint of anything untoward was that when Edmund, the second wagoner was interviewed, he said it was a bit odd that when they delivered to the docks, 'Jack always set off first and nearly every time, he arrives after me.'

'Does he ever say where he has been?' asked Nathaniel.

'Usually he says that he got held up in traffic or some other problem.'

'Seems a bit strange.'

'Yes but he always unloads the right amount onto the boat. He is probably stopping off for a drink or a chat.' said Edmund.

Nathaniel reacted as if he was not interested if that was all that happened, and just said, 'Thanks Edmund, it looks as if the stock sheets might have been wrong,' and as Edmund went back to his work, Nathaniel said quietly to himself, 'There is more to this than meets the eye, I am not letting this one go. I think someone is having a laugh.'

Nathaniel discussed the problem with Andrew over dinner back at the apartments that evening. 'I am convinced I counted those crates correctly and that four of them were stolen at some stage, but at the moment I have no idea where or when.'

'You have no clues at all then?' asked Andrew.

'No, the only slightly puzzling thing is that Jack, although he always sets off first is always the last to get there.'

'Well he probably stops off to see a girlfriend or some other simple reason.'

'Probably so, but why only when he is taking a load to the docks?'

'I don't know, but I think you had better keep a close eye on it. If you need any help give me a shout.'

***

The next time Nathaniel received an order which had to be delivered to the docks, he resolved to watch things more closely. The day before the delivery was due, he stayed behind after all the warehousemen had finished for the night on the pretext that he had a pile of paperwork to sort out. When it was quiet and he was on his own he did a thorough check of all the crates available for that specific order and found there were seventy-two. The order for the delivery to the docks was for sixty, all for the same boat.

Next day the goods were loaded onto two wagons again and Jack's wagon left the warehouse before Edmund had completed loading. Nathaniel informed Thomas that he was going to see Jonathan but would be back in the early afternoon, and set off to the docks to see if Jack was first to get there. When he arrived, he settled down for what he thought might be a long stay at a table in a dockside inn. As he relaxed with his ale he could clearly see the approach to the docks through the nearby window. Whoever turned up first would not matter as he had no intention of letting anyone know what was going on at this stage.

The road to the dock was extremely busy and he thought he might have difficulty recognising his wagons amid the teeming throng, but eventually he thought he caught a glimpse of one of his wagons and as it came nearer he could see it was Edmund. 'That's it for now,' he said. He drank the remains of his ale and left the inn making sure that he had not been seen. 'It's time for another stock check.'

The stock take did not take long and only nine crates were found. 'Three

191

missing,' he said to himself, 'don't panic Nathaniel, we are one step nearer a solution.'

***

'Do you think I should tell Jonathan first, Andrew or should I deal with it and tell him later?'

'Definitely tell him first. If things go wrong and he was not aware of what is going on, you could be in big trouble. Remember you are only here to learn and although you are doing a staff job, it is only temporary.'

'Thanks, I will try to see him tomorrow then.'

'Well make sure you have all the facts gathered for him to see and have a plan to present to him or he will only ask you to go away and prepare one.'

***

'Come in Nathaniel, take a seat and I will be with you in a couple of minutes.' Jonathan continued perusing some papers and soon tidied them up neatly. 'Sorry about that, what can I do for you this morning?'

Nathaniel explained the events of the last few days and his suspicions of who was taking the goods but as he was going to explain his plans to catch the thieves, Jonathan banged his fist on the table and exclaimed, 'Why the hell haven't you challenged them and given them the push? They will only do it again.'

'I have thought of that but I wanted you to consider the options that are available to me. The first is that I should stop the wagon in question as soon as it leaves the warehouse and check its load. This will only prove successful if they are loaded with the wrong amount of goods. I think it could prove a problem if they are not stealing on that particular trip it would only warn them of our suspicions. We want to catch them and get them out of our warehouse not just let them know we are watching them.'

'That's a good point what's your other option?'

'It's not just the wagon crew that is involved, someone in the warehouse must also be complicit when they load goods. What I suggest is that when we think it is going to happen again we get someone to follow them. Andrew is happy to do it and he is not likely to be recognised if he happens to be seen. We will need someone else to go with him as a witness. With a bit of luck we will catch the crooks, both our employees and the recipients and we will set an example to the workforce in general.'

'What happens if the wagon only stops for ale at their local inn?'

'Nothing is lost, they won't know they have been followed, so we keep our powder dry for another occasion.'

'I think you are right Nathaniel. We have lost a great deal of money through loss of goods over the last couple of years and we must put a stop to it. What we need is good hard evidence before we do anything drastic so I am

192

happy that you go ahead with your second option, but make sure you keep me informed.'

Nearly two weeks later a load of crates of kitchen utensils were due to be delivered to the docks and Nathaniel briefed Andrew and John, the managers of the other two warehouses who had volunteered to follow Jack's wagon. They were to see where it stopped and identify if goods were being offloaded somewhere on the route. Nathaniel carried out a stock take as before and found forty-five crates.

The next morning, Andrew and John were in place and ready to follow the wagon which should be carrying the order for thirty crates. Nathaniel tried to keep an eye on the loading of the wagon, but of course, had to be careful not make it obvious, nor could he stay watching all the time. He did, however note that there was only one warehouseman, Ben, assisting the two wagoners. Ben was a strong and able lad who would always do what he was told. Unfortunately, he was not the brightest pebble on the beach and was unable to read or write.

About half an hour later, Nathaniel saw Ben heading out to the back yard, 'What are you doing out here Ben?' Nathaniel asked

'Jack asked me to fetch a spare rein for the wagon, he says the main one looks a bit worn.'

'I see, have you finished loading then?'

'Not quite, Sir, but Jack says he can manage. They usually can, because I often have to fetch something for him before they set off.'

'Right Ben, you had better get on with it then.'

'So that's it then,' thought Nathaniel. 'Slip a few crates on when Ben's not there. Easy isn't it, and they don't have to share the proceeds with anyone in the warehouse.' As Ben went to search around the yard to find the reins, Nathaniel decided to see what Jack was up to. When he arrived at the loading bay, Jack and his mate were just putting the ropes on to secure the load. 'How is it going Jack, are you nearly ready to go?'

'Yes boss, we are just waiting for Ben to come back and then we are away.'

Nathaniel desperately wanted to check the wagon there and then, but he resisted the temptation. He wasn't changing the plan at the last minute, and anyway, Andrew and John were waiting somewhere outside ready to carry out their side of the plan, so he said, 'Well mind how you go, and don't forget to get the papers signed before you come back.'

As soon as the wagon had gone, Nathaniel called Ben over and told him that he needed to count the remaining stock. 'Why do you want to know boss?' enquired Ben.

'Because we have another order and I want to check that we have enough ready to send straight away today or wait until we get some more in.'

'Oh, I see.'

'Well Ben, I have counted twelve crates, are there any more hidden away?'

'No boss. That's the lot.'

'It looks as if I need to order some more then. Ben, could you get this lot tidied up for me and give the whole area a good sweep up, it's beginning to look a bit of a mess.'

Nathaniel was biting his nails for a couple of hours in anticipation of what Andrew and John had found out. He hoped things had gone as expected but there was no guarantee that he was correct in his assumptions and maybe, just maybe there was an innocent explanation for what had been going on.

By mid-afternoon, he was worried sick that he had heard nothing, when the wagon pulled into the yard and the driver, who Nathaniel did not recognise, asked to see Mr. Nathaniel Thorold.

'Good afternoon Sir, compliments of Mr. Andrew Lawson, I have returned your wagon and three crates. Thirty crates have been delivered to the docks and here is the receipt.'

'Thanks very much, but who are you and did Mr. Lawson send a message?'

'I am James, Mr. Lawson's warehouse supervisor. Mr. Lawson said to tell you, all is well and Mr. Adnitt is now in charge of proceedings. Mr. Lawson will call in to see you on his way home if he has time, if not he will see you tonight.'

'Thank you James, if you would just secure the horses, I will get someone to put the crates back into stock and stable the horses.'

***

When Andrew arrived back at the apartments, he immediately went to see Nathaniel and gave him a long account of the day's happenings.

'We followed the wagon for a good half hour in a direction away from the docks and it eventually entered a narrow alley where we had difficulty seeing what was going on. We took one of my lads with us to act as a runner because we thought we might need one, particularly as Jonathan had said he wanted to be in on any arrest. Luckily he arrived in time to apprehend Jack and his accomplice and a couple of dubious characters who were set to take the goods.'

'I didn't realise that Jonathan was involved in the plans. Why did he want to be there?'

'Obviously you don't know, Jonathan is a magistrate and although he won't be able to sit in judgement on this case, he will make sure one of his mates does.'

'No I didn't, but I know I wouldn't want to be in their shoes once Jonathan starts to pull the strings. Did they try to get out of it?'

'I was surprised that they didn't, considering initially there was only two of us but I think they were so surprised that the shock must have dulled their reactions. By the time they realised what was going on, Jonathan was there with his gang of men and all thoughts of resistance faded away.'

'What happened next?'

'It was quite funny really, Jonathan had them all tied with twine around their wrists and then a rope was used to tie them all together. Jonathan, in all his finery, led the group through the watching crowds, brandishing his walking cane and shouting, 'Clear the way, magistrate with prisoners coming through.' or some such slogan. It was very effective, the crowd opened up just like the 'parting of the waters' in the bible.'

'I wish I could have seen it.'

'You can always go to the hanging, there is bound to be a big crowd to see four hangings at the same time. By the way, Jonathan wants to see you in the morning. I am sure you are not in for a bollocking. Far from it, he was jubilant.'

***

When Nathaniel called in to see Jonathan, he was surprised to see Sir Samuel sitting in Jonathan's chair and Jonathan sitting on one of the two chairs usually used by visitors. 'Sit down Nathaniel,' said Sir Samuel pointing to the one vacant chair, 'I was delighted to hear the result of yesterday's little exercise. It seems that we have taken an important step in eliminating our biggest problem, and I am delighted to say that your work has proved to be crucial in apprehending the miscreants. Do you think we have caught them all?'

'Yes I think so, I thought there might be an accomplice in the warehouse but they seem to have taken advantage of the fact that poor old Ben is not the brightest of human beings. He is always willing to help anyone and do as he is told, but I am absolutely certain that he hasn't a clue that he was being used. I am also sure that if he was in on it, he will soon say or do something and give himself away.'

'I agree with Nathaniel, I have known Ben for a good few years and basically, he is a good, solid, reliable worker, but he hasn't the brains to be in on a scheme like this and then keep quiet about it. So Sir Samuel, I think we have managed to sort things out for the time being.'

'I am pleased to hear it. Now Nathaniel, how do you like being in charge of a big warehouse? It certainly looks as if you have things moving in the right direction.'

'I am getting there slowly I think. It was certainly daunting at first but systems are now working smoothly and most of the staff are happy and cooperative. The stock checking is certainly proving to be of value as evidenced by yesterday's results.'

'We are aware that you are there as a temporary stop gap and we are actively searching for a permanent manager. Jonathan thinks it is possible that he may have identified someone who is bright enough to do the job but would need intensive training on our systems. Would you be willing to train someone if it should prove necessary?'

'Yes, of course I would,' was Nathaniel's immediate response, 'but I would like to be back in Borton for the harvest.'

'That will not be a problem, I am sure Jonathan will have someone very soon.'

'No problem at all,' confirmed Jonathan.

'Well that's about all for today then. Well done Nathaniel you had better get back to Empire and explain to everyone what has happened. They probably know already but they will want to hear it from the horse's mouth.'

***

After the excitement of the sacking of the manager and the subsequent public hangings of the thieves and their associates, life at the Empire was very much routine. A new trainee manager was recruited and brought up to the required company standard by Nathaniel, with the aid of Andrew and John but life was beginning to seem repetitive and mundane.

Social life in London suited Nathaniel and he had become firm friends with Richard Pearson, the young gunmaker who lived in the apartments. Richard loved his games of poker and after playing a few games in the evenings at the apartments, it didn't take much effort to persuade Nathaniel to go with him to one or two of the games played at various venues around the town. By the time Nathaniel had sorted out the problems at Empire warehouse, he was playing regularly and as a result was accumulating debts which were beginning to cause him problems. This came to a head when Nathaniel wrote to Ephraim asking for his allowance to be increased to cover what he described as, 'the excessive cost of living in London.'

Ephraim of course, before making a decision, contacted Sir Samuel to clarify the position. When he received the reply, he was outraged to find that not only was Nathaniel getting an adequate allowance, but was also being paid by Sir Samuel for his job as a manager. Sir Samuel had also said, 'Please do not reply to Nathaniel's letter, I think we should let him stew for a couple of weeks and then I will sort him out myself. There are strong rumours that he is gambling again, a problem which his father had identified some time ago. If this is true, I will see Nathaniel personally and explain in clear language, which he will certainly understand, that this sort of behaviour is not acceptable in this organisation and we will not put up with it.' After Ephraim had cooled down a little, he passed Sir Samuel's letter to Joseph and George and asked what they thought they should do.

196

'Nothing,' said Joseph, 'you certainly should not send any money and nor should you respond to Nathaniel's request. Sir Samuel is in constant contact with Nathaniel and I am sure a good talking to from him will have far more effect than a letter from the three of us.'

'I agree,' said George, 'we can't control him from here and I am sure Sir Samuel will keep us fully informed of any action he takes.'

'It's so bloody annoying, did Nathaniel think we would send him funds without checking what was going on? I think he is trying to pull a fast one.'

'Calm down Ephraim, there is nothing we can do about it. Just be thankful someone else can save us all the trouble and do it for us. All we have to do is wait for Sir Samuel's letter, and if he wants us to take action on anything, we will consider it when the time comes,' was Joseph's calm response. 'You are right Joseph, it's stupid of me getting all wound up and upsetting myself, but does he think we were born yesterday?'

George interrupted Ephraim as he was about to start on another rant about Nathaniel and said, 'I don't know about you two but I am ready for something to eat. Shall we get off to *"The Angel"* before the mid-day rush begins?'

'I could do with a drink as well,' said Joseph, 'We could die of thirst if we stayed here much longer.'

***

'Jonathan, are we sure that Nathaniel's financial problems are being caused by gambling, or is he spending extravagantly on other things? Have you heard any rumours from the apartments or is he just trying it on with Woolaston?'

'Well I know that he is very close to Richard Pearson, one of the residents at the apartments and spends most of his free time with him. I am also aware that Richard likes his games of poker. Other than that, I am not certain what goes on, but it is certainly possible that Nathaniel is involved in the gambling'

'It is a problem with Nathaniel that cousin John identified some time ago, but we all thought it was just a passing phase and he had moved on. Let's hope he hasn't become involved again. This Richard, where does he work?'

'As far as I know he is still a gunmaker's apprentice at Knott's in the Minories, however he must be near the end of his training by now and may have already been approved as a journeyman gunmaker. I can certainly find out.'

'Don't bother, I know old Thomas Knott, I will have a word with him when I see him next week. When I have had a chat with him, we will see what Nathaniel has to say. If he *is* gambling heavily, we need to put a stop to it as soon as possible.'

'Well it would be such a shame if he gets involved with some of the gambling mobs around here, he could easily find himself in deep trouble.'

'He could, but this is just what his father was worried about. Could you make a few discreet enquiries among the residents of the apartments over the next few days, you never know, you might turn up a few snippets of useful information.'

***

'Well Jonathan, I have had a long chat with Thomas Knott and our young Pearson has quite a reputation. Richard was registered as a Master Gunmaker by the Worshipful Company of Gunmakers of London early last year. However, although he has a very successful business, it is not without its problems. His initial application for membership was rejected because he had submitted a proofpiece which, as the judging panel pointed out, the barrel had the mark of another maker on it. He was told to submit another piece of his own making and did so successfully later in the year.

A few months ago, Richard was in trouble again when the Gunmakers Company seized 59 pistol barrels which had been filed down after proof. A serious act which was potentially dangerous for anyone using them.'

***

Nathaniel was becoming increasingly worried about not having had a reply from Ephraim, when, as he was eating his lunch, he received a message from Sir Samuel requesting him to be at his office at six o'clock after finishing work for the day. 'Why should he want to see me in such a hurry?' thought Nathaniel. 'I have still got a couple of months to do and they all seem satisfied with my work.' He continued to think of what he could have done wrong and then suddenly thought that it was possible that he was going to be given another problem area to be sorted out. Such was his change of attitude that when he knocked on Sir Samuel's door he was in a bright, positive and enthusiastic frame of mind.

'Sit down Nathaniel, would you tell Jonathan and myself why you are pleading with Mr. Woolaston for more money?'

Nathaniel felt a gut wrenching pain in his stomach as the question sunk in. It was totally unexpected and hit him like a haymaker to the forehead. It scrambled his brain and his thought processes turned to a jumbled mass of soup.

'Well, do you have an answer?' barked Jonathan.

'I… er… em. well,' was all he could get out as he struggled to regain his composure.

'Come on then, let's have the truth. Spit it out lad!'

'Yes, and no excuses, we want to know why you need more money and we want to know *now*,' said Sir Samuel, emphasising the 'now' with a heavy thump on his desk, which jolted a quill from its stand.

Nathaniel's mind gradually worked its way up to speed and realised that these two experienced men probably already knew everything that they were asking to be told. This being the case he decided to tell the truth and get it all out at once rather than trying to lie his way out.

'I am afraid I have been gambling at poker over the last few weeks and have managed to build up a considerable debt. This debt is due to be paid off by the end of the month and I do not have the wherewithal to repay it without an increase in my allowance. I thought I would eventually have a good win and be able to repay quickly, but I lost more times than I won and now owe even more. I am now in the desperate situation I have just explained to you.'

'I believe your late father talked to you about gambling and its associated problems,' said Jonathan in a soft, calm voice.

'Yes he did tell me what could happen.'

'Well, why the bloody hell didn't you take any notice? You come here with pathetic, pitiful excuses but not one shred of regret for your behaviour. Where the hell do you think you will get the money from? Isn't your wage and your allowance enough?'

'Jonathan, I think we should have a word in private,' interrupted Sir Samuel. 'Would you go and wait in the main office Nathaniel, I think we may be some time before we call you back in.'

When Nathaniel closed the door behind him, Sir Samuel said, 'This is quite serious Jonathan, if we don't do something to get him back on track, he will go back to Borton and fritter all his money away with this silly, stupid behaviour. What do you suggest we do?'

'Well, we had planned to pull him out of the warehouse to work with Gerald Pickworth in your office for his last month or so.'

'Well why would he regard that as a punishment?'

'For a start, he doesn't know that we have planned to move him so he will see it as a demotion and if we stopped his wage, he would certainly see it as a punishment.'

'Now you are talking, Jonathan, what about his debt? Should we help him at all?'

'Well, we could pay it off for him, but if we do, we would, of course, want repaying.'

'That sounds fair to me. He will have to pay it back out of his allowance before he finishes his stay in London. He will certainly regard it as a punishment if we do that, won't he?'

'He will, and we will be in control, not some lowlife crook from a gambling den.'

'Alright, the only thing we need to do is send a message to Woolaston informing him what we have done and advising him not to increase Nathaniel's allowance until after he is back at Borton.'

'I will do that in the morning, shall I call him in now?'

'I think we should have a sherry first, don't you?' asked Sir Samuel as he got up from his chair and went over to the cabinet under the window. 'He can wait until we are ready can't he?'

**

All the staff in the outer office had left nearly an hour ago and Nathaniel sat on his own in a state of utter despair, overwhelmed by a feeling of hopelessness as he waited to be called back to learn his fate. He had been waiting for what felt like a lifetime when he heard Jonathan call from Sir Samuel's office, 'Nathaniel, you can come in now.'

Nathaniel walked slowly into the office and sat down on the chair he had vacated a couple of hours previously. His whole body was trembling in fear of what he was about to be told, he really thought he was going to be sent home in disgrace and vowed to himself, if he survived this mess then he would never, ever play poker again.

After what seemed a long silence, Sir Samuel spoke.

'Nathaniel, we are both deeply distressed by your recent behaviour. After a promising start and some extremely valuable contributions to the profitability of the company, that you should behave in such a way as to get yourself into debt, by of all things, gambling at cards, is deeply offensive to me. We have thought long and hard about what we should do and have made our decision. If you do not accept what Jonathan is going to tell you, then you will leave this office and our apartments tonight and we will not see each other again. The decision will be yours. Do you understand?'

'Yes, Sir Samuel,' was Nathaniel's muted reply.

'Alright Jonathan, please explain our decision.'

'Listen to me very carefully Nathaniel, I want you to understand what I am saying and if you need clarification please ask.' Nathaniel nodded his understanding and Jonathan carried on, 'First, tomorrow morning you will start work in Sir Samuel's office under the supervision of Gerald Pickworth. You will no longer be in charge of Empire Warehouse and you will no longer receive the wage for that post. With regard to your gambling debt, the company will take care of that and you will pay back an agreed weekly amount to ensure we have been repaid by the time you leave here. This, of course, will have to be paid out of your allowance which we can assure you will not be increased whilst you are with us. You will also be required to make a solemn vow never to play poker again for the remainder of your stay here. Do you understand what has been said and are you willing to accept the conditions attached to this agreement?'

With obvious relief in his voice Nathaniel responded, 'Yes, I agree to everything you have said and I am truly thankful for your understanding in

200

the matter.'

'Good, we will draw up a legal document covering what has been agreed and you will be required to sign it in when it has been drafted. You may go now.'

***

When Nathaniel arrived back at the lodgings, he went straight to his apartment, threw himself on his bed, and for a while, reverted to the old Nathaniel, cursing and blaming everyone but himself for his present predicament. Eventually, when he had considered the alternatives, he came round to the view that he had just had a very lucky escape. Yes, he was going to find it difficult with a lot less money at his disposal and he would have to be very careful with his spending over the next couple of months. The difficult part was the stipulation that there was to be no more poker, at least while he was in London. 'I am sure I would have won it all back given the chance,' was his stubborn view. 'If that old bastard, Woolaston had increased my allowance, and kept his mouth shut, I would have sorted it out.'

Nathaniel had arrived back too late for dinner and had gone directly to his apartment and as he was still mulling over events of the day, there was knock on the door and a voice called out, 'Is there a problem Mr. Thorold?'

'Come in Bernard, no I am alright.'

'I noticed you missed your meal tonight, Mr. Thorold. I kept something back in case you were working late, or did you eat out?'

'That's very kind of you Bernard, I will be down in ten minutes if that is alright.'

'Of course it is. See you in ten minutes then.'

Nathaniel was pleased that he did not see any of his fellow residents while he ate his meal and went back to his room immediately he had finished. The last thing he wanted was a question and answer session which he could well do without. He was still trying to work out how to break the news to his poker playing partner, Richard. It was pointless going to Richard's room, because he would almost certainly be out gambling in some dingy, smoke filled room.

***

Nathaniel was sorely tempted several times over his final two months in London, but he managed to stay away from the gambling set, mainly by avoiding Richard as much as possible. He spent much of his spare time riding out into the countryside with his friend Andrew. As the days stayed lighter for longer, they managed to venture further from the city and at weekends they would occasionally stay overnight at a convenient inn.

201

He found his work with Gerald, far from being a punishment, as he initially thought it was, turned out to be the most useful part of his stay with Sir Samuel. He was involved quite extensively with business dealings involving a whole range of influential people and he accompanied Sir Samuel to some very high level meetings.

Jonathan, Sir Samuel's direct, forceful and outspoken right hand man proved to be a mine of useful information on the managing of a business and was always willing to give advice when needed. By the end of his stay, Nathaniel had developed a lasting, friendly relationship with two of the most influential businessmen in the city and knew that he could always rely on them for an honest answer for any problems he might encounter in the future. His final week in London was hectic, both within the business and socially. He made the rounds of all the suppliers and customers that he had dealt with over the last few months, promising to keep in touch with them all. His fellow residents gave him a rousing send off with a special farewell dinner and he presented Bernard and Mrs. Smith with a small token of his appreciation for their services.

Whilst assisting Andrew at Thames Wharf, he saw the "*Juliet Star*" was tied up to the dockside so he went and asked if James Briggs was still in charge. 'Yes Mr. Thorold, he is. Shall I tell him you would like to see him?'

'Yes please, I would. How do you know my name? I don't recognise you.'

'I helped to clean up your companion after that rough passage through the channel.'

'So you did, I remember now, and I don't think my friend will ever forget.'

James welcomed Nathaniel with a massive hug and insisted he stay for his evening meal. 'We must have a long chat and a few drinks to remember your time on board.'

The next day was Nathaniel's last in London and Sir Samuel had insisted that Nathaniel came round for dinner. 'Mary will be terribly disappointed if you don't come. I will send my chariot to collect you at six-thirty, so no excuses please. I have already arranged for a cart to take your heavy trunks to Borton.'

'That's very kind of you Sir Samuel, It will be honour to join you.'

***

Nathaniel's final evening was extremely enjoyable and relaxing. Sir Samuel heaped praise on the work he had done for the company in the short space of time he had worked there, while Lady Mary quizzed Nathaniel about life on a farm in rural Lincolnshire. 'I have always enjoyed my visits there and I think it is delightful, but I am afraid it is much too quiet for me. I like the social life of London.'

202

'Yes, I understand what you say, but I find London very noisy and extremely smelly and I can't wait to get home. I suppose it is what you get used to over the years.'

'I am sure it is. Do you have a lady friend tucked away up there Nathaniel?'

'Now Mary, don't embarrass the young man,' and turning to Nathaniel, 'When do you take over from the trustees? Do you have long to wait?'

'I am still only twenty and I have to wait until I am twenty-five. It seems such a long way off.'

'Don't worry, it will pass quickly and if you get yourself involved and prove to them that you are capable, as I know you are, the trustees will sit back and let you get on with it.'

'Thank you Sir, I will certainly do my best.'

Chapter 15
July 1724 – 1728

Nathaniel was up bright and early the next morning but before he had time to dress, Bernard knocked on the door. 'There is a cart outside asking for your heavy luggage Mr Thorold.'

'Thank you Bernard, would you ask them to come up to collect it. It is all over there in the corner. I hope there are two of them, it is very bulky.'

Heavy footsteps on the stairs, then a short rap on the door announced the arrival of the two carters sent by Sir Samuel. Nathaniel called them in and said, 'I remember you two, its James and John isn't it? Didn't you deliver my luggage the last time I was down here?'

'Yes sir, we did.'

'Good, so you will know the way to Borton then. The trunks and all the luggage are over there.' he said, pointing to the corner. 'Make sure you don't take that bag over by the window. I will be taking that.'

By the time Nathaniel had dressed, James was at the door saying that they were ready to go, so after a quick check, the cart set off. 'Go carefully, James. I expect I will catch up with you before the day is out.'

As they set off, Nathaniel noticed that the cart was brand new. It was painted a bright glossy black with the sign, *Thorold of London,* highlighted in red letters, outlined in gold on both the side and rear panels. 'Very impressive,' he thought. 'That's a good bit of advertising, even though ninety per cent of the population can't read.'

After breakfast and having said his final farewells, Nathaniel gathered his few remaining belongings and was ready when his horse was brought round to the apartments at nine-thirty as arranged.

***

After a couple of days back at Borton, things had settled back to normal. Sylvia calmed down after her usual over-emotional welcome home. Work around the farm was gearing up for the annual harvest, tools and implements were checked and sharpened. Nothing seemed to have altered much during Nathaniel's brief absence and no outstanding events had been reported.

The cart had arrived late in the evening the day after Nathaniel, and James and John said that they had not encountered any trouble. The weather had been kind but they were feeling very tired and hungry. George Headland sorted out their horses and after a good meal, they both bedded down for the night in the loft above the stables.

***

Nathaniel thought it was about time he went to check things out with

Ephraim or he would soon be getting a nasty letter from him. He decided to go the next morning without making an appointment and trusting to luck that Ephraim would see him. He had plenty of other business to attend to anyway, so he would not be wasting his time even if Ephraim was unavailable.

It was a lovely summer morning with a clear, pale blue sky and the occasional thin, feathery cloud drifting on the gentle breeze as he rode towards Grantham. He was really enjoying himself as he progressed at a lazy trot through the peaceful, relaxing countryside. The air was full of birdsong accompanied by the occasional sound of voices of workers drifting from the fields as they went about their daily chores, and he reflected on the difference between life off the beaten track and the smelly, bustling, noisy rush of London. 'How very lucky I am to be back home and live in a place like this,' he thought. 'The city has some advantages, but at the moment I am at a loss to think of any.' and as he continued, he looked over the fields to the horizon and said to no one in particular, 'You just can't beat this!'

**

'Good morning Watson, what a lovely day.'

'Not so lovely if you are stuck in here Mr. Thorold. He's in a terrible mood this morning and has instructed me to refuse entry to anyone until this afternoon. Would you like to come back at two o'clock? He should be back from *"The Angel"* by then.'

'Two o'clock it is then.' said Nathaniel as he went back down the stairs, thinking he would see Ephraim in *"The Angel"* at lunch anyway.

Nathaniel spent some time at George Lawson's the saddler's discussing repairs that had recently been completed on a couple of harnesses and settled up the outstanding account. By the time he had finished his business at the saddler's, he decided that he would just about have time to call in at the blacksmith's shop before lunch. George Headland had asked him if he would call in and arrange with Jack Burr, for a time to take a couple of horses in to be fitted with new shoes. It was well known that Jack would only do work at a previously arranged time so it was essential to get an appointment agreed beforehand. Knowing that Jack was always referred to, with good reason, as a cantankerous old sod, Nathaniel raised his hat and said, 'Good morning Jack, I hope you are keeping well.'

'I 'ope you 'aint cum ere for a natter, I'm a busy man and I 'aint got time to waste.' was Jack's response.

'Not at all Jack, I would like to arrange to bring a couple of horses in for shoeing.'

'Ow many?'

'Two cart horses and a pony, Jack.'

'That's three then, not a couple. A couple is two where I cum from.'

'Quite right Jack, a couple is two, so when could I have the three of them brought in?'

'Well, we are really busy as you can see,' and rubbing his chin with a grubby hand, 'I will have to give it a good think.'

Nathaniel tried to suppress a smile as he waited for Jack to commence his regular routine for arranging appointments. It was quite obvious that Jack was not busy, he never was. He was semi-retired but he was a good and reliable blacksmith. George Headland always sent a few horses to keep the old boy in work.

As Jack looked around his forge, he picked up a hammer and banged it a couple of times on the anvil for effect. He then went to the bellows and pretended to boost the fire. Finally he said. 'Well Mr. Thorold, at a push, I should be able to fit you in tomorrow morning.'

Nathaniel thought it was time to get out before Jack thought of an excuse for changing his mind. 'Thank you Jack, I will make sure George has them here first thing in the morning.' he said as he hurried off to *"The Angel"*.

***

As he rounded the corner in to the main street, his eyes were drawn to a well-dressed gentleman walking leisurely in front of him. 'I know that man,' he thought, and increased his pace, 'it's George Montini, what is he doing all dressed up like a London dandy?'

He quickly caught up with him, tapped him on the shoulder and said, 'Morning George, what on earth are you doing, wandering the streets in the middle of the day dressed up like a dog's dinner?'

'Hi Nathaniel, how are you doing? I heard you had moved to London.'

'It was only temporary and I have just got back, but what are you doing now? Going by the way you are dressed, it doesn't look very much like hard work.'

'I am a man of leisure most of the time, but I enjoy playing poker regularly and am doing quite well at it. Do you still play?'

'Not now, after a bad experience down in London, I have learnt my lesson and don't play anymore.'

'What a pity, I will be playing in a big game on Saturday in Bourne and you would have been very welcome to join in.'

'Thanks all the same, but no thanks. I am just going to *"The Angel"* for some lunch. Have you eaten yet?'

'I was on my way to the *"Red Lion"*. I find it a lot quieter and I don't want to have to listen to old Woolaston, pontificating while I am eating. Why don't you come with me?'

'That's a good idea, at least we will be able to catch up on all our gossip without him taking over the conversation. I am seeing him later anyway.'

"The Red Lion" was only half full and they sat down at a table near a

window which overlooked a busy side street.

'What brings you to Grantham, George, it's a bit out of your territory, isn't it?'

'I had a late game last night and I stayed the night at a friend's house. I was a bit late getting up so I decided to have lunch here and then get off home this afternoon.'

'You look as if you are doing well anyway. You would fit in well down in London in those clothes.'

'Actually I bought this outfit in London a couple of months ago when I had done very well at the table. You have to look the part you know, even if you don't win every time.'

After a couple of hours of indulging in reminiscences and a few pots of ale to wash down their lunch, George suddenly stood up and said,

'My goodness is that the time? I should have picked up my horse over half an hour ago. Sorry but must dash,' and promptly headed to the door. 'Nice meeting you Nathaniel, we must arrange a night out and if you ever want a game you are always welcome. Don't forget, they are all very friendly,' were his parting words.

'Not when they are losing.' thought Nathaniel but, as the door slammed shut, said to himself with a degree of cynicism, 'Thanks George, give my regards to your family and tell Antonio I will be contacting him soon.'

'What the hell has got into him?' thought Nathaniel and as he finished his ale he realised that George had made no effort to pay his share of the bill.

***

Ephraim was waiting for Nathaniel, but as it was exactly two o'clock he made no comment about time keeping and welcomed him like a long lost friend. He indicated a chair and Nathaniel sat down while Ephraim shuffled a pile of papers and roared at Watson to get them sorted out. 'Well Nathaniel, you are looking very well and I have had some pleasing reports from Sir Samuel regarding your stay in London. It seems that you made quite a name for yourself, why don't you tell me about it?'

Ephraim leant back in his chair, crossed his legs and listened intently as Nathaniel spent quite some time relating what he had been doing. He emphasised the major tasks he had been responsible for but said nothing about the problems he had encountered with gambling and the debts he had accumulated. When he had finished, Ephraim pulled himself up closer to his desk, shuffled some more papers, coughed and said. 'Why did you find it necessary to ask for more money?'

Nathaniel was not surprised by the question, but was taken aback that it should have arisen so soon. He was fully aware that Ephraim knew about the gambling debts and that Sir Samuel had almost certainly told him everything that had happened, so he decided that it would be an absolute waste of time trying to fog the issue.

Ephraim paid particular attention to Nathaniel's story and as he listened he compared it to Sir Samuel's version. When he had heard it all he said. 'I am pleased you have told me the truth Nathaniel and I hope you will stick to your promise to stay clear of the poker tables from now on. However, there is something I must inform you of. Something of which you may not be fully aware. I know you are good friends with George Montini and I understand that you were seen with him in *"The Red Lion"*, earlier today. I am sure you know he is a very heavy gambler and dresses as if he is a big winner, however you probably don't know that it is all swank, he won those clothes at poker when his opponent could not pay. Also, he is very well known around here for not paying his bills and has tried to borrow from nearly all the businessmen in Grantham, with very little success I am glad to say. He is banned from *"The Angel"* and apparently he can't even buy a pot of ale in Bourne because he owes so much.'

'Good Lord,' exclaimed Nathaniel, 'I don't believe it.'

'It's true, and I am telling you all this because I know you are a friend of his and he is almost certain to ask you for money at some time or other so do be very careful about how you respond to any request, and please, I beg of you, keep your promise and never play poker again.'

This news came as a bit of a surprise to Nathaniel and it went a long way to explain George's quick departure from lunch, but he decided not to mention it to Ephraim and said, 'I am really upset to hear what you have said. I was completely taken in by what he said and his display of apparent wealth. Yes, he did invite me to a game next Saturday, but I am pleased to say I told him what had occurred in London and I don't gamble any more. I refused his invitation and I am also very pleased that you have given me this warning, Ephraim.'

'Thank goodness you said no, I really would be upset if you went down the same path as George, it would be an absolute disaster. Just remember, he is a bright lad and he is also a very smooth talker, so please do be careful.'

***

'Well Nathaniel, that's got my lecture of the day out of the way so let's get down to business. George and Joseph are obviously not here today because we had not arranged this meeting in advance. However I am sure if you are in agreement, they will not mind my telling you what we have discussed and the decisions we have made regarding your future and our working relationship with you.'

'That's fine by me.' replied Nathaniel, 'Why waste time setting up another meeting?'

'Good. The first thing is, everyone concerned has been delighted with

208

your efforts and dedication to the job in London – poker playing excepted. You have made some good management decisions and have proved you have the abilities to take on responsibilities which will be expected of you in the future at Borton. As a result of Sir Samuel's recent letter, we have decided to do as he recommends and let you do as much as you can with the least interference from us. How do you feel about that?'

'I look forward to it immensely,' Nathaniel said, and in an effort to polish up Ephraim's ego, he added, 'and I am sure you will always be there for advice and help when needed.'

'Of course we will. We have decided that for the next four years or so until your twenty-fifth birthday, we intend to take a back seat and be there for you when required. We will, according to your father's instructions, be in charge of the finances and will look at all the books on a regular basis but you will have as free a rein as we can let you and you will be involved in the annual financial review just as your father was. We will retain control of your personal allowance and it will be reviewed annually on your birthday. Basically you will run Borton the same way as the other managers are expected to run their farms and put in the annual financial report as all the managers do. You will also keep up to date with all the remainder of the estate and sort out any problems that the managers and tenants may have. Your allowance will be an agreed percentage of the estate profits so it is in your own interest to make sure things are going well.'

'That sounds alright to me but how will you decide on the starting percentage?' asked a rather mercenary Nathaniel.

'We have already worked that one out. We have taken your present allowance as a percentage of this year's profits as a base and have added five per cent. You will receive this new allowance from your birthday in November. That's only a few weeks away and it will be reviewed annually on your birthday. The more profits you make the larger your allowance , but beware, any sign of you putting personal expenses in as farm expenditure will be a negative influence when we carry out your annual review.'

'That sounds fair to me.'

'Yes, but you realise that you will have considerably more responsibilities than you have had so far, don't you?'

'Yes I do, and thank you Ephraim for your confidence and trust in me. I am really looking forward to the challenge.'

'I am glad to hear it, this is as near as you will get to taking over the whole business whilst it remains under the control of the three trustees. I can also tell you that Sir Samuel has expressed an interest in your future and wishes to be kept informed of your progress.'

'That's interesting, why does he want to know what I am doing?'

'I have no idea, it might be that he is interested as a family member or it might mean he has taken a shine to you as a future member of his team. You know these big business men always like to keep their options open and their contacts sweet.'

***

As Nathaniel rode steadily home from Grantham he had mixed feelings about his meeting with Ephraim and his mind was buzzing with contradictions. First he thought he had come away with a good result, he was going to be given a lot more freedom to run the estate. Then his feelings took a dive when he remembered that he was not going to take over properly for over four years. 'That fat bastard is still going to have the final say when it comes to spending my money.'

His mind was still in turmoil when he arrived home and he hardly remembered anything of the journey. He had totally ignored the friendly greetings of several people on the way including some of the workers on the farm, and suddenly snapped out of this brooding period of self-doubt when he realised that someone was talking to him in a rather loud voice.

'What the hell's up with you Nat, what are you doing?' Mo said, grabbing the reins and bringing Nathaniel's horse to a stop. 'You were staring into the distance and I thought you were drunk or even worse, sick.'

'Sorry Mo, I was just deep in thought but I am alright now. I think I could do with a nice jug of ale, something to eat and an early night. It's been a long, hard day '

***

After a good meal and a couple of stiff brandies, Nathaniel awoke with a bit of a thick head but in a comparatively good mood. He decided to make the best of his situation and concluded that he had come out of the meeting as well as he could have hoped for. If the trustees actually kept to their word, he would have the freedom to do most of the things he would like to do. 'I will do as Sir Samuel has trained me to do and always be prepared. I must have good logical reasons for any actions I take, or want to take. Get my facts right before I do things and I should get things done the way I want them to be done.'

***

Life for Nathaniel settled down quickly after his return to Borton and for the first couple of years he quite enjoyed the relative freedom of being his own boss. He worked hard and met all the guiding principles laid down by the trustees. The estates had run profitably and he had kept up his task of visiting all the tenants and managers and providing them with back up when appropriate. The trustees kept their word and apart from the annual reports and audits, only involved themselves when Nathaniel asked them. The expected pressures that he was prepared for never materialised and gradually he started to think about what it would be like when he reached the age of twenty-five years and took total control.

210

Foremost in his mind were three things, he needed plenty of money, an easy life with the minimum of responsibilities and above all, plenty of time to enjoy his wealth. His present situation provided him with a comfortable life and he was not short of money, but he had responsibility for nine farms in addition to his farm at Borton. These farms brought in a reasonable income but he realised that the rents from the four leased farms brought in almost as much as the nine managed farms without any direct responsibility on his part.

The more he thought about it, the more determined he was to change the status of the managed farms as soon as he possibly could. 'Why should I work my fingers to the bone when I could take it easy and increase my income at the same time?' he mused.

***

About eighteen months before he was due to take over from the trustees, Nathaniel received the news that Edwin Jones, the manager of Odder Lane farm at Gonerby had passed away in his sleep. It was not a surprise, as Edwin's health, which had been a problem for some time, had recently worsened and he had expressed the desire to retire as soon as possible.   On his way over to Gonerby to see Edwin's relatives and offer his condolences, his mind was in turmoil as to what he was going to say, he knew he was not very good at expressing sympathy. Choosing the right words for the occasion, and showing any emotion, was alien to him and in such circumstances he knew he came across as being aloof and somewhat remote. The only emotions he could manage were anger and self-pity and in the present situation he was aware that these were hardly appropriate.

When he arrived at Odder Lane Farm, work was continuing as normal although there was a general quietness, a lot less chatter and an absence of laughter. His meeting with Edwin's widow went better than he thought it would, and Nathaniel assured her that she would be helped through the difficult days ahead and would not be left wanting. She had already made the arrangements for the funeral and had decided to move in with her eldest daughter who lived in the village. After a suitable period Nathaniel left and said he would return for the funeral service on Sunday.

On his way into Grantham to discuss the situation with Ephraim, Nathaniel considered his next step. He would have loved to put the farm on the market and pocket the proceeds but he was fully aware that the trustees were legally bound to keeping the estate intact until they relinquished their duties. This being so he would have to find a new manager and as Robert Anderson was looking for a bigger farm he would give him first choice. A short diversion would take him to see Robert and so he called in before visiting Ephraim.

Robert had already heard about Edwin's death and was planning to see Nathaniel sometime in the next few days with a view to expressing his

211

interest in Odder Lane and was quite surprised to see Nathaniel ride into the yard so soon after Edwin's death.

'Good afternoon Nathaniel, what brings you here? Not bad news I hope.'

'Partly perhaps, I have just been to see Edwin's widow. Not a duty I enjoy at the best of times. You have heard about Edwin, I assume?'

'Yes I heard this morning. A very sad occasion for all I am sure. Come on in, I was just going in for a bite to eat, won't you join me?'

'Thank you, I will. I could do with a bit of light relief.'

As Nathaniel dismounted and handed his horse over to one of the yard hands, Robert led the way into the farmhouse where his wife was hurriedly laying an extra place at the kitchen table. 'Come in, Mr. Thorold.' she said, and as she pulled a stout wooden chair from the table, 'please sit down and make yourself comfortable. I hope you are hungry.'

'Thank you very much Charlotte, it's lovely to see you again. You are well I trust?'

***

Charlotte busied herself around the kitchen for a while and then left the two men to eat their meal and discuss business.

'Well Robert, you have expressed the desire to manage a larger farm many times in the past and you know Odder Lane is at least fifty per cent larger than yours. Would you be interested in moving over there?'

'To be honest, I have known for ages that Edwin was going to retire fairly soon and I have always thought it would be a good move for me, if and when he left.'

'That's fine. I am not looking for an answer today and I know you would want to look over the farm and check the books. I will have to recruit a new manager for a farm somewhere, be it at Odder or here, and as I am on my way to see Ephraim, I thought I would sound you out first.'

'Thanks Nathaniel, I am sure I would be happy there, but of course, you are right, I need to check it out thoroughly first.'

'There is also the option of leasing, it would give you more control and a bigger income. Have you thought of that?'

'I hadn't really thought of that, but I doubt if I could afford to buy the lease at the moment. I would be interested to see what it would cost though, and maybe it would be something I could consider in the future.'

'So far as I am concerned, whichever option you decide on Robert, I will be delighted for you to take over. I know the books will show you a well-run, profitable farm and the other good point is that yours is a nice small farm which should quickly attract a keen young man starting out in management.'

***

When Nathaniel arrived at the office in Grantham later in the

212

afternoon, he was surprised that Ephraim had not heard the news of Edwin's demise.

'Oh, I am sorry to hear it.' said Ephraim, 'He was a good man but I knew he was not well and had been suffering for some time. I expect I would have heard the news before the day was out, after all it is less than twenty four hours since the poor soul passed on.'

'I called in to see his widow and have put her mind at ease regarding any expenses involved. The funeral is arranged for Sunday and I will, of course, attend, although funerals are not high on my "like to" list. She informs me that she will be moving in with her eldest daughter who lives close by in the village so the farm house will be empty by next week.'

'We will have to put the feelers out and try to recruit a new manager pretty swiftly as we don't want to let things slide do we?' said Ephraim, shuffling papers around his desk.

Nathaniel told him of his visit to Robert at North Road Farm and explained what had been discussed and the conclusions they had reached.

'You don't let the grass grow under your feet do you?' exclaimed Ephraim. 'Robert would be the perfect man for the job. He is producing good profits, ambitious and a good people man. His record at North Road is exemplary. As regards the lease, I agree with you, I doubt if he could afford it at the moment, and anyway things must stay as they are whilst the estate is under the control of the trustees. However, I will produce some figures that will show him what he would probably have to pay for the purchase of a lease. It will show him what to expect and what he will have to save before he makes a move.'

'That's great, I will be seeing him at the funeral on Sunday and I will be able to arrange for him to see the necessary documents and have a good scout around the farm before he makes a final decision. Meanwhile, will you be spreading the word that we are looking for a new manager? '

'Yes Nathaniel, but I think you ought to check around our farms to see if we have any able and keen employees ready for promotion.'

'I am sure there are one or two ready, but I will certainly contact all the managers and leaseholders to see what they might turn up.'

***

Two weeks after Edwin's funeral, a delighted Robert Anderson took over as manager of Odder Lane Farm and Roger Kaye, was recruited to manage North Road Farm at Grantham. Roger was the son of Arthur Kaye, the leaseholder of Hillside Farm at Hough on the Hill. Roger had extensive experience working with his father and was keen to get some experience in management before trying to purchase a leasehold property in the future.

***

During his final year under the supervision of the trustees, Nathaniel privately formulated his plans for the future of the estate which he intended to implement as soon as he was in control. The idea of having to spend the rest of his life chasing around after a disparate group of farm managers, all with varying ideas and abilities did not appeal to him in the slightest. He quickly decided that to sell off the leases of as many of the farms as possible and then sit back and collect the annual rents would be far more to his liking than continuing with the present situation.

He had spent the last series of visits around the farms to evaluate their potential for leasing and had already identified two managers who he thought would be interested and were financially capable of taking advantage of the opportunity. He produced a detailed plan of action which included individual assessments identifying the positives and negatives of each of the managed farms which he planned to use as a basis for leasing off in due course. He also decided that he would deal with one farm at a time rather than all at once. He didn't want to create the impression that he was being forced into his actions by a shortage of funds.

He realised that there would be strong objections to his plans if he mentioned them to Ephraim and so he kept them to himself. 'Once I take over they will be powerless to do anything so why involve them in my plans? It's sod all to do with them,' he muttered to himself as he locked the incriminating evidence in his desk drawer.

***

The week before his twenty-fifth birthday was one of mounting excitement and Nathaniel could barely contain himself. He had received a note from Ephraim asking him to attend a meeting at ten o'clock on next Monday morning, the day after his twenty-fifth birthday, for the formal transfer of all the estate documents and responsibilities. Nathaniel was not best pleased and optimistically sent a note back suggesting the meeting was held on Friday. 'Why the hell should I have to wait until Monday?' he fumed. 'It's not as if it's going to make that much difference.'

***

Ephraim was also particularly keen to retain the Thorold business and was acutely aware that Nathaniel was under no obligation to continue using his services once he had taken over. This being the case, he thought he would have to be careful how he responded to Nathaniel's request and decided that it would be prudent to visit the farm at Borton and explain the refusal to change the date in person 'We will have to be very careful how we approach this one Watson, so you had better be on your best behaviour.'

***

The meeting did not go well for Nathaniel and even though Ephraim spelt out clearly, between bouts of deep, chesty coughing, that the legal requirements of the will stated that the transfer of responsibilities should take

214

place on, or as soon as possible after Nathaniel's birthday. As his birthday was on a Sunday the transfer would not take place until Monday. Nathaniel did not accept the decision gracefully, in fact he was in such a vile mood he didn't notice Ephraim was obviously in some discomfort, and had lost an awful amount of weight.

This mood continued for the next couple of days and on Saturday he decided he could do with a good night out. He set off to Bourne just before dusk, even though it was bitterly cold and there were regular flurries of snow drifting on the strong north-easterly wind.

As he was leaving the yard, Mo, on his way home from milking, called out 'Where are you off at this time of night boss? You don't want to be going far in this weather. It looks as if snow is setting in for the night.'

'Mind your own bloody business. I will go where and when I want without having to get your permission!' was the ungracious reply as he galloped out of the yard.

'Suit your bloody self. If that's how you feel, sod you.' thought Mo as turned towards his cottage.

***

As Nathaniel spurred his horse on, darkness came quickly with ever more snow laden clouds thickening and filling the evening sky. The flurries became more regular and gradually turned into a heavy storm of thick, soggy flakes which blotted out any indications of where he was. Covered in snow and having difficulty seeing where he was going, Nathaniel began to wonder what he was thinking of, setting out on such a night. 'What the hell am I doing out here, it's my birthday tomorrow and I should be looking forward to it, not stuck in the middle of nowhere frozen daft.'

Deep in thought, he tried to remember what had upset him so much and could not think of a rational answer, 'But I know I am behaving like a stupid, spoilt child.'

He turned his horse around and set off back to Borton. As he slowly made his way home the wind was blowing the snow directly into his face and making progress extremely uncomfortable. 'I can't go on behaving like this or I will go mad. I was extremely rude to my best mate and poor Sylvia must think I am an absolute bastard.'

Nathaniel was on his own in the bleak, silent countryside and had the chance to think things through and try to see things rationally. He knew that it all kicked off when he couldn't get Ephraim to change his mind regarding the handover of the estate, but the more he thought about it the more he realised that he was in the wrong and it would all be sorted on Monday. 'I will have to apologise to Mo and Ephraim as soon as I see them.' he thought, 'I can't get away with it this time.'

The storm continued for a while but gradually there were gaps appearing between the dark, scudding clouds where the moon had a chance to shine on the still, snow covered landscape. As he slowly progressed, muffled by the thick snow, his horse's hooves hardly made a sound. When he reached Borton all was quiet and still, not a single brave soul was abroad and there was no evidence of human movement in the virgin snow which covered the ground. The thatched roofs were completely hidden and the tower of the village church stood tall and strong in the moonlight. Even the dogs were quiet. 'I think a jug of ale in *"The Five Bells"* would be in order.' he thought.

As he approached *"The Five Bells"*, he could see that there was no sign of life, no footprints on the path to the front door and no lights shining through the small windows. 'Just my bloody luck,' he grumbled , 'no point in trying to get old Grimes to open up, I know exactly what he would say.'

When he passed *"The King's Head"* he found it was shut as well. 'Might as well go home,' he said patting his horse's head. 'Tomorrow is the first day of the rest of my life and I will be in control at last.'

Chapter 16

November 1728 – 1733

'Good morning Mr. Thorold, would you please go straight through, they are expecting you.'

'Thank you Watson, would you take my cloak please?'

As he entered the office, Joseph Godbold, Ephraim and George Heap were seated in a row behind the desk. Nathaniel saw Ephraim coughing heavily into his hands and looking extremely poorly. He had obviously lost an awful lot of weight recently and gave the impression of having shrunk in stature. Ephraim leant forward over the desk and waved a limp hand towards a vacant chair situated opposite the three of them and Nathaniel sat down. 'Good morning Nathaniel, I am pleased you managed to get here. I bet it was a difficult journey wasn't it?'

'Don't worry Ephraim, there was no way I was going to miss this meeting.' replied Nathaniel as Watson staggered into the office with four mugs of coffee and placed them on the table, slopping a considerable amount of the contents onto the work surface as he did so. 'I have been waiting five years for today, but even so, I had a long sleepless night last night tossing and turning and wondering what was likely to go wrong. I must say that a mug of hot coffee and a good fire blazing in the hearth is most welcome. The chance to get warm again is as welcome as the news I came here to receive.'

'For God's sake Watson get a cloth and wipe this lot up,' shouted Ephraim breaking into another bout of coughing, 'can't you do anything properly?'

***

The meeting passed smoothly and was carried out in good humour and was completed in a couple of hours. The executors and Nathaniel then adjourned to *"The Angel"* for a celebratory lunch where the discussion was mainly about Nathaniel's future plans. Ephraim was particularly keen to see if he would be able to continue dealing with the legal side of the estate's operation and Nathaniel told him, 'Well Ephraim, although I haven't made up my mind as yet, I have no intention of moving my business anywhere else in the foreseeable future.'

'Thank you Nathaniel, that's really good news, I have looked after your family affairs for a good number of years and look forward to a few more years yet.' was the reply through another outburst of coughing.

'I know we haven't seen eye to eye on a few occasions in the past Ephraim, but you have always been scrupulously fair and honest in your dealings with me, so you have no need to worry on that score.' Nathaniel purposely declined to inform them of his intentions to try to lease off the remaining farms and privately thought that Ephraim would be in no position to carry on work for much longer. His health was obviously deteriorating rapidly and reminded him very much of his father during the last few weeks of his life. 'It won't be long before I have to move my business anyway,' he thought. 'A younger man with an open mind will suit me better and I won't have the problem of Ephraim's objections which I know will be forceful.'

***

Over the next month or so Nathaniel revised his plans for the future until he thought he had them just about right. Now that he was in control he realised that there was no particular rush to get things done and that it was much more important to get things right. The final stage of his plan was to visit all the managed farms again and be as open as he could with the managers regarding what was going on. To this end he decided it was pointless going in the middle of winter and would take a couple of weeks out in late spring when the weather was better and the days were longer.

He also thought it would be prudent to seek the advice of Sir Samuel before putting his plans into action.

***

Everything at Borton was ticking over smoothly as usual and as Nathaniel was doing his regular morning tour of the farm he noticed a recent recruit was looking a bit worse for wear. The lad, a red headed Scot from Rosyth, and in his early twenties, was employed as a general farm labourer. He had left home to try to find farm work anywhere he could and came with good references. He was a capable lad and could be trusted with most jobs he was asked to do, but he also had a reputation as a ladies man.

When Nathaniel spoke to Mo, he mentioned that Jock was looking a bit rough and asked, 'What has been going on Mo?'

'Not a lot really,' said Mo. 'He tried it on with my sister Lillian and upset her, so I sorted him out, no problem.'

'What did you use, a sledge hammer?'

'I was just going to have a word with him but he said I should keep my fucking nose out as it was sod all to do with me, and if I didn't 'butt out' I would regret it.'

'Well it looks as if you sorted him out. Is Lillian alright?'

'Yes, she's fine. She said I shouldn't have hit him so hard.'

'Typical woman, I bet she feels sorry for him doesn't she?'

'She does. I just can't fathom out how the female mind works. I do her a favour and then I am in trouble'

'That's life Mo, but if you have any more trouble with him, just let me know and he will be out of here.'

'Right boss, I will. We don't need trouble with the women or anyone else for that matter.'

218

The weather during Nathaniel's first winter in charge was relatively mild. The snow came as usual but stayed, unusually, for a very short period of time. Routine winter tasks such as clearing ditches, ploughing fields and laying hedges were completed without disruption. All the stock animals survived and managed to get out to grass early in the spring.

Nathaniel was feeling rather pleased with general progress and as he strolled around he noticed how everyone seemed to be in a good mood, chatting and smiling as they carried out their tasks. 'Must be the sunshine.' he said to himself. He crossed the yard to talk to Mo. 'What's up with you Mo, you've got a face like a smacked arse. Have you got a problem?'

'Nothing I can't sort out, boss.'

'Come on then, let's hear it.'

'Well, when I went into the milking shed this morning, there was all hell on. Two of the young milkmaids were trying to tear lumps out of each other, there was hair everywhere. I had to pull them apart and try to calm them down which wasn't easy. When they had settled a bit, I told them to go home and sort themselves out and come back for afternoon milking. If it happened again they would be out of a job.'

'What was it all about?'

'They refused to tell me, but I have a damned good idea.'

'And what was that?'

'I think that bloody Jock is involved in it somehow or other.'

'Well keep your eyes and ears open, Mo, if he *is* involved, I will have to move him on. We can't have a disruptive, rampant young man loose among our women no matter how good a worker he is.'

'Thanks Nat, I will let you know if I find out anything.

'Well you know I am going to see all the estate managers at the end of next week and will probably be away for ten days or so. If you have any problems that you can't sort out they will wait until I get back.'

'What's all that screaming and shouting Sylvia?' asked Nathaniel as he was working at his desk.

'I am not sure, but I saw Robert Couling the miller from Smith's mill in the yard earlier and he looked very angry. You know Mo sent his daughter home yesterday so it might be something to do with that.'

'I bet it is. I know Mo can handle himself but I had better go and see what it's all about.' When Nathaniel reached the cart shed there was a crowd of workers gathered round and cheering what was obviously a fight. He forced his way through to the front and saw Robert kicking a man who was curled up in a protective ball on the ground, begging him to stop.

Mo was cheering along with the rest of the spectators and Nathaniel grabbed him and told him to 'Get in there and stop it before he kills him. Who the hell is it anyway?'

'It's that bloody Jock.' replied Mo as he enlisted the help of John Fowler and pulled Robert clear of his bloodied, cowering target.

'Everyone back to work now,' shouted Nathaniel. 'The show's over.'

***

'Bring them both to my office Mo, we have to get to the bottom of this now. I will see Robert first and find out what the hell got into him, he's normally such a quiet man. Jock can wait outside but make sure someone keeps an eye on him.'

***

'Good morning Robert, Can you explain why were you on my property causing mayhem among my workers?'

'I came to have a word with that bloody Jock. You sent my daughter Charlotte home yesterday for fighting with her friend Jane, well it was all because that bastard has been stringing them both along telling them that he loves them and God knows what else.'

'I think you were having more than a word Robert, from what I saw, it was more like war.'

'Well when I said I wanted a word he said, 'who the fuck are you?' I told him, and he said, 'well just keep your fucking nose out its sod all to do with you.' and then started to walk away.'

'Did you go after him then?'

'No, as I put my hand on his shoulder and turned him round, he took a swing and thumped me on the nose.' he said, wiping off a trace of blood with the back of his sleeve. 'That was enough for me, I set to and gave him a good thrashing. Nobody messes with my daughter, or treats me like that and gets away with it. He even called her a bloody trollop, what the hell was I supposed to do?'

'What did Charlotte say when you told her you were going to see him?'

'She begged me to stay away and says she loves him. She is besotted, and so is her friend Jane. He is playing one against the other and they both believe what he tells them. I dread to think what he is up to but I just hope we have caught things soon enough.'

'Well I understand your problem Robert, but to come here fighting on my property is just not on, whatever the reason.'

'I am very sorry Mr. Thorold but it won't happen again, I promise. Please forgive me and please don't tell Mr. Smith or he might give me the sack.'

'I won't tell him Robert, but I am sure he will hear about it. In fact, if the usual village gossip is up to speed, he will know already, but when he asks

220

me, as I know he will, I will tell him what you said and I am sure he will understand.'

'Thank you Mr. Thorold.' he said as Nathaniel showed him the door.

***

'Bring Jock in, Mo, let's get this sorted once and for all.'

Mo went out and returned with the bloody and bruised young man and John Fowler followed them in. 'I thought I would stay, just in case.' said John.

'Would you like to explain your behaviour Jock, and tell me why you were fighting with a villager who does not work here, in working hours and on my property?'

'I don't know who he is Sir, I have never seen him before and I don't know why he attacked me.'

'You know he was Charlotte's father and I understand you have been dallying with her. Is that correct?'

'I don't know what you are talking about, Sir. I don't know anyone called Charlotte.'

'I don't suppose you know Jane either, or that they are both milkmaids?'

'No Sir.'

'Then you don't know that they were good friends who ended up fighting over what you have been saying to them.'

'You shouldn't listen to what those lying cows are saying they are just a pair of rough trollops with vivid imaginations and can't be trusted to tell the truth.'

'Well I've done a great deal of listening today, and now it's your turn. Jock, you just listen to me. I doubt if you would recognise the truth if it hit you in the face and, in fact as I see it, your version of events bears no relationship to the truth. You have been a disruptive influence on this farm for far too long and despite having been beaten to a pulp at least twice, you have still not learnt your lesson. Pack your bags now and Mo, see him off the premises and make sure he keeps away from those two young girls we don't want him causing trouble before he leaves.'

'You can stuff your fucking job, I was leaving anyway.'

'Good. I would get a move on if I were you and remember, you will never get another job within fifty miles of here.'

As they left the room, Nathaniel called, 'Mo, come back and see me when he is well clear of the premises.'

***

'He was well down the Grantham road when we left him so I don't know where he will go boss,' said Mo when he came back. 'but from what he said as we packed him on his way he could well be back causing trouble given

221

half a chance.'

'Well you had better tell all your mates that if he shows up again, to let us know, his type cause more trouble than they are worth. Mo, I want you to find out, discretely mind, to what extent he has influenced those young girls. I know they will be tight lipped but just keep your ears open. I just hope they have had the sense to behave themselves.'

'Right boss. I will do my best but I doubt if I will find out much. Let's hope the first we know is not two large stomachs.'

'That's right Mo, we can certainly do without two little Jocks running around the farm.'

***

Nathaniel had been away for nearly a week at Saltfleetby All Saints with Michael Stitch, when late one evening he received a hand written note in Mo's scrawl, which said, 'Cum home now. playse on fyer' The young lad who delivered it said that a straw stack had caught fire in the night and burnt down. 'Mr. Clark said that you should come home quickly, Sir'

***

After a very early start the next morning, Nathaniel and the messenger made good time and were back at Borton by dusk. As they approached the farm, it was obvious that the fire had been much worse than he had first thought. Two straw stacks were completely burnt down and one end of the old cow shed was severely damaged. The thatch on one of the cottages also looked as if it had suffered some damage.

'Hi boss, I am pleased you got the message,' said Mo as he and John Fowler met Nathaniel and the lad.

'How much have we lost Mo, it looks pretty bad from here?'

'The two stacks of last year's straw have gone completely and the end of the old cow shed is damaged but we should be able to fix it. We have lost a sow and most of her litter. She had been bedded in the gap between the stacks and was burnt to death with six of her litter of nine. The three little ones that survived are all being taken care of by my sister so they should be alright. Luckily, all the cattle and horses were out in the fields so we were very fortunate.'

'What about the cottages?' asked Nathaniel

'Some sparks drifted over there on the breeze and started a few small fires but they were soon put out'

'Have you any idea how it started?' asked a very concerned Nathaniel.

'One of the stable lads thought he saw someone running away just before he saw flames.' said John. 'He wasn't certain, but he pretty sure it was Jock.'

'I thought he might come back. Have you alerted the neighbours and all your mates to keep an eye out for him?'

'We certainly have.' replied Mo 'and Brian Pell has him locked up over at Dunsby. He caught him trying to steal a horse and arrested him before he knew that we wanted him.'

'Do we know if he tried to contact either of the two girls?'

'I don't know,' said Mo, 'but I will find out at milking time tomorrow.'

'Good, I think I will get a good night's sleep and then go over to Dunsby in the morning see what the mad Scotsman has to say for himself.'

'If Brian is up to his usual tricks, he will have got a confession out of him by now and hung him up in a big tree before you get there.' said John, as Nathaniel thanked them and said goodnight.

***

Nathaniel was up early the next morning and rode the short distance to Dunsby where to his surprise there was a substantial and noisy crowd milling around in the normally peaceful village green. As he approached he discovered that they were all jeering and throwing all manner of detritus at an unfortunate individual in the village stocks. He was very hard to recognise with his filthy coating of rotting objects but he knew it was Jock.

He asked one of the merrymakers where he could find Mr. Pell and was directed to the farm just beyond the village church.

As he approached the farm he was met by a large strongly built man with a shock of grey hair. 'Good morning Nathaniel, I was expecting you, I take it you have seen the scoundrel. I thought it was a good idea to keep him there until you arrived.'

'Yes Brian, I have seen him and I think we should leave him there for the moment. It's ages since I saw you last, how are you keeping?'

'I am feeling great at the moment thanks.' replied Brian.

'How did you catch him?'

'We caught him trying to steal one of our horses down in the far paddock. Luckily one of my lads was suspicious when he saw someone heading across the fields, and alerted me. By the time I got there he was trying to climb onto one of our friskier cart horses and was dumped before he had managed to settle down. I brought him back here and locked him up, and soon afterwards I heard that you had suffered a stack fire and were looking for him.'

'Yes, we lost a couple of stacks and a sow with her litter of piglets. He was seen leaving the farm in a hurry just before the blaze took hold.'

Brian rubbed his chin thoughtfully and asked, 'What do you want to do with him Nathaniel? I would string him up now and give the villagers a bit of excitement. Horse stealing and arson are both hanging offences, so no one will complain if we did it ourselves.'

'We could, but I think we should make him suffer before he is hanged. We could tie him up well and put him in an open cart and send him off to Lincoln to be tried by the magistrates. If he survives the journey, old 'hang 'em'

223

Robert Dyer will love it, he likes nothing better than sending someone to the gallows.'

'...and they always get a good crowd at Lincoln.' observed Brian.

'We had better prepare statements for the magistrate and send them off with the escort, when we have prepared them we can remove him from the stocks and put him on a cart.' said Nathaniel.

The statements were prepared quickly and were brief and to the point. Brian organised three strong men to release Jock from the stocks and then deliver the felon and the statements to the magistrate at Lincoln. They experienced no resistance from the prisoner but the crowd were angry that he was being moved and thought he should be dealt with locally. They were very upset that they would miss the hanging as they would not be able to take time off work to get to Lincoln. Brian stood on a wooden bench and explained that he had to remove the prisoner and send him to a magistrate for sentencing and in order to placate the crowd he said, 'We will leave him here for another hour but we must take him today or we will not get to Lincoln before dark.'

There was a muted cheer from the crowd before the bombardment resumed in earnest.

By the time Nathaniel and Brian returned to collect the prisoner most of the crowd had dispersed and as he was secured on the cart, there were a few boos and shouts of disapproval but a bruised and battered Jock was pleased to be out of the firing line.

'He's in for a bloody rough ride,' said Brian, 'the cart will be treated as moving stocks as it passes through all the villages on the way and he will be pelted with anything that they can lay their hands on.'

'I just hope he survives until they get to Lincoln.' replied Nathaniel, 'A big public hanging is no more than he deserves.'

***

A few days later Nathaniel heard that Jock had been taken to the gallows just outside the walls of Lincoln Castle. In a note from the Magistrate, Robert Dyer thanked Nathaniel and Brian for their diligence in apprehending a common villain. He had been causing havoc around the farms in the north of England using several different aliases, and had avoided justice for several years. He noted, 'It was an agreeable hanging and people came from miles around to enjoy a good day out. He spread his profanities liberally around most of his previous employers, and the judiciary in particular, before stretching the rope.'

***

It was late June before he departed on his trip to London and Nathaniel was in some doubt as to whether he should implement his plans for the estate, partly because he knew Ephraim would tell him he was being stupid and partly because he was enjoying life as the country gentleman. Money was plentiful and work was not difficult, in fact, contrary to his expectations, he rather liked the life. He urgently needed to air his proposals and get the advice of an expert.

He knew Ephraim would do as he was asked but he was also aware that there would be strong opposition but despite not always seeing 'eye to eye' with him he respected his opinion on business matters. He urgently wanted to get Sir Samuel's advice before he made any firm moves and had requested a visit to London to discuss 'business development matters.' In reply, Sir Samuel said he would be 'delighted to see him' and had invited him to stay at his house in Ormond Street. Nathaniel was also looking forward to seeing his old friends from the apartments at some stage during the visit.

***

'Nice to see you Nathaniel, do come in.'

'Thank you Sir Samuel, it's lovely to see you again.'

'Come on through, I hope you have had a safe journey. When you have settled in we can have a good chat.' and to his butler, 'Capper, would you show Mr. Nathaniel to his room?'

'Certainly Sir,' said Capper, picking up Nathaniel's bags, 'please follow me Sir.'

***

After a very pleasant dinner, Sir Samuel and Nathaniel retired to the drawing room and over a glass of brandy Nathaniel explained his reasons for coming. Sir Samuel declined to make any recommendations and said, 'I think you will have to consider the consequences of your actions in a little more detail, it's not just a financial decision you are making. You are responsible for the welfare of all your employees and their families and must consider the effects of your actions on them. We are just going through a similar process and are having to make far reaching decisions on the future of our business. It is looking as if we might have to implement some radical, and probably unpopular changes. I think you should spend a couple of days with Jonathan. He is the driving force behind the project and he will explain how we are dealing with all the many aspects of business we have to consider before making any decisions.'

'That sounds very interesting.' replied Nathaniel. 'I realise we are operating in a very parochial business up at Borton and any independent input will, I am sure, be very useful.'

'What other plans have you made for your stay in London?'

'Not a lot really, but I intend to go and see my friends from the apartments and see how they are getting on although I think a couple of them have moved on.'

'Well I know Mr. and Mrs. Smith are still the housekeepers and Gerald Pickworth is still there but I am not sure who else of those that you know are

225

there.'

'I am sure Bernard and Brenda will be able to tell me all the goings on.' replied Nathaniel.

***

Nathaniel was apprehensive about his meeting with Jonathan but managed to be at the office early the next morning, keen to get it over with. 'I need unbiased advice,' he said to himself, 'and Jonathan is an employee, he is not a landowner. How does he know what is best for me?'

'Morning Nathaniel, nice to see you again. Come on in and sit down.' Jonathan breezed in, took off his coat and hung it on a peg. 'Now tell me what you are here for. All I have heard from Sir Samuel is that you are looking for some business advice.'

'I don't know if you will be able to help me but I have been preparing some plans to try to sort out my assets and responsibilities. I thought Sir Samuel might be able to advise me on which direction to take.' said Nathaniel, taking a wad of papers from a leather bound folder. 'If you care to take a look at these I will try to explain my thinking.'

'Well first of all why don't you give me a broad outline of what you have prepared and then we can get down to detail?' asked Jonathan.

***

Although very nervous initially, Nathaniel settled down and the two of them spent the rest of the morning going through Nathaniel's proposals. Jonathan spent most of the time listening and occasionally asking for clarification. He refrained from giving any advice but made copious notes throughout the morning. As lunch time approached he suggested that they adjourn and in the afternoon they would visit some of Sir Samuel's nearby business properties.

'That should be interesting,' replied Nathaniel. 'I am looking forward to it.'

'Well you are going to earn your keep,' said Jonathan, leaning back in his chair with his hands clasped behind his head, 'we want your ideas on what we should do. 'A great deal of what you suggest in your proposals applies to our current reorganisation. I will try to explain what our objectives are and your input will go into the mix at a meeting with Sir Samuel in the morning.'

'So I come seeking advice, and I end up giving it?'

'You do. Just think of it as a development exercise and take as much from it as you put in.'

Nathaniel was quiet for some time thinking things over. His first reaction was anger but he soon calmed down when he realised that what was being asked of him could indeed be very useful for him in his own situation. 'Whose idea was this, Jonathan?'

226

'Who do you think?' Jonathan asked, smiling. 'If you want something from Sir Samuel, you will never get it for nothing.'

During their lunchtime conversation Nathaniel mentioned that he had to visit the Bank of England during his stay in London as he had not made himself known since the trustees had handed over the estate.

'Well you must have a word with Sir Samuel before you visit the bank. He is a very good friend of Samuel Holden, the recently elected governor and also Sir Humphry Morice his predecessor. I am sure he would be delighted to introduce you to either, or both of them and you would be silly to miss such an opportunity.'

'Thanks Jonathan, that's very good news. I will certainly mention it when I see him tonight.'

***

Jonathan explained that the object of the current reorganisation was to streamline the business and operate more effectively to maximise profits. Nothing was ruled out and he expected Nathaniel to produce a draft plan of action. He explained that they wanted to expand the export business and ideas for fitting it into the existing setup should be included.

'Just like that?' said Nathaniel 'I expect you want it by the end of the afternoon as well, don't you?'

'Not quite.' replied Jonathan with a grin on his face, 'Today is Tuesday, so you must have it ready by Thursday morning when we will have a meeting with Sir Samuel.'

'Jonathan, be honest. I expect you have already sorted out what you are going to do, haven't you?'

'Yes, obviously we have a good idea of what will happen but we are always open to good ideas. In the past you have influenced some important operational decisions down here and your ideas are still working well.'

'Thank you, that's really good to hear.'

'Remember it is always wise to listen to good advice and no one ever knows everything. You have already taken the first step by seeking Sir Samuel's advice and he is very pleased that you contacted him. He is fully aware that you are largely on your own up in wild and desolate Lincolnshire and that good, unbiased, advice is at a premium.'

The afternoon passed very quickly for Nathaniel, he found it quite difficult to remember what he had seen and where it fitted in to the wider business. The variety of activities surprised Nathaniel, even though he had spent several months in London working for, and learning from the business. Their travels appeared to be random in that they didn't follow the progress of goods through the system but went from one site to the nearest one and so on. This haphazard route concerned Nathaniel and when he mentioned it to Jonathan, he replied. 'Well done Nathaniel, you have quickly spotted our biggest problem and probably the hardest to rectify. You see, the business has developed in a very random way, we have bought new premises when needed, but essentially because they were the right price, not because of where they were. This has now caught up with us and is starting to create problems.'

'I can see that,' said Nathaniel, 'I thought the warehousing was scattered all over the place when I was down here before.'

'I think Sir Samuel will be very interested in what you have to say on that subject. He is not totally convinced at the moment.' was Jonathan's comment as they arrived at what looked like a totally derelict site between two large old buildings which, although in use, looked equally derelict and had seen better days.

'This looks awful, what on earth is it doing in a state like this?' asked Nathaniel holding his nose, 'and what is that awful smell?'

Jonathan pointed to the larger of the two buildings, 'That's a slaughter house just over there and it has been there for years. We have tried to sell this land many times but no one will come near it.'

'Why did you buy it in the first place?'

'It came as part of a larger purchase so basically we have been stuck with it ever since.'

***

After dinner that evening, Nathaniel mentioned that he had to visit the Bank of England sometime during his stay in London and explained that Jonathan had said he 'Should have a chat with you first as you knew some important people in the bank.'

'Indeed I do,' said Sir Samuel, 'the current Governor, Samuel Holden is a very good friend of mine, as is Sir Humphry Morice, Samuel's predecessor. I will try to arrange an appointment for you with one of them, sometime tomorrow.'

'Thank you very much, indeed, that would be very kind of you.'

'Nonsense, you are family. Now, as I understand, you are working in Gerald Pickworth's office all day tomorrow. Is that correct?'

'Yes it is. I will be working on my report.'

'Good, then I will get a message to you as soon as I can. You know where the bank is don't you?'

'Yes, it's in the Grocer's Hall in Princes Street, isn't it?

'That's right, I will be there to meet you then. Now, would you like another brandy before bed?'

'No thank you sir, I had better be off to bed before I go to sleep.'

***

'Good morning Nathaniel, have you been waiting long?' Gerald said as he arrived at his office to see Nathaniel waiting outside the door.

'No, I have only just arrived.' Nathaniel replied.

228

After the usual pleasantries were exchanged, Nathaniel settled at the table Gerald had cleared for his use and read through the notes he had prepared. He had formulated a rough outline of what he was going to say at tomorrow's meeting but first he had to acquire a map of London. 'Gerald, do you know where I can get my hands on a map of London?' he asked. 'I need one fairly quickly if I am going to get this report sorted out in time.'

'I know there is one in Jonathan's office, but I don't know if there is a spare one available. Give me half an hour and I will see what I can do.'

'Well I could go and ask him myself and it will save a bit of time' said Nathaniel, keen to get started.

'It's no good going now Nathaniel, he is always in with Sir Samuel first thing and I am seeing him as soon as he finishes there.'

'Oh right. I will be getting on with something else then, I have got a lot to get through.'

***

Gerald managed to secure a map which suited Nathaniel's task perfectly. 'Thanks Gerald, that's brilliant. Where did you get it from?'

'Oh, Jonathan found it tucked away in his 'come in handy cupboard' He says he wants it back when you have finished with it.'

'That's no problem' said Nathaniel as he bent to his task. 'Look at this Gerald, had you noticed it was drawn up for Sir Samuel's brother George?'

'No, I hadn't. It must have been when he was Lord Mayor in 1720.'

'No wonder Jonathan wants it back, it's a family heirloom.' said Nathaniel. 'We had better take care of it.'

***

The morning passed very quickly and Nathaniel was very surprised when Gerald asked, 'Are you ready for lunch Nathaniel, my stomach is already rumbling.'

'I think you had better go Gerald, I intend to work straight through as I must get this finished today.'

'I can get you something if you like.'

'Well a pie would be very much appreciated, as I am quite hungry myself.'

'Alright, a pie it is.' said Gerald as he left the office.

***

Shortly after Nathaniel had finished his pie, there was a knock at the door and a nervous young man entered the office, screwing his cap in one hand and holding a piece of paper in the other, 'I have a message to give to Mr. Thorold, is that you Sir?'

'No, that's Mr. Thorold over at that table.' said Gerald, pointing towards Nathaniel who was sorting through a pile of papers.

'Thank you Sir.' said the young man as he walked over to Nathaniel and handed him a piece of paper. 'Will there be an answer, Sir?'

Nathaniel read the note and giving the lad a small tip, said 'No thank you, there is no reply.'

'I had forgotten all about that,' said Nathaniel, 'Sir Samuel wants to see me at the Bank of England at two o'clock this afternoon. I had better get a move on or I will be late.'

***

It was not far to the bank and Nathaniel arrived with a few minutes to spare. As he arrived he saw Sir Samuel's coach coming along Princes Street from the opposite direction so he waited for it to arrive. As it came to a halt a footman jumped down, lowered the step and held the door open for Sir Samuel to alight. 'Glad you are here on time Nathaniel, mustn't keep the Governor waiting, must we?'

Before Nathaniel could respond, 'Follow me,' Sir Samuel barked as he strode purposefully up the steps to the grand entrance. As Nathaniel followed Sir Samuel through the doors into the Grand Hall, porters and doormen genuflected as they passed.

'Most impressive,' thought Nathaniel 'I could do with more of this.'

They were ushered into a large, opulently furnished room where two extremely well dressed gentlemen were seated behind a large highly polished table. They had their backs to a window and it was difficult to see their faces which were in shadow.

'Welcome gentlemen,' said one of the faces in a rather high pitched boyish voice. 'So this is John Thorold's son is it? Welcome to the Bank of England Nathaniel, we have heard a great deal about you.' and pointing to the other side of the table, 'please take a seat.'

As Sir Samuel and Nathaniel sat down, the face continued, 'I am Samuel Holden, the Governor of the bank and this is Sir Humphry Morice, my predecessor in the job. We have all the papers here which were transferred into your name on the death of your father and we are here to do whatever you decide regarding investments and savings, indeed anything we can advise you on we will do so.'

'Thank you Sir.' replied Nathaniel, 'Any advice you can give me will be much appreciated.'

'First of all Nathaniel forget the 'Sir'. We are all businessmen here, I am Samuel, but if you wish you can call me Governor, and my colleague is Humphry. As regards your assets, you have a substantial sum of money lodged with the bank earning a basic rate of interest. Since the debacle of the South Sea Company, investments are strictly controlled by the government so there are very few areas where you are likely to make your fortune.'

'Yes, I have certainly heard of the *South Sea Bubble* and all its implications. Lots of people lost a fortune didn't they?' enquired Nathaniel.

'They certainly did, both of us included,' said Sir Humphry, 'It damn near ruined us both.'

'I am sorry to hear it, it must have been devastating,' said Nathaniel.

'It would have been worse if I had listened to the stupid idiot who was in charge here at the time. If I had cashed in my slave trade shares as I was advised to, I would have been in the poor house long ago.'

'I hadn't really thought of any investments in particular, all I really know is farming so if I decide to put money into any other business I will need really good advice.' Turning to Sir Samuel he said, 'What do you think Sir Samuel?'

'It's easy. Listen to their advice, go home, think about what they say and then do as you want. Remember it's your money and your decision how you spend it, not theirs.'

The meeting carried on for a while and ended with Nathaniel going away with a few ideas to discuss with Sir Samuel but nothing that he was really impressed with. His view of investments was that they looked like a big gamble and his experience of gambling was still etched in his mind. 'I think I would rather keep my money in the bank and spend it as I want.' he mused.

***

Nathaniel worked late that night preparing his presentation to Sir Samuel and Jonathan for the next morning. He had a fitful night, tossing and turning as he tried to think of things he might have missed. Eventually, when he fell asleep the sun was rising in the eastern sky and a blackbird was in full song outside his bedroom window. He awoke bleary eyed, still tired and quite worried about the morning meeting. He wanted to get on and check all his notes and get his arguments clear in his head before the meeting so after splashing his face with cold water from the jug on the dresser and wiping the sleep from his eyes, he went down to the breakfast room. Food was the last thing on his mind and breakfast was a hurried affair, a cup of coffee and a slice of bread and butter. He had finished and left the room before Sir Samuel appeared.

***

Nathaniel had been sitting outside Sir Samuel's office for twenty minutes before Jonathan arrived, 'How long have you been here Nathaniel.' he asked. 'all night?'

'Not long,' was the reply, 'I didn't want to be late, today of all days.'

'Well come on in and settle yourself down. Sir Samuel will be here in a few minutes.'

Sir Samuel strode in shortly after and gave Jonathan a few instructions to carry out after the meeting before trying to settle Nathaniel down. 'This is not a test Nathaniel, we would just like to hear what you think about our business and discuss any suggestions you may have to make on the way we do things. We know how you work and you have helped enormously in the past so I think we should all sit around the table and discuss your ideas informally. How does that sound?'

'That's great, I was getting a bit nervous but I am feeling better already.'

'Good,' said Sir Samuel, 'then let's get started. What's the map for?'

Nathaniel spread the map out on the table and said, 'You will see I have marked all the sites I visited yesterday on the map and noted what is carried out at each site. I didn't see all your sites and so the first thing we must do is put all your other sites on here and the activity carried out there. When we have them entered, we will be able to see how the goods and information flow through the business. We should also be able to identify any duplication of effort and where we could amalgamate processes. I have already identified several places where things could be improved but it's pointless doing anything about them until we get everything on the map.'

'That's a good start Nathaniel, let's get to work and get the rest of the sites recorded. I don't think we have ever looked at it in that way before,' said Sir Samuel, 'the business has just grown over the years and as we have bought in other businesses we carried on using those sites.'

After about an hour, all the sites and the activities carried out were recorded on the map and the area they covered was spread wide. There were also several vacant sites where nothing was carried out, one of them that Nathaniel had seen the previous day.

'That vacant plot of land near to the slaughter house seems to be wasted to me,' said Nathaniel, 'it is a large site, in sight of the river and on a main route. It seems to me to be a waste of a very well situated site.'

'But would you want to work next to a stinking slaughterhouse Nathaniel?' asked Jonathan.

'No I wouldn't, but you have an empty site half a mile away which has access to the countryside where the cattle are brought from. It also has a field as part of the site and would be ideal for a slaughterhouse.'

'That's brilliant,' said Jonathan, 'Purchase the slaughterhouse and offer the other site in exchange. We would kill two birds with one stone.'

'Do you think he will sell?' asked Sir Samuel. 'It would certainly help us in the long run.'

'I am sure we can find a way to convince him to come to an amicable agreement.' replied Jonathan.

'Well, I think we should consider everything and work out a plan for the whole business before we make any moves. We might just find we don't need that site at all.' said Nathaniel, trying to get the other two to concentrate on a comprehensive plan. 'We don't want to jump in and find at a later date, that we could have done it better.'

'Well said, Nathaniel. Let's do what we need to do and that's getting the whole thing sorted out, not a bit at a time.' said Sir Samuel.

Jonathan nodded his agreement, 'Yes, let's not rush into hasty decisions, we have waited long enough to tackle the problem so we must sort it out properly.'

As lunchtime approached, there was a general consensus that they had done as much as they could for the time being and Sir Samuel and Jonathan would take things further in due course.

Sir Samuel thanked Nathaniel for his contribution, 'You have concentrated our minds and have given us a few more ideas Nathaniel. If you ever want to come down here there will always be a job waiting for you.'

'Thank you very much. I might take you up on that sometime but I have plenty to occupy me up at Borton.'

I am sure you have and I haven't forgotten why you came here. Maybe tomorrow morning we could get together and see if I can help you with your plans.'

Thank you Sir Samuel, I am looking forward to that.'

Sir Samuel was heading off to another meeting and Jonathan asked Nathaniel if he was hungry. 'I certainly am,' he replied, 'I hardly had any breakfast as I was so nervous about the meeting and now I am absolutely famished.'

'Well let's go and get some lunch. There is an Inn just around the corner where I always get a good meal.'

***

As they finished their lunch, Jonathan asked if Nathaniel had anything planned for the afternoon. 'Not really,' said Nathaniel, 'but I thought I might take a good look around St Paul's. I had a fairly brief look around when I was last in London but I always wished I had spent a bit more time to take in the atmosphere of the place.'

'It's certainly worth spending some time there. You need at least an afternoon to take it all in and I am sure you will find it very impressive.'

'When I was here before, it had been open to the public for some time but there was still work going on, particularly on the outside where the final statues were still not all in place.'

'I think you will find it is complete and in all its glory by now.' said Jonathan as he paid the bill and prepared to leave.

***

Later in the afternoon Nathaniel decided to call in at the apartments to see some of his old mates. He had met a few of them on his tour with Jonathan a couple of days ago and knew that Michael Stevens had moved into his own lodgings with his family. He was also aware that Roger Gough had moved out eventually as expected. Gerald Pickworth had filled him in as regards any gossip he hadn't already picked up.

The door was open as he approached the apartments and as he entered, Bernard Smith was setting the table for dinner and when he saw who it was he came quickly round the table, hand out-stretched in welcome, 'Come in Nathaniel, good to see you,' and turning towards the kitchen he shouted, 'Brenda, put that ladle down and come and see who it is.'

'Good to see you again Bernard, it's been a …..' before he was interrupted by Brenda's shriek of delight,

'Nathaniel, how lovely to see you again.' she trilled and promptly wrapped her arms around him and gave him a chest squeezing hug.

'Put him down woman and let him breathe.' laughed Bernard. 'You will do him a mischief if you carry on like that.'

'Are you staying for your evening meal Nathaniel?' asked Brenda.

'No not tonight,' he replied. 'I have already planned to eat at my cousin's but I hope to have a night with the other chaps before I go home so I will probably see you then.'

They chatted for a while and Nathaniel had almost decided to leave a note for the others when Richard Pearson arrived. 'Are you staying?' asked Richard.

'No I have got to get back and change for dinner. I am expected to be on time as usual but I hope to come over tomorrow and have a bit of a night out if you are up to it.'

'Of course I am and I expect the others will be as well. Come over for dinner and we will go from there.'

'Thanks for the invite and I look forward very much to a good old night catching up with everyone but I must be off or I will be in trouble.'

Chapter 17

'Come in Nathaniel, get yourself a drink,' said Sir Samuel. 'Dinner will be in about ten minutes.'

'Thank you Samuel, I am sorry I am a little late.'

Nathaniel hadn't realised that there would be guests this evening but he saw Jonathan talking to Samuel's wife Mary. There was another lady next to Jonathan with her back towards Nathaniel who he assumed to be Jonathan's wife. As she turned around, it became obvious that it was not Jonathan's wife, he saw a beautiful young dark haired girl, no more than twenty years old. 'Who is that extremely attractive young lady?' he asked.

'Oh I am sorry, I forgot you haven't met, come on, I will introduce you,' replied Sir Samuel.

They crossed the room and Sir Samuel said, 'Excuse me ladies,' and turning towards the young lady, said 'Charlotte, may I introduce you to Nathaniel, a cousin of mine who is visiting us from his estate in Lincolnshire?'

'Nathaniel, this is Charlotte, Jonathan's niece. She is currently staying with Jonathan here in London.'

Samuel, Mary and Jonathan started to talk together and Nathaniel was left trying to make small talk to Charlotte. He was, rather unusually, finding it difficult to think of something to say and was pleased when they were all called in to dinner.

Nathaniel was delighted when he found he was seated next to Charlotte for dinner and soon overcame his reticence. He found himself very attracted to her and during dinner he found that they had much in common. She was the daughter of Jonathan's sister and she lived in the village of Colton Bassett in Nottinghamshire where her father owned several farms. 'I am surprised we've not met,' said Nathaniel, 'Colston Bassett is about the same distance on the other side of Grantham to where I live at Borton. Do you go into Grantham very often?'

'Hardly ever, but my uncle is a solicitor in Grantham and my father goes to see him quite regularly.'

'That wouldn't be old Ephraim Woolaston, would it?'

'Yes, that's him. Do you know him then?'

'I certainly do. My father was a client of his for years and Ephraim was one of the trustees of my estate until I reached the age of twenty-five and he is still the family solicitor.'

'What an extraordinary coincidence,' exclaimed Charlotte. 'Have you seen him recently?'

'I saw him only last week, just before I came to London,' said Nathaniel. 'I think Ephraim and Sir Samuel between them know more about me than I know myself.'

'I had better have a word with them then,' she said, laughing out loud.

After dinner they all had a stroll around the gardens and Nathaniel spent most of the time in Charlotte's company. He was oblivious of the other three diners although they occasionally attempted to talk to the young couple. All too soon, Jonathan told Charlotte that it was time to go. Nathaniel expressed the fact that he would love to see Charlotte again although she made no promises or firm commitment before departing with a wave of the hand from the carriage window.

***

After a sleepless night, tossing and turning and thinking of nothing but Charlotte, he arose and tried to turn his mind, with little success, to the morning's meeting with Sir Samuel regarding his plans for the future.

'Good morning, Nathaniel,' said Sir Samuel, 'you must have been early for breakfast. Couldn't you sleep?'

'Well I did have a fairly restless night. I must have eaten too much.'

'I don't think it was the food do you? It was more likely to be that beautiful young Charlotte. It was obvious you were smitten,' he chuckled.

'Well she is very attractive and such a personable young lady and we did get on together.'

'Did she tell you she was stepping out with a young man?'

Nathaniel's heart missed a beat and he felt physically sick. He could not believe what he had just heard and failed to take in what Sir Samuel was still saying.

'Jonathan tells me it is not serious but we assumed that she would have said something,' and seeing Nathaniel's distress he said, 'Come on Nathaniel, all's not lost. She was obviously attracted to you, we could all see it in her demeanour.'

'I just wish she had told me, I don't know what to do now,' said Nathaniel, trying to hide his disappointment.

'Don't worry about it Nathaniel, she obviously likes you so don't give up yet. Now let's get on with the business at hand, shall we?'

'You have my outline plans and know that my preference is to lease as much of my property as possible. However, since I have taken over, much to my surprise I have found I am quite content with things as they are.'

'I am pleased to hear it, Nathaniel. Your review of my business was comprehensive and very perceptive in its conclusions. It was also interesting to find that you made no recommendations to sell or lease our under-used, vacant properties, particularly as that was the main theme of your plans for your own estate.'

'That's true, I thought as you had not finalised your plans with regard to expanding your business, it would be silly to lose control of something you

236

may need in the future.'

'Exactly,' said Sir Samuel, 'if you sell you lose control, and the same applies if you lease property out. Leasing would bring you a regular income but you no longer have the flexibility you may require in the future and that is why our business policy is never lease any land or buildings. Renting will bring you an income and you retain more control.'

'Is that what you think of my proposals?' asked Nathaniel.

'I would leave things as they are for a couple of years until you have a definite plan for the future and some idea of what you need the money for. After all, it is very early days and you haven't been in charge for a year as yet.'

'It's funny really, all the time I was under the control of the trustees I wanted to get rid of as much as could and live off the cash it brought in but after I took over control I have gradually moved towards the idea of keeping and developing what I have. What you said has given me the nudge that I needed and I won't have to have a fight with old Ephraim. Incidentally, did you know that he is related to Jonathan through his sister's husband?'

'I did, he met Ephraim at his daughter's wedding but I don't think they have met since.'

'I was extremely surprised when Charlotte told me. I have always had a love-hate relationship with Ephraim but he can be trusted to give honest practical advice.'

'Have you decided when you are going back to Lincolnshire?'

'Yes I will be going back tomorrow, all being well. I have arranged to have a night with the chaps from the apartments so I will probably be late back tonight. I intend to go back to the house now to pack my belongings and I have to tell Mary that I won't be in for dinner tonight.

'Don't forget Nathaniel, you are welcome to stay as long as you like, you don't have to rush home just because we have finished our business. I am sure you could find plenty to occupy yourself for a few days in an interesting city like London.'

'Thank you for the offer Samuel, but I will have a lot to catch up with when I get back to Borton.'

***

When he arrived back at the mansion in Ormond Street, he was met by Mary who told him there was a message for him in the drawing room. 'It must be from the chaps at the apartments saying that tonight is off. I was going to tell you I won't be in for dinner tonight but that may have changed.'

'It was delivered this morning by a liveried footman so I don't think it's from the apartments,' said Mary.

As Nathaniel eased the folded paper from its seal a card fell out on to the floor and before picking it up he read the short message on the paper: 'Charlotte asked me to invite you,' it was signed Jonathan. His heart started to pound as he quickly picked up the embossed card. His hands shaking he read, 'Jonathan Adnitt requests the Pleasure of your Company at dinner tomorrow evening at seven-thirty. *RSVP. Carriages, Ten Thirty.*'

'You knew who it was from, didn't you Mary?'

'Of course I did, I know all of Jonathan's staff, but I couldn't tell you could I?'

'I suppose not, but this is wonderful. I must get a reply off straight away.'

'Don't worry I will get Capper to send it round when you are ready. I take it you *are* going?' she said with a smile.

'It means I will not be heading for home tomorrow morning as I had planned, but what difference does a couple of days make? Plans are made to be changed aren't they?' said Nathaniel grinning from ear to ear.

'So you will definitely not be here for dinner tomorrow then, and what about tonight?' queried Mary.

'I will not be here tonight and I might be fairly late back?' said Nathaniel, as he bounded up the stairs to his room to write the acceptance note.

***

'What the hell is the matter with you Nathaniel?' asked Richard. 'You've hardly spoken a word and your plate is still full. Are you ill or something?'

'More like woman trouble,' commented Andrew.

They were all having a good laugh and everyone was enjoying the meal but Nathaniel was deep in thought about his unexpected invitation, especially as Charlotte was rumoured to be involved with another man. 'I do hope she is not stringing me along,' he thought.

'I think he has fallen in love,' said Gerald, 'Jonathan told me this morning he had taken his niece to Sir Samuel's for dinner and Nathaniel was there. Weren't you Nathaniel?' he said accusingly.

'Yes I was. She is a beautiful young girl and I got on very well with her.'

'Do you think you will see her again? It's a long way to London from where you live,' asked Andrew.

'I am seeing her tomorrow at Jonathan's house so let's change the subject shall we?'

***

The evening was a bit of a waste of time, Nathaniel could not get his mind away from Charlotte and hardly participated in the conversation at all. They all noticed it and there was general agreement that it would be a waste of time going out for the evening, after all, the gathering was to meet and get up to date with Nathaniel again but his mind was miles away.

238

It was the same all the next day, he had nothing particular to do and so time hung heavily on his mind. The minutes seemed like hours and to try and pass the time Nathaniel went for a long walk but he had no interest in his surroundings or the people he bumped into. His mind was in turmoil, all he could think of was Charlotte and the other young man. He had fallen madly in love and was extremely jealous of a man he knew nothing about. 'Please God, it's only a rumour,' he thought. Just occasionally his spirits were lifted when he remembered that Jonathan had said it was Charlotte who wanted to see him, but these positive thoughts were constantly being engulfed by a flood of negative feelings.

The day dragged on. By the time he was ready to go, Nathaniel was in a state of nervous exhaustion and as he made his way to the door, Sir Samuel saw him and said, 'Are you going already Nathaniel? It's not half past six yet. Come in here and have a brandy, you look as if you need it.'

They made their way into Sir Samuel's study and pointing to the armchair in the bay window, said firmly, 'Sit down there Nathaniel.'

'I think I would rather stand, Samuel.' Nathaniel replied.

'I said sit down,' and handing Nathaniel a brandy, said, 'Get that down you and relax. If you go to dinner in that state you will make a fool of yourself. You don't want to do that do you?'

'Of course I don't.'

'You were perfectly relaxed at dinner when you met Charlotte, so what is the difference this time?'

'Well I didn't know there was another chap on the scene, did I?'

'Oh him, so that's what it's all about. Well I have it on good authority that he is an occasional companion and nothing more. There is no romance as far as Charlotte is concerned.'

'Why didn't you tell me before?'

'Because I only found out this afternoon, and by the way, don't mention him to Charlotte, she will tell you in her own time if she wants to.'

The brandy and Sir Samuel's pep talk was having its effect on Nathaniel and he was beginning to relax. 'Thanks for the advice and the brandy, I feel a bit more positive now but I had better be on my way.'

'Are you going on foot, Nathaniel?'

'Yes, I think it will give me the chance to get things sorted out in my mind.'

'That sounds a good idea. I will send my carriage to pick you up at ten-thirty so enjoy yourself and the best of luck.'

'Thank you Samuel, you are very kind.'

***

As Nathaniel nervously approached Jonathan's house, his feelings of trepidation increased until he began to feel physically sick again. As he neared the front door he said out loud, 'For goodness sake pull yourself together. No one is going to hurt you, you have been invited for dinner by a beautiful young lady so relax and enjoy it.'

Jonathan appeared at the door and said, 'Talking to yourself Nathaniel? That's the first sign of madness. Come on in, you are the first to arrive.'

'Not too early I hope,' said Nathaniel, 'I gave myself plenty of time.'

'You know my wife, Jane don't you and of course you've met Charlotte.'

***

It took Nathaniel a few minutes to gain his composure after seeming to lose his voice whilst in the presence of Charlotte but things settled down fairly quickly. Charlotte was a confident young lady who was easy to talk to and proved to be a calming influence on Nathaniel. All his previous feelings of dread rapidly disappeared and were replaced with extreme happiness.

Before he realised it, the dinner was over and it was time to depart. The young couple had been so engrossed with each other they had hardly spoken to any of the other guests. Nathaniel had sought Jonathan's permission to walk out with Charlotte over the weekend and he had approved. She had not mentioned the other man at all and Nathaniel had come to the conclusion that there was nothing serious going on. He had also learnt that Charlotte was going to her sister's in Oxford on Monday so he must make the most of the very short period of time he would be able to spend with her.

***

Before he knew it the weekend had passed. It was Monday morning and Nathaniel, after a sleepless night arose early and despite having already said his farewells, decided to try to get to Jonathan's house to see Charlotte one more time before she left for Oxford. His feelings for her were overwhelming and he knew she had similar feelings for him. They had promised to see each other as soon as possible and Nathaniel would seek Charlotte's father's permission for them to continue seeing each other, but he had to see her one more time before she left.

He dressed quickly and headed off at a brisk walk and as he approached he saw a carriage at Jonathan's front door being loaded with several heavy trunks by two elderly, heavily perspiring servants. 'Well she hasn't gone yet,' he said to himself, 'What am I going to say when Jonathan wants to know what I am doing here at this time of the morning?'

'Still talking to yourself Nathaniel?' asked Jonathan as he appeared from behind the coach. 'I am getting a little worried about you. I suppose you have come to say goodbye to Charlotte have you?'

'Yes, I couldn't sleep so I thought I would come to see her off.'

'What a pity, you have just missed her. She set off early on horseback and went on ahead saying she likes to ride in the quiet hours after dawn.'

Nathaniel's heart sank as he forced himself to hold back the tears. As he turned and started to walk away, Jonathan laughed and said, 'Only joking, she will be down in a few minutes and I am sure she will be pleased to see you.'

'You bastard Jonathan, I suppose you think that was funny,' and turning towards the two servants, 'You two can wipe the smiles off your faces as well or you will be in trouble.'

'Well it did get you going didn't it,' said Jonathan, 'I couldn't resist the temptation.'

***

Nathaniel and Charlotte had just enough time to walk around the garden in private before she set off and they vowed to see each other as soon as she was back at Colton Bassett. 'I am sure Daddy will let you see me,' said Charlotte, 'I know Uncle Jonathan will speak well of you and Uncle Ephraim knows you as well as anyone doesn't he.'

The parting was tearful. Charlotte waved from the carriage as she wiped tears from her eyes and Nathaniel tried his hardest not to let Charlotte see that he was unable to prevent tears himself. As he walked back to Sir Samuel's, he thought he would pack up his belongings and leave that very morning. 'There is nothing here for me now,' he said. 'The sooner I leave the sooner I will be home.'

'You were out early this morning Nathaniel. Have you had any breakfast?' asked Mary.

'No, I don't really want any thank you Mary. I am just going up to pack my things and I will be on my way home as soon as I am ready.'

'She has really got at you hasn't she? She is a lovely girl and I know she thinks a lot about you but you mustn't let it take over your mind completely. You know we have all been through what you are feeling now but you still have to carry on with your normal life so you just go and sort your things out and when you are ready I will arrange that you get a good breakfast before you go.'

***

Back at Borton things soon settled back into a regular routine. Nathaniel's relationship with Charlotte blossomed and her family were delighted that she had met a gentleman with good family connections. Even Ephraim was delighted and approved wholeheartedly.

The estate was also operating on a firm footing and Nathaniel had concentrated on developing the existing farms and had relegated his thoughts on leasing to the dustbin long ago. His relationship with Sir Samuel had blossomed and while Nathaniel was a regular visitor to London, Sir Samuel always called in at Borton whenever he was in Lincolnshire.

The romance went from strength to strength and in the summer of 1732, just over three years after they first met, and much to the delight of all concerned, Nathaniel and Charlotte got engaged. There was a big celebration at Colston Bassett and even Ephraim, despite being frail and somewhat hard of hearing managed to attend. Speculation as to a date for the wedding were rife and although Nathaniel would 'get married tomorrow,' a two year engagement was considered to be most likely.

The following week, Nathaniel arranged a party for all the workers at Borton and their families to celebrate his engagement. The big barn was cleared and plenty of food and drink was supplied and a group of musicians from Grantham was hired to provide the entertainment. Nathaniel and Charlotte stayed for a couple of hours but left the revellers to carry on until late in the night. Nathaniel took Charlotte over to Grantham so that she could stay overnight at her Uncle Ephraim's. When he arrived back at Borton the party was still going strong and as he went into the house, he thought, 'It's good to hear them all enjoying themselves, they deserve an occasional break from routine.'

***

Nearly a year after the engagement celebrations, Nathaniel had just finished a letter to Sir Samuel and thought he would walk around to "The Five Bells" for a jar of ale. When he arrived he joined Mo who was sitting outside enjoying the evening sun. 'Do you want another, Mo?' he asked.

Mo nodded his confirmation and emptied his pot. 'Thanks very much, Nat. It seems a long time since you bought me a drink.'

'Yes, I suppose last Thursday is a long time ago, isn't it?' said Nathaniel as they both settled down and relaxed.

Nathaniel had nearly finished his first drink when John Fowler approached them, looking a bit flustered. 'Nathaniel, Sylvia says can you come home quickly, it's very important.'

'What does she want?'

'I don't know, but a man arrived on horseback and Sylvia took him into the house.'

Nathaniel hurried home to see Charlotte's brother sitting at the kitchen table drinking a pot of coffee. Thinking the worst he said, 'Hello Charles, what has happened?'

'I'm afraid it's bad news Nathaniel, it's Charlotte. She was out riding this morning and the horse stumbled and fell. Unfortunately she was trapped underneath for some time until the horse could be moved.'

'Oh my God, how is she?'

'She is very poorly indeed, but she keeps asking for you.'

'Let's go then, I must get there quickly,' and turning to Sylvia, 'Sylvia, get George Headland to saddle up my horse as quickly as he can and bring it round. And tell him to move the saddle on Charles' horse to one of ours, he will need a fresh one tonight and we can't waste any time.' As he left the kitchen he said, 'Just wait here Charles, I am going to pack an overnight bag. I will be back in a minute.'

'I think Sylvia has already packed it. Isn't that it on the chair?' said Charles.

***

As they sped on their way to Colston Bassett, Nathaniel's mind was in turmoil. There was no conversation between the two riders as they were both deep in thought and, at the same time, trying to concentrate on the road ahead in the darkening gloom. It was well past midnight as they arrived and candles were flickering in the windows indicating that people were still up and about.

They were met at the door by Charlotte's father who had obviously been crying and as they entered the front room, all the ladies were sobbing and comforting each other as best they could. 'I am terribly sorry Nathaniel, but Charlotte passed away about two hours ago. The last thing she said was, tell Nathaniel I love him,' he said and burst into floods of tears.

Nathaniel collapsed on the floor and sobbed uncontrollably on receiving the devastating news. His sobbing subsided gradually and eventually he asked, 'Please can I see her now?'

'Of course you can,' said her father. 'Come with me.'

As they went up the stairs, Nathaniel, who was emotionally drained and distraught with grief, was also worried what he would see. Had she been badly disfigured or worse, would he even recognise her? 'I will leave you now Nathaniel,' said Charlotte's father as he stood aside to let Nathaniel into the candlelit bedroom, 'stay as long as you wish, we will all be in the parlour when you come down.'

As he entered the room he saw that there was a candle either side of the bed illuminating his beloved Charlotte's face. Her hair was spread over the crisp white pillow, its long black tresses shining as the light was reflected from the candles. She looked as if she was in a deep peaceful sleep and there was no indication that she had been involved in a tragic accident.

Nathaniel, tears streaming from his eyes, knelt beside the bed, leant over and kissed her on the lips. 'Oh my darling Charlotte,' he cried, 'I love you so much. What am I going to do without you?'

He stayed with her for what must have been hours, stroking her hair and her brow and talking to her continually and when he finally said goodbye and went down to see the others, dawn was breaking and the candles had nearly burnt out. When he went downstairs to the parlour it was in darkness and he thought everyone had gone to bed but a voice came out of the gloom. 'I am pleased you could come Nathaniel. She loved you very much and was always talking about you.'

243

'I loved her with all my heart and she has changed my life completely. The last four years have been sublime and I don't know what I am going to do without her.'

'You must get some rest Nathaniel, there is a bed made up for you in the back room and you are welcome to stay as long as you wish.'

'I don't think I could sleep now, my mind is full of thoughts of poor Charlotte,' and he burst into a flood of tears again.

Here drink this,' said Charlotte's father, passing him a large brandy, 'it will help you to rest for a while.'

Nathaniel drank the brandy slowly and eventually he fell into a fitful sleep in the chair. Charlotte's father covered him with a blanket and then went upstairs to sit with Charlotte.

Chapter 18

1733 -1734

After Charlotte's funeral, Nathaniel withdrew into himself and was not seen out of the house for several weeks. Sylvia's life was made miserable by his aggressive outbursts and refusal to eat regularly. She understood the reasons for his depressive behaviour but she was very worried about his gradual reliance on alcohol. Her efforts to encourage him to get out occasionally always fell onto deaf ears and even when she asked Mo to help, his efforts were rebuffed, usually with a foul mouthed tirade.

Eventually he made the effort to get out and see what was going on, even then, nearly everyone he spoke to were sympathetic and offered their condolences. This only took him back to that awful day when he saw his beloved Charlotte lying motionless and cold in the darkened bedroom, 'I can't stand any more of this,' he screamed, banging his fist against the kitchen table, 'I have got to get out of here for a break away from this hell hole! They will never let me forget if I stay here.'

He packed his bags that evening and in the morning told Sylvia he was going to London for a break. 'What on earth for?' she, asked. 'All your friends are here in Borton and you have got to get yourself back into the routine of the estate. You have done nothing but mope around for nearly a month and relied on others to do your work for you. It's time you took charge again.'

'But Sylvia, people round here won't let me forget,' he pleaded.

'No one is trying to upset you, they are very sorry for you and understand your grief. Don't forget, they have been waiting all this time for the chance to tell you what they feel and now they have seen you they won't remind you again.'

'I suppose so, but it really upsets me. I don't know if I'll ever get over it.'

'Believe me, you will eventually and you will remember all the good times you had together. I just don't think clearing off to London will help at all.'

'I understand what you are saying, but you have no idea how much it hurts me to know I will never see her again,' he said putting his head in his hands and sobbing like a baby.

Sylvia put her arm around his shoulder as he sat at the table and as he calmed down and dried his eyes, said 'Please don't go to London Nathaniel, not yet anyway. Stay here and see how you feel in a couple more weeks.'

***

Nathaniel took Sylvia's advice and decided not to go to London immediately but after three weeks of continuing turmoil he set off to see his

245

mates in London. The visit to London did not help very much. All his friends were very sympathetic but of course were working most of the time and Nathaniel was left on his own with his thoughts and memories. He saw Sir Samuel and Jonathan but again they were working most of the time. They did suggest that Nathaniel did some work for them to occupy his time and his mind but he refused, saying if he wanted to work he would have stayed at home and done some of the jobs he had been putting off since the funeral.

Nathaniel only stayed in London for a week and on his last night Sir Samuel invited him over for a meal. After the meal Sir Samuel took Nathaniel into his study and tried to impress on him that memories will fade eventually but will never disappear. 'You will gradually get over this traumatic period of your life, but only if you put your mind to something else and try to work your way through it.'

'That's what they all say, but they don't know what it is like. It's never happened to them, has it?'

'Well it has you know. Jonathan was married before and his first wife died in similar circumstances to Charlotte. Mary and I had a small boy, Richard, who died when he was two years old. We were absolutely devastated, just like you, but time helped and gradually the pain eased but it never goes away completely. Sometimes it all comes flooding back when we see a small boy playing with his dog or with a group of other small children.'

'I didn't know that, I am very sorry.'

'I know you are Nathaniel, but you must accept that people are very sorry for you, and you must let them tell you. They are behaving perfectly normally in such a situation.'

'I know, but it upsets me so much and I will never forget Charlotte.'

'Of course you won't and no one expects you to, but remember, Charlotte would never have wanted you to withdraw yourself. I am sure she would have wanted you to carry on as best you can. After all, she knew that the livelihoods of your entire workforce and their families rely on your estates running smoothly and profitably.'

'It's so difficult but I hear what you say and I must try to get back to work quickly.'

'Good. Now let's have a brandy and consider the lecture over and done with.'

***

Over the next month or so Nathaniel tried to work his way through his pain and it gradually started to ease. He also stopped his heavy drinking and had only the occasional night out at *"The Five Bells"* with Mo. Sometimes, if he wanted a quiet drink on his own he would ride over to Bourne, have a couple of pots of ale and ride back home.

On one winter Saturday he had been in Bourne on business when the weather closed in and the snows came suddenly and quickly. Everything had ground to a standstill and there was no way Nathaniel was going to get home before dark so he booked a bed for the night at *"The Nag's Head"*.

'What have we to eat tonight, Molly?' Nathaniel asked as he sat down for his evening meal, 'I hope it's not fatty bacon again.'

'Yes it is, Mr. Thorold, but we have some roast beef as well if you prefer that.'

'Roast beef and a pot of your delicious ale would be just fine,' said Nathaniel settling down at a small table near the window.

As he watched the snow blowing around outside covering all traces of movement, Molly returned with his ale. 'Your roast will be here in a moment, Sir,' she said, looking over Nathaniel's shoulder. 'I am pleased I am not out there in that lot.'

***

George Montini had also been stranded at the *"Nag's Head"* and as he came down the stairs he saw Nathaniel drinking his ale. 'Can I join you Nathaniel?' he asked, 'I assume you are stranded as well.'

'Hello George, of course you can. Take a seat' and pulling back the other chair said 'It seems ages since I last saw you,' his mind frantically trying to remember Ephraim's warnings about George's reputation regarding his finances. 'Just be very careful,' he thought. 'What have you been doing with yourself lately?'

'I have been helping my father on the farm when he needs me, but mostly I have been over in Nottingham where I have a couple of small business ventures. They help to keep the wolf from the door. What about you, are you married yet?'

It was like another kick in the stomach for Nathaniel but he tried not to show it. He was convinced that George knew all about Charlotte and her untimely demise. Certainly the Montini family were aware as he had written them a note and they had sent their condolences, so what sort of game was George trying to play? 'Not yet,' he replied 'Have you ordered your meal yet, George? It's fatty bacon, your favourite,' he said with a note of irony.

'Your roast beef looks nice,' replied George ignoring Nathaniel's comment. 'I think I will have some of that.'

As the evening progressed and having a few more ales, Nathaniel relaxed and all Ephraim's warnings about being careful were forgotten. 'I think it's going to be a long night,' said George. 'I have organised a game for later on, would you like to join in to make up the numbers? We have a room upstairs and there are a couple of gentlemen up from London who would like a game.'

'No thank you George, I learned some time ago that poker is a mug's game.'

'It's up to you, there is a seat if you want one.'

'No thanks George,' and calling to Molly, 'Two more ales please Molly.'

***

The evening went quite well but Nathaniel was still wondering why George had not mentioned anything about Charlotte. He was about to raise the subject when two gentlemen came through from the public bar and spoke to George. 'Have you managed to get a fourth player for our game tonight, George?' one of them asked.

'Not yet I am afraid, but I am still trying to persuade Nathaniel here to join us. He is an accomplished player but he has sworn off the game as a result of some heavy losses in the past.'

'Well he can't lose much with us,' replied the smaller of the two men. He was a rather rotund young man with small piercing blue eyes set in a round, florid face. 'We only play for very small stakes and no one makes much money either.'

'There's nothing else to do here tonight so why don't you join us Nathaniel?' said his companion, 'you can't be going to bed at this time of night.'

George looked directly at Nathaniel and said, 'Come on Nathaniel, just for once, you know that it won't do you any harm and you are not likely to lose your fortune tonight, are you?'

Nathaniel was severely tempted and remembered his promise to Sir Samuel, but thought to himself, 'He will never know, and it will pass a couple of hours before bed.' So he turned to the two visitors and said, 'Right, you are on. Let's get started.'

***

Molly kept the players supplied with drinks and food and they continued the game until nearly dawn. It only stopped when one of the visitors had nothing left to gamble with and his friend was also nearly broke. Nathaniel however, was completely elated and had won a large amount of cash and a few promissory notes. George said he had broken even, but Nathaniel thought that he was being rather economical with the truth and had lost a tidy sum.

After a few hours in bed Nathaniel went down for breakfast and George was already there. 'Morning Nathaniel, did you enjoy the game?'

'I certainly did, what about your friends from London, have they got up yet?

'They have "up and gone" already, I don't think they bothered with breakfast,' said George, 'they didn't seem too happy when I saw them.'

'They won't get very far in all this snow it must be knee deep out there.'

'Haven't you had a look outside, it's nearly all gone. It turned to rain

248

just after we started the game last night so most of it has gone.'

'That's good news George, I thought we would be stuck here for another night with your unhappy friends.'

'They will be back sometime. They won't give up after just one heavy loss and they certainly won't forget you either, they don't like losing. *Ever.*'

After breakfast, George left early and when Nathaniel went to pay his bill he thought it was a bit expensive. When he asked Molly why it was so large, she said. 'Mr. Montini said that you had agreed to settle his account and said to thank you very much.'

'The bloody cheek of the man,' he thought to himself, 'But it still seems to be quite a large amount Molly, are you sure it is correct?'

'Yes Mr. Thorold, there were some outstanding things on his account from a few weeks ago but he said you would understand.'

'I *do* understand, but in the future will you ask me before you let him out of your sight?' He replied with anger in his voice.

'I will Mr. Thorold, but Mr. Montini said you knew all about it, and left very quickly.'

'I am sorry I was a bit abrupt Molly, I know it was not your fault. I will sort it out in good time.'

***

It was a cold wet ride home and Nathaniel was experiencing mixed emotions, on the one hand he was elated with his success at the poker table and on the other, Ephraim's warning about George and his devious ways kept recurring. He was furious with himself for getting caught out and vowed never to let it happen again although he realised the only way he could prevent it, was to warn the hotel staff to refuse any such request. 'I will get even with that cheating little pipsqueak if it's the last thing I do,' and he smiled as he said to himself, 'even so, I came out of it very well, didn't I?'

By the time he arrived at Borton he was getting quite concerned about George's remarks about the other two gamblers. What did he mean about 'They will be back,' and 'they don't like losing, *ever.*' especially the emphasis on the word ever. How did George know these men? Were they regular gamblers and had George tried to set him up in some way so that he would lose a lot of money to them? The more he thought about it, the more he thought it was a set up. George had an awful lot of explaining to do.

***

Several weeks later, Nathaniel had to arrange a trip to London on business and he was invited to stay at the apartments. He expected to be down there for a few weeks and he was looking forward to seeing his old mates again. Nathaniel thought he owed them an apology for his behaviour the last time he had seen them and although he knew it would bring back traumatic memories he thought he was strong enough now to talk openly about

Charlotte.

As they sat down for his first evening meal at the apartments, Nathaniel had a brief feeling of panic, but fortunately it passed and they all had a very pleasant time. Towards the end, Richard Pearson asked, 'Do you still play a good hand of poker, Nathaniel?'

'Not very often, Richard, but I did have a good win a few weeks ago. Do you still play?'

'Yes, I do play occasionally in fact we are having a game here tomorrow evening. Just a few of my pals come over and we always finish well before bed time.'

Nathaniel was a bit dubious about it but in the end thought that if it was here and only a friendly game he would like to join in, but knowing Sir Samuel's opinion of gambling asked, 'What does Sir Samuel think about your gambling on his premises?'

'He doesn't know. We always use my room and don't make a noise so no one has ever found out.'

'Alright Richard, I would love to have a game provided it is just a friendly get together.'

'You will enjoy it Nathaniel. The stakes are not high and no one loses or wins very much.'

***

Nathaniel enjoyed his games of poker and during his stay he played two or three times, and over the period found he had roughly broken even as far as stakes were concerned. He convinced himself that he had his old problem with gambling well under control and was absolutely certain that he would never get in such a difficult situation ever again.

Nathaniel concluded his business fairly quickly and also paid a courtesy visit to Sir Samuel and his wife. He had a pleasant evening with them. They were very understanding regarding Charlotte's accident and they were very pleased to see that Nathaniel was being more positive about things than the last time he was in London.

On his last evening he was enjoying a pot of ale with Richard when his friend said, 'You remember that pair of pistols I was going to let you have when you were down here some time ago, well I still have them if you are interested.'

'Well I could do with a new pair, mine are still usable but they are a bit damaged. I had forgotten you had offered them to me.'

'Well I have never used them and they are still brand new. You can have them at cost if you are interested. I will just go up to my room and get them, and you can have a look.'

Richard soon came back with the pistols. 'Here they are Nathaniel. Have a good look and see what you think.'

Nathaniel opened the polished wooden carrying case and the two pistols were sitting on velvet in shaped recesses. He took out one to inspect and weighed it in his hand, 'It's very nicely balanced Richard,' he said.

'Of course it is, and so is the other one, they were my inspection pieces to get my qualifications so they have been checked by the experts.'

Nathaniel continued his appraisal of the pistols. The stocks were made of walnut and the extensive decorations were of silver and silver wire inlay. The pistols had sidelocks and each one was also fitted with a sliding safety catch. A ramrod was fitted to each barrel. The barrels were of smooth circular section of 0.65inch calibre. 'They are a pair of lovely pistols, Richard, you should be proud of your work and I would be delighted to purchase them if the price is right.' said Nathaniel.

Negotiations were quickly concluded and deal was made. Nathaniel would pay half now and the remainder on his next visit which was planned for May.

'You have a bargain there Nathaniel, they have only been fired once and that was when they were proof tested,' said Richard as they shook hands to seal the deal.

***

Back at Borton things carried on as normal and in early April, Nathaniel did a routine visit round all the farms and collected the annual reports. The results were much better than the previous year at all the farms and Nathaniel was very pleased that he had not leased or sold any of them off. He was beginning to reap the benefits of owning the properties outright. All the farm managers, much to their delight, received an increase in their salaries.

Edward Wood, the manager at Frieston was still interested in owning a farm of his own and was very disappointed when Nathaniel told him that he had decided not to sell or lease Holt Hall Farm. 'But you said that you were keen to lease off some of your farms Nathaniel,' he complained, 'You even encouraged me to believe that you wanted me to buy the lease.'

'I know Edward, but things have changed since I took over and it is not in my interest to lease or sell anything at the moment.'

'I am very disappointed Nathaniel. I have been saving hard and thought I would have enough money saved to lease the farm this year or next and now you tell me it's off. I am really upset.'

'I am very sorry but that is how things are now. It may change in the future but I can't make any promises.'

'If that's how it is, then I will have to start looking around. I can't wait for ever you know.'

'I understand how you feel Edward, but if you are sure you will be moving, then I wish you all the luck in the world. All I ask is that you give me adequate warning before you go.'

'Of course I will and I just hope we remain good friends whatever happens.'

'We will, and if I hear of a suitable property coming up for sale I will let you know immediately.'

***

'Good morning Nathaniel,' wheezed Ephraim, 'I hope you are feeling better than I am.'

'Morning Ephraim, you do look a bit rough. What's the problem?'

'I can't shake off this blasted chesty cough. I have had it since before Christmastide and it just won't clear up and I can't seem to keep warm.'

'You should go to bed for a few days and give yourself a chance to recover.' advised Nathaniel.

'I can't do that I am on my own here. Watson has taken to his bed and I don't think we will see him again.'

'I wondered where he was. How long has he been off work?'

'It's three weeks tomorrow and I am banging my head against a stone wall trying to keep up with things. It's beginning to get a bit desperate.'

'You have to get some help Ephraim, you can't go on like this.'

'I know. I have already decided that I will retire later in the year and have arranged for Charles, my nephew to take over the business but he is still doing his exams and won't be starting here for at least two weeks. You know Charles, don't you? Charlotte's brother.'

Nathaniel's heart missed a beat as all the thoughts of Charles coming to Borton to tell of Charlotte's accident, flooded back. 'He's a good man Ephraim,' he said, trying to hide his emotions. 'I hope he is as good as you,' and then, 'but you need a replacement for Watson immediately. You can't carry on like this.'

'I know, I would like to get someone settled in before Charles arrives and I have already seen a couple of young men who have been to school. Both look as if they would be able to learn the ropes quickly. What I really need Nathaniel, is someone else to give their opinion. You know the job and so I wondered if you would have a word with them before I make up my mind? I would be extremely grateful for your comments on their suitability.'

Nathaniel was taken aback by Ephraim's request and the trust in him that it demonstrated. 'Of course I would Ephraim, I will be delighted to help in any way I can. When do you want me to see them?'

'I can get a message to them tonight, would tomorrow morning be convenient?'

'Tomorrow's fine, say about ten o'clock.'

'That's wonderful Nathaniel, I will have them here ready and waiting for you at ten.'

'Well to save them hanging around, can you have one here at ten and the other half an hour later and then I won't have to rush things.'

'That's a good idea. I will see to it.' replied Ephraim.

***

Nathaniel had already been with Ephraim for over an hour and he thought he ought to start on the business he came to deal with. 'I have collected all the farm reports, Ephraim,' he said, 'and I think you will be pleased with what you see. I have also increased the salaries in line with the agreement we made with the managers. I know you are extremely busy and at the same time without an assistant so I will understand if you are a bit late with your report.'

'I promise that I will go through them as soon as I can Nathaniel, but I might wait until Charles arrives so that he can get a grip of things quickly. You are my largest account and I want to make sure there are no problems after he settles in.'

'That's alright Ephraim, now before I go home, would you like to tell me a little about these two young men I am seeing tomorrow?'

'Well the first one is Michael Lawson , he is the second son of George Lawson the saddler. He's a bright lad but the family business will eventually go to his elder brother John. He attended the Church School, as did the other lad, Luke Buxton.'

'I think I know both of these young men, I certainly know their fathers. Luke is Edward Buxton's son isn't he?' said Nathaniel.

'Yes he is, as you know, Edward has the haberdashers in the London Road and Luke is his youngest son.'

'I thought so, and if you can arrange the meetings for me, I look forward to seeing them both tomorrow.'

'That's alright then, are you ready for lunch?'

'Not today, I am afraid, Ephraim. I have to get back to Borton. I have a lot of work to do in preparation for my visit to London next week.'

'That's a pity, but thanks for your help Nathaniel. I am looking forward to your opinions on the two lads and I hope you think at least one of them is suitable.'

***

Nathaniel saw both the candidates for the job as Ephraim's clerk, as planned. Both young men impressed Nathaniel and he was pleased by their attitude, their obvious abilities and their interest in the job. 'I think this is a decision that Ephraim must make.' he said to himself, 'Both could do the job so it's down to Ephraim to pick the one he thinks he could best work with.'

***

'Well, which one is it Nathaniel?' Ephraim asked as Nathaniel sat down at the desk.

'I think you presented two very bright lads for me to interview Ephraim, and I complement you on your choice. Which one would *you* have chosen if I hadn't been involved?'

'It was difficult, but I think I would have chosen Luke myself, he was a bit easier to get on with and I think he was "quicker on the uptake," but you still haven't told me who you thought would be best, have you?'

'Well Ephraim, you have chosen the one that suits you. I was going to say the only way they could be separated was for you to choose the one you got on with best, and that is obviously Luke.'

'Thanks very much Nathaniel, you have put my mind at rest and I will get him started immediately. I just needed another opinion as I have never recruited anyone in my life. Watson was already here when I took over the business and I will certainly miss him.'

'I think when Charles comes he will be pleased that he will have a clerk who is young and not too set in his ways. I somehow think Watson would have been a problem for him.'

'Probably so,' said Ephraim as he showed Nathaniel to the door. 'Enjoy your visit to London.'

***

It was early in May when Nathaniel arrived in London. He had settled in quickly at the apartments and had meetings planned for the next four days. He had decided to mix business with pleasure and hoped to have time to enjoy the sights of London and maybe treat himself to a new fashionable suit of clothes. It was not long before Richard Pearson convinced Nathaniel to join in a game of poker and as usual Nathaniel lost sometimes and won others. Stakes were small and so losses, when they occurred, were not really a problem.

Nathaniel concluded all his business successfully and had packed all his purchases ready for the trip back to Borton when Richard said, 'We are having a big game at a friend's house tonight, are you interested?'

'I am going home tomorrow so I don't want a late night, otherwise I would love to come.'

'We are never late,' said Richard, 'you will still get your beauty sleep.'

'Well, if you are sure. What time do we start?'

'I will be going at about six o'clock so be ready by then and I will show you where we are going.'

***

'This is the place,' said Richard, as he rapped on the rickety door with his cane. 'The others are probably upstairs waiting.'

'I hope it is alright,' said Nathaniel uneasily, 'it looks a bit rough to me.'

'Don't worry, I have been here dozens of times and have never had any trouble,' he said as the door creaked open and a rough looking, thin faced man with gaps between his black crooked teeth peered around the edge of the door and said, 'Come in Mr. Pearson, they are waiting for you.'

254

'Thank you Jake, I am not late am I?'

'No Sir, just follow me and mind the gaps on the stairs.'

'Where the hell are we Richard? I don't like the feel of this place,' said a very nervous Nathaniel.

When they arrived at the top of the stairs, Jake opened a door and stepped to one side as he ushered the two gentlemen into a dimly lit room. There were two men standing near the small window and as Richard and Nathaniel entered the room, the taller of the two men said, with a mirthless smile on his face, 'Good evening Mr. Thorold, nice to meet you again. I hope you haven't come all the way from Bourne expecting to win again have you?' The taller man continued, 'I am Mr. Smith,' and pointing to his rotund friend, 'this is Mr. Brown.'

Nathaniel's mind flashed back to the last thing George had said after Nathaniel's big win that winter's night at Bourne. 'They don't like losing, *ever*.' He realised that these two gamblers were out to get even with him and he was going to have to be very careful. 'Why on earth did I let Richard talk me into this?' he thought.

***

Nathaniel was extremely nervous as the games progressed and was having difficulty concentrating, but Richard seemed quite relaxed and was winning. Smith and Brown were both friendly enough and Nathaniel started to relax and enjoy himself and was pleasantly surprised when Mr. Brown, the short rotund one, asked if anyone would like a coffee. Everyone agreed that it would be a good idea and Brown called Jake and said, 'Four coffees please Jake and make two of them strong. We don't want our guests going to sleep, do we?'

As the evening progressed, Nathaniel began to lose very heavily and at one stage put one of his small farms as a stake. Fortunately he managed to win a few hands and retrieved his losses. Time was passing quickly and he thought he should be thinking about going back to get an early night but he didn't want to go when he had started to win. Richard was losing heavily and was feeling very tired. 'I can't keep my eyes open and my head is throbbing like a drum.' he said, 'I have had enough and am going home to bed.' He got up from the table and staggered to the door. 'Are you coming Nathaniel or are you staying a bit longer?' he asked.

'I think I will stay a bit longer, but I won't be late,' was the reply. 'I can't leave while I am winning, can I?'

'No he can't, he has to give us a chance to get some of our money back. He owes us the chance, doesn't he Brown?'

'He certainly does. He cleaned us out last time,' replied Mr. Brown, his piercing blue eyes staring directly at Nathaniel. 'So let's get on with it!'

***

Soon after Richard had departed, Nathaniel was finding it difficult to concentrate and his head was throbbing. Brown and Smith took on the appearance of a couple of macabre apparitions who were constantly moving in and out of focus. 'I am going home,' he tried to say and heard one of the other two say, 'Oh no you're not, we haven't finished with you yet!'

**

Light was streaming through the small, cobweb covered window onto a bare wooden table when Nathaniel opened his eyes. He was alone in the room as he tried hard to remember where he was. The door on his left was swinging open on its squeaky hinges and there was no sign of anyone anywhere. Slowly it dawned on him that he had been playing poker with Richard and the two gamblers he had first met at Bourne, but why was he here all alone?

His head was really hurting and the strong sunlight coming through the window made it difficult to open his eyes and his head felt as if it had been hit with a hammer. 'What the hell has been going on, I don't remember having a drink at all so it can't be a hangover,' and then, once more, he remembered George's warning, 'they don't like losing, *ever*.'

'They must have put something in the coffee,' he thought, 'Richard was having trouble as well, that's why he left early.'

He quickly checked his pockets and purse, they were all empty. 'The bastards,' he exploded, and then he found the note pinned to his waistcoat…

Chapter 19

1734 – Continued

'Where are you going in such a rush Nathaniel?' Sylvia pleaded, trying to find out what was going on and why was everyone in such a panic.

'I don't bloody well know, but it will be a long way from here,' he said as he rushed out of the door. 'I'll let you know when I get there. Just remember to send the mob to Ephraim, he will sort it out.'

***

'Where are we going boss?' asked Mo as they galloped out of the gates towards Grantham and then eventually onto the muddy, rutted road towards the small town of Sleaford.

'As far away from Borton as we can get, but I want to get to Boston and I don't want to go by the obvious route. I will need your help when we are on the back lanes because I haven't a clue.'

'It's a good thing we brought George with us then. He knows his way over the fens like the back of his hands.'

'What do you think George? Which will be the best way to go?' asked Nathaniel.

George Headland rubbed his stubble covered chin as the horses slowed to a gentle trot. 'Well Mr. Thorold, if you want to get there quickly then I suggest you stick to the main roads. If you start going on the unmarked country lanes you could be in real trouble. There are lots of rivers and deep streams to cross and most of them you will have to get the horses to swim.'

'Don't they have ferries?'

'No Sir, mostly you have to pay a local boatman, if you can find one, and even then they can't carry a horse.'

'Well it might take longer, but at least we will get there without being followed,' countered Nathaniel.

'Don't you believe it,' interjected Mo. 'The word will be all over the county that three men on horseback are rushing along back roads towards Boston and your friends from London will be waiting for you when you get there!'

'It's true Sir, word spreads very quickly and it will take at least twice as long to get there if you go on the local tracks,' said George.

'Alright, if you are both convinced that the main route is the best one to follow then let's get onto it as soon as possible. Which way do you suggest Mo?'

'I think we should stay on this road until we get to Sleaford and then there is a fairly good road to Boston. It will be a bit muddy in places after all the rain we have had but we should make good progress.'

'Do you agree, George? asked Nathaniel.

'Well it's not a bad idea. But if we turn off about four miles before we get to Sleaford, there is a route which is almost as good. It goes through Threekingham and Donington and is a few miles shorter. I think we should try that one and we would get there a bit quicker.'

'I think you are right George,' said Mo, 'and we don't have to fight our way through Sleaford.'

'That's it then. You lead the way George.'

***

It was just after noon when six riders arrived at the big house at Borton. A tall thin man dismounted while the others remained on their horses. He ignored the few workers in the yard and strode to the front door of the house and rapped on the door with the handle of his whip. There was no reply so he banged on the door with his fist and shouted, 'Open up Thorold, before we break the door down, you know why we are here.' He was about to bang on the door again when there was movement inside. He heard the door being unbolted before it opened slowly and Sylvia asked politely.

'Can I help you Sir?'

'Yes you can. Get Nathaniel Thorold out here immediately or he will be in deep trouble.'

'I am afraid Mr. Thorold is away on business and won't be back for a while, Sir.'

'What do you mean, "for a while," will he be back today or has he gone for longer?'

'I am afraid, I can't tell you Sir, he said if anyone came they should talk to his solicitor.'

'Did he now, and who is this solicitor who deals with all his problems?'

'He is Mr. Ephraim Woolaston from Grantham.'

'When exactly did Mr. Thorold leave, may I ask?'

'He left early this morning, Sir.'

'You have no idea where he has gone then?'

'He mentioned the farm at Hough on the Hill last night so he might have gone there,' said Sylvia thinking she would try and send them off on a 'wild goose chase'

'Really!' said the tall man sarcastically, and turning towards one of the farm hands, 'You there, get my horses fed and watered. Quickly now, we haven't got all day.'

In an arrogant voice he said for all to hear, 'Now girl, just get something to eat and drink for me and my men, and be quick about it.'

'Of course Sir, please come inside and sit down.' She asked them to sit at the kitchen table and then went to the pantry to prepare some food.

As they were eating their food the tall thin man kept telling his companions to 'Hurry along,' as he wanted to get things sorted today. At the same time he persistently questioned Sylvia about where Nathaniel had gone, but she insisted she knew no more than she had already told them. He also sent one of his men out to the stables to try and find out if anyone in the yard knew where the master had gone.

When he returned, all he had found out was that Nathaniel and two others had left the farm early that morning and had trotted gently off down the Grantham Road.

'Two others, eh, who were they?' asked the tall man.

'Apparently they were the head cowman and the ostler, and as its market day in Grantham they thought that that's where they were heading.'

'I see,' and turning to Sylvia, 'which way would they go, to where was it, Hough on the Hill?'

'They would have to go through Grantham Sir.'

'Right, get the horses and let's get off to Grantham. Now!'

***

'Come on Brown, it's only a few steps, you're not that incapable,' said Smith as the portly Mr. Brown wheezed his slow climb up the steps to Woolaston's office. 'What was that solicitor's name?'

'It was Woolaston, Mr. Smith.' He replied between big gulps of laboured breath.

'I know it is Woolaston, you damn fool, that's what it says on the door. What's his first bloody name?'

'I think the woman said Ephraim, Mr. Smith.'

Smith banged on the door at the top of the stairs and a frightened young lad stood in his way and said. 'Have you an appointment Sir?'

'No I haven't, I want to see Mr. Ephraim Woolaston, now. It's urgent.'

'I am afraid Mr. Ephraim Woolaston is not here today Sir. Can I...'

'Charles, on hearing the loud voice of Mr. Smith had come out of his office. 'It's alright Luke, please carry on with your work. Now Sir, how can I help?'

'I wish to see Mr. Ephraim Woolaston, is that you?'

'No I am Mr. Charles Woolaston, a partner in this business. How can I help you?'

'I am here to discuss some private business regarding Mr. Nathaniel Thorold and I believe you are his representative.'

'Yes we are, please come in and sit down,' said Charles, 'but Mr. Thorold has given us no instructions recently Mr.. .....?'

'My name is Smith and this is my associate, Mr. Brown and I think you should see this,' he said, and with a flourish produced a crumpled sheet of paper and passed it over the table for Charles to study. 'What are you going to do about that then?' asked Smith.

After a quick glance over the paper, Charles dipped his quill into an inkpot and wrote a short note. He folded it in two, and said, 'Luke, would you take this note to Mr. Thomson please, it's urgent'

'Yes Sir.' said Luke as he left the office.

'Sorry about that gentlemen, but I just remembered I had an urgent meeting and you have caused me to miss it. Now where was I? Oh yes, your note. Well, I am doing absolutely nothing about it.'

'What do you mean, nothing, You can see quite clearly, he has transferred Priory Farm, Bartan over to us by default of a debt he incurred two months ago. It is signed under his hand and dated all legal like.'

'Yes I can see what it says, but as far as I am concerned, it is worthless.'

Mr. Smith started to shout and thump the table and Charles just leant back in his chair until calm was restored. 'Now gentlemen, when did Mr. Thorold sign this paper, you say it's "all dated legal like" but I can't find a date anywhere. Can you point it out to me?'

'Well he had enjoyed quite a lot of drink when he signed it,' said Brown, smirking as if it was funny.

With a quick interjection, Mr. Smith said, 'But he wasn't drunk.'

The outside door banged and Luke came in followed by a smartly dressed, elderly gentleman. 'Ah, sit down Brian. Gentlemen I would like to introduce Mr. Thomson he is our magistrate for Grantham. Brian what do you think of this?' he said, handing the paper to the magistrate.

Mr. Thomson studied the paper for what seemed an age and as the two visitors began to squirm in their seats. 'What is it gentlemen, are you feeling uncomfortable?' asked Charles, but both, looking decidedly guilty, remained silent.

'Well Charles,' said Brian. 'As forgeries go this is a very poor one. First I know of no such farm anywhere around here, and also I have never heard of a place called Bartan. As for the signature, it is certainly not Nathaniel's. The other thing you may *not* have realised Charles, is that Mr. Brown and Mr. Smith are not their real names and both are wanted in Bourne for fraudulent activities along with their friend George Montini, who you *do* know.' Turning to the pair of miscreants who were just getting out of their chairs he said, 'Don't bother rushing off chaps, my men are waiting for you at the bottom of the stairs. We have already arrested your four companions.'

***

'I will call back later when I have dealt with this rabble and discuss what we should do next,' said Brian. 'We ought to inform Nathaniel what has been going on, but from what I understand he knows nothing. According to the men we arrested downstairs, he left Borton in a hurry early this morning, telling no one where he was going.'

'I will send a message to Borton first thing in the morning after I have had a word with Ephraim,' replied Charles. 'If he is not at home we might get some idea as to where he has gone and anyway, Ephraim may well know what is going on.'

***

Nathaniel, Mo and George had just passed the small hamlet of Bicker when Nathaniel's horse stumbled in a rain filled pothole and started to show signs of distress. 'I could do without this,' Nathaniel pronounced as he checked the horses legs. 'I think it has a badly sprained ankle. We will have to leave it behind and try to get another one.'

'It will be a bit difficult to get another one round here,' said Mo, 'I think we will have to go back and try our luck in Bicker.'

Nathaniel stamped his feet and swore. 'If we don't get a move on those bastards from London will catch us up and then I will be in it up to my neck.'

'Well let's get going,' said George calmly, 'I'll walk with your horse sir, and you can go on with Mo and start checking around to see what can be done. I should try at that little inn we passed, they should know who to talk to.'

'Well done George, that's a good idea.' said Mo, and to Nathaniel, 'Shall we get going then Nat?'

***

After they had departed, George was walking slowly with Nathaniel's horse past a small copse near a boggy field when a man appeared on horseback. George had no idea where he came from, as he had approached quietly from behind the horse he was leading.

'What have we here?' asked the stranger pointing a pistol at a very nervous George. Who does that fine looking horse belong to? It's obvious that it's not yours.'

'It's my Master's sir. He has gone on ahead with his man but they will be back soon.'

'Yes I saw them go. Now you be a sensible man and move away from that horse while I check his saddle bags. I don't want to have to use this pistol.' and more menacingly, '*so move, -now*'

George did as he was told and backed away from the horse as the stranger rummaged through Nathaniel's baggage. 'Ah, what's this?' he asked as he pulled out the smart, polished wooden box containing the pistols. He opened the box slowly, keeping his eyes on George. 'What a beautifully balanced pair, they must have cost a fortune. They look as if they have never been fired.' He pointed his own pistol at George and told him to move further back and 'Don't you dare move. I am going to load these two beauties and try them out.'

It took him a few minutes to load and get them ready, all the time

261

making sure George stayed well away. When he was ready he started to look for something to fire at and as he did so he heard Nathaniel and Mo coming back at a gallop with a young lad on a third horse. 'What's going on over there?' asked Mo? 'It looks as if George has company.'

'It looks like a hold up Mo, that man's got a pistol and it's pointing at George. Get yours out, I left mine in my saddlebag.'

'Don't come any nearer,' shouted the stranger, as he climbed carefully back onto his horse, 'I have two loaded pistols ready to fire. If you come any nearer I will let you have both barrels.'

'Spread out Mo, and you lad, stay here until this is sorted. He can't hit all of us, even if he is a brilliant shot and gets lucky.'

'I said don't come any nearer, do you wish to be gunned down with your own pistols?' said the stranger, waving the pistols menacingly.

Nathaniel said, 'Go left Mo and I will move towards George. Just be ready to move when I say so.'

'That's near enough, I have warned you twice.'

Nathaniel looked past the highwayman towards where George was standing. *'Now, George,'* he shouted. The stranger, thinking George was going to charge him swung round and fired a shot. There was an almighty explosion and the barrel of the pistol burst, sending shards of metal in all directions and taking the strangers hand with it. The combination of the explosion and his screams caused his horse to bolt and as it continued on its frantic chase, the highwayman's screams receded as the distance grew.

'Are you alright George?' Nathaniel shouted

'I'm OK. What the hell happened?' George asked looking on with a bewildered expression on his face. 'I thought he was going to kill me, what on earth did you want me to do?'

'Nothing George, I just wanted to distract him.'

Mo had dismounted and was picking up bits of the pistol, 'It's a bloody good job you had not fired these yourself Nat, where on earth did you get them?'

'I got them from a friend, Richard Pearson, a gunsmith in London.'

'He will soon run out of customers if all his pistols are like that one.' said Mo examining the handful of remaining bits he had picked up.

'Well, when I was in London, he was a good mate of mine and I had heard that in the early part of his career he had been tampering with proofed pistol barrels but I never believed it. No wonder he never asked me for the remainder of the money,' and pointing to the remaining pistol lying in the mud, 'Throw that pistol in the river Mo, we don't want any more accidents do we?'

'No boss, we certainly don't.'

'Right, it's time we moved. We can't afford to waste any more time,' said Nathaniel. 'George, can you transfer the saddle and all the bags from my horse to the spare one that young Jack has brought? Jack will walk my mount back to the inn and you can collect it on your way back in a day or two. Hopefully it will have rested well and you can take it home.'

'Aren't you coming back with us, then?' asked Mo.

'I don't know what I am doing yet, but I don't think I will be home for a while.'

***

After Jack had set off back to Bicker, they continued their journey and Mo asked, 'Are you going to tell us how far we are going?'

'I am not sure yet, but I think you will be able to go home once we have reached Boston and I have sorted things out. I won't need your help after that.'

'Aren't you going to tell us where you are going then?'

'I don't know myself as yet and it is best for us all that you have no idea what is going on. I'll give you a message to take to Mr. Woolaston at his office in Grantham and he will give you any instructions he deems to be appropriate.'

***

It was mid-afternoon when they arrived at Boston and Nathaniel booked in for the night at *"The Anchor"*. After settling the horses into the stables, Mo and George were booked into a small boarding house just around the corner. Nathaniel's final words to the two, were, 'Be in the bar of *"The Anchor"* at noon tomorrow and I will tell you what is going on. I have some sorting out to do before then, so you can have the rest of the time to yourselves, but don't get drunk and don't be late!'

***

Nathaniel left *"The Anchor"* and headed directly to Max Hoboer's office only to find it closed. A few questions to a couple of young lads loitering around the area ascertained that Max had headed towards the docks shortly before Nathaniel had arrived. After a short walk, it did not take him long to find his friend. Max, who was just leaving a small, tidy brig from which a strong smell of fish permeated the whole area.

'Nathaniel, what the hell are you doing here?' he boomed as he came down the gangway, 'have you given up farming?'

'Nice to see you too,' replied Nathaniel with a touch of sarcasm. 'Actually I am in desperate need of help and I think you are the man best suited to provide it.'

'If I can help, you know I will. Now tell me, what's the problem?'

Nathaniel explained as briefly as possible the situation he was involved in and said, 'What I need is a passage to anywhere, as quickly as possible. I won't feel safe until I am out of the country, so have you any vessels

263

due out in the immediate future?'

'Well if you can put up with the smell and be ready in three hours, the *"Alesund"* here leaves on the next tide. There are no other sailings for the next three days that have vacancies for passengers'

'Where is she going?' asked Nathaniel.

'I thought you said you were happy to go anywhere.'

'I am, but I am also interested where it's going.'

'You are in luck Nathaniel, it's heading to warmer climes. It's actually going to Lisbon in Portugal but will be stopping at a few ports on the way. I know he is not carrying any passengers so if you are interested, I am sure he will be happy to accommodate you.'

'I will go and get my baggage from *"The Anchor"* straight away,' said Nathaniel, wanting to get going as soon as possible.

'I think we had better check with Captain Horgesand first, don't you? You would look a bit silly turning up with your kit and find there was no berth. Now come on, let's go and ask.'

***

It didn't take Nathaniel long to agree terms and confirm his passage on the *"Alesund"* and Captain Horgesand was delighted to have some company for the trip. The option for Nathaniel to disembark at one of the ports on the way was agreed, but the berth to Lisbon was his if he so required.

As Nathaniel walked back to Max's office he asked if Max would send someone to *"The Anchor"* to collect his belongings. 'I don't want Mo and George seeing me move out and asking awkward questions. They will probably still be in the bar drinking.'

'When are you going to tell them?' asked Max. 'You have got to tell them sometime.'

'I want to be out of here before they find out,' replied Nathaniel. 'I have told them to be in the bar at noon tomorrow and they will find out all they need to know then.'

'So who is going to tell them?' Max asked, saying, 'You will be long gone!'

'I was hoping that you would be kind enough to tell them that I had already gone and you had no idea where to, or when I would be back,' and pulling a sealed package from his waistcoat handed it to Max and said. 'Would you ask Mo to deliver this to Ephraim Woolaston at Grantham as soon as he gets the opportunity?'

'Don't you think you should tell them where you are going?' asked Max.

Nathaniel explained his reasons for secrecy and gave some instructions for Max to pass on to Mo and George. Max despatched two of his men to *"The Anchor"* to collect Nathaniel's belongings and gave them strict instructions to go through the back door and not go into the bar.

'Come on Nathaniel, let's go for something to eat, I am famished. We have plenty of time before you need to get on board.'

***

Mo and George arrived at *"The Anchor"* in plenty of time and settled down in a quiet corner with a pot of ale to await instructions. Noon came and went and there was no sign of Nathaniel. 'Where on earth has he got to?' queried George.

'I don't know, but we will stay here until he shows up. It looks like we are in for a storm and at least we won't get wet in here,' replied Mo. 'Your turn to fill up George,' he said as they settled down for what could be a long wait.

About an hour later, a big built, red bearded man entered the bar and looked around before approaching their table. 'Are you two gentlemen waiting for Mr. Thorold?' he asked.

'Yes sir, we are.' replied Mo, 'Is he alright?'

'Yes he's alright. Can I sit down?' he asked as the barman came over with a pot of ale and put it on the table.

'Your usual Mr. Hoboer?' he asked, and cleared up some empty pots before returning to the bar.

'I am Max Hoboer, and I have some instructions for you from Mr. Thorold,' he said. 'Unfortunately Mr. Thorold can't be here himself as he took passage in a boat out of here on last night's tide.'

'Where has he gone, and why didn't he tell us himself?' asked Mo.

'I am not at liberty to tell you, but I am sure you will understand that the less you know, the better, but he has given me some instructions for you.'

'Well we know he is in trouble and there is a gang looking for him so I suppose there isn't much more to tell,' said George.

Max fiddled around with some papers he was carrying and produced a few coins from his pocket. 'Mr. Thorold would like you to take the horse he borrowed, back to the inn at Bicker and collect his horse to take back to Borton. You must be very careful not to make any damage to the horse's ankle worse. There is enough money here to pay your way home and cover for any emergencies. He also says you must give the lad, Jack at Bicker, this penny for his troubles. He must have been a very frightened boy. There is also a letter for you to give to Mr. Ephraim Woolaston at the earliest opportunity.'

'I think we knew all that anyway,' George said as he emptied his pot. 'Don't you have any idea where he has gone or how long he will be?'

'I know where he has gone but I have no idea how long he will be away, but he is certain you will be in danger if you know any more. He said he will be in touch as soon as he thinks it will be safe for you to know. That's all I can tell you.'

'Well, I suppose we had better get started then,' said Mo. 'We might as well be on our way, eh George?'

'I suppose so,' George replied somewhat grumpily, 'but I have just ordered another pot of ale each'

'You have no need to rush, Mr. Thorold has paid for your accommodation for tonight so you might as well start off early tomorrow. Relax for the rest of the day and get a good night's sleep,' said Max, getting up from the table. 'Have a safe journey and don't forget that letter to Mr. Woolaston.'

As he left "The Anchor", George said, 'What do you make of that Mo? It's a bit strange, isn't it?'

***

'Good morning Charles,' said Ephraim. 'I see we have had your note to Nathaniel returned. No one seems to know where he is at all.'

'Yes, Sylvia Butler kept it for three days hoping he would be back, but decided to return it to us when she had not received any news.'

'Well we can only assume he knows nothing of the arrests and thinks he is still on the run. Let's hope we hear from him soon so that we can put his mind at rest,' said Ephraim. 'It certainly looks as if his gambling has got the better of him, even after all his promises.'

***

Two days later, Maurice Clark arrived at the Woolaston's office with Nathaniel's note. He handed it over to Ephraim and said, 'Will that be all Sir? I have to see some people in town before I go back to Borton.'

'That's alright Mr. Clark but please call back before you go home as there might be a reply.' Ephraim passed the note to Charles. 'Here you are Charles, you read it. Your eyes are better than mine.'

Ephraim leant back in his chair and relaxed as Charles carefully eased the seal, unfolded the sheet of paper and started to read:

'*Dear Ephraim and Charles,*

May I humbly apologise for leaving in such a hurry and not informing you of my problems beforehand. I have no idea what I committed myself to whilst in London, but the note I found when I awoke on that morning was very threatening. I know I had been gambling but I can't understand why I have no memory of the events of that particular evening. My friend, Richard Pearson, also awoke with no recollection of the evening's events so he was no help to me whatsoever.

When I heard that the gang were expected to arrive at Borton I decided that it would be prudent to leave until things quietened down and hoped that you, with your legal expertise and skills, would be able to fend them off. I know it was cowardly and inconsiderate of me but I am afraid I was, and still am, very frightened.

I am leaving Boston in a Swedish brig on the next tide and will inform you of my whereabouts in due course. I suspect I may be away for some considerable time and so I would be extremely grateful if you would take over the control of the estate until my return.'

Charles paused and said, 'There are the usual felicitations, and that's about it. No clue of where he is or his intentions for the future. He didn't even date it, so we will have to ask Maurice Clark to see if he can help.'

'Gambling will ruin that young man,' said Ephraim, 'he knows full well that he must have been given something to send him to sleep and that he was dealing with a bunch of crooks. In some ways it was a good decision to run away, at least with Brian's help, we managed to take them off the streets.'

'That's true but it will be some time before Nathaniel finds out that he is not being pursued, so he will have to sweat it out a bit longer.'

'It won't do him any harm to suffer for a while and he might realise what a fool he has been,' replied Ephraim, 'There's absolutely nothing we can do until we hear from him, is there?'

***

Soon after leaving harbour, the *"Alesund"* started to experience heavy weather and Nathaniel took to his tiny bunk situated in an airless compartment in the stern of the ship. As the storm worsened, Nathaniel began to feel very poorly and he slid into one of his 'sorry for himself' moods. Between bouts of sickness, he reflected on his life of wasted opportunities and bouts of juvenile behaviour.

By the second night, with no improvement in the weather, he was seriously depressed and Captain Horgesand was getting very worried about his passenger. Every time he checked to see if he was alright he was told in no uncertain terms to 'bugger off.' Nathaniel's mind was in turmoil, the way he disrespected his father, his problems with gambling, his wild behaviour as a young man, the loss of his beloved Charlotte, the way he had treated his friends and colleagues and now the loss of a substantial part of his estate. At every stage of his life he knew he had ignored good, sound advice and he hugely regretted it. He lay, curled up in his bunk, sobbing, and being violently sick, 'If only I had listened, but no! I carried on in my own stupid, pig-headed way and now my life is finished, what the hell am I going to do? Stuck here in this wretched stinking hovel not knowing where I am heading or what's going to happen to me. I've got no future, and for all the good I have done in this world, I might as well be dead.'

The storm showed no signs of easing and Nathaniel, still in his bunk, continued his troubled assessment of his life. Finally, totally depressed and in a state of self-pity, he climbed out of his heaving bunk determined to 'finish it, once and for all.' It was in the early hours of the morning, and in complete darkness, he staggered onto the upper deck and, grabbing any hand hold he could, stumbled towards the stern rail.

The seas were washing over the boat and occasionally the sea would break violently and make it impossible to hold on safely. His progress was

267

slow and continually broken by waves lashing across the wet boards of the deck forcing him to grab anything he could.

Captain Horgesand was on the bridge and saw Nathaniel staggering around. 'What the hell does he think he is doing now?' he said, and then shouted as loudly as he could, 'get back below decks you bloody fool.'

Nathaniel continued to stagger towards the stern rails, oblivious of anyone or anything and totally immersed in his own self-pity.

Captain Horgesand watched spellbound as Nathaniel was picked up and buried under a tumultuous wall of water. 'NATHAN-I-E-L!!' he screamed and his voice was blown away on the wind and into the black of the raging night.

***

As Nathaniel neared the stern of the boat he was picked up bodily by a massive and powerful wall of water, and just before he lost all consciousness, Nathaniel thought he heard someone call his name. In his confused state of mind, he thought it was his beloved Charlotte...

'Wait for me darling, I am on my way.' he called out, as he was washed away...

PART 2

Somewhere In The Vineyard

Chapter 20

1734 - Continued

'The bloody fool,' exploded Captain Horgesand, trying to keep his balance as the ship rolled violently in the heavy seas. 'That's the last we will see of him.'

Horgesand was the captain of the Swedish brig, *"Alesund"* and had just seen his only passenger washed overboard during a violent night time storm

***

Nathaniel Thorold was a gentleman farmer who had come aboard at Boston, desperate to evade a crowd of thugs who were chasing him for a considerable sum of money which he had lost at poker on one of his visits to London. The *"Alesund"* had sailed straight into a violent storm and Nathaniel had spent two days in his bunk suffering from sea sickness and feeling sorry for himself and blaming everyone but himself for his current predicament. He had descended into a deep black depression and had eventually decided he would be better off dead. The last time he had been seen was when Captain Horgesand had seen him disappearing under a wall of water washing over the stern of the brig.

***

'Captain, sir, I think he's still down there,' shouted an excited lookout, trying to make himself heard above the noise of the storm. 'I just saw something.'

Horgesand went to the see what the fuss was about and, when the stern lifted out of the water as it crested another huge wave, he saw something wedged against a deck locker. 'It can't be him,' he thought. 'If it is, he will certainly be dead.'

He kept a close watch on the spot and the next time he saw it he decided it was a body and it should be brought back to somewhere safe, regardless of whether he was alive or not. He instructed three sailors to get some safety lines and collect the lifeless Thorold. 'We can't leave him out there, he deserves a decent burial whatever he has done. Just go carefully lads and don't take risks.'

After a struggle Nathaniel's lifeless body was brought back to safety and the captain instructed the sailors to: 'Put him back in his bunk until the weather eases, and then we will give him a decent burial. You had better put a rope round him, we don't want him falling off the bunk and rolling round the deck.'

***

By the next afternoon, it was still fairly uncomfortable aboard the *"Alesund"* as she fought her way through the tail of the storm. Gradually, as the wind eased and the seas calmed down, two sailors were dispatched to get a canvas sheet and some ballast to prepare Mr. Thorold for burial.

Within a few minutes, one of the sailors rushed back on deck and shouted up to the captain, 'Captain, sir, he's still breathing. Come quick!'

'You must be mistaken,' said a disbelieving captain as he made his way to Nathaniel's cabin. 'He was dead last night.'

The other sailor was waiting outside the cabin door and in an excited state, declared, 'He is sir, he's definitely breathing.'

Captain Horgesand entered the cabin and peering through the semi-darkness, looked at the body in the bunk and saw a sheet-white face with a very large lump on his forehead and an open wound on his left shoulder. 'Looks dead to me,' he said. 'What makes you think he is still alive?'

'He was definitely breathing sir; we could see his chest move.'

The captain looked closer, and just as he had decided his first assessment was correct, he thought he saw some movement. 'I don't believe in miracles, but get Olaf to bandage his wound then cover him up and keep him warm. One of you stay here and keep your eyes on him. Make sure you tell me if there is any change.'

***

By dawn the next day it was obvious that Nathaniel was still alive and was slowly showing signs of improvement. By mid-morning he had opened his eyes and was asking for water. As the weather improved, Nathaniel, who had spent most of the time in his bunk, gradually recovered and began to relax.

When Captain Horgesand asked 'What on earth were you doing on the upper deck in such a violent storm, Nathaniel? You could have gone over the side and that would have been the end of it!'

'I have no idea Lars, I remember feeling very poorly and miserable but then I woke up in my bunk, wet through. My mind is a complete blank as far as that goes, but I can remember feeling very sick and unhappy.'

'Well you are very lucky to be alive. We all thought you were dead and were about to prepare you for a watery grave.'

***

Nathaniel realised he had had a narrow escape but once he had got out of his bunk, eaten a couple of meals and relaxed on deck, he began to enjoy the trip.

He was still very apprehensive as regards what would happen to his considerable estate in Lincolnshire whilst he was away from home, but he was very pleased that he had sent a note to Ephraim Woolaston. Ephraim was the family's legal representative who for many years had proved to be totally loyal and trustworthy. Ephraim's nephew had recently joined the practice with the intention of taking over when his uncle retired in the near future.

His thoughts began to concentrate on what his future actions should be. 'I can't go back,' he thought, 'those crooks will still be chasing me, but I haven't a clue what I am going to do in some foreign land.' He knew the brig's final destination was Lisbon but he still had plenty of time to make up his mind where to disembark before it reached its first port of call, which he knew was Ostend.

Lars Horgesand enjoyed having Nathaniel as company on the trip and whenever it was convenient they relaxed in the comfort of Lars' cabin and enjoyed long stimulating conversations. Nathaniel was particularly interested in the strong smelling cargo. 'Lars, tell me, why are you carrying such a foul smelling cargo of fish all the way from Norway to Portugal when they have plenty of fish of their own?'

'Lots of people ask me that,' he said, prodding the tobacco firmly into his pipe. 'The fish we are carrying is dried salted cod and is known in Norway as "Klippfish" but the Portuguese have their own name for it and it is known there as "Baccalhau."'

'Why don't they make their own then?'

'It's not so easy, you need good cold water cod for it to be successful. The Portuguese have tried to salt and dry all sorts of species of fish but have never been able to get the desired results. They have also tried to preserve without salt and have produced "Baccalhau Fresco" which is edible but a poor substitute for our product.'

'Do you deliver to order then?'

'No we just load up the brig and sail for Portugal. So far we have always managed to sell everything we've carried.'

'Are you the only one doing this trade then, Lars?'

'Good Lord, no. Our company has five brigs continually working this business and there are a couple more small firms also involved.'

They must be busy up in Norway then, salting and drying to keep you all busy.'

'Yes, and nearly all of it is carried out in Kristiansund in the North of the country.'

'Why do the Portuguese eat the dried salted stuff when they can get as much fresh fish as they want?' asked Nathaniel, still not understanding the reasons behind such a big trade.

'It's all to do with religion,' said Lars after a long pull on his tar coated pipe. 'They're all Romans and they are not allowed to eat meat on a Friday. The people round the coast are alright because they can eat fresh fish, but those further inland where the fresh fish is not available eat either dried fish or go without. Nearly all of this cargo will be moved inland as soon as it is off-loaded.'

'Well I never,' said Nathaniel, 'you learn something new every day.'

After relighting his pipe with a taper, Lars asked, 'What are you going to do when you leave us, Nathaniel?'

'I don't really know, but I have toyed with the idea of going on to Livorno in Italy where I have some good friends. It's a nice place and I know I will be able to relax there. Where do you go after Lisbon, do you go home empty?'

'I have to pay a visit to the shipping agent and see if he has a cargo for me, if not I will have to wait until something suitable turns up. I will get a load soon enough but I never know where we will be going next.'

'You don't go straight back to Norway then?'

'Sometimes we do, but not very often.'

***

After his conversation with Lars, Nathaniel decided to stay with the *"Alesund"* until it reached Lisbon and thought that as it might take months for things to settle down at home, and anyway, Ephraim and Charles Woolaston could handle things comfortably. Thoughts of paying a visit to Livorno were firming up in his mind and he was also beginning to form the idea of a business venture which might prove a lucrative side-line whilst in Italy. His friend Fabio Montini the shipping agent in Livorno was also featuring prominently in his plans. 'I will have to have a word with Lars,' he thought. 'if the Portuguese like it, why shouldn't the Italians?'

***

At dinner a couple of nights after leaving Ostend, Nathaniel asked Lars if he could purchase three or four barrels of "Baccalhau" when they arrived at Lisbon. 'Of course you can Nathaniel. You can buy all you want, but I didn't realise you loved it so much.'

Nathaniel smiled and started to explain his plans. 'Well, I am being a bit devious really. I have a friend in Livorno who told me when I was staying with him that those away from the coast were in the same situation as your clients in Portugal and for the same reasons. I intend to give him these barrels of "Baccalhau" as a present because I know he will pass them on to relatives far from the coast. If they express any interest in having more then I will be in business, probably with my friend Fabio'

'Sounds a good idea to me,' replied Lars 'but how do you propose to get your "Baccalhau"?

'Well I hope you will be able to supply it, Lars. Who else would I get it from?'

'I have no idea.' said Lars with a grin.

***

Nathaniel spent a great deal of the remainder of the trip in deep discussions with Lars on how to develop their ideas and trying to predict the possible pitfalls. To save months of delay Lars said he would try to pick up a

273

cargo in Lisbon for Livorno or a port in the general direction and if an order looked likely he could get back to Kristiansund and set the wheels in motion. Nathaniel was delighted with the prospect of such positive help and could see distinct advantages for both of them. A quick resolution depended on Lars picking up a cargo for Livorno, but if not, he would still go ahead as he had originally planned.

Nathaniel was elated with the outcome of his talks with Lars and forgot entirely the problems he was running away from. He was experiencing an excitement and challenge he had not felt since working in London with Sir Samuel Thorold, developing his business skills, and he loved it. All he could think of was the challenge he was setting for himself and being involved with such a project was occupying all his waking hours. 'This is great and I love it, it's so different from the routine of estate management.'

**

By the time they arrived in Lisbon, Nathaniel was so excited and enthusiastic about his plans that he was beginning to infuriate Lars. Soon after tying alongside the jetty, Nathaniel asked Lars if he had managed to secure a cargo and received the angry retort, 'For God's sake Nathaniel, calm down and be patient. I haven't been ashore yet and I have to sell this lot before I can take another load!'

'I am sorry Lars, but I am so excited, I can't help it.'

'Well if you carry on like this you will drive me mad. Now, I have got work to do so why don't you go ashore and stretch your legs and get out of my way!' Lars turned away and strode down the gangway heading to the port office, ignoring Nathaniel's apologies.

It was a week before the bulk of the "Baccalhau" was sold and a new cargo brought on board. Lars had managed to secure a part load to Valencia and the rest of the hold was filled and to be delivered to Barcelona. Both Lars and Nathaniel were very pleased as this would set them well on the way to Livorno.

They had managed to keep six barrels for Nathaniel to see how things worked out and he had decided to give Fabio two of the six barrels. They would try to sell the rest for the best price they could get.

'I like it, it will be a good way to test the market.' said Lars.

**

The trip from Lisbon to Livorno eventually took just over a month. They had picked up cargo at Barcelona for Toulon, and then eventually a near full cargo for Livorno.

They eased their way into the bustling harbour as the sun was just setting over the azure blue Mediterranean. Nathaniel excitedly pointed out some of the main landmarks and Lars said, 'It's a long way out of my usual territory, but at least I am still making money. I hope I can pick up a return

274

load as I don't want to be stranded this far from home.'

'Well I am sure Fabio will be able to help you as he is the shipping office manager here. If he can't sort you out then no one can.'

***

The next morning Nathaniel went in search of Fabio and met him just outside his office in deep discussions with a group of French seaman. It was obviously important so Nathaniel stood and waited. It wasn't long before Fabio saw him and he called out, 'Nathaniel where have you appeared from? Why didn't you let me know you were here?'

'Hello Fabio, nice to see you. I only arrived last night so I waited until now before looking you up. I have such a lot to tell you and so perhaps we can talk over lunch.'

'That's a good idea, be at my office by midday and we can visit my favourite restaurant. Meanwhile I have a lot to do so if you don't mind, I must get on.'

***

Over lunch, Nathaniel explained why he had left home in a rush and the plans he had developed during his trip from Boston. Fabio listened intently and eventually said, 'First things first Nathaniel, get all your baggage together and I will send someone to bring it round here later this afternoon and we will get you moved in at my place until we decide what to do.'

'That's very kind of you Fabio. What about the two barrels of "Baccalhau?"

'I will get a cart round this afternoon to collect them and take them home. As for the other barrels you mentioned, we can arrange storage until we need them.'

'That's wonderful, really appreciated. Is there any chance of helping Lars to get cargo back to a North Sea port?'

'Of course there is, we always need long distant carriers. It's easy enough to get transport within the Mediterranean but beyond Gibraltar is not so easy.'

'Thanks for that, Lars will be very pleased to hear it. I think he was a bit worried about having to work his way back in short stages.'

'Just ask him to call around whenever is convenient and we will sort something out.'

'I will, but he won't be in too much of a rush as he wants to see the outcome of our experiment. He would be very happy to get an order for a full load of "Baccalhau" before he sets off, and so would I.'

'That's sorted then. It's been a long time since we last met Nathaniel, did you hear that I married Maria a couple of years after you left?'

'Yes I did, I thought you would take the plunge eventually. Have you

275

any children yet?'

'We have. Two lovely young boys, Julio who is three years old and Roberto who is two. We didn't think we were going to have any but thankfully our prayers were finally answered and Roberto came very quickly after Julio.'

'Wonderful. I look forward to meeting them all. I hope they are well.'

'Thankfully yes, and I am sure Maria will be delighted to see you again.'

***

Back on board the *"Alesund"*, Lars was busy supervising the offloading of cargo and when Nathaniel arrived back after lunch he managed to get a few minutes to tell him of the good news. He also told him that 'A cart will be around to collect two barrels of "Baccalhau" sometime this afternoon to take to Fabio's home.'

'Where have you been Nathaniel, it's already been and gone.'

'Good Lord, that was quick, I didn't hear him give anyone the instructions.'

'He's obviously switched on, that chum of yours.' said Lars, as he kept an eye on the cargo being carried ashore.

'Well I hope he is not too quick off the mark when he sends someone round to collect my baggage, I haven't started packing yet.'

'By the way, what are we going to do with the remaining four barrels?' asked Lars.

'Fabio is finding somewhere to store them so no doubt there will be a cart around tomorrow morning to collect them.'

***

'I don't remember this road.' said Nathaniel.

'No I don't think you have been this way before. Soon after Maria and I got married, we bought a new villa out of town. It's in a peaceful spot with lovely views. It will be ideal for the children as they grow. I am sure you will like it.'

'They turned off the main road onto a narrow precarious track which passed through an olive grove. The gnarled ancient olive trees stretched away up the hillside to the right and down to a dried riverbed to the left.

'Nearly there.' said Fabio.

As they turned down a gentle slope on the left a smallish, modern red roofed villa came into view and Maria appeared at the entrance with the youngest boy in her arms and the other standing by her side. 'How lovely to see you again Nathaniel. It was such a surprise to get Fabio's note this morning. Come inside and relax.' and then to Fabio, 'Those two barrels you sent smell awfully fishy so I have had them put in the outhouse.'

'That's alright darling, I will sort them out later.'

'Come on Nathaniel, let's go and have a glass of wine on the veranda.'

276

As Nathaniel and Fabio enjoyed a glass of local red wine in the warm evening sun, Nathaniel said, 'What a wonderful place you have here Fabio. Sitting here watching the sun go down over the olive groves and the beautiful blue Mediterranean in the distance, it's a million miles from Borton. I could settle down here and never ever wish to go back home, ever again.'

'You would get bored to tears Nathaniel and I bet you would soon get lonely with no one else around to talk to.'

'I suppose you are right, but I can dream, can't I?'

'This idea of yours Nathaniel, just go through it again will you?' said Fabio, topping up their glasses.

Nathaniel explained his ideas again and stressed the need to spread the "Baccalhau" to as wide a group of people as possible to get an idea if there is a market for it.

'I can tell you now there is a need and I am fairly sure you are on to a winner. However, I might be wrong. I will get my brother Silvio to take a barrel out to relatives tomorrow and see what they think. You should have a good idea by the end of the week.'

'I don't think I have met Silvio, have I? Is he reliable?'

'I don't think you have, he has only been here for about a month and is desperate for a job. He will be very keen to make a good impression and he is certainly reliable. He will be here first thing in the morning so you can tell him exactly what you need him to do.'

They relaxed and talked together and eventually were joined by Maria who had been settling the boys in bed. 'What are you going to do with those two barrels of smelly fish, Fabio?' asked Maria.

'Nathaniel hopes to make his fortune by selling them all over Italy for Friday dinners.'

Using the Italian word for dried fish, Maria said, 'But we can get "Baccala" anyway so why bother?'

'These are top quality codfish, not the tiny little tiddlers you can sometimes get here in Livorno and they keep for months at a time.' explained Fabio.

'I think we should open one of the barrels in the morning.' said Nathaniel. 'We had better check the stock before we start moving out with it.'

Maria was still a bit apprehensive and asked, 'but what do you do with it? It smells a bit strong to me.'

'It's best to soak it overnight to get rid of most of the salt and then you cook it as you would any other fish. It's very tasty, we had it a few times on the "Alesund". I am sure people will buy it once they have sampled it.'

***

When Silvio arrived the next morning, Nathaniel explained what was to be done and although Silvio was surprised that he was to give the "Baccala" away he soon understood the reasoning behind it. When they opened one of the barrels, both Fabio and Silvio were surprised at the size of the fish. They were whole large Cod, split and gutted. 'I didn't expect them to be as big as that.' said Fabio, 'If they are all like this one, I am sure they will sell quickly. I think you might be on to something here Nathaniel.'

'Where exactly will you be going Silvio. Is it very far?' asked Nathaniel.

'Our Auntie Anna lives way up in the hills where they farm goats and if I leave before midday today I should get there tomorrow afternoon. I will be stopping overnight on the way so I will be able to give my hosts some to sample and check with them on the way back.'

'When do you expect to get back?'

'I should be away for a few days, so expect me back in about a week.'

Nathaniel turned to Fabio, 'I would love to go with him, do you think I could?'

'That's a brilliant idea, I will let you have a horse and you can use it or travel on the cart. You will be able to see for yourself what sort of reaction you get to your "Baccala."

***

Fabio set off for work leaving Nathaniel and Silvio to get organised and away on their trip. 'Don't forget to speak to Lars today,' shouted Nathaniel as Fabio set off, 'he will need to get those other barrels stored and out of his way very soon.'

'Don't you worry Nathaniel, I'll sort it out. Just get off and enjoy yourselves.'

***

It didn't take long for Nathaniel and Silvio to load the cart and prepare the horses for the journey. They made sure they had enough food and drink to cover any hold ups on the way, said goodbye to Maria, and set off.

It was a lovely day, and the sun shone from a cloudless sky as they made their steady way east from Livorno towards the hills in the far distance. They soon were well into the sparsely populated countryside and people were few and far between. 'It's a bit quiet out here,' said Nathaniel, 'I don't think there will be much need for our "Baccala", do you?'

'Don't worry Nathaniel, there are plenty of people, all with very large, hungry families. As soon as they see what we are bringing, they will want more. Believe me, you won't be able to supply enough.'

'I hope you are right.' replied Nathaniel, beginning to think he was wasting his time. After a couple of hours they stopped for refreshments near a small group of houses situated by the side of the track. Several dogs barked loudly as they approached and a group of children who were playing in the road quietened the dogs and surrounded the travellers.

Nathaniel's understanding of the Italian language was very limited but he understood some of the basics and obviously the children wanted to know what these strangers were doing and more importantly, did they have anything to give them. Meanwhile the mother of some of the children came out and Silvio engaged her in conversation and eventually she went back to her cottage and returned with a welcome jug of rough red wine.

As they leant back on a grassy bank in the shade of a lemon tree, Nathaniel closed his eyes and said, 'This is very nice, the wine's a bit rough but it's very welcome.'

Silvio was laughing as the children chatted to him in their speedy language and turned to Nathaniel and said, 'There are nearly forty people spread among these few houses here, do you think it is worth leaving some "Baccala" for them to try. We can check their reaction on our way back, can't we?'

'Why not?' replied Nathaniel, 'although they look a pretty poor lot to me. Do you think they could afford to buy some?'

'Of course they can. These people sell their sheep and produce in town and are not short of ready money.'

***

After a short stay, the two travellers set off again and apart from a few solitary cottages and the rare traveller they were very much on their own. Eventually they arrived at a fairly large village and made enquiries regarding their overnight accommodation. They were directed to a villa on the other side of the village which they were told, took in travellers. It almost certainly had vacancies and also provided stabling for the horses.

The accommodation proved to be very comfortable and the owner, Mr. Santi had a very large farm with both animals and extensive fruit orchards. He also traded in a variety of goods and operated a carters business transporting goods and livestock all over the area. He showed particular interest when Nathaniel and Silvio explained the purpose of their journey and agreed to take a few samples of the "Baccala" and give his opinion when they called in on their return journey.

***

They set out early the next morning and after a long, hot and sticky day the two travellers arrived at Silvio's aunt Anna's farm. It was late in the afternoon and the sun, although still very hot, was beginning to ease its way down towards the distant horizon. Alerted by the farm dogs barking their warning, a noisy group of excited youngsters ran out to meet them followed by a tall wiry lady who Nathaniel soon realised was Silvio's Aunt Anna.

As Silvio was trying to extricate himself from the children, Anna said, 'What a surprise. What on earth are you doing here Silvio, you should have let

279

us know you were coming.'

'Lovely to see you Anna, I am afraid it was arranged at very short notice and my good friend Nathaniel and I are here on business.'

'If its business then you had better talk to Mario, but come on in, you must be very thirsty after your long journey.' and to one of the farm hands, 'See to the horses Claudio, and tell the master we have guests.'

They followed Anna to the patio where a long table was situated under the shade of an enormous vine weighed down with numerous bunches of red grapes. 'Please sit down and I will get you a nice cool drink. Then you can tell me all the family news from Livorno, it seems ages since I last went there.'

They settled down in comfortable chairs and relaxed in the evening sun. The children had sent been off to play elsewhere and Anna was keen to get all the gossip and news before husband Mario arrived, 'How are Fabio and Maria and their children? I haven't seen them since little Roberto was a few months old, and now he must be at least two.'

'They are all well Anna and they send their good wishes, and yes, Roberto is two years old and no longer a little baby.'

'My goodness, how time flies. I must get Mario to take me down to see them soon. It can get quite lonely up here.'

The sun was just disappearing behind the distant hills when Mario came in. He was a big, jovial man with black curly hair and a wide smiling mouth below a thick black moustache which appeared to support a large hooked nose. He greeted them warmly and after settling down with his glass of wine said, 'What brings you all the way up here Silvio, not bad news I hope.'

'Not at all,' replied Silvio, 'we are here to bring you gifts and at the same time pick your brains.'

'Oh really, as far as I am aware no one travels all the way out from the coast to bring free gifts and not expect something in return. Are you going to tell me you are different?'

'Yes I am.' replied Silvio and went on to explain Nathaniel's ideas and they thought it would be very useful to get the opinions of people who were a long way from the coast who found it difficult and costly to get fish to eat on a Friday.

'Well, let's have a look at it while it is still light enough, shall we?' said Mario getting up from his chair. 'I will be off to the fields early in the morning, probably long before you two have managed to get out of your beds.'

'I think Claudio has put the barrels in the store next to the stables,' said Anna as the two visitors followed Mario into the yard.

***

'This looks good,' said Mario as he pulled out a large specimen of "Baccala" and held it up to the light. 'How well does it keep?'

'How old is this barrel?' Silvio asked Nathaniel in English.

'It must have been dried at least three months ago, probably a lot more. Don't forget it was dried and packed in Norway and has travelled all the way here. Tell Mario that it will stay in good condition for several months more if it is kept in a fairly cool, dry place.'

Silvio explained to Mario what he had been told and Mario seemed quite impressed.

As Mario turned the sample over between his large calloused hands, he asked, 'How do you cook it and what does it taste like?'

Silvio explained as best he could and Nathaniel suggested that they put some in to soak overnight and Anna could cook some for when Mario came home for his meal after work.

'Sounds a good idea to me,' replied Mario, 'and we could invite our friends around to try it as well. The more people who try it, the better idea you will have of its chances of success.'

Before they went back to tell Anna of their proposals, they took some "Baccala" out of the barrel to soak overnight. They made sure they had enough to feed all their friends before they carried it to the wine cellar, where they put it in a large stone trough and covered it with fresh water from the well. 'I am pleased you turned up today Silvio,' said Mario, 'tomorrow's Friday and we would normally have a vegetable stew.'

***

'Do you think it has been soaking long enough?' asked Anna, 'I don't like things too salty.'

'It should be alright,' replied Silvio, 'It's been in quite a long time.'

It was about mid-day and Anna was starting to prepare the evenings meal. She was a little concerned about how to deal with such large pieces of fish and the amount that had been in soak. 'How do you think I should cook it?' she asked.

'Just treat it as you would any other piece of fish. Cook it the way Mario likes it and you won't go far wrong.'

'I think we should let Anna get on with it Silvio, she won't want us getting in the way and she is perfectly capable of doing it herself.' said Nathaniel. 'Why don't we go for a stroll through the orchards?'

***

When Nathaniel and Silvio returned after a long walk around the local area they found that some of the neighbours had already arrived. They were in small groups on the patio, some seated and a few standing, but all talking very loudly trying to make themselves heard. As they approached they could see no sign of Anna and wondered where she was. 'I hope she is alright,' said Nathaniel, 'and hasn't got herself into a panic.'

Fortunately for them, Anna appeared from inside with two other ladies who had obviously been sampling the "Baccala" as they were still eating and wiping their mouths. 'It's very good, and the girls like it too,' Anna said before introducing her friends. 'Help yourselves to drinks,' she added before disappearing back into the house, 'I have to see to the food and Mario will be here very soon. He has just gone to get cleaned up'

***

After all the guests had gone, Mario said, 'Well Nathaniel, your "Baccala" seemed to be a resounding success, well done.'

'I am very pleased to hear it. Do you think it would sell if I started to import it?'

'No doubt at all, it cooks well, it meets the religious requirements and the indications are that it keeps well. I think you are on to a winner if you can get it at the right price.'

'Well I have a good reliable supplier keen to be involved, he is in Livorno at the moment and waiting for me to make a decision.'

'That's good then, so what's stopping you?'

'It's the church and their attitude that worries me somewhat. Are you sure that they will be happy for it to be eaten on a Friday?'

'Of course I am, didn't you see Father Francis last night? He was here enjoying it like everyone else.'

***

They set off on their way back to Livorno early the next morning having left the remainder of the "Baccala" for Mario to distribute or use as he wished. 'The more people who know about it the better, said Nathaniel, 'I know Mario will spread the word and so will all his guests, I didn't meet anyone who didn't like it.'

'Let's hope Mr. Santi has had time to try it before we get there tonight,' replied Silvio, 'I think he will want to set up a distribution system if he thinks it will take off.'

'I think you are right,' said Nathaniel, 'he could be very useful to us if we can get him on our side.'

***

Silvio's prophecy proved to be correct and soon after their arrival Carlo Santi was expressing great interest in Nathaniel's venture. 'This could be the best selling new product I have seen in a long time, Nathaniel. If there is any way I could assist or advise you on the potential sales in this area, I would be very happy to oblige.'

'Thank you Carlo, I am delighted you think it will sell out here. Did many people get a chance to try it out?

'Yes they did, I had a large group of friends around yesterday and I am sure I could have sold a barrel to every single one of them. They loved it!'

Nathaniel was excited at the thought of the project taking off and was also aware that he could not get it going without some local help. All his money was tied up at home and his ready cash was dwindling quite quickly. It looked as if Carlo would fit in nicely with his plans, he would bring a ready-made distribution set up, plenty of local knowledge and a good chance of some money to invest.

Over a glass of wine and a good meal, Nathaniel, Silvio and Carlo talked late into the evening and Carlo hinted more than once that he would like the opportunity to be involved, and possibly be the agent for his area.

***

When they were on the way down to breakfast, Silvio asked, 'Why didn't you give Carlo a chance to act as agent last night Nathaniel, it was obvious that he would like it?'

'Just wait and see if he bites when I throw him the bait this morning.'

'You devious so and so, Nathaniel. Are you making him an offer?'

'Not yet, but I am going to investigate his business during the day before we go back to Livorno tomorrow.'

***

'Good morning Nathaniel,' said Carlo indicating the spare seats at the table. 'Have you any plans for today?'

'Nothing in particular Carlo, but we thought if it is alright, we would like to stay another night with you. We are both quite weary after our travels and the effects of that lovely wine of yours.'

'Of course you can, I would be delighted with your company and I could show you around my organisation if you wished.'

'I would love that.' replied Nathaniel, wiping his mouth to hide a grin as Silvio gave a wink and a surreptitious 'thumbs up'. 'It will be better than travelling on a Sunday.'

***

Back in Livorno, Fabio met with Lars and told him that he had just been informed that a cargo of tiles for delivery to London had been booked and if he could be ready to load on Friday, the cargo was his. 'I know it's Monday today and Nathaniel is not back yet. Are you willing to take the chance and hope he turns up before then?'

'I can't stay here for ever, can I?' he replied. 'He said he would be back this week so he still has a few days to spare. I think we should discuss prices and if we can agree terms, I will take it.'

'Well whatever Nathaniel does or doesn't do, you must sail on Saturday with this particular cargo if you accept it.'

'No problems, how do they pack the tiles Fabio? It would help if I had some idea as I have never carried them before.'

'Well there is a load ready for shipping in the upper warehouse. We could go and have a look at them if you wish.'

Lars accepted the invitation and found the tiles were all wrapped, ten

283

to a pack, in hessian and then into large wooden crates. 'These will be much easier to store on board than barrels of "Baccala" Fabio.' said Lars. 'Where is this lot going?'

'Not far. They are going to Malta on Thursday.

Chapter 21

The Start of a new Life

Nathaniel and Silvio arrived back at Fabio's villa late on Monday evening and Fabio explained to Nathaniel that Lars had committed to taking a cargo of tiles to London and would be sailing on Saturday morning. After his few days away, Nathaniel realised he had an awful lot of work to sort out before Saturday and as he had already made up his mind to go ahead with his new venture, he had not much time to come to an agreement with Lars regarding the purchase of a regular supply of "Baccala". He was fully aware of the pitfalls that could occur and that he would have to be very careful how he was going to take things forward. He intended to see Lars the first thing in the morning and set things in motion.

He had a restless night and hardly managed to get any sleep at all. Things were constantly flitting through his mind and problems seemed to come thick and fast. He had just dozed off when he sat up suddenly and said to himself, 'Oh my Good Lord. I haven't written to Ephraim since I left Boston. He will be going berserk!' He got out of bed and lit a candle with the intention of writing a letter immediately but as he stumbled around he realised it was futile doing it now. It could wait until tomorrow and he would give it to Lars to forward when he got to London. He would also need to give Lars a note to present to the bank in London to authorise the collection of his money.

The remainder of the night passed slowly and he had just managed to get to sleep when Fabio banged on his bedroom door and called loudly, 'Come on Nathaniel, if you want to get into town today you had better get a move on.'

***

On the way into Livorno, Nathaniel explained that if things were going to progress as he wished, he would need suitable premises and most importantly he would need accommodation somewhere within a reasonable distance of the docks.

'Don't worry about that, Nathaniel, you know you are welcome to stay with us as long as you like. Maria and the boys love having someone new around the house.'

'That's extremely kind of you, Fabio, but I am sure I will be working long and irregular hours until things are up and running. I think it will be much better for all concerned if I am close to my place of work.'

'Probably so, but you don't have to rush, do you?'

They continued in silence for a while until Fabio asked, 'What sort of place were you thinking about Nathaniel?'

'I haven't really given it much thought up to now but somewhere simple which is clean and comfortable but above all, serves good, simple food.'

'Well, I don't know anywhere at the moment, but I will keep my ears open and ask around if you wish.'

'Thanks Fabio that will be much appreciated,' replied Nathaniel, as his mind drifted off into thoughts of what might lay ahead.

***

When they arrived at Fabio's office, Nathaniel walked around the dock to the "*Alesund*" and went aboard where he found Lars in his cabin going through some papers. 'Come in Nathaniel,' he said, and pointing to a chair, 'Sit down and make yourself comfortable. How was your trip?'

'It went really well Lars, everyone spoke very positively about the "Baccala" and I am sure it will be a good seller.'

'So, have you made your mind up then?'

'Yes I have, I am going to give it my best and hope it takes off.'

'That's great, so we need to get some talking done and sorted before I sail on Saturday then?'

'We certainly do.' said Nathaniel. 'So I suggest we get started right away.'

***

They spent the remainder of the morning discussing quantities, costs, delivery dates and payment details and by lunchtime they had come to an amicable agreement. Nathaniel had written a letter to his bank in London authorising payment and Lars would present it for payment on his arrival.

'I have to write a letter to my legal representative in Grantham so would you take it to England for me Lars?'

'Of course I will. I can arrange for it to be forwarded from London when I get there'

'That would be very good of you. I should have sent it ages ago but with all the excitement of the last few weeks, it completely slipped my mind.'

'Don't worry about it. Just make sure you give it to me before Saturday.'

'I will. Now how about something to eat? I am absolutely famished as I hardly had any breakfast.'

'That's a good idea. Just give me a minute to tidy these papers and I will be with you, I promised to meet Fabio for lunch so we can collect him on the way.'

***

Fabio joined them for lunch and he naturally enquired about progress with the project and was pleased to hear things were going ahead when Nathaniel asked, 'Fabio, do you know a gentleman called Carlo Santi?'

'Of course I do, everyone around here knows Carlo. Why do you ask?'

'I met him last week and he hinted quite strongly that he would like to be involved with my business. Do you think he is reliable?'

286

'He is a very successful businessman and as far as I know he is honest and totally reliable. If he worked with you, I would think he would be a great asset.'

'Well I accept I will need some local knowledge and from what you say, he sounds as if he could provide what I need.'

'I agree,' said Fabio 'and I don't think you will find anyone more suitable.'

'Thank you Fabio, I will contact him soon and see what we can arrange.'

'Well, why don't you write him a note? There will certainly be some of his delivery men in town over the next few days so you can give them the letter. Carlo is frequently in town so you should be able to see him soon.'

***

Nathaniel spent the next day in Fabio's office writing letters and trying to find information on suitable properties for his business enterprise. At the same time he started making enquiries about somewhere to call home for the foreseeable future.

The day before the "*Alesund*" sailed, Nathaniel gave Lars the letter for Ephraim and also one for Sir Samuel. He thought it important to keep Sir Samuel informed as he could prove useful at some time in the future. The note he had written for Carlo had been handed to one of his carters earlier in the day so he as hoping for a response early the next week.

***

On Saturday Nathaniel was up early and headed for the docks to see Lars sail. The "*Alesund*" was due to sail on the high tide which was just before noon so Nathaniel made sure he had plenty of time to check that Lars was happy with the arrangements. Hopefully he would get a rough idea of when Lars would be back with his cargo of "Baccala", but when he broached the subject the only answer was, 'At a guess, somewhere between two and four months. It definitely won't be less than two and hopefully less than four.'

'Serves me right for asking,' replied Nathaniel who already knew that the answer would be vague. 'Have a safe trip Lars, and I will see you eventually.'

'I hope so, now it's time for you to get ashore if you don't want to come with us. You don't want us to miss the tide do you?'

Nathaniel stood on the dockside and watched as the "*Alesund*" was helped away from the dockside into the main stream. Gradually she unfurled her sails one by one until she was out of the small harbour and on her way. As she disappeared around the headland, Fabio said. 'That's it Nathaniel, you can't stop things now. You are a business man in a foreign land.'

'I am, and I have no premises, no workforce, nowhere to live and very little money. My whole future is in the master of that small ship that has just sailed.'

***

It was nearly two weeks before Nathaniel had a reply from Carlo and when they met, Carlo didn't seem as keen as he was at their earlier meeting. However, he promised he would be available to give help and advice anytime Nathaniel needed it. When he learnt that Nathaniel still had four barrels of "Baccala" he was very keen to buy some and said that he would buy them all if he could. After some discussion, a price was agreed but Nathaniel refused to sell him more than two of the barrels. 'I need some here in Livorno to use as samples for the locals, after all this is where my business will be based.'

'I can see that,' said Carlo. 'But if you decide to sell the other two just put them on one of my carts and I will pay you the same price for them.'

'I will Carlo, but you are a business man and you know I need them here.'

'OK. All I ask is that you contact me as soon as your ship turns up and I will see if we can do some business.'

'You know I will Carlo. Now did you say you knew of some properties that might be suitable for me?'

'I know of one and I also have an empty warehouse that I think would be just the job. Would you like to have a look at them now?'

'I have plenty of time before I will need the space but would love to have a look if you can spare the time.'

'Let's go then, there's nothing like the present.'

***

'How did you get on with Carlo?' asked Maria later that evening. 'Did he want to get involved?'

'He was quite evasive when we first met this afternoon, but he opened up as the time went by, but he didn't want to commit to any firm deal.'

'But I thought he had indicated that he was very interested when you met at his home.'

'That's right, but he definitely wants to buy the "Baccala" and he bought two barrels and wanted more. If I didn't need the last two barrels myself, he would have had them as well.'

'I bet he will go and sell them on when he gets home,' said Fabio taking a long sip of wine. 'He won't lose out on the deal either.'

'Well, he paid a very good price for what he bought and if I can get that sort of money for a ship load, I will be a very rich man, very quickly.'

'Did he know of any properties?' asked Fabio.

'Yes, he took me to two warehouses, one of his and another not far from your office. I think the second one was the best for me. The one Carlo owns was a bit too big at this stage and I only need enough space to take one boat load at a time.'

288

'Are the rents reasonable?'

'Yes, they are much cheaper than I had thought but I don't intend to take one up at the moment and expect I will wait for six weeks or so before I commit myself.'

'What about workers,' asked Maria, 'Will you need to take on many people?'

'Not really, I don't think I will need more than one good strong lad.'

'I am sure you will need more than one, Nathaniel.'

'It's possible, but I can hire carters to take the barrels from the ship to the warehouse and offload them where I want them stored. After that I would expect the purchasers to collect the barrels using their own transport. All I will need is a good reliable warehouseman.'

'Sounds a good idea to me.' said Fabio closing his eyes as he dozed off.

'You seem to have things well under control.' said Maria. 'I think I am about ready for bed. Come on Fabio you can't sleep here all night.'

***

The next six weeks or so seemed to flash by. Nathaniel had spent his time searching out prospective clients for his "Baccala" and had managed to convince several traders to place orders, and in some cases to pay a deposit. The reaction to the "Baccala" had been very positive and all Nathaniel had to do was provide the goods he had promised and he would be able to make a substantial profit. He took the lease on the warehouse he had seen initially, and with the help of Silvio, they prepared the place for business. Silvio had been unemployed since their trip to the hills during Nathaniel's first week, and Nathaniel had taken him on as a temporary employee for a trial period. He could not offer him anything more permanent until he had seen how the business was likely to progress.

When the second month since Lars had sailed, passed by, he started showing signs of a fair degree of anxiety. 'You will have to calm down Nathaniel,' Maria told him. 'It is only just two months since Lars left and you know he said it would not be less than that before he would be back.'

'I know, but it is quite a strain in the circumstances. You know I am the worrying type, and the longer it goes on, the more difficult it gets.'

'I am sure that's right, but what have you done, if anything, to take your mind off it all?'

'Nothing really, but what *can* I do?'

'Have you found somewhere to live yet?'

'Why, are you trying to tell me something?'

'Don't be silly Nathaniel, I only ask because you have plenty of free time now and searching for somewhere suitable to live would help to keep your mind occupied while you are waiting.'

'I am sorry I snapped at you Maria, I know you are trying to help. You and Fabio have been so very kind to me and I will always be grateful for your kindness, but you are right, I must get down to it and start looking. I will need to be somewhere near to my work as soon as Lars turns up.'

***

Nathaniel spent the next couple of weeks pottering around, the warehouse was clean and ready, all his "Baccala" had been distributed and there was very little left for him to do. Silvio had been laid off until Lars arrived with the cargo and Nathaniel's search for accommodation had ground to a halt. Although nothing more had been said, he had the distinct feeling he had overstayed his welcome with Fabio and Maria.

Fabio was taking quite an active role in Nathaniel's search and regularly came up with information about vacant rooms but none had so far proved to be suitable. 'I think you are going to have to lower your expectations Nathaniel,' said an exasperated Fabio. 'You are never going to find the perfect place around here. That place I took you to last week looked perfectly alright to me.'

'It wasn't bad.' replied Nathaniel, 'but it was fairly grubby and with all those children running around screaming their heads off, I would go mad after a couple of weeks with that lot.'

'Well I suppose you have a point. We will just have to keep looking.'

'We will. I must get something sorted before Lars gets here. Things are getting quite desperate,' concluded Nathaniel.

***

A few days later, Nathaniel joined Fabio for lunch and Fabio said he had just heard of a place that might be suitable.

'Tell me about it.' said Nathaniel, 'Have you seen it?'

'I have never been in the house but I have known the owner for years. He is a pharmacist and has had a business here as long as I can remember but I think business is suffering at the moment. He doesn't have any children, but a couple of years ago he married a young girl less than half his age so he might be hoping for a successor to appear on the scene.'

'It sounds interesting, at least he is a professional gentleman so it could be a possibility. When can we go and have a look?'

'I am sure I could arrange it for this afternoon, if that's alright with you.'

'The sooner the better as far as I am concerned.'

'I will get a message round straight after lunch and see what happens.'

'Good, what's the pharmacist's name, Fabio?'

'It's Antonino Canale, but I am not sure what his wife is called. I think it might be Anna.'

***

'This looks more like it.' said Nathaniel as they approached a large

290

house situated on the outskirts of Livorno. 'Very impressive indeed.'

They dismounted and tied their horses to the rail at the side of the house and an elderly gentleman came to greet them at the front door. He was a thin old man with a shock of unkempt, nearly white hair whose body was bent with age and was supported by a stick. He looked as if he had once been a tall, smart and confident man but the years had had a telling effect on him.

'Good afternoon gentlemen, I am Antonino Canale, welcome to my home. I know you Mr. Montini and you, sir, must be Mr. Thorold.' said Antonino, leaning heavily on his stick.

'Yes, I am Nathaniel Thorold, and it's a pleasure to meet you Mr. Canale. I am the one looking for accommodation and my friend Fabio here advises me that you might have rooms for rent.

'Yes I have, but please call me Antonino. Unfortunately my wife is not at home at the moment, but if you follow me I will show you what is available.'

Nathaniel and Fabio followed the old man slowly up the stairs and they were shown the two rooms which were for rent. There was a large airy, sunlit sitting room with table and chairs and two comfortable easy chairs, one either side of a large fireplace in the centre of the wall to the left. There were double doors which opened on to a small balcony which overlooked an orchard at the rear of the house, and also a large window which had the same aspect. Nathaniel stood on the balcony and admired the view and away to his left he could see the sea shimmering in the sunlight. 'This is exactly what I am looking for.' he thought.

'If you come through here Mr. Thorold,' the old man said heading to a door to the right of the fireplace, 'I will show you the bedchamber.'

Nathaniel followed dutifully and entered another large, well-furnished room. The large bed was against the wall over to the left and immediately in front of him was another pair of double doors leading onto a much larger balcony where the view of the distant sea was now directly in front of him. A small window looked over the same orchard as that in the sitting room. 'It is a very pleasant apartment Antonino,' said Nathaniel. 'It is a very large house, do you have any other guests staying here?'

'Oh no, there is just my wife Anna and myself, we have only recently decided to let these rooms off and have no intentions of letting any others. We feel it could be too noisy with a lot of guests and neither of us like a lot of noise.'

'That's good, I can't stand noisy people. I like a certain amount of solitude so it should suit me.'

After another quick check around they left the bedroom by another door which opened on to the landing near to the door through which they had first entered. Mr. Canale took them downstairs and showed them the dining room and then to a beautifully furnished room where they sat down and discussed rent and general terms and conditions. Nathaniel was delighted with what he was told and said, 'This will suit me admirably Antonino and if you are in agreement, I will move my possessions in on Monday next.'

***

As they rode back to Fabio's office, Nathaniel said, 'It looks as if I have fallen on my feet there Fabio, everything laid on as well.'

'And loads of space for you to relax from your busy life.' said Fabio, raising a sardonic eyebrow, 'seriously though, you couldn't have done any better, it's a lovely place.'

'I know, it is better than I expected and it's not far to travel each day either.'

They continued on their way in silence until they were nearly back at the docks and Fabio said, 'I wonder how long you will have to wait?'

'I said I would move in on Monday.'

'No. I was thinking about Lars and his cargo. They could be here anytime soon.'

'Or several weeks yet.' replied Nathaniel, reverting to silence.'

***

On Sunday evening, Fabio and Maria had arranged a surprise farewell party for Nathaniel and all their neighbours and friends turned up. Everyone had a lovely time and as a 'thank you' for her hospitality, Nathaniel presented Maria with a cameo broach set in gold which he had bought on a visit to a local engraver's workshop.

'It's beautiful, Nathaniel. You shouldn't have, but I will treasure it for the rest of my life.' she said, bursting into floods of tears.

'You have been wonderful and so patient with me for all of my stay, Maria, but I am only going into town so you won't be getting rid of me that easily.'

'Promise you will come and see us Nathaniel,' she said between sobs.

'Of course I will, you just try to keep me away.'

***

Early on Monday Nathaniel supervised as all his possessions were being loaded onto a cart to be delivered to his new home. Fabio had made sure the two young men in charge of the cart knew exactly where to go and had given strict instructions that they were to go direct and there were to be no deviations for private business. 'Mr. Thorold will be waiting for you and he doesn't want to be hanging around for hours on end.'

'We'll get there as quickly as we can Mr. Montini, I promise.' said the older of the two carters as he climbed onto the driving seat. He gave a sharp crack of his whip and the two horses leant forward, took the weight of the cart, and set off to the Canale residence.

Nathaniel said his goodbyes to Maria and the boys and set off to town

292

with Fabio. 'I will go to your office and pick up a few of my bits and pieces before I go around to the apartment,' said Nathaniel, 'and I suppose I had better check out the warehouse as well. I have asked Silvio to come in and check that everything is still neat and tidy and ready for when Lars cares to put in an appearance.'

'Don't worry about Lars, Nathaniel, it could be another month or six weeks before he gets here.' said Fabio. 'You never know, he might have decided to spend your money on drink and wild women.'

'For goodness sake, Fabio, can't you be serious for once. I have enough to worry about without you trying to stir things up.'

***

They rode the remainder of the journey in comparative silence and when they arrived at his office, there was a man waiting for Fabio with a small package. 'Good morning Mr. Montini, compliments of the master of the brig "Westminster", just arrived from London and Gibraltar. He says to deliver this by hand and will be around to see you when he has unloaded.'

'Thank you, young man, tell him I look forward to seeing him later.' and to Nathaniel, 'This is addressed to me "for the attention of a Mr. Nathaniel Thorold." I think that might be you.' he said handing over the packet.

'It's from Sir Samuel,' said Nathaniel, breaking the red seal on the back. 'I wonder what he has got to say.'

'He will probably tell you that you are out of your mind running off like you did and then trying to set up a business in a foreign country.'

'Nathaniel carefully opened the packet and started to read the first of two sheets of paper.'

'Come on Nathaniel, read it out loud, let's hear what he has to say.'

Nathaniel continued to read it to himself and finally said to Fabio, 'Basically he thinks I am an idiot for gambling and not facing up to my problems. Running away solves nothing especially as the collectors were found to be crooks and have been arrested. Nevertheless, he wishes me well in my project and says I have a good business head which needs to be put to use. If I ever need help or advice then he will be happy to provide it.'

'That's generous of him, I thought he would disinherit you.'

He also says that the crooks who were threatening me were tried at Lincoln and were subsequently hanged. Also, there is some very disturbing news for you Fabio, and there is no easy way to tell you. Apparently your cousin George was heavily involved with the crooks and was tried with them. He was also found guilty and hanged.'

'Oh my God, poor Uncle Paulo and Aunt Emma, they must be devastated. How am I going to tell all the family?'

'I am so sorry Fabio, but that's what gambling did for George. I knew he was in financial trouble ages ago and I suppose he was taken in by these crooks and he has paid the ultimate price.'

'Poor George, he had such a bright future and wasted it.'

'I know, he had good start in life and he completely wasted it. I also realise that it could so easily have been me.' said a very contemplative Nathaniel. Nathaniel left Fabio sitting at his desk, with his head in his hands and deep in thought. 'What a stupid man you were George. What a waste.' he muttered to himself.

***

Nathaniel arrived at the Canale house just as the carters were leaving. 'Where did you put my belongings?' he asked the elder of the two men.

'The gentleman at the house told us to put it all in your room sir, so it's all up there ready for you to unpack.'

'Thank you very much, lads.' he replied, and gave them a tip for their trouble as they went on their way.

***

Nathaniel untied the saddlebags containing the belongings he had brought from Fabio's office and headed to the front door. 'I should tell Mr. Canale I am here.' he said to himself and rapped on the door with the handle of his whip. He waited a short while until he heard Antonino approaching. The tapping of the old man's stick on the hard tiled floor echoed around the large hall as he progressed.

'Come in Mr. Thorold, no need for you to wait out here, this is your home for as long as you care to stay. Your things have been placed in your room so just go on up, you know where it is. When you are ready, come down and I will introduce you to my wife. You haven't met her yet, have you?'

'No I haven't, she was not at home when I came the last time.'

'I will see you soon, then. We will be out on the patio, so just come straight through.' he said as he disappeared through a door at the side of the stairs which Nathaniel remembered lead to the dining room.

As Nathaniel went up the stairs, he realised how lucky he was getting accommodation in a house like this. None of the places he had seen over the last two months had been anything like as good and most of them were considerably more expensive. As he entered his apartment, the balcony doors were open and although the room was in shade and cooled by a gentle breeze, the view from the room was breath-taking. Nathaniel just stood and stared, 'This is even better than the view from Fabio's patio.' he thought. 'How lucky can I get?'

It didn't take Nathaniel long to sort out his belongings and he found that he had more space for things now than at any time since he left home. 'This is wonderful,' he said, and sat down on one of the fireside chairs, 'but I should go down and meet Mrs. Canale or they will wonder what has happened to me.'

Nathaniel entered the lounge and headed for the patio doors. 'Out here Nathaniel, don't be shy,' called Antonino. 'Come and meet my wife.'

As he approached the door, he could see Antonino sitting in the shade but it was not until he was on the patio that he saw Anna, Antonino's wife. When he saw her, he thought he was going to be sick, so powerful was the shock. His head was spinning and he felt weak at the knees. A horse kicking him in the stomach could not have hit him harder. He saw his beloved Charlotte, even though her skin was a slightly darker shade, her black shiny hair was set in the same style and her physical features were very similar.

'Are you alright Nathaniel?' asked Antonino, concern showing on his lined face.

'Er, um, yes. I just felt a little dizzy. Perhaps a glass of water will help.'

'Of course, sit down and take things easy for a few minutes.'

He sat down and Anna poured a glass of cool water. As she passed it to him, she innocently felt his brow to see if he had temperature and Nathaniel felt another powerful sensation and spilt some water on to his lap.

'Are you sure you are alright?' asked Antonino. 'Do you think you should go and lie down until you feel better?'

'I'm sorry, I think it must be a touch of the sun. I should be alright in a couple of minutes.' replied Nathaniel, taking another sip of water. He closed his eyes and sat quietly for a few minutes and thought of his beloved Charlotte and all that had happened to him over the last year or so. He thought he had managed to get her out of his mind but this had come as a complete shock to him and had hit him very hard. After a few minutes, when he thought he had sufficiently recovered, he composed himself, emptied the glass of water and said, 'I am very sorry about that, but I think I am alright now.'

'Yes, but you must take things easy for the rest of the day. You have probably been doing too much lately.' said Antonino. 'Now, although you have already met, may I introduce my wife, Anna.

Nathaniel slept fitfully that first night in his new apartment. Charlotte was never far away and Anna had awakened all his feelings for the woman he lost in such tragic circumstances. 'What on earth am I going to do, why does this foreign woman awaken such painful memories?' he thought.

As he tried to sleep, he found no answers. Long before dawn he gave up trying to get to sleep and sat out on the balcony, listening to the sounds of the night and thinking over his old life in a very different, far off, Lincolnshire.

Chapter 22

1735 - The First Cargo

Since first moving in with the Canale's, apart from a couple of days at Christmas, Nathaniel had spent most of his time either relaxing at the apartment or visiting prospective customers. He was still amazed at the likeness between Anna and his beloved Charlotte but was beginning to realise that the similarities were only superficial. Anna had an outgoing personality and was more forthright in her dealings with people. She was also much more talkative and was quite willing to discuss personal issues openly.

With Antonino busy at his apothecaries business, Anna and Nathaniel would often spend the afternoons on the patio discussing all manner of topics. Initially, the conversations would be about Nathaniel's business plans but gradually they became more personal, Nathaniel talked about life in England and told Anna about Charlotte and her terrible accident.

In return, Anna talked about her childhood and her mother's early death. How her father was desperate to get her married so that she would not be a drain on the families meagre earnings.

'Is that why you married a man much older than yourself?' asked Nathaniel who had not dared to ask such a question earlier.

'Yes, my father said Mr. Canale had expressed as desire to get to know me better and I should grab the opportunity of a comfortable life. The option, he said, was to go into Holy Orders and spend the rest of my life in a nunnery.'

'But you are an extremely beautiful woman, surely you could have found someone your own age.'

'Not a man who was willing to pay my father money for his permission to marry me.'

'How could a father do that to his daughter? Surely you must hate him.'

'I did at first, but Antonino is a kind and generous man who makes no demands and anyway, my father died shortly after we married so hate would be pointless.'

'Why did Antonino want a young wife, surely he could have found someone nearer his own age?'

'I don't really know but I am sure it was to impress people. He feels good with a young wife on his arm when we are out in public.'

'Are you a real wife to him?' Nathaniel asked, hoping he hadn't asked too much already.

'Oh no, we have had separate bedchambers ever since the second week of our marriage.'

'Don't you get lonely here all on your own?'

'Not really, the servants and the cook are always around and Antonino doesn't spend so much time at work as he used to.'

'Has he talked about retiring, after all he is quite old isn't he?'

'He hasn't mentioned it but I know the business is not doing very well at the moment. A young apothecary has opened up in competition not far from Antonino's and has taken a great deal of our business. That's one of the reasons that we decided to rent out the rooms.'

'So money is fairly short at the moment?'

'Yes, and it's getting worse by the day He doesn't say much but I know that he is getting worried.'

***

After a long frustrating wait and doubts that it would ever happen, in mid-February, one of Fabio's men arrived with the news that the 'Alesund' was at anchor just outside the harbour entrance and waiting for the tide to change. 'Mr. Montini said would you care to join him for lunch and then we can be there when she docks.'

***

After lunch, Nathaniel and Fabio went down to the docks and arrived just as the "Alesund" was being secured alongside the wharf. As soon as it was secured and a gangway put in place they went on board and met Lars. Apart from his cargo of "Baccala", Lars had a package for Nathaniel from his solicitors in Grantham. 'I was in Boston for some urgent repairs on the way here, and your mate, Max suggested that we get in touch with Ephraim to see if he wanted to forward a note to you. This arrived in Boston as we were getting ready to sail.'

'Thanks Lars, how was that scoundrel Max?'

'Oh, he was the same as usual.' and then addressing Fabio, 'Will you have anything for me in the next few days?'

'I think there might be a full load in about ten days, otherwise it will be a lot of small stuff for a few different places, it will be up to you which you take.'

'I'll take the full load then.' he replied. 'When will you be collecting *this* load, Nathaniel?'

'Fabio's men will offload it first thing in the morning and I will get it stored as it comes off.'

'That's alright then. So if you gentlemen will excuse me, I will get this ship cleaned up and ready for stocking supplies for the return journey.' said Lars as he turned his attention to more immediate matters.

***

When Nathaniel left the "Alesund" he went directly to the warehouse and together with Silvio, they contacted as many of their customers as they possibly could to inform them that they would be able to collect their goods from the warehouse 'the day after tomorrow'. They also wrote notes to anyone who could not be contacted directly and despatched them by hand.

After a night of high tension, Nathaniel was at the warehouse early. When he was satisfied that Silvio was fully aware of what to do, he made his way to the docks and saw the first fully loaded carts on their way.

It was late afternoon before the precious cargo was safely stored and Nathaniel could relax. Even so, he did not relax for long. He started to worry about whether anyone would turn up to fulfil their promises and take their orders.

***

That evening over dinner, Antonino, who by now regarded Nathaniel as one of the family, asked, 'What are you so tense about, Nathaniel?'

'I'm beginning to wonder if I have done the right thing. If no one turns up tomorrow I could be in deep financial trouble, all my money is tied up in that warehouse.'

'You were the same a few weeks ago when you thought Lars wouldn't turn up. But he did.' said Anna.

'I know, but I can't help it. I worry too much.'

Anna laid a comforting hand on his arm and said 'Just relax Nathaniel, get a good nights sleep and forget about it. You can't change thing now, no matter how much you fret.'

***

When Nathaniel arrived at the warehouse in the morning, there were three carts waiting outside as Silvio opened up. They were quickly loaded and despatched and were followed by a steady stream of carts throughout the rest of the morning and into early afternoon. 'Things are going very well Silvio, at this rate we will have sold everything by next week.'

'It won't keep at this pace for much longer, Nathaniel, things will ease off very quickly. We have seen most of the dealers and they will only come back when or if they sell what they have already taken.'

'I know, it's just me being unrealistic. I will just have to have a bit more patience.'

As they were beginning to tidy the warehouse and getting ready to go home, Lars and Fabio arrived to see how things were progressing. 'You left this in my office Nathaniel,' said Fabio handing over the unopened package from Grantham, 'and Lars wants to know if you will be reordering. I have told him there is no rush, as his next load will not be ready for another week.'

'Thanks for that Fabio, I had completely forgotten about it in all the excitement of the last two days.' said Nathaniel putting the package down on his office desk. 'As for another order, I will definitely be reordering, but I will let you know how much well before you sail, Lars. Things look very promising at the moment.'

298

After Fabio and Lars had left, Nathaniel opened the package expecting a dressing down from Ephraim but was quite shocked to hear that Ephraim had passed away just before Christmas and that Charles was now the sole proprietor of the business.

He was pleased to hear that all the farms were operating smoothly and there were no unexpected disasters to report. However, Edward Wood was beginning to get a bit impatient in his request to buy the lease of Holt Hall Farm. Charles thought the time was right to do the deal and Edward was financially placed to complete the transaction. 'I will sleep on it and make up my mind before Lars sails,' thought Nathaniel. 'There are plenty of other things to think about before I reply.'

***

Over half of the stock had been sold and moved out before Nathaniel placed an order for another full load. He was very optimistic about the future and even though he had no indication that there would be repeat orders, he was prepared to take the risk. He had made what he considered was a very handsome profit so far, and with minimal effort. 'If this continues I am going to be a very wealthy man.' he told Fabio. 'and if sales take off, it will be a double order next time.'

'Don't get ahead off yourself, Nathaniel. You still have plenty of stock in the warehouse to be sold and only when you start to get repeat orders will you be able to tell how things are going to progress.'

'I understand what you are saying, Fabio, but it's going better than I ever thought it would.'

'I know it is and I think you did the right thing ordering another load. You have another few months to go before it arrives and that's plenty of time to sell the rest.'

***

'You are in a very jolly mood this evening, Nathaniel,' said Anna at dinner. 'Have you had a good day?'

'Yes I have. It is six weeks since the "Baccala" arrived and today I sold the last of my stock. The word is spreading and the merchants are continuing to ask for more. Next time I will have to order double the amount.'

'Are you making a good profit Nathaniel?' asked Antonino. 'There are plenty of sharks out there who will try to do you down, especially if they see you doing well.'

'Yes I know, and I have already had a couple of them trying to take advantage but I think I am aware of most of their crooked ways.'

'Well, just be careful Nathaniel, and don't trust anyone,' said Anna with a smile, 'we don't want to lose such a good tenant, do we Antonino?'

After dinner they retired to the patio and, at Antonino's suggestion, they celebrated Nathaniel's success with a few more glasses of wine.

Eventually the old man decided to go to bed and left Anna and Nathaniel to relax and enjoy the calm, gentle, balmy evening. They sat, talked a little but spent most of the time in silence, enjoying the sounds of nature.

Eventually Nathaniel decided to retire. He thanked Anna for a lovely evening, said goodnight and went up to his room. He prepared himself for bed but still felt quite awake and so he sat on the balcony for a while. His thoughts kept returning to Anna. How on earth such a beautiful and vibrant young woman could be married to a man nearly old enough to be her grandfather baffled him. 'Surely she must have some regrets. She spends most of her time on her own and now she finds that they are running short of money. It's not an ideal situation for a young woman'

When he finally got into bed he was still thinking of Anna and the thoughts were much more personal. He tried to banish them from his mind as he knew it was totally wrong to think of such things about a married woman. 'She's not married in any normal way,' he thought, trying to convince himself that it wasn't wrong to have such thoughts, even though he knew he had strong feelings for her. With his mind in turmoil he finally fell into a fitful sleep.

**

He seemed to have only just managed to get to sleep when something awoke him. He thought he had heard someone or something moving outside his bedchamber. He lay as still as possible and strained his ears to see if he could hear anything. After a few minutes he decided it must have been his imagination and turned over to go back to sleep, but as he was dozing off he heard what sounded like a footstep on a creaky floorboard outside his door. 'There it is again.' he thought, 'there *is* something out there.'

The bedroom was bathed in the silvery light of the full moon and as he lay there wondering what he could do if it was a prowler intent on mischief, the handle on the door turned and the door started to open very slowly. 'Who is it?' Nathaniel called out nervously as he began to fear for his safety. 'Show yourself or you will regret it!'

'Shush,' was the soft whispered reply. 'It is only me, Anna.'

Nathaniel's heart missed a beat and said in a whispered reply, 'Anna, what is the matter?' His heart pounded as he saw her silhouette, ghostlike in her white silk night attire, softly tip toe across the room. He sat up and watched in awe and extreme excitement as she approached the bed.

'I am so lonely Nathaniel,' she said pulling back the bedcover and climbing in. 'Please hold me. Please hold me tightly.'

Nathaniel needed no more encouragement and for the first time in well over a year, embraced tightly a very willing, beautiful woman.

**

When he awoke in the morning Anna had gone and Nathaniel began to think the events of the previous night were all a dream, but a bracelet on his bedside cabinet told him that it was true and had really happened. His mind was in turmoil, but he realised that his life could now have changed for ever. Even in his wildest dreams he would never have thought this could happen, but it had, and he was euphoric.

Chapter 23

Months passed and Nathaniel's relationship with Anna blossomed, but Antonino preferred to ignore it. The apothecary business was in deep financial trouble and Nathaniel had been helping out financially as much as he could, however, Antonino had no desire to change the current situation. Anna was happy, Nathaniel was happy, and with help from his lodger, Antonino was still living to his accustomed standards. All he required was that Anna behaved as his wife when they were out in public together.

However, it was not all so easy going, tongues were beginning to wag. Nathaniel and Anna were regularly seen out together in his carriage and the sight of a young married lady and her unmarried gentleman companion was not altogether appreciated by the devoutly catholic local community. Anna's open affair with Nathaniel caused the church authorities grave offence, particularly as Nathaniel was not a catholic. The church's reaction was to set in motion a policy of persecution of the offenders despite Antonino's declaration of his wife's faithfulness and his friend's innocence.

***

Nathaniel had now been in business for well over a year and all the stockfish he bought was sold very quickly. The "Baccala" was very popular in the area and a dish of "Baccala", soaked and cooked with onions, tomatoes, olive oil and spices became known as 'Baccala alla Livornese' and was now an accepted, inexpensive and delicious Friday meal. Money was rolling in and he discovered that some of the traders with whom he was dealing, were sending the "Baccala" as far away as Naples. In discussions with Silvio they decided that it would be more beneficial to cut out the middle man by having "Baccala" imported directly into Naples. This would require some more research and setting up warehousing in the area. 'It might solve a personal problem as well.' said Nathaniel, 'The local priest is upsetting Anna and I must say she has a point. She is already talking about wanting to move away from town'

'What will you do with this place if you move?' asked Silvio. 'I am not keen on moving all the way down there and my family definitely won't want to move.'

'I have no intention of closing down the business here, Silvio and I hope you will stay and run it for me. You are practically doing the job now and you are the obvious choice to take over.' said Nathaniel. 'Obviously we would have to come to some financial arrangement, but how would you like to give it a go?'

'That would be brilliant, I would love it. Thank you very much

***

When Nathaniel arrived home that evening, Anna came to his room in tears. 'What on earth is wrong darling?' Nathaniel asked, 'has that priest been around again?'

'No, thank goodness, it's not that.'

'What is it then, what has upset you?'

'I have been waiting all day to tell you. Nathaniel, I am pregnant and I am so happy I just can't stop crying.'

'That's wonderful darling, but what will Antonino say.'

'I haven't told him yet but I don't think he will be upset, after all he has known what we have been doing for quite some time. Will you come with me and so that we can get it over now?'

***

'I didn't expect that did you?' said Nathaniel, 'but if that's the way he wants it, it's fine by me.

'Well I am his wife and if he insists that he is the father, so be it,' she replied. 'I suppose the church will have to accept it as his. If we indicated that it is ours, they would never admit the poor thing into the church, would they?'

'Yes, you are right. He is a stubborn but honourable old man and I can see his reasoning, however, I doubt if the church will give up their campaign of persecution. They will just ignore his assertions.'

'I know,' said Anna, 'that's what worries me the most. Those people smirking and spreading foul gossip. It is getting increasingly more difficult to be seen in public without someone making disparaging remarks.'

'I may have some good news for you on that subject, Anna. As business is booming, I have discussed the possibility of opening another warehouse in Naples. Silvio would be delighted to carry on here in Livorno and we could go to Naples to run the business there.'

'That would be fantastic, Nathaniel, and it would get us away from these bigots who are blighting our lives here.'

'How do you think Antonino will react?'

'I think he will jump at the opportunity to pack up work. His heart has not been in it for ages.'

'He hasn't many friends here now has he?'

'No, most of them have passed on and so long as he is comfortable I am sure he will be alright.'

***

As Anna's pregnancy began to show, the gossip mongers and the church increased their campaign and it was getting so bad that Anna very rarely left the house. The local priest was trying to improve the situation as he saw it by pressurising Nathaniel into converting to Catholicism. He was continually visiting Nathaniel both at home and at work but Nathaniel had absolutely no intention of submitting to the pressure. The only reaction the

303

priest ever received was an abrupt 'pazienza' and a polite goodbye. Even so, the constant attention of the priest and the effect it was having on both himself and Anna was beginning to tell. They both looked forward to the day they would be moving to Naples.

***

Setting up the new branch in Naples was progressing satisfactorily but unfortunately it would not be able to open until after the expected birth of Anna's child in late December or early January. Nathaniel had secured a suitable warehouse and having interviewed several men for the post of warehouse manager, he finally decided on Marco Montini, a younger cousin of Silvio. He had ordered two full loads of "Baccala" with Lars and asked for them to arrive a month apart, the first of which was due to arrive in March or April 1737.

Marco had arrived in Livorno early in January and was staying with Silvio whilst he learnt all the procedures employed in the warehouse. Nathaniel planned to go to Naples in February and take Marco back with him to make the final arrangements and to publicise his business. He also had to ensure he had suitable accommodation for Anna and the baby, and of course, her husband who was very keen to get out of Livorno.

***

Nathaniel had some very important decisions to make as well as those concerning his new life and business in Italy. He had a good profitable estate back home in England and a potentially very profitable set up in Italy, miles away from his native home. Although Anna was the wife of another man and that man lived with him as part of a dysfunctional family, he regarded Anna as his wife. A further complication was that he was now going to be a father but the child would never be able to carry his name. Although Antonino was now in his seventieth year and would not be there for ever, it could be many years before he passed on. Even when eventually he did depart this world the problem would still be there, marrying Anna was never going to be an option as the church would never condone her marrying a protestant, and as he had said many times, 'There is no way I will *ever* convert to Catholicism.'

First he had to make up his mind as to where he was going to make his permanent home, England or Italy, and then some more decisions had to be made about his properties and possessions. At the moment he was staying in Italy but there was no rush and a decision could be deferred for a year or so to see how things turned out. Whatever happened he said, 'One thing I should never be short of money, but when I do make a decision it will involve having to make a trip back to England at some time in the near future.'

***

Baby Maria was born on New Year's Day 1737 and had a head of dark

304

wavy hair and deep brown eyes like her mother. Her skin was paler than either Anna or Antonino and anyone could see who the father was. Both Nathaniel and Anna were ecstatic and even Antonino was delighted and they were surprised when Antonino repeatedly referred to 'My baby Maria.'

After he had gone back to his room, Anna said, 'Do you think that Antonino really thinks the baby is his, Nathaniel?'

'I don't know, but he does tend to live in his own small world and with all the effort he has made to convince the church, he may have actually convinced himself.'

'Yes I think he has. He has always kept his feelings well hidden and he has no other living blood relations to talk about. He has probably persuaded himself that he is the father, and he is certainly in denial about our relationship, so he thinks he is the only one who can possibly be the father.'

'Well I don't see it as a problem that will affect us, do you?' asked Nathaniel.

'Not at all, Maria will be lucky to have two fathers doting on her, won't she?

***

The next couple of months were quiet as far as the business was involved, the warehouse was almost empty and so Nathaniel spent a great deal of time at home with Anna and baby Maria. They had employed a nanny who helped with the basic chores and was particularly useful at night when she would take over and comfort the baby ensuring that Nathaniel and Anna were not disturbed. Anna was not looking forward to Nathaniel going to Naples to prepare the business, but he reassured her that as far as he was concerned, his main task was to find suitable accommodation for them all. 'I want us to be together as soon as possible,' he said 'I don't want us to be apart any more than you do.'

'I believe you,' she replied, 'and I understand why you must go but I will miss you so much.'

'Don't worry darling, I will send for you as soon as possible and I will get you away from these bigots at the first opportunity.'

***

The day before he was due to go to Naples, Nathaniel had spent all day at the warehouse He made sure that Silvio was well briefed and was aware of all the possible events that he could think of. After starting the day feeling very nervous and somewhat apprehensive, Silvio had settled down well and realised that, with plenty of encouragement from Nathaniel he was perfectly capable of doing the job. 'It's just that I have never been in a job where I have been in charge,' said Silvio 'and you won't be here to sort things out if they go wrong.'

'Don't worry so much, Silvio, you have been doing the job ever since we set the place up and you know more about the day to day running than I do.'

'I suppose so. It's just that I am a bit worried that I won't be able to contact you quickly in an emergency.'

The only area of concern that Nathaniel had with Silvio was his lack of experience of the financial side of the operation and to that end he tested Silvio on as many aspects as could think of. To his credit Silvio answered impeccably and Nathaniel was suitably impressed. Nevertheless he had already discussed his thoughts with Fabio who had promised to help in any way he could.

'Well if you do have any problems have a word with Fabio, he will be able to help. The main thing you need to sort out before the next shipment arrives is to recruit an assistant. You know the type of person we need well enough. He should be just like you and willing to learn.'

It was quite late by the time Nathaniel had finished with Silvio and before heading home he wished him the best of luck, shook hands and said, 'Don't forget, if you have any problems, however small, seek help. If you carry on blindly you will only make a fool of yourself.'

'Thanks boss, I will try my best and I promise I won't let you down.'

Chapter 24

In early February, after a tearful farewell with Anna and Maria, Nathaniel set off for Naples with Marco. He was not very happy the way things had turned out last night. He had intended to have a quiet romantic evening but he was late home, and the meal was ruined by the time he arrived. Anna was in a tearful mood and accused him of staying out late with his mates. Eventually Anna calmed down and the evening passed without any more problems. Nathaniel realised that Anna was upset regarding his trip to Naples and that the real problem was that they had no idea how long they would be apart. It all depended on how long it took to secure suitable accommodation.

Anna had decided not to come down to the docks to see them set off and as Nathaniel made his way he thought, 'I know I shouldn't, but I feel guilty about leaving Anna and Maria here to fend for themselves.'

Marco interrupted Nathaniel's thoughts and said, 'Is everything alright Nathaniel? You look a bit worried about something.'

'Yes, I am fine, thank you Marco. I just hope we are going to have a smooth trip to Naples.'

'How long do you think it will take to get there?'

'Fabio says it usually takes between two and three days, depending on the weather and which way the wind decides to blow.'

'Well I hope it's not too rough, I am not a very good sailor.'

'Me neither.'

***

The trip south went quite smoothly and they arrived in Naples in the evening of the third day and after managing to secure transport for all their baggage, they set off to Marco's home. Marco still lived with his parents, father Luigi and mother Rosa. Nathaniel had met them on his last visit to Naples and had been made very welcome. Luigi was particularly thankful for giving Marco a job and as he said, 'getting him from under my feet.'

Luigi was on the patio and came out to greet them as soon as he heard the dogs barking, 'How nice to see you again Nathaniel,' he said as he shook hands energetically, and turning to Marco, 'Welcome home son.'

As the luggage was unloaded they sat down with a glass of wine and Rosa asked, 'What are your plans Nathaniel?'

'For goodness sake Rosa, they have only just arrived, give them a chance to relax.' said Luigi.

'It's alright Luigi,' said Nathaniel, 'We start tomorrow, Marco will start to sort the warehouse out and I will go house hunting. I have to get Anna down here as soon as possible and we must be prepared for the arrival of our

"Baccala".'

'Don't rush around looking for a place, you have plenty of time and you are welcome to stay here as long as you wish.'

'That's very kind of you but it will be a lot easier with a place of our own and of course, Anna is very keen to join me.'

***

Marco worked hard at getting the warehouse ready, clearing piles of rubbish and carrying out repairs to the structure whilst Nathaniel looked over dozens of properties. Eventually, after two weeks of searching, Nathaniel found a villa which suited his purpose. There was room for everyone, plenty of space for Nathaniel and Anna, a separate self-contained apartment for Antonino and room for the nanny to live in.

As soon as the purchase of the villa was agreed Nathaniel wrote a short note to Anna telling her to come as quickly as she could.

My Dearest Anna,

'Hurrah! I have secured accommodation for us at last. There is enough furniture and household equipment for you to live comfortably and there is plenty of space for Antonino. Any items you particularly want but can't carry with you, make sure they are put to one side to be forwarded at a later date. If Antonino wishes to accompany you and the nanny, do not discourage him. However if he wishes to stay until the house has been disposed of, I will understand. Whatever you decide, I desperately want to see you again soon. I miss you every hour and every minute of every day.

Nathaniel

As soon as he had finished writing, he sealed it with red wax and promptly went down to the docks to find the next boat going to Livorno. Luckily he found one going on the first tide the next morning and paid the captain handsomely to see that his message was delivered with no delays.

***

About a week after sending the message to Anna, Nathaniel moved into his new home. He had spent most of his days ensuring that everything was neat and tidy and ready for the arrival of his 'family.' Days began to drag as he waited to hear from Anna and he was limited as to what he could do whilst waiting for his first cargo of "Baccala". The warehouse was ready, and he kept in close contact with all his prospective buyers. He spent most of his spare time pacing around the docks hoping to get advance warning of boats coming from Livorno and of course Norway. It was, he knew, a fruitless task, the first he would hear of any arrival would be when the boat appeared outside the harbour.

He was sitting on the patio one evening about two weeks after moving in, just relaxing enjoying a glass of local red wine hoping that Anna had

308

received his message, when there was a loud knocking on the front door. The sudden noise in such a peaceful situation quite startled him and brought him back to reality and he went to see who could be visiting at this time in the evening. 'Excuse me sir, are you Mr. Nathaniel Thorold?' asked a uniformed man.

'I am, and how can I help you?' he asked, looking over the visitor's shoulder at a carriage parked on the drive. 'Oh my goodness, Anna,' he shouted as he saw his beloved's head peer out of the carriage window. As he ran to the carriage he saw Antonino sitting next to the nanny opposite Anna, and swiftly changing his approach and said, 'Welcome to your new home Antonino, how was your journey?' and to Anna, 'and how is your beautiful little Maria?'

***

The family were quickly settled into their new home and Anna soon had the place as she wanted it. Antonino loved his separate accommodation and joined Anna and Nathaniel for meals and other family occasions but retreated to his rooms most of the time. He still maintained the pretence of married life, but during summer, Anna was often seen out, either walking or riding in their carriage with Nathaniel and the baby Maria, and the picture of a normal marriage with Antonino was beginning to fade and tongues had started to wag.

Nathaniel's business had taken off as quickly as it had in Livorno and he had placed orders with Lars for deliveries to be made on a regular basis of one ship load per month. In August Nathaniel paid a visit to Livorno to see how Silvio was getting on and was very pleased with what he found. Silvio had recruited a very able young man as his assistant and they were handling increased trade very well. Silvio had also increased the customer base and had some suggestions to make regarding the efficient use of the warehouse and maybe importing some additional stock lines.

Nathaniel was very impressed but said, 'I like your ideas Silvio but I think we should wait a few more months. If you could do some research and find out what our customers would like then we can talk about it on my next visit.'

'That's alright. I will ask a few more questions and get it all down on paper for you. But we certainly have extra capacity here that we could be using.'

'I appreciate that and I like your attitude, but if we let optimism get in the way of the facts, the whole project could end in disaster. However, I am delighted with the profitability of the first half of the year since I last saw you, and with all the hard work you have put in, you thoroughly deserve your bonus.'

***

After what seemed a whirlwind visit to Livorno, Nathaniel arrived back home in Naples to find that a representative of the church had called to have a polite chat with Antonino. He didn't mention it to Nathaniel but when the priest arrived unannounced at the house, Anna was very suspicious. 'Antonino took the priest out onto the patio and I got them some drinks and then I left. I guessed what it was all about so I made a point of sitting quietly behind the door and listening. I am sure Antonino knew I was there because he talked quite loudly and asked the priest to speak up because he said he was a little bit hard of hearing. I nearly burst out laughing.'

'What did they say?'

'Well it was all very polite at the start, but then the priest gradually started to mention our little walks and rides around the area and wanted to know why Antonino wasn't there.'

'What did he say to that?'

'Well, he got quite angry. He said he thought the world of you, and I was the best wife anyone could possibly have. Just because he wasn't keen on walks or carriage rides, was it wrong for his friend to offer himself as my escort?'

He didn't tell him to mind his own business then?'

'Not then, but when he asked if little Maria was his, he went mad. I thought he was going to hit him, he was furious. He jumped up and accused the priest of listening to local gossip mongers, and hadn't he anything better to do than try to make things worse. Hounding a loving father, his wife and their very good friend, instead of castigating the propagators of scandalous and untrue speculation.'

'Goodness, I bet the priest didn't expect a mouthful like that.'

'I have never seen a priest move so quickly, he left here nearly tripping over his vestments.'

'What did Antonino say to you?'

'He has said absolutely nothing. He just smiled when he saw me and walked off to his room.'

'Should I go and have a word with him?'

'I don't think so. He will tell us eventually if he wants to. I just hope that this isn't going to be a repeat of what went on in Livorno.' said a worried Anna.

'Let's hope not. It makes you wonder who starts these rumours, doesn't it.'

**

It was now approaching a year since his first sales in Naples and Nathaniel was pleased and very excited with the way the business was progressing. His sales were good and his staff were handling things just as he had hoped, and so he was able to concentrate on calling on customers and spreading the word. He had also recently received a note from Sir Samuel asking if he wished to buy any Cornish Winter Pilchards which would be ready for shipment next December.

Nathaniel had been putting off a trip back to England to sort out his business interests and Sir Samuel's note had spurred him on to make a decision. He had discussed it with Anna and they agreed that he should go in the summer. Anna had said she was happy as long as he didn't stay too long as she would miss him terribly.

Two weeks after he had received Sir Samuel's note, Nathaniel had a distressing letter from Jonathan Adnitt. He sat down to read it with tears in his eyes.

***

10

January 1738

Dear Nathaniel,

I am deeply sorry to have to inform you that on the first day of January, Sir Samuel Thorold passed away peacefully in his sleep. After a suitable lying in state at his residence in Ormond Street, he will be carried to Harmston where he will be interred on 19th January.

I have to inform you that you have received some benefit in his will and you will be informed of your entitlement in due course.

I appreciate that you will not be able to attend the interment but may I strongly suggest that you make every effort to come back to London to finalise all aspects of your inheritance.

Your humble servant,
Jonathan Adnitt

***

'This changes everything Anna, I will have to go as soon as I can arrange a passage.' Nathaniel explained during their evening meal. 'At least I can get it over with and then I will be able to spend the Summer months here in the warm.'

'It is very important that you go at the first opportunity Nathaniel,' said Antonino. 'A death in the family is a very upsetting experience and you must pay your respects as soon as you can.'

Anna remained quiet for a while and then said, rather grudgingly, 'Yes, you must go Nathaniel.'

***

The only boat going to London in the foreseeable future was not due to leave until the end of the week and Nathaniel managed to secure a not very comfortable birth.

'How long will you be away, Nathaniel?' asked Anna. 'You won't be long will you?'

311

'I will be as quick as possible, but don't expect me back until at least June. It's a long trip and I will have a lot to do before I can return.'

'But it's only March now, what am I going to do?' she cried, and promptly burst into tears.

Chapter 25

The journey from Naples to London was very uncomfortable for both crew and the few passengers on board. They experienced a series of quite violent storms from the moment they set sail until they arrived in London. Nathaniel was never so pleased as he was on the day they finally arrived.

He disembarked and made his way directly to Sir Samuels's office where Jonathan greeted him cheerfully. 'Good afternoon Nathaniel, you look a bit weary, have you had a good trip?'

'No, I am sorry to say, I haven't. It was the worst trip I have ever made, high winds and raging seas nearly all the way. I have never been so pleased to get off a ship in my life.'

'I am sure you were very sorry to hear of Sir Samuel's death and I am sorry that it was me that had to tell you.'

'It came as a complete shock to me,' said Nathaniel 'I never expected such news. I thought he would live forever.'

'Well he lived a good life and he died peacefully in his sleep at the age of sixty-five years.'

'I didn't think he was as old as that, but I suppose I had never even thought of how old he was.'

'I don't know what your plans are Nathaniel but you will be most welcome to stay with us until you have made up your mind.'

'Well, I will be going to spend some time in Lincolnshire, but I expect someone will want to see me regarding the will whilst I am in London.'

'The executors for Sir Samuel's will are Mrs. Millicent Neate and Fotherly Baker both of whom I think you know.'

'Yes I do, but I thought Millicent was the wife of a vicar somewhere down in the West Country.'

'She is, but she is staying in London until the will has been sorted out. Fotherley has an office here in town and I will send him a message to say that we will be at his office tomorrow at two pm, if that is convenient.'

***

Nathaniel and Jonathan braved the unusually chilly wind as they walked the short distance to Fotherley Baker's chambers. 'It's a bit chilly for April, isn't it?' asked Nathaniel. 'I thought we should be getting into Spring by now.'

'Yes it is, we are suffering a bit of a late Spring this year.'

They entered a small doorway which opened into a surprisingly large vestibule. 'I think you may be in for a bit of a surprise,' said Jonathan as they handed their capes to an attendant. 'You should make sure you are sitting down before he reads the will.'

'Come on in,' said a small portly gentleman who Jonathan introduced as Fotherley Baker. 'I am pleased you managed to get here so quickly Nathaniel. I haven't seen you for years.'

'No, it must be at least five, and I wouldn't have recognised you if I had seen you in the street.' replied Nathaniel, thinking, 'he has put on a great deal of weight.'

'Sit down please gentlemen and we will get on with the task we are here for. Unfortunately Mrs. Neate is unable to be here today but her attendance is not essential.' He proceeded to untie a red ribbon which held together a pile of papers, laid it carefully to one side, and started to read aloud, *'In the name of God, Amen. I Sir Samuel Thorold, Bart., being of sound mind, memory and understanding, praised be to God for the same, do make and declare this to be my last will and testament as follows.......'*

As Fotherly started to describe what was being left to whom, Nathaniel realised that the main thrust of the will was to leave all the Harmston estates, including Harmston Hall which had been built by Sir Samuel's brother Charles, to him. He was also to receive the sum of eight thousand pounds. The estate in the village of Rowston was left for the use of Mrs. Neate for the remainder of her life. On her death, that would also revert to him. Jonathan had inherited Sir Samuel's half share of the London business.

It took some time for Fotherley to complete the reading. There were many minor bequests but Nathaniel's mind was on the estates he had inherited. He had no idea what he was going to do as, when he left Naples, he was seriously thinking of selling off all his existing estates and leaving England for Italy. Now he found himself with an even bigger estate, and a bigger decision. 'I will have to take my time and think this through very carefully.' he mused.

***

Nathaniel's mind was in turmoil and when they returned to Jonathan's office, Jonathan sat him down and asked 'What's the problem Nathaniel, I thought you would be delighted.'

'Well it was such a surprise, and there is so much to take in. When I arrived in London yesterday I had made other plans for my future. This news has now thrown them into total disarray.'

'Do you want to tell me about it?'

Nathaniel thought about it for a while and Jonathan remained silent. He knew that he would have to talk to someone and Jonathan was probably the only person he knew who he could trust totally. 'I know I can trust you Jonathan, but it will take quite some time. There is a lot to tell and I definitely need an honest unbiased opinion'

'Well let's go home and we can sit down and you can tell me all. You know Jane will be out this evening so we will not be disturbed.'

Thanks very much Jonathan,' said Nathaniel as he was passed a glass of rum, 'I need that.' He took a good draft from the glass and continued, 'I don't really know how to tell you, but I will begin with Charlotte's death and my departure from England.'

'I can understand your anguish at that time Nathaniel, we all miss her terribly, she was such a lovely girl.'

'She was, and I will never ever forget her. I doubt if I will ever marry now.'

'You can't say that Nathaniel, you can never predict the future.'

'I don't think I could ever risk suffering feelings like that again, Jonathan. *Ever.*'

Seeing the signs of distress Nathaniel was displaying, Jonathan leant forward, placed a comforting hand on Nathaniel's wrist and said quietly, 'Just tell me in your own time, there is no rush.'

Nathaniel spent over an hour telling Jonathan everything that had happened and what he had done since Charlotte's accident. His running away, and his failed effort at trying to end his life. His subsequent stumbling on the "Baccala" and its potential for exploitation. The development and success of his business in Livorno. His lodgings and the resulting relationship with Anna and the denial of her husband. How they had been run out of town by a bigoted church and its cohorts. His expanding business in Naples and the child Maria, he had fathered with Anna. How old Antonino has reacted to his obvious relationship with Anna. How he had planned to come to England this summer and sell up his estates, return to Italy and remain there for the rest of his life. How the news of Sir Samuel's death had meant he had returned to England early. How today's news had made things far more difficult and not easier, as most people would suspect.

'You can see that I am a bit out of my depth at the moment. I need to get things straight in my mind before I come to a decision.'

Jonathan, who had remained silent for the whole of Nathaniel's monologue, said, 'Em, I can see your problem. I think what you need now is a period of quiet reflection before you make any decisions.'

'I am quite keen to hear what you think, Jonathan. You know I respect your opinions.'

'I am sure you do Nathaniel, but I think I need a period of quiet reflection as well. I will need to think of a sensible way out of this problem and I can't do it instantly.'

'Thanks for listening Jonathan, just sitting there and letting me ramble on has helped already. I have been bottling it up for months but now it doesn't seem so much of a problem after all.'

'I think we should have another glass of rum and then think about going to bed. Don't you?'

***

Over breakfast, Nathaniel said he was still uncertain as to what he should do and Jonathan quickly told him to arrange a meeting with Sir Samuel's legal representatives in London. 'You can't do anything without seeing them first and at the moment you know absolutely nothing about the Harmston estate and all its complexities.'

'That's true, all I know is that it is a bigger estate than the one I already have, and I don't know everything about that either.'

'I will send one of my men around to set up a meeting for later this morning. I am sure they will see you immediately. You are now a very big client of theirs.'

'Thank you Jonathan, is there anything else you have thought I should do immediately.'

'A letter to Charles at Grantham wouldn't go amiss. I am sure he would like to know what is going on. He has been deeply involved in your business ever since you disappeared and he hasn't seen you for nearly four years.'

'That's true, and I feel so guilty. I will get a note off to him today, probably after I have seen the legal representatives.'

***

They alighted from Jonathan's carriage outside a modern building and stepped into a cold cutting wind. The building had large marble columns either side of the heavy main entrance door which was strengthened by wrought iron bars and had a small iron grill situated at eye level. Two uniformed doormen, stood aside as the door opened as if by magic, and they were ushered inside. They entered into a vast marble floored area and two well-dressed gentlemen came forward to greet them. 'Good morning Jonathan, I presume that this is Sir Nathaniel.'

'Indeed it is, although I don't think he realises it yet. Nathaniel, may I introduce Mr. Edmund Fullerton and Mr. Richard Smythe.'

The introductory formalities were dealt with quickly and they retired to Edmund's chamber to discuss Nathaniel's inheritance and Nathaniel's first question was, 'What was that Sir Nathaniel all about then. Were you having a laugh?'

'On the contrary, His Gracious Majesty, King George the Second confirmed you were the rightful successor to the title on the death of Sir Samuel, and you are now known as "Sir Nathaniel Thorold of Harmston in the County of Lincolnshire." Hadn't you heard before now?'

'Not at all, it was news to me until you mentioned it down stairs earlier on.'

316

The briefing from the two legal gentlemen proved quite difficult for Nathaniel to take in and he was completely taken aback with the size of the estate, and he expressed his concern at the detail and complexity of what he was being told.

'You mustn't worry too much Sir Nathaniel,' said Edmund, 'Kenneth Parman the estate manager is a very competent fellow. He has been manager for nearly ten years now and all of that time Sir Samuel lived in London so no matter where you have your normal daily residence, things will carry on as normal up at Harmston.'

'Well, that's very pleasing to hear, I was getting very worried until you told me that.'

***

Back at Jonathan's house, Nathaniel relaxed and was feeling somewhat better than he had felt at breakfast. The knowledge that the Harmston estate was in good competent hands would allow him more flexibility in his decision making over the next few weeks.

'What have you planned for tomorrow Nathaniel?'

'There are lots of things I need to do and fitting them in may be a problem. I need to get a new set of clothes, the ones I have brought with me are designed for warmer climes and I am suffering in this cold, damp weather. I have also to see the Governor of the bank fairly soon, I have a lot of sorting out to do. By the way, who's in charge now? It was Samuel Holden the last time I called in but I expect he has retired by now.'

'I shouldn't worry too much about the weather, it's not likely to stay like this for much longer, said Jonathan. 'Yes, Samuel retired a few months ago and it's a chap called Thomas Cooke now. I don't know him very well, but he seems a decent enough man.'

'I don't know him do I? '

'I doubt it, he was not at any of Sir Samuel's gatherings as far as I know, so it's very unlikely.'

'Oh well, not to worry, I will soon find out won't I?'

'Yes and I will introduce you to my tailor once we have sorted out your banking situation. You will need to get measured for your new outfit quickly as it will take time to get everything made up.'

***

The meeting at the bank was very enlightening for Nathaniel. Although he knew he was already a wealthy man, he soon realised he was far more wealthy than he had ever thought. Apart from the cash he had inherited, there were investments in coal and goods which provided a substantial regular income from His Majesty's Exchequer.

By the time the meeting was over, Nathaniel's head was in a spin. In addition to the news of his newly acquired estates, he was informed that the profits he had accumulated from his business in Lincolnshire had grown steadily during his absence and he should think about investing some of his assets.

***

After the meeting Jonathan introduced Nathaniel to his tailor and then left to go back to his office. Nathaniel spent the remainder of the afternoon discussing styles and being measured for a complete new outfit of clothes. He also bought a couple of readymade outfits which he could wear until his order had been made. 'I have spent a small fortune.' he told Jonathan that evening.

'Well you have a fortune to spend, haven't you?' was the somewhat sarcastic reply.

'No need to be like that, Jonathan.'

'I'm sorry Nathaniel, I didn't mean to be rude. I just meant you will have to get used to being a very wealthy man. Money is no object to you now.'

After they had finished their evening meal, Nathaniel sat down and wrote a long letter to Anna explaining all his news and telling her that he would probably have to stay in England longer than he had expected. He explained that he was missing her terribly and would return as soon as he possibly could. She was not to worry. He longed to be back with her in his arms and there was no chance of him staying in this freezing cold country a moment longer than was necessary. He promised to write to her regularly and keep her up to date with all his news.

***

Nathaniel stayed in London for a month before heading north to his home at Borton where he hoped to get a few things sorted out. At the insistence of Jonathan, he was accompanied by Richard Houghton, a good strong reliable worker and a young William Gilbert who was an assistant to Jonathan's valet.

It hadn't taken long for Jonathan to persuade Nathaniel that it would be better on horseback. 'You will need a manservant to help you and make sure you have everything to hand. Also it is not safe travelling on your own these days and Richard can be relied on to help keep you safe.'

'I had heard that coaches were travelling up north these days, Jonathan.'

'Well I know there are a few setting up in business but they are so slow and uncomfortable that it's not worth the trouble. They are also very vulnerable to being held up by highwaymen who are very active especially where coaches are concerned.'

'So you don't recommend them then?'

'I don't. You will definitely be better off on horseback. I will provide your horses and Richard and William can stay with you until you return to London.'

318

'That's extremely kind of you.'

'It's the least I could do. You are going to be very busy for the next few weeks.'

***

The journey North took several days but thankfully the weather had improved dramatically and they experienced warm sunny days with a gentle breeze coming from the West. Nathaniel had plenty of time to think as they plodded on their way. Conversation was very sparse and they rode in silence for mile after mile soaking up the sun and enjoying the sounds of the country.

After a couple of days into the journey, Nathaniel had decided on his plans for the future. The Harmston Estate, if he found that Kenneth Parman was doing as good a job as he had been told, would stay unchanged.

The Borton estate was a bit different, he would lease off any farms where the manager wished to buy the lease and then get a manager for the Borton farm who would also act as estate manager for however many farms remained in the fold.

Whatever happened there was no way that he was going to stay around Lincolnshire a minute longer than was absolutely necessary. 'I have to get back to Italy and my darling Anna as soon as possible.'

Chapter 26

As they approached Borton, Nathaniel was feeling a certain amount of trepidation. He had left in a hurry nearly four years ago giving neither warning nor explanation to any of his staff. He deeply regretted the fact that he had been very rude and abrupt with Sylvia who had always been a loyal, devoted servant and friend. As they drew nearer he thought to himself, 'I have changed since I was here last, I will have to make up for some very poor behaviour over the years. What on earth must they think of me?'

**

It was mid-morning when they rode into the farm at Borton and hitched their horses to the rail in front of the house. The place seemed deserted, no-one in sight anywhere. 'They must all be in the fields.' said Nathaniel, 'but I am surprised Sylvia hasn't appeared.' The outer front door was open but the inner one was closed.

As Nathaniel dismounted, a dog barked in the house and the door opened. Sylvia appeared looking quite shocked. 'Nathaniel,' she gasped. 'Why didn't you warn us you were coming? We didn't expect you for another week or two,' but before Nathaniel could answer, she had rushed forward and flung her arms around his neck and burst into tears. 'I've missed you so much Nathaniel and it's lovely to see you again. I hope you are not going to disappear like that again.'

**

Once Nathaniel had ensured his two travelling companions had been shown to their accommodation and their horses had been taken care of, he settled down in the kitchen to talk to Sylvia. He felt some serious explaining was in order and first, asked her what she had been told about his sudden disappearance.

'All we were told was that you were in debt and some men were coming to get their money. When they arrived there were about six of them and they were very rude. They were not very happy when they found you were not here and they went to Grantham to see Mr. Woolaston.'

· 'Did you tell them that's where I was?'

'No, I said I thought you had gone to the market with Mo and so that's where they would find you.'

'I am very sorry I put you in such an awkward situation Sylvia but I was a very worried man. I thought they would kill me if they found me. Did you find out any more after that day?'

Sylvia said she had the entire story from Ephraim a couple of weeks later and asked, 'Why didn't you come back once you found out that they were crooks?'

'I couldn't, Sylvia. I didn't find out for nearly a year and by then I was setting up a business in Italy.'

'Well I had heard you were in Italy, and you certainly look as if you have spent some time in the sun.'

***

Nathaniel went on to tell her his story and what had happened in the four years since his departure. He also told her his visit was only temporary and what he would be doing while in Lincolnshire.

'How long will you be staying here Nathaniel, but I suppose I will have to call you Sir, from now on won't I?'

'Don't be silly Sylvia, I will still be Nathaniel to you, but if we have guests in the house just call me Sir as you have always done.' and carried on, 'As for how long I will be staying, I expect I will be here for about a week and then I will have to go to Harmston to find out what is going on there.'

Sylvia looked downcast as she realised he was going away so soon, when Nathaniel said. 'That's enough about me, tell me what's been happening here.'

'Nothing much, really, everything has been running as normal.'

'Surely someone's died or married and there must have been a few new births over the four years.'

'Oh yes, I forgot to tell you in all the excitement. Mo's married a farmer's daughter from Barkston in the Willows. They married just over two years ago and have a baby boy. Guess what they call him.'

'I have no idea, Sylvia. Tell me.'

'They call him Nat!'

'Nat!' he exclaimed. 'I wonder where they got that from?'

'And the vicar married Charlotte Headland about a year after you left. They have a lovely little girl called Kate.'

'And you said nothing much has happened. I must have a word with Mo. Where is he working at the moment?'

'I am not sure but he should be back for milking in about an hour, but before you see him I think you should know, Mo has been running this farm more or less on his own for about two years. John Fowler has been very poorly and has been unable to work most of the time and even when he can get to work, he can't do very much.'

After he had spent some time with Sylvia, Nathaniel went round to the milking parlour to see Mo. Mo was delighted to see him and because he was very busy supervising the milking he asked if could talk to him when he had finished.

'Of course you can Mo, just call around at the house when you are ready.'

When Mo knocked on the door Nathaniel shook his hand vigorously and said, 'I was very pleased to hear your news Mo. A family man now eh? That came as a bit of a surprise.'

'Well you weren't here were you? We have a little boy as well. Guess what we call him.'

'I know, Sylvia told me. How old is little Nat now?'

'Just over a year. He was born on New Year's day last year.'

'I don't believe it!' exclaimed Nathaniel. 'That is the same day as my little Maria was born.'

They sat down in the kitchen for an hour or so and continued to discuss everything that had taken place since they last saw each other. The bond they had formed growing up together as young boys was still there and after a bit of leg pulling, Mo referred to Nathaniel as 'Sir Nathaniel,' and was promptly informed, 'You have always called me "Nat," and as far as I am concerned you will always call me "Nat." You are the only person in the world who does and no one else ever will.'

As time went on Mo appeared to be getting restless and Nathaniel asked him if he was alright.

'Well it's just that Nell will have my tea ready, and she will be worrying where I am.'

'You had better get on then Mo, we don't want your tea getting spoiled do we?'

'Why don't you call around later this evening, Nat? I would love you to meet Nell and young Nat and being a father, you know what its like.'

***

The next morning after an early breakfast, Nathaniel set out for Grantham to see Charles, his legal representative. He had taken Jonathan's advice and decided it was prudent to be accompanied wherever he went, even though he was well known in the area. His elevated status meant he could be the target of footpads and vagabonds and so Richard and William were to stay with him at all times when away from his home.

When he arrived at Grantham he pointed out the stabling where the horses could be watered and fed, told them to wait for him close by and went up the clutter-free stairs to Charles office. Things had changed considerably, there was a new door with a neat new sign proclaiming '*Charles Woolaston, Solicitor at Law. Oaths Taken.*' As Nathaniel approached the top of the stairs, the door opened and a smiling Luke Buxton said 'Good morning, Sir Nathaniel. Mr. Woolaston will see you straight away.' and ushered Nathaniel into Charles's neat and tidy office.

'Come in Sir Nathaniel, and take a seat. Luke, get Sir Nathaniel a coffee please, and one for me as well.'

'I can see you have been busy Charles, the place looks very business-like and young Luke seems to have settled in well.'

'Yes I am pleased with the way things have gone. It took some sorting out as you can imagine, but after Watson had left and old Ephraim had departed we had to go through everything. Luke was an inspired choice, he has a very tidy way of working and is a very quick learner.'

'Well it certainly looks as if you have worked wonders, I don't know how Ephraim and Watson ever managed to get things done.'

'Well to be honest, I think yours was the only account that was in any sort of order and in fact, he hardly had any other accounts at all. I have had to work hard to build up the client list and now, at last, we are in a more stable position.'

'I am pleased to hear it Charles.'

Luke brought the coffees, and as he left the room, Charles thanked him and said, 'Close the door please Luke.'

***

Apart from a break for lunch at *"The Angel"*, the meeting continued on well into the afternoon and Nathaniel was very happy with the outcome. The position of manager at Borton would be offered to Mo if John Fowler's health showed no signs of improvement. Three of the managed farms were also expressing an interest in taking them on a lease and if all these were actually taken up then there would be no need for an estate manager. Charles said that the remaining six farms could be supervised directly from his office – as he had proved over the last four years.

'I will visit the three managers showing interest within the next few weeks and see if we can get things moving. If you can get some figures put together so that I can have something to discuss with them, it will be helpful.'

'No problem Nathaniel, I should have them ready by the weekend. I have already started and all they need is a bit of tidying up.'

'Well why don't you come over to Borton for lunch on Friday and we can go through them together. It would be a good opportunity to catch up as well.'

***

Charles arrived mid-morning on Friday and had brought all the papers he had promised. Nathaniel was very impressed by Charles's work and complemented him on his efforts. 'I am writing a note to the three managers who are interested and told them I will be calling in to see them within the next ten days,' said Nathaniel, 'at least they will have the chance to prepare their case.'

'I think you will find they are well prepared already. I have told them to seek legal advice and so you should expect to have to deal with some well

323

thought out negotiations.'

'Do you think their representatives will be there?' asked Nathaniel, sounding more than a little nervous.

'Quite possibly. I know I would if I was entering into a binding long term contract.'

'Well do you think you should come with me Charles? I would be a good deal happier if you were there.'

'I would be happy to be there Nathaniel, but when you write to the managers you must tell them I will be there and specify the days you will be seeing each of them.'

'That's no problem, I will get the messages off this afternoon. Have you any days you would prefer?'

'We will have to be away for two or three days to do Frieston and Saltfleetby but Gonerby is close enough to deal with in my office. If you let me know the days you decide on I will fit in with you.'

'Alright, let's say we will go a week on Monday, three days should do it. We can deal with Gonerby when we get back.

'That's fine.' replied Charles, 'I will have everything ready for Monday morning and you can call in at the office on your way if you wish.'

***

Nathaniel and Charles had a successful trip and concluded the agreements to the satisfaction of all concerned. Charles had not been to that part of the county before and thought it was a bit wild and desolate, however he had really enjoyed the stay at Holt Farm. After they had concluded their business, Edward Wood had invited his legal representative to stay for dinner with Nathaniel and Charles. 'It would be a lovely way to seal the contract and I am sure you will enjoy the company.' he said.

The four of them were enjoying a pre-dinner drink when a coach pulled up at the house, followed swiftly by a loud banging on the door. 'Oh didn't I mention it, I have also invited a special friend of mine to join us,' said Edward as they heard the maid welcoming the guest.

They all heard the guest shout, 'Where the hell is that reprobate Nathaniel?' as the door flew open and in came Max Hoboer.

Charles looked on in amazement and thought. 'Who the hell is this, does he think we are deaf?'

'For the Lords sake Max, we are not deaf,' said Nathaniel, and putting his health at risk, he allowed Max to give him a great big bear hug. When he had regained his breath, Nathaniel introduced Charles who, when Max released his hand, took several minutes to get the circulation back into his fingers.

The next morning they had planned to get to Saltfleetby as early as possible but both Nathaniel and Charles were late getting up and were suffering from the effects of the large amounts of alcohol they had consumed. 'Good morning gentlemen,' said Edward as he greeted his guests in the dining room. 'You both look a bit fragile this morning. What do you fancy for breakfast?'

They both asked for coffee and nothing else. 'We have to get going soon.' said Nathaniel 'we promised Michael we would not be late.'

'Well, Richard and William have the horses ready for you and are ready to go.'

'Thanks Edward, we will go as soon as we have finished our coffee. We will stop somewhere for something to eat when feel a bit more disposed to it.'

Charles rubbed his brow and said,' How does Max do it? I have never seen anyone drink so much and stay seemingly quite sober.'

'Lots of practice.' replied Nathaniel finishing his coffee.

***

They arrived back at Charles's office on Thursday afternoon and Nathaniel stayed long enough to go through all the agreements and also to plan a meeting with Robert Anderson, the manager of Odder Lane Farm at Gonerby. Charles suggested that the meeting be arranged for Tuesday 'in my office' and he would get a note delivered to Robert immediately.

'Make sure you tell him to bring his legal representative.' said Nathaniel. 'We don't want any unnecessary delays, do we?'

'No we don't. From what you have told me, you want to get over to Harmston as soon as possible don't you?'

'I certainly do. I hope to get over there a week on Monday as I expect I will have a great deal to do. I expect it will be a few weeks before I can get away and set off back home to Naples.'

'Who is the legal representative at Harmston at the moment, Nathaniel?'

'According to Fullerton and Smythe in London, it's a firm called Wilson and Partner from Lincoln.'

'Well, if you find out they are not up to it, you know you can rely on me.'

'We will see. I am not making any promises but it might be beneficial to only have one legal firm to deal with.' concluded Nathaniel.

***

Back at Borton, Sylvia was delighted to see Nathaniel and fussed around as if he had been away for months. 'For goodness sake Sylvia, I am not a schoolboy now,' said a rather grumpy Nathaniel and then immediately regretted it. 'I'm sorry Sylvia, I didn't mean to criticise. You look after me very well and I really do appreciate your concern and dedication to your job.' He was worried about how he was going to tell her that he was going away again,

325

very soon. He knew he would be away for several weeks, and how was he going to tell her that when he had finished at Harmston he would be returning to Italy, probably for ever?

***

The day before Nathaniel's trip to Harmston, Sylvia spent most of the time sniffing and blowing her nose in between bursts of tears. She hardly spoke to Nathaniel as she prepared his clothes and checked everything was clean and tidy. Afraid of Sylvia's reaction, Nathaniel had repeatedly delayed telling her about his permanent return to Italy until earlier that day.

'Why didn't you tell me before?' she sobbed. 'At least I would have had time to get used to it.'

'It's not as if I am going to Italy tomorrow, Sylvia. I will be coming back here for a few days when I have finished at Harmston so I think I have given you fair warning.'

'Well you could have told me weeks ago, couldn't you?'

'Yes, I could have done, but I would have had to put up with your tears for the past few weeks, wouldn't I?'

'That's not fair,' she said, bursting into tears once more and rushing from the room, 'I sometimes think you hate me.'

Something Ephraim had once said came to Nathaniel's mind. 'That Miss Butler regards you as her son Nathaniel. Her whole life revolves around you and you never even notice.'

He said to himself, 'He was probably correct and I should be more considerate in the way I deal with her.'

326

Chapter 27

Nathaniel had never been to Harmston before and approached the whole trip with some trepidation. He had no idea of what to expect and as they had gone to see Charles at Grantham before setting out, it was beginning to turn into a long drawn out day. When they left Grantham they followed the track of the old Roman Ermine Street. As they left, Charles had said, 'Stick to the Roman road as near as you can and you will come directly to Harmston.' As they entered Boothby Graffoe, Nathaniel said to his two companions, 'We must be getting somewhere near by now. I think Mr. Woolaston said it was the next village.'

A short distance later they came upon a very small village where there appeared to be no sign of life and certainly no sign of a Hall. As they approached the village church there was an old man sitting on a tree stump smoking a pipe. He wore what looked like a piece of hessian sacking, which covered his shoulders and was held together under his chin by a piece of sharpened wood. A worn, shapeless, old felt hat covered his head and his grimy trousers were held in place by a frayed cord around his waist. A scruffy black and white dog sat at his feet and started to wag its tail as the three riders approached.

When the old man realised that the horsemen were approaching him, he struggled to his feet, doffed his old felt hat screwed it up in his hand and holding it close to his chest, said 'Good morning sir, nice day isn't it?'

'It certainly is. Now tell me, is this the village of Harmston?'

'No sir, this is Coleby, Harmston is the very next village, hardly a mile from here.'

***

After what seemed more like three miles, they saw the Hall. Nathaniel could hardly believe his eyes. 'I can't believe it. It's absolutely magnificent.' he exclaimed as he stared at the nearly new building which glowed a pinky red colour in the late afternoon light. 'How am I going to take care of *that*?'

***

As three travellers turned left through the front gates he stared aghast, 'Look at the size of it,' and then 'Oh my goodness!' when he saw rows of people lined up in front of the main entrance. 'Who told them we would be arriving today?' he thought. 'It could only have been Charles, just wait until I see him again.'

A smartly dressed man stepped forward as Nathaniel approached the reception party. 'Good afternoon Sir Nathaniel, I am Kenneth Parman your Estate Manager and may I welcome you to Harmston Hall.'

'Thank you very much Parman, it's a pleasure to meet you at last. I

327

have heard a lot about you.'

Kenneth introduced all the staff individually, and by the time introductions were complete Nathaniel was totally confused. However, he managed to give a brief speech by way of introducing himself and before dismissing the welcome party, Nathaniel asked Kenneth to make sure Richard and William were allocated suitable accommodation. He also explained that they were always to be available whenever he required them.

'Certainly Sir, I will see to it straight away.'

'Good. Then if you will make yourself available, I will see you at nine o'clock tomorrow morning.' He turned to the butler who was standing next to him, and said, 'I really need to freshen myself up, Jones, so would you please show me to my chambers.'

***

Although he had a very comfortable bed, Nathaniel's mind was in a total spin and he slept fitfully. He had been quite relaxed about his inheritance, in fact he had been looking forward to this day ever since his arrival back in England. Now that he was actually at Harmston, the size of the estate was so much larger than he had ever thought and the house itself was enormous. He hadn't counted the household staff at the time of the introductions, but there must have been at least forty, and that didn't include the gardeners. 'It's not at all like Borton with just Sylvia and a couple of housemaids. I hope someone knows what goes on here.'

As he contemplated the enormity of his situation and tried to decide what to do, there was a tap on his bedchamber door and William Gilbert entered pushing a trolley with a wash bowl and a large jug of hot water. 'Good morning sir,' said William as he placed the bowl and jug on the dresser. He moved over to the window and as he opened the drapes he said 'Can I lay your clothes out for you sir or is there anything else you would like me to do?'

'Thank you William, just get me something comfortable. What's the weather like this morning?'

'It looks as if it could be a nice day sir. The sun is shining and there is a gentle breeze at the moment.'

William completed his tasks and as he was leaving he said, 'Cook says breakfast will be ready in the dining room in half an hour, sir.'

'Thank you William,' and then realising he hadn't a clue where the dining room was, said, 'I think you should ask someone to come to my room and show me where to go.'

'Certainly, sir. I will have a word with Mr. Jones immediately.'

***

After breakfast, Nathaniel went into the library to spend a few minutes before setting out on his tour with Kenneth. It was a very large room and although there were several large bookshelves, there didn't seem to be a great deal of books. There was a large globe placed in the window and as he tried to spin it round, he found that it was seized solid. 'No one's looked at this for a few years,' he thought, 'and I don't expect anyone will look at it for a long time to come.'

There was a gentle tap on the door and a young maid entered and said, 'Complements of Mr. Parman Sir, but he is in the hall ready for you as requested.'

Having ascertained the young girl's name, he said. 'Thank you Rebecca, please tell him I will be with him directly.'

***

The next three days were hectic for Nathaniel, it seemed to be a nonstop tour of a whole series of local villages where he had an interest. As well as Harmston there were the villages of Colby, Boothby Graffoe, Aubourne and Waddington where he had extensive property and in some areas he owned the whole of the village. Nathaniel also decided that, although he would not inherit Rowston during her lifetime, he should take a day to go and make himself known to Mrs. Neate who owned the title for as long as she lived. Unfortunately Mrs. Neate was not in residence and had not yet visited Rowston since Sir Samuel's death, but Nathaniel found it was another village where everything had been owned by Sir Samuel.

***

After his tour of most of the properties, Nathaniel spent a couple of days getting to know his way around the Hall and its multitude of employees. He made copious notes of what he had learnt of the scope of his properties in preparation for a planned meeting with his local legal representatives. He had met Edmund Fullerton and Richard Smythe in London and they dealt with the Harmston part of Sir Samuel's estates. They had informed him that Hubert Wilson and Partner were the local agents who dealt with all local work. Unless there were any serious problems they only reported to London once every six months.

Nathaniel went over all the available estate papers with Kenneth, whose knowledge of the business proved to be very helpful. 'What involvement does Wilson and Partner have in your regular estate work, Kenneth?' asked Nathaniel. 'Do they ever visit or offer you advice if you need it?'

'I have been here nearly ten years and they have never visited the estate in that time and I doubt if they ever have.'

'How are the accounts prepared for all the farms and what happens to them before they are sent to London.'

'I visit all the tenants and farm managers, gather all the information, put them in order and check them against what information I already have. I

329

then produce an annual report and take it to Wilson's for whatever they have to do with it.'

'Is this what has always happened?' asked Nathaniel.

'Yes, that's how I was told to do it and it has always worked that way.'

'I see.' Nathaniel rubbed his chin thoughtfully, 'so you produce a full set of accounts for Wilson and Partner to pass on to London.'

'Yes, that seems to be about it.'

'Do you keep copies of your reports?'

'Not the full reports, just the main points and the financial figures.'

'We will have to see what they are doing for their money, won't we. Their bills seem excessive for very little work to me.'

'I have always thought they were, but have been met with indifference and a certain amount of legal bluster when I have raised the subject. I have always had to check their bills thoroughly when they come and I always have to ask for clarification on something or other.'

Nathaniel suspicions were aroused but he just said, 'Well it's a big estate and I expect some things could slip your memory.'

'No, it's made absolutely clear to all managers that no one spends money without my explicit approval. The only area I do not deal with is household expenses. Mr. Jones the Butler and Mrs. Mills the housekeeper deal with that side of things.'

'Well then, I had better have a word with them before we go to see Mr. Wilson and his partner, hadn't I?' said Nathaniel.

'I think you had, Sir.' was the response from Kenneth.

***

After his meeting with Jones, Nathaniel decided that he needed to look a bit deeper into the financial state of the business and asked Kenneth to bring him all his reports. When he was in London, Nathaniel had made copies of the reports that Edmund Fullerton and Richard Smythe had received from Wilson and Partner and he thought it important that he should check for any discrepancies.

'Come in Kenneth, sit down and let's have a look and see what is going on.' Nathaniel spread the two piles of papers on the table and sorted them into date order. Picking the top one from each pile, Nathaniel said, 'Let's look at the last report you sent with the one that was sent to London and see how they compare.'

'This is the final figure I agreed with Wilson's after some argument over their fee. 'said Kenneth.

'And look at this,' said Nathaniel, pointing to a much smaller figure on Wilson's submission to London. 'Let's check a few more.'

It soon became obvious that Wilson and Partner were sending false reports to London and swindling large sums of money from the estate. 'What can you do about it?' asked Kenneth.

'Well, we know what is going on and they don't know that we are aware of their behaviour so we will have a good advantage when we meet. We will have to play things quietly and lead them into a corner where they will have to admit their dirty deeds.'

'Do you want me to be at the meeting, Sir?'

'Of course, Kenneth, I am sure you will enjoy it, but before you go let's just add up the amount of money they have put in their bank that should be in ours.'

***

As they made their way to Lincoln, along the wide open heath, Nathaniel asked, 'Do you visit their office very often, Kenneth?'

'Yes, I visit every year with the reports but that's all. They have chambers next to the Stone Bow.'

'Are there stables nearby?'

'Yes, they are more or less next door.'

'I don't think I have been to Lincoln more than once, and that was when I was quite small. I came with my father so I am afraid you will have to be my guide. The only thing I can remember is the cathedral towering over the city, just as we can see it now.'

As they continued on their way and Nathaniel turned to Richard and asked 'I don't suppose you have seen it before, have you?'

'No Sir, I never expected to see a building as big as that in such a desolate county.'

'We are full of surprises around here, aren't we Kenneth?' and then to Richard, 'When you have settled the horses Richard, you can have a look around. We should be at least an hour so be ready for us by then, otherwise the time is your own.'

'Thank you very much Sir.'

***

As they came down the hill into Lincoln, the roads gradually became more congested, and as they crossed the High Bridge, Nathaniel recognised the Stonebow directly in front of him. 'I remember that archway from when I came here with my father,' he said. 'Doesn't the Cathedral look magnificent on the hill?'

'It does, and the castle looks minute in comparison.' replied Kenneth

They went through the arch and Kenneth indicated that they had arrived. As they dismounted Kenneth pointed out a sign with an arrow showing that Hubert Wilson's office was on the next floor. Nathaniel and Kenneth went up the stairs as Richard took the horses to the stables.

331

A young clerk ushered them into the office where they were welcomed by a tall, grey haired, slimly built, middle aged man. 'Good morning, Sir Nathaniel, I am Hubert Wilson. My partner and I are pleased to be involved in helping you with the running of your business. We have a long association with the Harmston Estate and hope it will continue well into the future. We were very sorry to hear of Sir Samuel's early demise and offer our sincere condolences.'

'Thank you very much Mr. Wilson, as you will appreciate I am reviewing all aspects of our dealings with outside organisations and decisions will have to be made as appropriate. I can assure you, however, that no hasty decisions will be made.'

'My partner will be with us shortly, he is attending to other business at the moment. Perhaps we can start without him?'

Nathaniel was about to reply when a short, round man came in and breathing heavily, sat down with a bump opposite him. He looked familiar to Nathaniel but the bald head, fringed with unruly red hair didn't match anyone he could remember. 'Gentlemen, may I introduce my partner, Peter Gardner,' said Hubert Wilson.

Nathaniel immediately realised where he had seen him. He was the hated prefect he had met on his first day at school in Bourne, and thought to himself, 'These accounts will definitely need close scrutiny.' and then out loud, 'Good morning Peter, it's been a long time.'

***

The colour of Peter's face changed from a pale, pasty grey to a shade closely resembling his hair as he stuttered, 'I am sorry, Sir, but I don't think we have met.'

'Oh yes we have. You were a prefect at Bourne Grammar School,' and with animosity creeping into his voice, 'and as I recall, a particular favourite of Mr. Myers, the headmaster.'

'I remember now, you were a gambling partner of that Montini character who was hanged not so very long ago. I went to join the crowds to see the execution and it was a real good turnout. I think they hung three of them that day, they were all gamblers'

'Actually, they were executed for fraud Mr. Gardner, just you remember that.'

Mr.Wilson promptly changed the subject and offered them coffee and suggested they get on with the business they had convened for.

***

Nathaniel asked for all the papers and went through them methodically. Both Wilson and Gardner began to squirm and show signs of panic. Eventually when confronted with overwhelming evidence of their misdemeanours, Wilson burst into tears and Gardner rushed out of the office and stumbled down the stairs in his rush to get away.

'He won't get far, will he Kenneth?' said Nathaniel with a smile. 'Mr. Wilson, we took the precaution of warning the Sheriff, and he is waiting outside to lock you both up. He will be calling for you in a few minutes. As for your chances of continuing as the representative for the Harmston Estates, what do *you* think?'

The Sheriff soon arrived to arrest Wilson and as he was marched away, Nathaniel said, 'If you see your friend Gardner, just say I hope he has a good crowd at his hanging.'

***

Nathaniel was extremely busy for the next week or so. He took Kenneth to Grantham to transfer all his Harmston business over to Charles. Charles explained to Kenneth how he had been dealing with the Borton business and Kenneth was very happy with the new arrangements. Nathaniel also pointed out that his estates were no longer part of Sir Samuel's empire and that he was going to discuss with Fullerton and Smythe the need to continue with their involvement with the London office.

'I agree.' said Charles. 'We can do everything here and it will save paying two sets of legal advisors.'

'At least I will know who to get in touch with if we have any problems,' said Kenneth 'it will make it much easier for Mr. Jones and myself.'

After the meeting Nathaniel decided against spending the night at Borton and headed back to Harmston. 'I have to go to Lincoln tomorrow to give a statement to the Sheriff about our problems with Wilson and Gardner. The sooner I get that sorted, the quicker I can get back to London and a boat back to Naples.'

Will you be back at Borton before going to London?' asked Charles.

'Yes I will be staying a few days but I am not looking forward to it. Sylvia is going to be in one of her moods and saying goodbye to all the workers will not be easy. 'I will see you sometime before I go to London, though. There are bound to be some last minute things to discuss.'

'You are not going away for ever, are you?'

'Well I can't see me returning very often, my life is in Italy now, Charles. I was devastated when your sister Charlotte died and it took me ages to get back to living normally again. Don't get me wrong, I still think of Charlotte every day and wonder what my life would have been like, but Anna rescued me from my misery and I have a lovely life now but I am afraid it is in Naples, not in Borton or Harmston.'

'I understand, Nathaniel. We all miss Charlotte but you have to have a life and I am pleased you have found someone to be happy with.'

'Thank you Charles, I am pleased you understand.'

Nathaniel completed his visit to Harmston and also gave his statement to the Sheriff. He suspected Wilson and Gardner would be paying a visit to the gallows in the very near future and the Sheriff commented that 'They would have gone on cheating for years if poor old Sir Samuel had not passed away. He was such a gentleman.'

As he left Harmston, all the staff once again lined up in front of the Hall to say their goodbyes and Nathaniel suspected that they were relieved to see him go. 'It will be a few years before I come back here and they will probably regard my visits as an intrusion.'

Borton was a bit more difficult, he was only there for a week before setting off to London with Richard and William, both of whom were looking forward to going home. A lot of time had been spent with Charles and the final decision on the transfer of the responsibilities from London had yet to be made. Sylvia was, as he had forecast, in a state of perpetual turmoil and Nathaniel tried his best to keep well out of her way.

Much to Mo's delight he was promoted to farm manager at Borton, and he quickly moved his family into the large cottage attached to rear of the manor house. He was fulsome in his thanks to Nathaniel and wished him well for his future in Italy. 'I'll be back from time to time Mo. You can't get rid of me forever.'

'I hope not, I thought we had seen the last of you when I said goodbye at Boston about four years ago and here you are, a Knight of the Realm.'

'I know, it was a big shock to me when I found out. I never expected to inherit from Sir Samuel. Life's full of surprises isn't it?'

***

Business in London was concluded smoothly and quickly. Fullerton and Smythe were happy to relinquish the administration of Harmston to Charles at Grantham but they thought they were probably in a better position to recommend suitable places for his investment. They had always offered Sir Samuel good advice and Jonathan confirmed they had. Nathaniel therefore decided to retain their services for investment advice on a commission only basis. They were also happy to advise Charles on queries or difficulties he might experience.

Nathaniel managed to secure a passage to Naples due to depart in eight days so it gave him time to see all his old colleagues and even when invited to a game of poker politely refused. He stayed with Jonathan and they had ample time to discuss business and the prospects of future cooperation. Nathaniel asked Jonathan if he knew that Sir Samuel had enquired about exporting some Cornish Pilchards to Naples.

'Yes, he discussed it with me at the time. He had a part share in two boats, which of course, I now own. We have the ability and knowledge to export anything you ever require and I am sure you have contacts able to supply return cargoes.'

'When could I expect these Cornish Pilchards, Jonathan?'

'The new harvest would be ready for dispatch in December or January.'

'That sounds alright, I will be home in plenty of time to make sure everyone is expecting them and get some orders in place before they arrive.'

'Good, then I will put the order in the system.' said Jonathan, 'By the way, I thought you said you were just setting up home in Naples.'

'You know I am.'

'Well I thought you would be buying some decent furniture while you were in London. There is a very good selection here and it's comparatively reasonable in price. Why don't you have a look around?'

'To be honest, I hadn't given it a thought, but I will go and have a look around tomorrow. I will also have a look for a nice present for Anna.'

***

Nathaniel spent the next few days purchasing a large number of items of furniture and a selection of soft furnishing for his home in Naples. Jonathan's wife, Jane accompanied him on his expeditions and her advice was well received, particularly regarding the soft furnishings.

He also enlisted Jane's help when he went to expensive jewellers to buy Anna a present. After much debating and many changes of mind he eventually bought a diamond encrusted gold brooch and matching bracelet. 'She will absolutely adore that Nathaniel,' said Jane. 'She is a very lucky lady.'

Chapter 28

Four years had passed since Nathaniel had returned from England and events had moved on very quickly. Both in Naples and Livorno business had grown far more successfully than he had ever thought possible and his family had grown with the addition of two more daughters, Nancy and Anna.

Antonino was still living with them and still denying any misconduct by Anna, who, where it was obvious for everyone to see, was living as Nathaniel's wife. The church in Naples was even more active in their condemnation of the activities of Nathaniel and Anna, and were constantly calling at the house to state their case. Nathaniel was very worried about the effect this harassment was having on his beloved Anna and was rapidly coming to some decisions about their future together and the future of his businesses.

'We don't have to suffer this campaign of interference from the Bishop and his cohorts, darling,' complained Nathaniel, 'we could live anywhere we choose and be well out of the way of all of them and their bigoted ideas. What would *you* like to do?'

'You know I hate their constant pressure, but we can't keep on running away from them, can we?'

'No we can't, but we can't stay here for the rest of our lives in constant fear of a knock at the door. We should find somewhere where we would be respected and left to ourselves without the church interfering with our lives. You know the area far better than I do, so can you think of anywhere we could escape to?'

Anna thought about it for a while and then replied, 'I spent a few months at my Grandmother's house on the Island of Capri when I was a young girl. It was beautiful there, and so peaceful and friendly.'

'I've never been to Capri at all and it's not so far away. Do you think we should go and have a look?'

'It sounds lovely, but I don't think you could control your business from there do you? It would mean you living in Naples for most of the time and me being stuck over there. I would miss you *too* much and be very lonely.' said Anna with a slight catch in her voice.

'Don't worry about that, I have a plan which I am working on and I think you will like it.'

***

Nathaniel sent a short note to Silvio in Livorno asking him to come down to Naples as soon as possible when he would have a proposition to put to both him and Marco. 'I think you will like what I have to say to you both.' he wrote.

***

Silvio arrived in Naples about ten days after Nathaniel had sent the note and Nathaniel sat down with his two managers and put his proposals to them. 'You are both well aware of my recent inheritance of a large estate in England and along with what I already own, it provides me with a substantial income. I have no intention of deserting the businesses I have built with your valued assistance, but I have decided to put the following proposals to you which I think will be of considerable benefit to you over the coming years. Firstly, I have no intention of separating the Naples and Livorno sites as I think that would put one site in competition with the other and I would regard that as a bad move.'

He then told them of the problems they were having with the church and how Anna was reacting to the pressure. 'We are planning a move to the Island of Capri in the near future but I have no intention of giving up my control all together. What I am proposing is that for the next five years, and as long as you both continue to work for me, I will transfer shares in the company to you until you own forty-nine percent of the company between you. I will retain the remaining fifty one percent. The shares will be transferred as follows: At the end of year one, Five percent, a further ten percent at the end of years two and three, and twelve percent at the end of years four and five. All shares transferred will be divided equally between the two of you and after three years you will both be expected to become directors of the company with all the responsibilities that will entail.' He paused for them to take it in and then said, 'I would like you to go away now and think over what I have said and then tomorrow we will talk it over and clear up any questions you may have.'

They thanked him for the offer and as they walked away, Nathaniel heard Silvio say, 'I don't believe it. I never expected anything like that in a million years.'

'Nor me. I'm speechless.' replied Marco.

***

'How did Marco and Silvio react to your proposals, Nathaniel?'

'I think they like what they heard, but I asked them to go home and sleep on it and let me know tomorrow.'

'I really hope they accept your offer, I so want to get away from Naples.'

'Well, as soon as they agree we can go over to Capri and spend a few days looking for somewhere to stay. I suppose Antonino will be happy wherever we decide to stay. I know he is getting tired of those priests continually pestering him. They seem to be paying him more attention than they do you.'

'They think that he will give in quickly but I know that once he has made up his mind it will be impossible to get him to change,' said Anna.

'Thank goodness he accepts what is going on. If he didn't we would find ourselves in an impossible situation,' said a reflective Nathaniel.

***

As expected, both Marco and Silvio were very keen to seize the opportunity Nathaniel had offered them and Anna was even more delighted when Nathaniel told her. He also told her that he had arranged for them to go to Capri in two days' time and they would stay for three days to search out a place to live.

'Thank you so much Nathaniel, I am really looking forward to going and I am sure we will find something suitable.'

'Don't get too excited darling, I have heard that housing is generally quite poor and we may have a struggle to find something up to the standard we are used to.'

'Well we will find out soon enough won't we.' Anna replied. 'We will never know if we don't look, will we?'

The trip to Capri was uneventful. The sea shimmered in the bright sunlight, twinkling on the ripples created by the gentle, warm breeze. As they approached the island, Nathaniel was struck by the sheer beauty of the place. Houses at first seemed to be built on vertical cliffs but as they slowly got nearer he could distinguish footpaths and narrow lanes amidst the scattered dwellings. 'This looks like heaven,' gushed Nathaniel. 'In all my travels I have never seen anywhere as beautiful.'

The sails were lowered one by one and the boat drifted gently onto the sandy beach in the harbour. There was a slight shudder as it came to a halt and assisted by some men on the beach, the crew lowered a wide plank to form a bridge to the beach. Their baggage was passed over before Nathanial and Anna were helped ashore.

***

Capri proved to a difficult place to rent a property but eventually they decided to take a house in a quiet part of the main town on a short let. Nathaniel would rather have not taken it but Anna was getting desperate to get away from Naples. 'It will be much easier to search if we are here, and we will get to know quickly if a suitable property becomes available,' she argued.

'Yes, darling, you are right as usual. It does make sense, so I will arrange for us to move here next week.'

***

It was a very hectic week for everyone, Nathaniel had to make sure he could be away from his business for a few weeks, and as the house on Capri was fully furnished, all the furniture they owned in Naples had to be put into storage until it was required. Anna supervised all the work at the house and ensured everything that was needed was packed and marked up for easy access. Antonino was not the slightest bit interested and just watched the frenzied activities from a safe distance. The children were kept well out of the way by the nanny but were all excitedly looking forward to a trip 'over the sea on a boat.'

On the day before the move day, all the crates and boxes were sent down to the docks to be loaded on board. As Nathaniel was ensuring everything had been loaded on the wagon, he looked up and saw a priest coming down the path, 'Well Father Phillippe, I suppose you are satisfied now, aren't you?' said Nathaniel, his anger clear in his voice. 'Now that you have succeeded in driving us out, you will have to find someone else to persecute, won't you.'

'I am not pleased at all,' replied the priest, 'we would still want you to behave in a way that the Good Lord says you should, wherever you live.'

'Just kindly go away and leave us in peace.' said Nathaniel, biting his tongue before he said something he regretted.

The priest turned to leave and said, 'We are all sinners Nathaniel, but I wish you all the very best and may God bless you.'

Anna, who had seen the incident, came out of the house to see what was going on and asked Nathaniel if he had been rude to the priest.

'Of course I have, if I had lost my temper I would have booted him off our property.'

***

Those items that were required overnight were kept back in readiness for a very early start in the morning. Nathaniel had carried out his final checks and given final instructions to the staff, the children were all ready and chattering amongst themselves. Anna was stressed but hoping that things might improve once they had moved, while Antonino quietly tagged along with the move and did not appear to be taking much interest at all.

They arrived at the docks just after dawn and Nathaniel commented that he couldn't remember the last time he had been up and about so early. 'It still seems to be the middle of the night,' replied Antonino with his only comment of the morning so far.

***

On the first morning in their new house, they were all late rising and awoke to a bright sunny day with only the faintest trace of a cloud in the sky. The children were all excited and Nathaniel said they could go for a walk with the nanny while their mother sorted things into some sort of order. Nathaniel was still not totally impressed with the house they had acquired and went into town to make sure all the local professional people knew he was here and was looking for much better accommodation.

***

After six long months of searching and experiencing several disappointments, they eventually found somewhere suitable. Even so,

Nathaniel was not convinced that he was in the one he really wanted and still kept his eye open for a better place. By this time, he was spending less and less time at the warehouse and was beginning to live the life of a moneyed gentleman and was accepted by the local Caprese as such.

The experiences and frustrations of trying to find the perfect home finally convinced him that the only way he was going to get what he wanted was to build one himself. He had seen an old wreck of a building near Due Mari which was once owned by the seventeenth Bishop Gallo and had been used many years previously as a hostel for Nuns. It was on a large site on the hillside overlooking the sea and the property also included a neglected vineyard. He discussed the possible purchase of the site with Anna but when he took her to see it she was not at all enthusiastic. 'I love the view from here,' she said, 'but it's an absolute wreck and would cost a fortune to get it how we want it. Anyway I am perfectly happy with where we are now.

'Well I have a fortune, in fact I have three fortunes, so I am sure I can afford anything I want, my darling,' was his rather abrupt reply, 'and all I want is the very best for my family, and where we are now is not the best.'

After explaining that all she was worried about was the cost and if Nathaniel could afford a new villa she would love it there. 'A new villa on that site would be absolutely perfect.' she said.

***

The next six months were an exciting time for Nathaniel and Anna and they spent many hours with Marziale Desiderio consolidating their ideas on what the new villa should look like and how it would be laid out. They considered that Desiderio was an inspired choice who came with a glowing reputation both as a designer and a builder, and were delighted that he accepted the challenge. His ideas proved crucial to the final design and he used the situation of the site on the hillside to its maximum advantage. The actual building work was to be carried out by Michele Gargiulo and his brother, both local builders, who were highly recommended by Desiderio who would be in overall charge of the project. 'These two are the best builders in the area and we are lucky they will be available when we need to start building.'

As soon as he had bought the ruins, Nathaniel had employed some local workers and set them to work on restoring the vineyard. Keen to produce wine of his own, he had taken advice on the way forward and decided it was something he could be getting on with. All indications were that it would take two or three years to start producing some decent wine.

Chapter 29

Building of the villa started just over a year after they had moved to Capri. Nathaniel, who had spent most of this time in Naples, and with the occasional visit to the warehouse in Livorno, soon came to the conclusion that he would be much happier spending more time on the island. With that in mind he had encouraged both Silvio and Marco to take more responsibility and had informed them that he wouldn't be around quite so much in the future. Both knew that they would always be able to contact Nathaniel fairly quickly in an emergency and accepted this decision with glee, and as Silvio said, 'It won't make much difference to me as I have been doing the job since you left Livorno.'

'You have Silvio, you have both been doing a very good job and I appreciate it very much,' replied Nathaniel, 'if you carry on like you have been doing, I will be delighted.'

***

By this time Nathaniel and Anna were living as man and wife and although Antonino was seldom seen with Anna, on his rare trips out of the house he continued to tell anyone who asked, that there was nothing wrong with his marriage. The local Capriotes were fully aware of the situation and accepted it for what it was, and they regarded Antonino as a little bit delusional. The local church, however were obviously not happy about the situation but had stayed quiet so far.

As building progressed, Anna convinced Nathaniel that a decision had to be made soon regarding furnishing the house. 'It's no good waiting until the place is finished before we start looking for suitable furniture, Nathaniel.'

'Of course my darling, you are right as usual, so what do you suggest?'

'Well the first thing we should do is sit down and decide what we need and then go into Naples for a few days to have a look around to see what is available.'

'Well, let's get on with it then,' said Nathaniel. 'We will need a lot of furniture to fill the place, have you seen the size of the floor area now that they have levelled it off?'

'Yes I have, I saw it yesterday and it looks absolutely massive.'

***

Furniture buying proved to be a much more complex procedure than Nathaniel had ever envisaged. Three days spent in Naples resulted in the purchase of a total of just three beds and some trinkets for the nursery. 'That was a bit of a waste of time,' said a disgruntled Nathaniel, 'surely there must be a better way than this, and we didn't even get a bed for ourselves. If we continue as we are, we will never get the place furnished.'

'I know,' replied Anna, 'but what can we do?'

'I think I should have a word with Desiderio. He has built many large villas and will know how other people get their ideas and the best way of doing things.'

'Sounds a sensible idea to me, you must have a word with him tomorrow.'

'I will as soon as he gets back. He's away for a few days so it will have to wait till then.'

'Well, a few days will make no difference, but we can't go through all that again. We will get absolutely nowhere.' said Anna who didn't relish going through the experience again.

***

Nathaniel invited Desiderio to the house the following week and after discussing general progress he asked him about the purchase of suitable furniture.

'No problem,' said Desiderio, 'There are two very good agents in Naples who will provide excellent advice and who are certain to be able to help you. I will arrange for them to come and see you and your good lady as soon as possible and they will gladly tell you what is currently fashionable. They both represent the best manufacturers and do everything for you, once you have made up your minds.'

'Where do most people get their furniture from?'

'Oh, all over the world, from France, England and of course here in Italy. The agents will bring their catalogues and you can choose what you want. It will be manufactured to your requirements and shipped over from wherever you wish.'

'Do you think it will be here before the villa is ready?'

'Of course it will. They will have it here waiting for us to finish.'

'That sounds alright then, so would you get these agents over here as soon as you can, we don't want to waste any more time,' and to Anna, 'do we darling?'

'You look very relieved Nathaniel, much better than you did a couple of days ago.' said Anna, ruffling Nathaniel's hair. 'I think that's the best news you've heard for some time, isn't it.'

'It couldn't be better darling!' and turning to Desiderio, 'Thank you Desiderio, I will leave the arrangements to you, just let us know when we can expect to see them.'

***

A few days later Desiderio came to the house to see them, 'I am afraid I have only been able to arrange for one of the agents to see you, Sir Nathaniel. One of the agents has gone to London on a business trip and won't be back for at least two months, but Georgio Cappello will be able to come and see you

342

next Tuesday. He will be arriving late on Monday and I have promised to reserve a room for him so that he can be with you early the next day. Georgio is probably the most experienced of the two so I am sure he will provide you with what you need. I have worked closely with him on several big projects and his advice and guidance always proves invaluable. He is the best there is.

'Thank you very much,' said Nathaniel, 'I am looking forward to seeing him, and I am sure Anna is too. She needs to be in on the discussions as I am sure I would get it wrong if it was left to me.'

'Yes I agree, and you will need to have your copy of the plans of the villa available so that Mr. Cappello can make some sensible recommendations.'

***

Mr. Cappello arrived as expected and brought with him a large folder of drawings and samples of fabrics. Anna went immediately to the pile of fabrics while Nathaniel started to look through the drawings.

'I think you will find a good selection of the latest designs from London, Sir Nathaniel. There is also a wide choice of the more traditional furniture for you to peruse.' said Cappello. 'The fabrics are the finest available from both London and Paris and you won't find a better selection anywhere in Italy.'

'You certainly present a wide and impressive range, Mr. Cappello, but where do you think we should start?'

'The logical way, I think, is go over the plans and decide what is the purpose of each room and how many rooms need to be fitted out. I can advise you on all aspects of design and content but naturally, the final decision will always be yours. '

The samples and drawings were put to one side and the remainder of the morning was spent making a comprehensive list of everything that was required. After lunch a start was made on identifying the type and style of the furniture and as Nathaniel sorted through Cappello's drawings, he held up a set of drawings and exclaimed, 'We've got some of these chairs Anna. They are identical to those I bought in London!'

'Which ones are those?' asked Cappello, reaching over for the drawing. 'Oh yes, they are beautiful aren't they? They are by a young and upcoming furniture designer called Chippendale. He is making quite a name for himself and his style and designs are already beginning to be copied.'

'We both like them very much,' said Anna 'especially the padded seats. I am sure the style will suit several of our rooms and I love the fabrics you have brought for us to see.'

***

It was early the next evening before they completed the mammoth task and both Anna and Nathaniel were happy with their choices. Nathaniel had chosen sturdy traditional English oak furniture for his study and library and

343

the rest of the house was to be fitted out in the latest style in a variety of materials including mahogany, walnut and cherry, with no expense spared.

Nathaniel invited Mr. Cappello to stay for dinner and over post dinner drinks they tied up all the loose ends and the contract was sealed. The goods would all be delivered and fitted in their designed position in the villa on completion of building. Mr. Desiderio would keep Mr. Cappello informed of the progress of building and would give him ample warning of the completion date. 'Thank you very much for your help Mr. Capello, it has been a busy couple of days but goodness knows how long it would have taken without your knowledge and advice.'

'It has been a pleasure Sir Nathaniel. I look forward to seeing the project completed. I am sure it will be the most sumptuous villa within many miles of Naples.'

***

A couple of months after the order was placed, Nathaniel informed Anna that he would have to go to England to check on his investments and collect the remainder of his personal belongings to bring back with him. 'My home is here now Anna darling, I have to go and I want to be back well before the villa is ready.'

'Well I will miss you terribly,' she said, 'but you won't be away as long as last time, will you?'

'No I won't. I have no intention of staying longer than absolutely necessary this time.'

'When you are in London do you think you will be able to check on the progress of our order?'

'If I have the time, I will try to check on progress, but I must remember to check with Mr. Cappello and find out exactly where the furniture is being made.'

***

The construction of the villa had been going for about a year when Nathaniel set off on his visit to England in the spring of 1744. Anna was obviously upset at his departure but was also getting very worried about the interest the Bishop was taking in their relationship. Although the general population were not very interested, Monsignor Rocco, the Bishop of Capri was occasionally sending a priest around to inform the couple that their behaviour was thought of as sinful and heretic, particularly as Nathaniel was not a Catholic. Nathaniel had sworn he would never convert to Catholicism and when the priest raised the subject, as he inevitably did, Nathaniel always replied 'pazienza', or used his favourite response, 'bye and bye.'

'Don't worry too much darling, so long as old Antonino insists he is your devoted husband, there is nothing the church can do, is there?'

'I suppose not, but I will be very pleased when you get back. I don't

344

like being on my own very much and I hate it when you are away, even when it's only one night.'

***

He had decided to go to Harmston first and encountered extremely difficult conditions on the way. The roads were knee deep in mud and progress was very slow. Whilst at Harmston, Nathaniel was thrown from his horse as it stumbled and he hurt his back, confining him to his bed for three weeks.

It took another two weeks to recover and eventually get back to fitness, much to the relief of his staff. Despite this setback, Nathaniel managed to get the possessions he required sorted and left instructions on how they were to be packed and where it was to be sent. Happy that everyone knew what to do, he set off to Borton to do a similar exercise.

When he arrived at Borton, Sylvia met him at the door and Nathaniel was shocked by her appearance. He remembered her as a young woman and although, when he last saw her she had aged, she was still a fit and active woman. Now, however, she had taken on the aspects of an old woman, bent, stooping shoulders and moving slowly supported by a stick. Nathaniel gave her a hug and noticed that she was no longer the well-padded Sylvia he had always known but frail with very little meat on her old bones. 'Sit down Sylvia,' he said as she went to make a coffee. 'Sit down and tell me how things are with you. That can wait.' Nathaniel was surprised that Sylvia did as he said, 'She wouldn't have done that the last time I saw her.' he thought.

'I am afraid I am getting old and a bit crotchety,' she said, 'and things are not getting any easier, but I struggle on as best as I can.'

'How long have you been feeling like this?' asked Nathaniel, with genuine concern in his voice.

'It's been getting steadily worse over the last couple of years, and I have not been eating too well just lately.'

'Well I must get you some help before I leave, I can't have you struggling along like this. You will have to take things easier in the future.'

***

Over the next few days, Nathaniel kept his eyes on Sylvia. Mo had told him that she was putting on a brave face for his benefit, and was in fact a lot worse than she was admitting. As a result of his observations, and information gathered from other members of staff, Nathaniel decided drastic action was needed. He had seen that Sylvia's assistant, Susan, had been doing most of the work and appeared to be a competent young woman, so he decided to retire Sylvia and promote Susan. He thought this would be a difficult task and expected a strong reaction from Sylvia, but when he raised the subject, it was obvious that Sylvia was relieved to be free of her responsibilities. She was even more pleased when Nathaniel told her that she could stay in her quarters in the house for as long as she wanted, and she could continue to eat with the rest of the staff for no cost.

'Thank you so much Nathaniel,' she said, trying to get up to hug him, 'you are so very kind.'

'It's the least I could do Sylvia. You have spent your whole life looking after me and I am not going to see you thrown out just because you are getting older.'

***

Leaving Borton was a bit of a wrench, and as he rode out of the village, heading South toward the Great North Road at Stamford, Nathaniel wondered if he would ever see his real home again. He had planned to visit regularly every few years, but thinking about Sylvia's rapid decline he realised you couldn't predict the future. One thing he was very grateful for was that he knew all his estates were in good, capable hands and he didn't have to worry in that regard.

Chapter 30

Nathaniel arrived back in Capri on a blustery December day having been away for longer than he had hoped. Anna met him at the dockside, and in a very public display of affection, put her arms around his neck and kissed him full on the lips. As he extricated himself from her embrace, Nathaniel said, 'Well, that will be reported to the Bishop's residence before we reach home.'

'It doesn't worry me in the slightest,' said an obviously excited Anna. 'I couldn't care less now I have you home again, my darling.'

'Neither could I,' replied Nathaniel, 'but I bet we have a visit from one of his priests tomorrow morning.'

'He had better not come too early then, or he will catch us in bed,' giggled Anna.

***

Nathaniel awoke late the next morning, apart from being in bed with Anna, he was luxuriating in the comfort of a proper bed at last. 'You have no idea how uncomfortable those berths on a boat can be,' he told Anna, 'if I didn't have to go to check on progress at the villa, I could stay here all day.'

'Yes please,' she replied sliding down under the sheets, 'so could I!'

***

Just as Nathaniel had made ready to go to the villa, the expected emissary from Bishop Rocco arrived and requested an interview with Nathaniel and Anna. Nathaniel politely refused the request and sent him back with a message for the Bishop.

'Would you kindly tell Bishop Rocco that if he has anything to say I would be delighted to hear it directly from him. I feel sure that as an English nobleman I am at least due that level of respect.'

'Rocco won't be pleased with that,' said Anna. 'He thinks he is above being requested to do anything.'

'Well if he won't come here I certainly won't be visiting him. Just make sure you don't let any of his entourage into the house when I am not here Anna. I will not talk to anyone other than Rocco so if he won't come here he will get precisely nowhere.'

'He won't get anywhere if he does come here unless Antonino changes his story.' replied Anna.

***

The next couple of weeks were hectic for Nathaniel, apart from the progress checks on the villa he went to the warehouse in Naples and paid a visit to Mr. Cappello. Marco reported all was well at the warehouse and sales were continuing to improve. Another cargo of Cornish pilchards was due anytime soon and if sales went as well as last year it was agreed to double the next order. Marco informed Nathaniel that Silvio and his family were due in Naples for a short break in a couple of days' time and with luck they might meet before Nathaniel went back to Capri.

The visit to Mr. Cappello was arranged for Nathaniel's last day. 'There is no need to worry Sir Nathaniel, everything is well in hand and I don't expect any delays. Mr. Desiderio is keeping me informed of progress on the building and I have visited the villa recently.' said Cappello, 'You are certainly getting a magnificent home, Sir Nathaniel. The setting is perfect and with such wonderful views you will be the envy of everyone who sees it.' The orders for furniture had all been confirmed by the manufacturers and dates for shipment agreed. The soft furnishings had also been confirmed and in some cases materials had already been delivered to Naples and were available to be made up into curtains, drapes and bed covers. As a result of the meeting Nathaniel would be able to tell Anna that things were progressing well, and on time.

By the time Nathaniel was ready to go back to Capri, Silvio had still not arrived in Naples. He had hoped to see both Marco and Silvio together to invite them and their families over to the island for a few days as a reward for the way they had worked during his absence. 'Tell Silvio, no excuses, we would both love to see you all, and our children would love playing with your broods. I will arrange for a boat to bring you all over.'

'I look forward to it and I am sure my family will too. Thank you very much Nathaniel.'

'Good, then that's settled. Just make sure Silvio comes and tell him not to worry about the warehouse. A few days off won't make much difference.'

***

The next few months saw Nathaniel start to relax and take much more time away from his business and concentrate on making sure work on the villa was progressing according to plan. He was extremely pleased with the results so far and Mr. Desiderio was proving to be as good as his reputation had suggested. Mr. Cappello was a regular visitor and suggested a few more additions to add 'that final touch.'

Nathaniel's belongings from England arrived in late Spring and Anna took extreme delight in going through what she laughingly said was 'a load of old rubbish.' At the bottom of one large crate she pulled out a heavy, wooden object, wrapped in a woollen blanket. 'What on earth is this?' she asked, as she started to uncover a brightly painted, carved object.

'That's my family coat of arms.' said Nathaniel proudly as he helped to extricate it from the blanket. The King of England allows me, and no one else to use it. It shows my family's position in society.'

'Well what are you going to do with it, Nathaniel?'

'It will be positioned prominently over the front entrance to our new home.' replied Nathaniel proudly. 'Everyone who calls, will ask what it means, and I will tell them.'

'It will certainly stand out, won't it?' and then she laughed as she said, 'They will probably think you are a goat herder with those three goats on it!'

'They are not goats,' he said, pretending to be hurt. 'They are stags!'

As they continued unpacking they failed to find much that would suit their new home although there were a couple of paintings which Anna liked. The first was a country scene which Nathaniel said reminded him of Borton. As he studied it, Anna picked up the other one and asked, 'What is this magnificent building, Nathaniel?'

'Oh, that's Lincoln Cathedral, it's a beautiful building isn't it? We will definitely find somewhere for that, and the other one can go in my study.'

'Have you ever thought about having your portrait painted?' asked Anna. 'I think you should have it done and it can take pride of place in our new home.'

'That's a brilliant idea, darling, we can both have one done.'

'I don't think that would be very kind on Antonino. I think if I had mine done and hung it next to you he would be upset, don't you? We don't want to humiliate him, do we?'

'No, perhaps you are right.'

***

It had been a few months since Nathaniel had despatched the priest with a request to talk to Bishop Rocco, directly or not at all. 'We haven't heard from the Bishop for ages, darling. Do you think he has forgotten us?' asked Nathaniel.

'He hasn't called round here, but I know his priest is spreading gossip among the staff. Luckily they are very loyal and take no notice. They know the truth and enjoy working here but Rocco has certainly not forgotten us.'

'I think I will make a point of talking to the priest next time I see him wandering around. A few home truths could come in useful.'

'What do you mean? Do you know something I don't?'

'Let's just say that there are more rumours about him, than there are about us.'

***

Towards the end of Summer, Nathaniel and Anna were enjoying a pleasant evening on the patio having a glass of red wine when Anna turned to Nathaniel and rubbing her tummy, said, 'I think we have another addition to the family on the way, darling.'

'That's brilliant,' he said, leaning over and giving her a kiss. 'Do you think it will arrive before the villa is finished?'

'I don't really know, but it doesn't matter does it?'

'Not at all, but I just thought it would be nice if it was here when we move in.'

349

They sat silently for a while and then Anna asked, 'Would you like a boy this time or another girl?'

'I don't really mind, but it would be wonderful if we had a son to inherit the business and my estates. Even if it's a girl this time, we are still both young and I am sure we will have a boy eventually.'

'I haven't told Antonino yet. Will you come with me to tell him?'

'Of course I will. I am sure he will be delighted, he loves children doesn't he?'

***

As they expected, when they eventually told Antonino, he was delighted. 'What wonderful news, Anna, another Canale, but I hope you can produce a boy this time'

'I hope so too,' Anna replied,'a boy would make our family complete.'

'I am so pleased you told me Anna, but make sure you look after yourself, won't you?'

***

'He's such a nice old man, and has such a lonely life even though we are here every day.' said Anna as they left Antonino's room. 'You do realise Nathaniel, that if he had been a lot nearer my age, you wouldn't be with me now.'

'Well, he isn't and I am, and I couldn't be happier. You are the best thing that ever happened to me, and although I like Antonino very much I am pleased that he is old.'

'Yes, so am I, but I fear he is ageing very rapidly and spending much more time in his room.'

'Well when we move to the villa he will have a lovely apartment all to himself. He will be able to sit and admire the beautiful view or stroll on the terrace just as he pleases.'

'You do realise that this will be the signal for another attack by the Bishop, don't you Nathaniel?'

'How will he know? I won't be telling him, and I don't suppose you will, so it will be a few more months before it's obvious.'

'The priest visits Antonino quite regularly and he will tell him at some stage. He is so pleased for me and he will never keep it secret for long.'

'Well thank goodness he is sticking to the story that he is the father. You did notice that he referred to "another Canale," didn't you?' and after a pause, 'I didn't know that the priest was a regular visitor, Anna.'

'As far as I know, he hangs around the area until he knows you are out of the house and then comes in through the servant's door.'

'I think it's time we had a quiet chat with the priest, don't you? Let's invite him round for lunch one day soon and have an interesting conversation on neighbourliness.' said Nathaniel, as he refilled their glasses. 'Cheers, here's

350

to the latest addition to the Thorold dynasty.'

***

The lunch with the Bishops representative was friendly enough, but the situation with Anna was soon raised. Everyone on the island knew what was going on and the priest was no different. He said that his task, under the direction of the Bishop was to continue his efforts to get Nathaniel to convert to Catholicism and to stabilise Anna's marriage to Antonino. 'Bishop Rocco regards this as his major priority and will never give up. He sees your behaviour as a disruptive influence on his flock and at this moment, would dearly love you to leave the island.'

'I think you should remind your bishop of what he already knows. First that I will *never* convert to Catholicism. Second, you have heard my friend Antonino's strong assertion that he is the father of the children, and that they are all confirmed members of the Catholic Church, confirmed by the Bishop, no less.

As for my leaving the island, my stay here is not for negotiation. I will be here for the rest of my life, and the local Caprese accept me as their friend and good employer. Why does he think I am building a beautiful new villa just down the road? It's for me and my friend Antonino's family to spend the rest of our lives.'

The lunch concluded with both sides well aware of the others entrenched position and no sign of any movement towards agreement.

'Well we all know where we stand Anna, let's hope Antonino doesn't change his story.' said Nathaniel as the priest set off to the Bishop's Palace.

'I am sure he won't, he is too settled to want any changes. If he wasn't here with us he would have nothing and he would never cope. After his business failed, he has become totally reliant on your generosity for his comfortable life.'

***

Anna gave birth to a son, Pietro in July 1745, a couple of months before the villa was due to be completed. She had experienced a difficult birth and was confined to bed until just before they were due to move. Both Nathaniel and Antonino were very concerned about her condition and were very relieved when she recovered, however there were worries about Pietro who was not showing signs of normal development and not taking food as they would have expected.

351

Chapter 31

The month before they moved into the villa proved to be very hectic. Once Desiderio had completed all his work and Nathaniel had agreed that it was done to his satisfaction, Giorgio Cappello arranged for all the furniture and fittings to be brought in from the warehouse where they had been stored safely for the last few weeks.

'There is one major problem, Sir Nathaniel, I am afraid your large order with Mr. Paul de Lamerie for silver tableware has not arrived yet but we are hoping it will be here very soon. However, I recommend that we carry on and get the villa fitted out and we can bring the silverware as soon as it arrives.'

'Where the hell has it got to Capello? I expected everything to be ready as soon as Desiderio had completed his work.'

'I am afraid it is completely out of our control. I know that de Lamerie was extremely busy when we placed the order, but he did promise it would all be completed on time.'

'Well I am extremely angry and this is ruining all your good work. I paid a fortune for that order and I expect you to find out where the hell it is.'

'Calm down Nathaniel, Mr. Capello won't know where it is until it actually arrives. There is nothing he can do, is there?'

A few days after the furniture and fittings started to be transferred to the villa but Nathaniel's presence was beginning to get on Capello's nerves. Nathaniel thought he should be there every day to supervise the operation, but Cappello, who was experienced in this sort of interference, had a few diplomatic words on individual responsibilities.

When Nathaniel complained to Anna about Cappello's attitude, she said, 'You employed Mr. Cappello to design and set up the villa so you must let him get on with it.'

'I was only trying to make sure everything gets done properly and surely I need to be there to do that, don't I?'

'No you don't. You know nothing about furnishing a villa, so let the expert get on with it. When he is ready, he will come and tell you and you can then go and see that he has done it to your satisfaction.'

'I suppose you are right, but it is costing a fortune and I want to make sure he gets it right.'

'Well let him earn his fortune. Now let's hear no more about it, and come and sit down and have a drink.'

***

When everything was complete to Mr. Cappello's satisfaction, apart from the silverware which had still not arrived, Nathaniel, Anna and Antonino went to inspect his work. Anna was completely taken aback by the sheer scale of the building. 'This is the first time I have seen it since before Pietro was born. It's absolutely fabulous.' she said as they walked over the elevated drive to the villa.

The building was built to a rectangular plan and was divided symmetrically along the short side in order to take advantage of the general ambience of the site. Being situated between the mountains and the sea, it had two entrances, one facing the mountains and the other towards the coast. It was built to incorporate traditional elements of the architecture of Capri, such as the trellis work, with a 1700's Neapolitan style terrazzo. The entrance facing the mountains gave views towards Rome and the access to this entrance jutted out from the façade and was built on top of three tall arches. The impression you gained as you approached the villa was of walking through the tops of the lemon trees. This was the entrance they were using and Anna turned to Nathaniel and said, 'The whole place looks stunning and your coat of arms fits in beautifully. There's nothing else like it on Capri and it will certainly impress the locals.'

As Mr. Cappello showed them around the accommodation Anna became more and more excited and had difficulty in taking it all in. All the living areas were light and airy and most rooms had access to the terrazzo which stretched the whole of the seaward side of the building. There was a separate suite of rooms for Antonino and when he saw where he was going to live he burst into tears and declared. 'I can't thank you enough, Nathaniel. You have been so kind and generous to me I could never, ever pay you back.'

'Don't be silly Antonino, I don't want paying back. You were very kind to me when I first moved to Livorno and we are all one big family now, aren't we?'

***

The next week or so was a very busy time for everyone, all their belonging were sorted and taken to the villa. Antonino was the first to move in, and had taken up residence two days before the remainder of the family. The three young daughters, under the supervision of the nanny and household staff had a wonderful time exploring their new home. With so much space they could play almost anywhere, and spent a great deal of time in the garden and the large vineyard on the slope at the rear of the villa.

The interest in the villa shown by the locals was intense and Anna suggested that they should invite all their friends to the house to let them have a look at what they were longing to see. 'I think that's a brilliant idea,' agreed Nathaniel. 'There is plenty of space for a whole hoard of them and they have all been so welcoming to us. Yes, I think it would be good to invite as many as we can and let them see how much they mean to us, in fact I think we should include Bishop Rocco, don't you?'

'Are you serious? I don't think he would dare come, do you?' replied Anna with a grin.

'Well, if he comes he will be made welcome, and if he doesn't, it will be no loss. We will invite him anyway'

***

The gathering was a great success and all the people of note on the island attended, including the Bishop. Nathaniel had almost given up on him coming but he turned up, dressed in all his finery an hour after everyone else and brought four priests with him. After Nathaniel welcomed the Bishop and his group, the Bishop circulated among the guests but avoided Nathaniel at every opportunity. He did, however, ask Anna where Antonino was. 'Oh he was very tired and went back to his room. He can't stand for long and the noise of chatter gives him a headache.'

'Oh what a shame,' replied the Bishop, 'I would have liked to have met him.'

'If you had been here earlier you could have had a chat with him. He was looking forward to meeting you.' she replied rather sharply.

Turning away and ensuring his priests were within hearing, the Bishop said, 'I am afraid I will have to leave soon, Mrs. Canale, as I have a lot of work to do.' and while pretending to look around the room, 'I can't see Sir Nathaniel so would you thank him for me. It was very kind of him to invite me.'

***

'Has he gone already?' asked Nathaniel, he wasn't here more than half an hour.

Anna told him what the Bishop had said and how he had expressed interest in talking to Antonino.

'He hasn't the guts to talk to me, has he?'

'No, and he made a deliberate point of calling me Mrs. Canale.'

'Pompous old prig, he is missing a real good party and he is becoming the laughing stock of the island.'

'Everyone else is enjoying themselves and they all love the villa.'

'They do. Do you know what they are calling it already?'

'No I don't. I hope it's not something rude or naughty, Nathaniel. I would hate that.'

'It's not naughty at all. They are calling it *"Palazzo Inglese"* the English Palace.'

'Oh, how lovely. I bet that makes you feel proud, doesn't it?' she said giving him a hug and a peck on the cheek.

***

The party was the talk of the island for weeks afterwards and Nathaniel was continually stopped on his walks in the lanes around the island, for a chat. Praise was heaped on him when the house was discussed, it was

354

considered to be the most opulent residence ever seen and a great credit to Capri. They were all hugely impressed by Nathaniel's portrait which took pride of place in the main reception area. Not many people on the island had a portrait of themselves, and the few who did, could not have afforded one by the celebrated artist, Battone.

Bishop Rocco seemed to have called off his campaign to get Nathaniel to join the church. It had been a couple of months since the party and all seemed quiet but Nathaniel was not convinced. 'He hasn't finished with me yet, Anna. Just you wait and see.'

'I think you are right, did you see how he took note of everyone who came.'

'I did and I am sure that he brought those four priests to make sure they didn't miss anyone.'

'Yes, I heard that he gave a very strong sermon on the subject of infidelity at mass just after the party and it was pretty obvious to the congregation what he was referring to.'

***

The euphoria surrounding the party was not long lived as Pietro's development had been very slow and bedevilled with a variety of problems. Unfortunately, much to Nathaniel's dismay, he passed away in his sleep. His death devastated the family, particularly the eldest daughter, Maria. She had formed a very close affection for the baby and it took her some time to get over it. 'Don't worry Maria, my darling, maybe we will have another brother for you sometime soon.' said Nathaniel as he tried to comfort her.

***

As Spring turned to Summer, Nathaniel decided to have another party, and judging by the hints people were dropping, it seemed to be his turn. There had been parties at regular intervals throughout the winter and he agreed with the general sentiment. He also wanted to introduce to locals to the first sample of his own wine, which he thought was now ready to drink. He was confident it was up to a decent standard and if he could get the approval of the locals he would be delighted. He knew they would be forthcoming with advice, however good or bad it proved to be.

'You will also be able to show off all your beautiful silver as well, won't you, darling?' said Anna, gently massaging his ego.

'Just so long as no one takes some home with them.' he laughed. 'I suppose we had better get some invitations sent out soon then, hadn't we?'

'Well don't you dare invite Rocco this time, he is a real killjoy and casts a big black cloud over the proceedings.'

'I agree but I think I will invite Silvio and Marco this time. There is plenty of room here and the children get on well together. They can stay as long as they like.'

'That is a great idea, they work very hard for you, don't they?'

'They do, but don't forget, they are directors now, so they are working for themselves as well.'

'When will they own the full forty-nine per cent? Is it this year?'

'No, they have just one more year to go and then it will be time for me to make some decisions.'

'What do you mean, Nathaniel?'

'Well I wouldn't be surprised if they don't approach me to sell them enough shares to take total control.'

'Would you do that?' asked Anna.

'That's a decision I expect I will have to make next year,' replied Nathaniel.

***

News of the party spread around the island quickly and invitations were sent to all their friends and associates, but not, this time to the Bishop and his priests. However, within a week of the announcement of the party a priest was seen by one of the staff entering Antonino's apartment. This was soon relayed to Anna who told Nathaniel.

'Has he gone yet?' asked Nathaniel.

'I don't think so,' replied Anna. 'As far as I know he has only just arrived.'

'Right, I will sort this out, once and for all,' he snapped, and turned to make his way to the other end of the villa.

'Don't upset Antonino.' called Anna as Nathaniel disappeared through the doorway.

Nathaniel stationed himself outside Antonino's apartment and after quite a long wait was beginning to get a bit frustrated when there was no sign of the priest. Thinking he must have missed him, he decided to knock on the door to see if Antonino was alright. 'Come in,' called Antonino in response to Nathaniel's knock. On entering the apartment he was very surprised to see the priest sitting opposite Antonino engrossed in a game of chess.

'Oh, I will call in when you have finished. Sorry I interrupted your game.' said Nathaniel, taken aback by what he had seen.

'That's alright Nathaniel, just pop in when Father Giuseppe has gone. I wanted a word with you anyway.'

***

After he had told Anna what he had seen, she said, 'Don't worry about it Nathaniel. It seems perfectly innocent to me.'

'I don't know, I wouldn't put it past old Rocco to be trying to soften Antonino up to get him to tell the truth.'

'I am sure we will find out soon enough. Now just relax until we find out.'

'What will we do if he decides to tell the Bishop everything?'

'We will carry on as normal, Nathaniel. After all, everyone knows the truth anyway so it won't make the slightest difference to us, will it?'

'I suppose not, but we could do without any more interference from the Bishop.'

As they carried on the discussion, they saw the priest walking away from the house via the back door. Nathaniel went immediately to Antonino's apartment and knocked gently on the door. Antonino called him in and said, 'Please sit down Nathaniel, I have something to tell you and I must ask for your complete co-operation.'

'You haven't???....' began Nathaniel and was immediately interrupted by Antonino.

'No I haven't but I must insist that you say absolutely nothing about my games of chess with Father Giuseppe. The Bishop sends him here to try to get me to tell him false things about you, but he is not interested and much prefers a game of chess.'

'That's a relief, I thought you had finally agreed to tell him what he wanted to hear.'

'Not a chance, but Giuseppe is a good chess player and we do enjoy our regular games. But you *do* understand, the Bishop must *never* know.'

'Of course I do, but I didn't realise how isolated the Bishop was. Even his own priests don't agree with him.'

'I wouldn't be so sure about that Nathaniel. They are not all like Father Giuseppe so don't trust any of the others. The Bishop will not give up easily and I am sure he has not given up yet.'

***

The party was as successful as the first one and everyone, with the exception of two of the Bishop's youngest priests, thoroughly enjoyed themselves. The first guests to arrive informed Nathaniel that there was a priest watching at both front and back entrances. They stayed until the party had finished, and as the last guests departed Nathaniel invited the priests to come in for a drink but they both refused and made it clear that they didn't want to suffer the Bishop's wrath.

As Anna and Nathaniel prepared for bed, Nathaniel said, 'I wish I knew what the Bishop is going to do next, but I know he is never going to let things go.'

'He can't hurt us darling, so forget about him and come to bed.' she replied, suppressing a tired yawn.

357

Chapter 32

1748 - 1749

In the spring of 1748 Nathaniel met Silvio and Marco in Naples and signed over the last tranche of shares to his partners and thanked them both for their hard work and dedication. He also declared that he was going to take things easy from now on. 'I am enjoying the relaxing life on Capri with my family and you don't need me watching you all the time. I will still be in contact with Jonathan in London as I have other business there. In fact I intend to take another trip to London this summer, so if you want me to order anything special, just let me know.'

The meeting went well and the two partners expressed their thanks for Sir Nathaniel's generosity, however, no mention was made of any purchase of further shares.

***

Back in Capri, Nathaniel was telling Anna about the meeting and said he should be paying another visit to London sometime in the summer if everything was alright.

Anna looked a little concerned and said, 'I have a feeling that you may wish to stay here when you hear what I have to say.'

'You aren't, are you?' asked an excited Nathaniel.

'Yes I think I am, darling.'

'That's wonderful.' he said, pulling her towards him and kissing her passionately. 'I do hope it's a boy this time.'

'So do I, but will you still be going to London?'

'Of course not, I must be here for you. London can wait.'

***

Nathaniel spent the summer relaxing and enjoying walks through the winding lanes and meeting the locals. He enjoyed just sitting in the sunshine admiring the wonderful views, and getting the chance to improve his ability to speak Italian. Only occasionally did he make the trip to Naples to check on his business. 'This is the life I have always wanted,' he thought. 'I would have hated it if I had been stuck in Borton for the rest of my life, and oh, those English winters.'

Because of the problems associated with Pietro's birth, Nathaniel was very concerned about Anna's health. Fortunately, as her pregnancy progressed, Anna was keeping well and in good health and in January 1749, to the delight of the parents and Antonino, she gave birth to a healthy baby boy. They had all previously agreed that if they had a boy it would be called Samuel in memory of Sir Samuel who had left his fortune to Nathaniel.

***

Early in the New Year when he was satisfied he could leave Anna, Nathaniel decided to take his delayed trip to London. It was over three years since his last visit and things had progressed considerably, both in England and in Italy. He needed to sort out his finances and set up a system for regular transfer of assets from his bank in London to Naples. He planned to restrict his visits to London and run things as far as possible from Italy where he had decided to make his permanent home. He realised he had some serious decisions to make and he would probably be away for several months. Anna was not looking forward to him being away but knew that it had to be done. She also reminded Nathaniel that Samuel would need to be baptised very soon.

'Well it would probably be best if you get that sorted while I am away,' said Nathaniel, 'you know I don't attend those occasions.'

'It's such a shame you can't be there Nathaniel.'

'You know my feelings about the Catholic Church, Anna darling, I will never change as long as I live, and anyway, Antonino loves to be there and take the credit.'

'I know darling, it would have been lovely to have you there but I realise it's impossible.

***

Nathaniel set off in mid-May. A tearful Anna, the three girls and baby Samuel waved him off from Capri. His first stop was Naples where he planned to stay two days to discuss business before he sailed for London. Everything proved to be going well and Marco had things well under control, so when he set sail for England, he was in a relaxed, contented mood. This was helped by the fact that it was a bright, clear morning with a calm sea only ruffled by a light breeze. 'This is how I like,' he thought. 'Let's hope it stays like this.'

On arrival in London, Nathaniel sent a messenger to Ormond Street to let Mary, Sir Samuel's widow, know that he had arrived and would be taking up her offer of accommodation later in the day.

As he packed his belongings and made ready for going ashore, he was surprised to find Jonathan's carriage had arrived to pick him up. When he asked why he had been sent, the coachman said, 'I don't know why, Sir. I just have to deliver you and your luggage straight to Mr. Adnitt's house.'

As they turned into the drive, Jonathan came out of the house to meet the coach. 'Nice to see you Nathaniel, have you had a pleasant trip?'

'Yes thank you Jonathan, but why have you brought me here?

'I have some sad news Nathaniel, but let's go inside and I will tell you all.'

***

Jonathan ushered Nathaniel into the drawing room where Jane met them and asked them to sit down.

'Nathaniel, I know you had arranged to stay with Sir Samuel's widow

359

Mary, and so I had to make sure you didn't go straight to Ormond Street. You see, unfortunately Mary passed away three weeks ago, while you were on the way here.' said Jonathan.

'That's terrible news,' replied Nathaniel, 'was it expected?'

'Not at all. It came as a complete surprise to everyone. She died in her sleep.'

'Well I am shocked, she always seemed so full of life, and I am very thankful for intercepting me and preventing any embarrassment.'

'Well you must stay with us now, Nathaniel. Your baggage has already been taken to your room.' said Jane.

'Thank you so much Jane, and you Jonathan. I would have been a bit lost if I had turned up at Ormond Street and found the house closed.

***

Nathaniel stayed in London for a couple of weeks and concluded most of his business quite quickly, he was pleasantly surprised by the way Edmund Fullerton and Richard Smythe had handled his investments and successfully agreed a safe method of paying bills from his London bank in his absence. He would continue to operate with two separate banks, one in London and one in Naples.

Once he had sorted out his financial position, he bought himself a complete outfit of clothes, bought a few items of furniture and presents for Anna and the children, and decided on a quick trip to Lincolnshire. He had hoped that this would not be necessary but Jonathan had hinted that he had heard that not everything was going smoothly in parts of his estates.

'I haven't heard anything definite but Charles has mentioned one or two things were occurring which needed sorting out.'

'Have you seen Charles recently, then?' asked Nathaniel, more than a little worried.

'Yes he was in London a few months back, he came down for his annual discussion with Edmund Fullerton and Richard Smythe.'

'I thought Charles took over the running of the estate affairs from them when I was here last time.'

'He did, but they convinced him that he would get better advice on his private investments from London rather than an advisor in Grantham.'

'Edmund and Richard didn't mention any problems on the estate when I was with them a couple of days ago.'

'Well they wouldn't, would they? Charles was here on private business and wouldn't talk about other affairs, would he?'

'I suppose not, but did he give any clues?'

'Nothing definite, but he did mention things at Borton were not as good as expected.'

'Nothing else? Did he mention Maurice Clark?' Nathaniel was

wondering what Mo had been doing if Borton was falling behind.

'No he didn't mention any names, but is Maurice the man you promoted to manager?' asked Jonathan.

'Yes he is and he is a good man. Something must have gone wrong.'

Chapter 33

Nathaniel was lucky with the weather on his trip North, dry all the way and in the long light evenings they made good time. Jonathan had arranged for Richard Houghton to accompany Nathaniel on his trip as he had done the last time he visited Lincolnshire. Richard was an able assistant and Nathaniel was delighted to get someone he knew, and thanked Jonathan for his generosity and thoughtfulness.

***

Nathaniel approached Borton with very mixed feelings. All the places he knew so well still appeared exactly the same as they were the last time he was there and he felt the warm glow of arriving home at the place of his childhood. However, at the same time he was very apprehensive about what he would find when he arrived at the farm. He was still no wiser what the possible problems would be but he knew he would soon find out.

'It all seems very quiet, Richard,' said Nathaniel as they rode up the short drive to the manor house. 'I wonder where everyone is?'

***

As he started to dismount a dog started to bark somewhere in one of the buildings and then, 'What the hell are you doing here Nat? I thought you had gone for good,' called Mo as he came out of the cow shed.

'Nice to see you as well,' replied Nathaniel. 'It's a bit quiet round here. What's going on?'

'They are all out in the fields, busy with the harvest and it looks as if we might have a good one for a change.'

'Right, I will get settled in and then you can bring me up to date. I am sure you have plenty to tell me.'

'OK boss, I will see you soon.'

***

Susan the housekeeper busied herself sorting out Nathaniel's belongings while Nathaniel cleaned himself up after the journey. When he asked Susan how Sylvia was enjoying her retirement, she had to explain that unfortunately Sylvia had passed away nearly a year ago.

Nathaniel was devastated by the news and sat down at the kitchen table with his head in his hand and wept. 'Why didn't anyone tell me,' he cried, 'surely someone realised how much she meant to me.'

'I don't know sir, but no one here can write properly and you were such a long way away. We thought Mr. Woolaston would have told you.' replied Susan.

'It's not your fault Susan so don't worry. I knew she was not very well but I thought she would live for ever.'

After a few minutes Nathaniel dried his eyes and said, 'Susan would you send someone to find Maurice and ask him to come round to see me now.'

***

'Sit down Mo,' said Nathaniel as Mo entered the library, 'I think we have a lot of catching up to do.'

'Yes we have, it's been a long time since you were last here and I have a lot to tell you.'

At Nathaniel's prompting, Mo told him he was still enjoying married life and his wife, Nell had given birth to a lovely daughter six months ago. They had called her Sylvia after their good friend who had passed away a couple of months previously.

'I only heard about Sylvia from Susan and it really upset me. I was surprised no one had told me.' said Nathaniel, 'but I am really pleased for you and Nell. I will have to come around and see them soon. Nathaniel will be quite the young man now won't he? I bet he is growing up fast.'

'He certainly is, and how is your family coming along?'

Nathaniel told him how things were in Capri and that his current visit may well be his last but he intended to keep all his properties in England for the foreseeable future. Having covered the domestic situation, Nathaniel asked Mo what had been happening at Borton.

'Well until last winter we had been making good progress, but as you probably know, we had another terribly long, cold, icy spell right through from November to the end of January. We lost two of our four cows in mid-December and another finally gave up before the end of January. The survivor was too weak to be put to the bull so we had to go out to get some more stock for the summer. It was quite a problem but we managed to get two·cows in calf and another one which we put to the bull is well on the way to calving. Hopefully we will be back to normal for the winter. It was a very depressing time for us all and as Mr. Woolaston will tell you, very expensive.'

***

The next morning, Nathaniel started his day with what had always been his old pre breakfast routine. He arose early and took a stroll around the farm checking things out and chatting with the workforce. He recognised and spoke to most of the employees and they were all keen to talk to him, but there were quite a few new faces that he realised had started since he left Borton.

After a leisurely breakfast he set off for Grantham to pay Charles Woolaston a visit. While Richard Houghton took care of their horses, Nathaniel strolled round to Charles's office and was very surprised to find the place locked up, and apparently deserted. When he peered through a grimy window he saw piece of dried up paper on which he could just make out, *'moved to 28 London Road.'* It was hard to tell whether it was *28 or 23*, but as he set off down London Road he soon found a smart, freshly painted, swinging sign which

363

said, *'Charles Woolaston, Solicitor.'*

'This looks a lot smarter than the old place.' thought Nathaniel, 'It looks as if Charles has started to sort things out.'

***

The front door let Nathaniel into a small waiting room where there was a bell on a shelf and next to it a sign saying, *'Please ring for attention.'* He picked up the bell and gave a couple of rings and thought. 'Just like being at school'

Luke promptly appeared from a back office. 'Good morning, Sir Nathaniel, how can I help you?'

'Good morning Luke. Is Mr. Woolaston free?'

'I will just check Sir, would you like to take a seat?'

***

'I do like your new premises Charles, very smart indeed.'

'Thank you Nathaniel, it is certainly more conducive to efficient business. I don't know how old Ephraim managed in that derelict dump.'

'Well don't forget Charles, when Ephraim moved in it was probably as modern as this is now.'

'You are right Nathaniel, but anyway welcome to my new office. It's lovely to see you again after such a long time.'

As Nathaniel was explaining his reasons for the visit, Luke brought them a coffee and went back to his own small room. 'When I was in London, Jonathan thought he had detected that something was not quite in order when you were in London a few months ago. I thought it was imperative that I come up whilst I was in England and see for myself if there was anything that might need my attention.'

'I suppose Maurice will have told you about the cows, hasn't he?'

'Yes Mo told me last night and things seem to be under control now.'

'Well my visit to London was right at the time we were having those problems and I suppose it showed in my behaviour but I regarded it as a normal farming problem which we would sort out. I planned to inform you in my next report, and in fact, I actually sent the report two weeks ago.'

'No problem, Charles. How are you getting on with Kenneth Parman at Harmston?'

'He is a great estate manager and meticulous in every way. His reports are spot on and once you sorted out the problems at Lincoln your bank deposits have increased dramatically.'

That's good news, then.'

'It is, but when are you going over to Harmston.'

'Actually I had no intention of coming up to Lincolnshire at all until Jonathan mentioned possible problems at Borton.

'So you aren't going to Harmston then?'

364

'No, I am perfectly happy to stay at Borton.'

'Do you think that is wise?'

'Well, I never feel comfortable there. I know it's my main residence but it's not, and never will be home to me.'

'I bet the staff at Harmston will be very upset if they know you have been here and not even visited them.'

'How will they find out?'

'Well Kenneth is due to come to Grantham early next week so if you are still here I expect you would like to meet him.'

'I would, indeed. I didn't think I would get the chance to see him but that would fit in really well.'

'How long are you staying in Borton?'

'Probably another ten days, maybe a bit less. It depends on what crops up.'

'If you want my opinion, I think you should make the effort to visit Harmston while you are here, even if you have to extend your stay in England for a few more days.'

'Maybe you are right, but I haven't anything special to go there for, have I? What is Kenneth coming for?'

'Actually Kenneth has become a good friend of mine and will be staying with Rebecca and myself for a couple of nights and we would be delighted if you could come around and have a meal with us.'

'That sounds wonderful, I would be delighted and thank you very much.'

'Good. I will send him a note and he can be prepared for a meeting during the day and we can relax at my house afterwards.'

'One more thing Charles, have you had any more enquiries from the managers about leasing their farms?'

'Yes, nothing definite, but it does crop up occasionally. I think we sorted out the main contenders at your last visit.'

'Well if you get any firm interest I am quite willing for new leases to be agreed. This only applies to farms on the Borton estate with the exception of Borton itself. This arrangement is not to include any properties on the Harmston Estate.'

'Are you saying you would like me to negotiate these leases if they should occur?'

'Of course. You would be sorting them out if I was here, wouldn't you, so why not, even if I am in Capri?'

'I suppose I would, and it's nice to know that you can trust me.'

On his way home after the meeting Nathaniel thought hard about what Charles had said regarding a visit to Harmston and could see the possible implications of not going. 'I think I had better show an interest and go and spend a few days with them. I still have plenty of time up here and I might as well spend my time there as at Borton.' he mused.

***

The meeting with Kenneth Parman went smoothly with no surprises and Nathaniel was pleased with his manager's knowledge and ability to explain things in simple terms. Financially the Harmston Estate was on a much sounder footing than it was under Sir Samuel. 'Those crooks in Lincoln had it too easy for too long,' said Nathaniel 'they certainly deserved their punishment.'

'They certainly did and I made the effort to go to Lincoln and see justice done. There was a very large crowd assembled and all in all it was a very satisfactory day.' replied Kenneth.

***

'I am pleased you came down to Grantham Kenneth, it has given us time to talk through things in a neutral situation. You appear to be running the estate very profitably and I am delighted with your performance. Now, is there anything else which you think we need to discuss before we adjourn?'

'Only one thing, I have seen a number of the larger landowners starting to enclose their estates and I think it would be beneficial if we started to do something about it. I know new legislation is being considered and I am sure you don't want to miss out.'

'To tell you the truth I haven't really thought about it. Perhaps we should talk to Charles and see what the legal implications might be. I understand that you will be staying with Charles and Rebecca until Friday so we could get together sometime before you go back to Harmston. Also, I plan to pay a visit on Monday so it will give you a couple of days to warn the staff of my visit.'

'I am sure they will all be delighted to see you Nathaniel, how long do you think you will be staying?'

'If all goes well I will return to Borton on Friday and then set off back to London on the Wednesday.'

***

Back at Borton, Nathaniel made a point of visiting the village churchyard to put some flowers on Sylvia's grave and was very disappointed to find there was no headstone in place. In fact he had tried unsuccessfully to find the Reverend Spratt to make sure he was at the correct grave.

When he had placed the flowers he saw the vicar approaching the churchyard gate. 'Nathaniel I am so pleased to see you again, it seems such a long time since you were last here. Have you time to come in and meet Charlotte and my two lovely daughters?'

Nathaniel realised the mention of the name Charlotte had no longer affected him in the way it did before and replied, 'Of course Roger, I would

366

love to meet your family.'

As they walked over to the vicarage, Nathaniel said, 'I am going to Harmston in the next few days Roger and I would like you to do me a big favour.'

'Of course I will Nathaniel, just name it.'

'I would like you to arrange for a decent headstone to be erected on Sylvia's grave as soon as you can. I will write down what I would like engraved on it and of course, I will pay for it in full.'

Roger chuckled and said, 'Certainly I will, and now I will tell you the real reason I asked you for a chat. Would you believe, I was actually going to ask you if you would be kind enough to contribute to a headstone for Miss Butler's grave.'

They were both laughing as they entered the vicarage and as Charlotte welcomed Nathaniel, she said, 'You both seem very jolly, come in and sit down. I will go and fetch the girls. You haven't met little Jane have you?'

***

Nathaniel took advantage of his short trip to Harmston to firm up his plans for enclosure and as he toured the estate Kenneth explained where he thought they should concentrate in the initial stages. Nathaniel stressed that none of the employees should be disadvantaged in any way by changes they might introduce. 'We must not incur the type of problems that some other landowners have suffered, Kenneth. Do you understand?'

'Yes I do Sir Nathaniel. We have a generally contented workforce at the moment and the last thing we want to do is spoil it.'

That's right, and if you could firm up what we have talked about, I think you should discuss your plans with Charles. Then if he is happy that you are operating within the current rules, I think you can get on with it.'

'Thank you Sir Nathaniel, I will get on to it as soon as I can.'

'I will brief Charles so that he is expecting you to call sometime soon.'

***

During his stay at the Hall, the domestic staff had scurried around and made sure he wanted for nothing, but Nathaniel eventually left with the distinct feeling that they were delighted to see him go. He felt as if he was disrupting their ordered lives in the running of the house. It was as if he was a stranger in the place and the fact that it was all his, made no impression whatsoever.

As he rode out of the gates after saying goodbye to the assembled staff, he thought, 'This will be the last time I come here, and I won't miss it one little bit.'

***

Nathaniel spent another week at Borton and during that time he said his goodbyes to all his close friends and associates. When he met Reverend

Spratt he was pleased to hear that the manufacture of Sylvia's headstone was progressing well and would be ready to be put in its place the day before he would be leaving.

'I am delighted to hear it Roger,' said Nathaniel, 'I am so glad that I will be able to see it in place before I go.'

***

Nathaniel had almost forgotten that he had promised the Montini's in Italy that he would call in and see their family at Corby Glen. He had to make a visit at very short notice on the day before leaving for London and came away with numerous letters and packages to be delivered when he arrived back in Naples. Tony was very envious that Nathaniel was going back to Italy and said he wished that he was going too.

Nathaniel reminded him that it was a long sea trip and asked, 'You know what you think of sea travel don't you?'

Saying goodbye to Mo was going to be difficult so Nathaniel arranged to go for a final drink in the *"Five Bells"* when he returned from Corby Glen.

***

'Sorry I'm late Nat. I was late home from work and Nell was upset because my tea was cold. Then young Nathaniel was playing up a bit.'

'You should get onto your boss. We can't have you working late when you are supposed to be having a drink with him can we?' laughed Nat. 'Sit down and get that down you.'

'Thanks boss, I can't stay late I have an early start in the morning.'

'So have I. I need to be on the road very early and want to get to London as soon as possible.'

'When are you setting off for Italy then?'

'I don't know yet. I will have to get down to the docks as soon as I get to London to book the first suitable boat.'

'Will you get a berth that takes you all the way?'

'I doubt it very much. The chances are that I will have to change somewhere on the way. Boats going all the way to Italy don't go very often.'

'You said when you first came back to Borton that this might be your last visit. Were you serious?'

'I am afraid I was Mo. I have a lovely family in Capri and also a very profitable business. The weather is beautifully warm all the year round and I don't really have to work. I have built a fantastic house overlooking the sea and can sit on the patio with a glass of wine and watch the sun go down over a calm blue sea.'

'You make it sound like heaven, Nat.'

'It is, and I regard it as my home now, so yes, I am sure this will be my last visit to Borton.'

'We will all miss you Nat, especially your household staff.'

'And I will miss you all too, but I have to be realistic. I am not getting any younger and it's a hell of a long, tedious, and at times very uncomfortable journey and I don't think my arthritis would stand another English winter. '

'What will you do with all your property in the county?'

'I am not going to sell if that's what you think, it's well run now and there is no reason to suspect it will change. You will have a job as long as you want, so you have no worries as far as that is concerned.'

'Thanks Nat, but we will still miss you.'

***

After a rather soggy journey from Borton to London, when the weather never improved from a constant drenching downpour, his first two weeks at Jonathan's were spent in agony in his bed. The pain in his wrists and knees were the worst he could remember and as a consequence the business he had planned was delayed, as was his departure for Naples. By the time Nathaniel set sail for Italy he had been staying with Jonathan for five weeks, far longer than he had planned.

Chapter 34

1750

It was the first week in February 1750 when he finally arrived in Naples and as he disembarked he swore to himself that he 'would never, ever, do that journey again.' The only saving grace was that since they had approached Gibraltar and the weather had improved, the problems with his joints had gradually eased and by the time he reached Naples he was completely free of pain.

When he landed his main priority was to get back to Capri and be with his family. After he had arranged for the goods he had brought for Marco to be sent to the warehouse Nathaniel went immediately to book a passage to Capri. He managed to secure a berth for early that evening and once he had arranged for all his baggage to be transferred to the ferry, he made his way to the warehouse to see Marco.

***

Nathaniel found Marco in a nearly empty warehouse supervising a young man he had never seen before. 'Good morning Nathaniel, this is a surprise. When did you get back?'

'Only a couple of hours ago so I am still trying to get used to walking on land. How have things been going here whilst I have been away?'

'Things are going extremely well and it is difficult to keep up with the demand. As you can see we have sold nearly all of our last delivery and we are not expecting any more for a couple of weeks.

'..and who is the young man?' asked Nathaniel. 'I don't think I have met him, have I?'

'This is Massimo, Giuseppe decided he didn't like Naples and moved to Rome to try and make his fortune. Massimo has been here for about a month and is settling in well.'

'Good,' replied Nathaniel, and said to Massimo, 'Welcome to our business Massimo. If you work hard and do what is asked of you I am sure you will be very well rewarded here. Now Marco, is there anything important I should be aware of before I head off home?'

'Not really, everything here is running smoothly, but Anna will be pleased to see you.'

'Have you seen her then?'

'Yes, I took the family over to see her about two months ago and she was hoping you would be home soon.'

'Is she still having problems with the church?' asked Nathaniel, concern evident in his voice.

'I think so but she didn't say much. She also said something about trouble at little Samuel's christening.'

'Is that all she told you?'

'Yes and I don't know if it is connected, but something strange happened about two months after you had gone. A priest turned up here at the warehouse one morning and said he was pleased to hear you had gone back to England and we wouldn't be seeing you again.'

Nathaniel's temper kicked in and as he lashed out angrily at a nearby barrel, he shouted, 'I'll kill that bloody Bishop if he has upset my family again,' and stormed out of the warehouse without saying goodbye.

'I heard he had a temper but that's the first time I have seen it. We will have to be careful in future Massimo, won't we?' observed Marco.

Massimo said nothing.

***

The passage to Capri was torture for Nathaniel even though the sea was calm. His mind was constantly on Anna and the children and what the Bishop and his cohorts had been doing to upset them. He deeply regretted having to go to England and swore he would never leave his family again. By the time he arrived he was absolutely tired out, the mix of constant worry and lack of sleep was getting him down and all could think of was sorting out that bastard of a Bishop.

***

Before disembarking Nathaniel ensured all his belongings were gathered together and arrangements made to deliver them to the villa. He was not expecting anyone to meet him as there was no way would his arrival have been expected so he decided to walk home and gather his thoughts while enjoying the peace and quiet of this beautiful island.

As he left the harbour, he heard someone calling his name, and as he turned to see who it was, he was surprised to see the children's nanny Flavia hurrying towards him from the other end of the wharf with his three daughters and baby Samuel in his carriage. They were all waving and calling him as he rushed over to meet them. 'How did you know I was coming?' he gasped as the girls, all excitedly chattering at the same time, rushed to embrace him.

'We didn't know you were coming sir and we only came down to watch the boats coming in. Madame will be very pleased to see you.' gushed Flavia

'I am going to tell her.' called out Maria as she ran off in the direction of home.

Nathaniel looked into the baby's carriage, 'Gosh hasn't Samuel grown? It's such a shame I missed his birthday.'

***

They all talked excitedly as they climbed the steep slope towards the villa and as they turned the final corner, Anna came running down the lane

371

towards them followed by Maria. She nearly knocked him down as she rushed into Nathaniel's arms, tears streaming down her cheeks. They embraced passionately and smothered each other in kisses; Anna sobbing uncontrollably tried to talk but was so emotional that Nathaniel could not understand what she was saying. 'It's alright darling I am home now and I will never leave you again. Just let it out and you can tell me all when we get home.'

As they turned to go home Nathaniel saw a priest watching them from a short distance away. 'That's it, first thing tomorrow I am going to sort out that bloody Bishop.' he said to himself as they made their way back to the villa.

***

It was difficult for Nathaniel to concentrate on Anna until he had distributed the presents he had brought for the children and they had all gone to the nursery with Flavia. Although Anna had been smiling and talking to the children it was obvious to Nathaniel that she was still upset and as soon as the children had gone he asked, concern evident in his voice, 'What's happened my darling, has that Bishop been harassing you again?'

Between sobs, Anna explained that from the moment Nathaniel had left for England, her every movement had been watched. 'There was always at least one priest outside the villa and sometimes one at the front of the villa, one at the back and another knocking at the door wanting to come in and talk to me. They even threatened to ban Samuel's christening until Antonino said he would go to Rome and sort things out there.'

'Marco told me that the Bishop was spreading rumours that I was never coming back. Is that true?'

'Yes it is. A priest stopped me when I was out walking and said that the Bishop had heard you would never be coming back to Italy and I should attend church and admit all my sins as soon as possible. It was horrible.' she said bursting into floods of tears again.

'Did you believe him?'

'Not really, it helped when Antonino explained it was just another of the Bishop's tactics to get me to confess, but I was very pleased when I received your first letter because I had been quite worried until then.'

Anna continued to pour out all her pent up feelings and gradually, as she eventually began to calm down, Nathaniel convinced her he would never leave her on her own again and this would be his final trip to England. 'I have made arrangements to enable me to conduct all my business from here.' he said as he held her closely while wiping the tears from her eyes and cheeks.

'Thank you darling I missed you so terribly and I don't think I could stand another long parting.'

'Neither could I,' replied Nathaniel. 'I am home now and I am never going to leave my wonderful family, ever again.'

***

372

When things had quietened down Nathaniel went to see Antonino and was very surprised to see how the old man had aged during his absence in England. After a pleasant conversation Nathaniel thought, 'He might look old but his mind is still as sharp as a tack.' Antonino had explained that whatever Bishop Rocco had said or done he still maintained that he was the rightful father of the children and would always do so. 'I still have my regular games of chess with Father Giuseppe and the Bishop still hasn't a clue.' he said with a chuckle. 'We both really enjoy our games and really Giuseppe is the only contact I have from outside the villa.'

'Don't you get out much these days Antonino?' asked Nathaniel

'Not really, I am gradually finding it more difficult to move around now as my knees give me a lot of trouble. I don't mind too much because I enjoy sitting on the terrace in the shade just watching the boats in the harbour. It's just so peaceful here and I am extremely thankful to you for providing me with such a lovely home Nathaniel. I don't miss Livorno in the slightest.'

'Think nothing of it Antonino, it's your home as well as mine and we all love it here, don't we?'

'We certainly do.'

***

'Anna tells me there was some trouble when you wanted to get Samuel christened. What was that all about?'

'The Bishop tried to say that I wasn't the father and the child was a bastard who looked just like you. I asked him if he had seen the child, and told him that if he had, then his eyesight must be fading as anyone could see the boy is the image of me. I also mentioned some gossip about his behaviour with one of his priests that was common knowledge around the island and if that was true then someone might decide to inform his holiness the Pope.'

'What did he say to that?'

'He said he had not seen Samuel so he was probably wrong about the child.'

'That was a quick change wasn't it? I won't ask who told you about him but it seemed to work didn't it.'

Antonino smiled and answered, 'It certainly did and I have a few more rumours in reserve if we need them. Giuseppe is a very good friend, but for a priest, he is not very discreet.'

'I am seriously thinking of paying Monsignor Rocco a visit. It is against my better judgement but I think his vendetta has gone far enough and needs to be put to rest.'

'I think it would be unwise Nathaniel you might give him more devious ideas to work on if you try to get him to change his attitude. I suggest you stay well away from him. You know he is powerless whilst you are here on the island and I am sure he will not trouble Anna again. I have a distinct feeling that it is you who will start to feel his wrath if you continue to antagonise him.'

'You may be right Antonino, but I will find it difficult not to react to his actions. He has upset Anna terribly and I find it inexcusable that a senior member of the clergy can act in such a cavalier way to an innocent lady.'

'Just think carefully before you act Nathaniel. The decision is yours but think of the consequences and their effect on the family.'

'I will Antonino and thank you for your considered advice, but one thing I will never do is convert to his religion so I can't really see a solution that will ever be to his satisfaction.'

***

'What did Antonino have to say?'

'Well he has convinced me that I should do nothing to antagonise the Bishop and I should wait for him to act next. He is convinced he will not pester you while I am here but he is sure that some devious plot will be hatched before long.'

'What did you think when you first saw Antonino, Nathaniel?'

'I thought he looked a lot older than I remembered him but he is still as bright as ever. He says he is finding it more difficult to get around and he does not go out often but he is not getting any younger is he?'

'No he isn't and I know he has difficulty walking now. He tries not to show it but I see him struggling quite often and I know father Giuseppe helps him when he is here'

'I like Giuseppe. He is a good friend to Antonino and I am sure it is him who provides all the gossip, particularly about the Bishop.'

Chapter 35

Nathaniel took his semi-retirement to heart and very rarely visited his business in Naples and only went to Livorno once a year. He spent most of his time enjoying the life of a gentleman and whilst he took great pride in the quality of the wine produced in his vineyard, he was a devoted father to his growing children. When not involved with family and his vineyard he enjoyed his time sitting in a shady spot with the old men he met on his long walks in the lanes around his villa. Gradually over the years he had become firm friends with the locals who no longer regarded him as a foreigner, so much so that he even became friends with most of the priests on the island who were always reminding him that their instructions were to get him to convert to Catholicism. The majority of the priests would regularly raise the subject and Nathaniel's reply was usually a polite 'bye and bye' and the topic would be dropped amid general laughter.

His relationship with the priests was very advantageous in that as they were still under strict orders to visit the Pallazzo Inglese to try to get the residents to admit to sinning against the church they knew that they were never likely to succeed. Nevertheless, whilst they complied with the Bishop's instructions, they nearly all gave Nathaniel or Anna prior warning of any planned visits.

However, despite a certain amount of disinterest among the religious community, Bishop Rocco was still adamant that he would get Nathaniel to convert to Catholicism and admit his discretions. But of course, through the regular priestly visits, Nathaniel was warned of Rocco's impatience and his intentions to inform the Pope in the very near future..

'What does he think the Pope can do?' he asked Anna. 'I am not one of his flock so how does he think he can get me to change my mind?'

'I think he is desperate by now, darling. He thought he could win you over soon after we arrived here and he regards it as a challenge that he must win at all costs.'

'He must be desperate. Even his own priests couldn't care less and are telling him untruths.'

'I know but what are you going to do about it?'

'Well I am not converting to his religion so I think I will invite him around to have a chat.'

'He won't come you know.' she replied.

'He will if I hint that I might change my mind.'

***

A couple of days later when Nathaniel was sitting on an old log watching the world go by, he was approached by Antonino's old friend and

375

chess opponent Father Giuseppe who sat down rather heavily next to him.

'Good morning Father Giuseppe, how is the world treating you this lovely day?'

The priest sighed and said, 'I'm not too bad but the Bishop continues to complain that none of us are making much progress on his pet project and he is beginning to lose his temper with us.'

'I assume that his pet subject concerns the Canale's and myself then?'

'Yes it does and he is still threatening to write to the Pope. None of us thinks that will change things and we have told him so, but he stills goes on about it.'

Will you tell him from me that I am extremely happy to talk to him about his problem. You know, he has hardly ever spoken to me since I came to Capri even when he came to my party he avoided me all evening.'

'Shall I tell him that you will come to see him then?'

'No, tell him he is welcome to call in and see me any time he wishes, but he must come alone. This will be a discussion just between the two of us.'

***

A week passed and still Nathaniel had not heard from the Bishop and the next time Father Giuseppe called to play chess with Antonino he took the opportunity to ask him how the Bishop reacted to his invitation.

'Not too well Nathaniel. When he gave us our daily tasks this morning he said we must keep the pressure on you and the Canale's to admit your sins. He also indicated that he still intended writing to the Pope as he has threatened in the past.'

'Just as I thought,' said Nathaniel. 'he is a coward who can't do his own dirty work.'

The next time that Giuseppe came to play chess, he asked to see Nathaniel before going to Antonino's apartment.

'Come in Giuseppe,' Nathaniel called as he saw Giuseppe outside the open door, 'what news have you brought this time? Is Rocco on his way here?'

'No such luck Nathaniel, he has sent the letter to Rome for the attention of His Holiness the Pope.'

'Has he really, and do you know what he has said?'

'In short he has complained that, in his words, *A scandal has been caused on the island by the co-habitation of a certain married woman with an heretic English nobleman and that they are continually behaving in a flagrant manner in public causing distress and dismay among the population*, and he is seeking advice on what to do to remedy the problem.'

Nathaniel laughed and called in Anna from the patio, 'Listen to this Anna, he's finally done it, the silly old fool.'

Giuseppe told Anna what the Bishop was complaining about and she asked, 'What are you going to do now, Nathaniel?'

'Absolutely nothing, we will just wait for his next move, but I can't see that there is anything more that he can do.'

'Whatever the Pope says I don't think he will give up, do you darling?'

'I am sure he won't, but the more he tries, the more he will look silly in the eyes of the local population.'

***

About six months later word quickly spread around the island that an emissary from the Vatican had arrived on the island and had been seen entering the Bishop's Palace.

When Nathaniel was told he said to Anna, 'It won't be long before we have a visitor from the Bishop's Palace darling and we will soon have to prepare for his next move.'

'Well we will just have to wait and see won't we. It's pointless trying to guess what the Pope has said and what Rocco's response will be.' replied Anna. 'It's been quiet since he sent the letter so let's hope it stays that way.'

***

Rocco eased the seal from the packet and unfolded the letter carefully smoothing it out on his desk. As he read the short note his anger grew, '*Dear Rocco,*' it said '*His Holiness considers your problem is purely domestic and wishes you good fortune. He reminds you that utmost care should be taken when dealing with a foreign nobleman.*'

The note was signed on behalf of *Benedictus Quartus Decimus* with an undecipherable signature and dated August 1754.

***

Rocco could not believe what he had just read. He flew into a rage and sent for the emissary for an explanation. When none was forthcoming he locked the poor man in his room with the threat that he would stay there until he provided a satisfactory answer.

The few priests who had seen what had happened pleaded with Rocco not to be so stupid and tried to get him to change his mind. The emissary had not written the letter he had only delivered it. Despite the pleadings of the priests Rocco would not relent, 'I will see him again tomorrow, meanwhile he will stay where he is and if he refuses to explain he will spend another day there. Now get out all of you and leave me alone!'

Word quickly spread around the island and Nathaniel heard the rumours that the emissary had been locked up from Father Giuseppe the next day.

'Are you sure Giuseppe?' asked a concerned Nathaniel. 'If it's true that will be the end of Rocco when Rome finds out.'

'I am sure it is. I was told by member of staff who took food to the room this morning that the emissary was locked up. The rumours were already circulating late last night.'

377

'Have you any idea what the Pope's letter said?'

'No I haven't heard yet but it must have been quite serious to send Rocco into such a temper.'

'Have you any idea when Rocco will release him?'

'None at all but Rocco says he will be released when he explains the reason for the letter. However he plans to see him again this afternoon and unless the Bishop finally realises that he was only the messenger and knows nothing of the content I think he will stay locked up.'

'It won't take Rome long to find out what has happened and that will be the end of Rocco and his vendetta.' said Nathaniel. 'I must tell Anna, she will be pleased.'

'I am sure she will, now I must go to see Antonino I promised him a game today.'

***

The Bishop's Palace was in turmoil and the senior priests had agreed to send a strong deputation to the bishop to try and defuse the 'stalemate' his actions had caused. At first Rocco flew into a rage again and refused to see them but eventually, after his most trusted advisor was given time to explain, he agreed to see a deputation of just three priests.

The meeting was initially stormy with Rocco flatly refusing to believe that the messenger would not have known the content of the note. The priests were beginning to despair until one of them pointed out that the messenger was the Pope's representative and everyone on the island already knew that he was locked up and it would not be long before the news reached Rome. If he remained locked up any longer then the Bishop would definitely be called to Rome to explain his behaviour.

The priests, now seeing they were beginning to get the upper hand told Rocco that he must free the messenger immediately and apologise profusely before sending him on his way back to Rome.

'Apologise …. Never.' was Rocco's response. 'Just release him and send him on his way. I don't want to see him again.'

'If you want him to forget his experience on Capri you must apologise profusely and treat him as a gentleman while he is your guest.' said Rocco's advisor.

'Never!' shouted Rocco as he thumped his fist on his desk, 'just get him out of here.'

'If you want him to tell Rome of your actions, just send him away. If you apologise and treat him with respect you just might be able to convince him to keep quiet.'

Rocco sat with his elbows resting on his desk and his head in his cupped hands for some time and eventually it dawned on him that he was in a very serious situation. He decided that he didn't really want to be hauled

378

before an enquiry in Rome and possibly lose his position and status in the Church. He placed his hands palm down on his desk and looking very tired said, 'Thank you gentlemen, bring the man to me and we will lunch together before he departs.'

***

'So Rocco didn't hang on to him for long, did he Giuseppe? I hear the emissary left yesterday afternoon.'

'Yes he did. Apparently it took the delegation from the priests quite some time to convince the Bishop he was doing himself no good at all by holding the poor innocent man any longer.'

'Has the Bishop bribed him to keep quiet?'

'I think that might be so as they had lunch together before he left the island, but that might not prove enough as word could have easily reached Rome before the poor chap left here.'

'Have you found out the contents of the letter yet?'

'No not yet but I am sure it will be all over the island before long. There is already speculation that he is being withdrawn from Capri.'

'I think we had better wait and see don't you? I don't expect us to be that lucky.'

***

Nathaniel and Anna had noticed a distinct difference in the activities of the local priests over the three months since the visit from the Popes' representative. Whilst they still mentioned that it would be of great benefit to the family's integration into island society if Nathaniel converted to Catholicism they were a lot less aggressive in their tactics. Father Giuseppe told them that Rocco only mentioned the subject very occasionally at his morning briefings and then usually as an aside. He also said that Rocco had been noticeably subdued in his general attitude since the emissaries visit and speculation was still rife that his future was still under some sort of threat.

Early in December, Giuseppe told Antonino that there had been a lot of activity at the Bishop's Palace and it looked as if someone was making preparations for a trip to the mainland. There were signs that at least three priests were involved but they were being segregated from general duties and so it was extremely difficult to find out what was going on.

'Very interesting Giuseppe, I suppose rumours are spreading like wildfire.' said Antonino, 'Do you think it's anything to do with Bishop Rocco?'

'Almost certainly,' was the priest's curt reply, 'but I am sure we will find out very soon.'

'Well whatever happens they will find it impossible to leave the island without being seen by half the population, won't they?'

'They will and I expect with the speed rumours travel around, there will be a big crowd at the harbour to see them off.'

379

Early the next morning two carts left the Bishop's Palace and headed down to the harbour escorted by two priests. Both carts were obviously well loaded with various items and each one had a rough woollen sheet hiding the contents from prying eyes. When they reached the jetty and removed the sheets it was obvious someone from the palace was expecting to be away from the island for a considerable length of time. The two priests supervised the transfer of the luggage and by the time it was all stowed safely on the boat the ever increasing crowd turned to see a procession approaching. The Bishop was leading, dressed in his ceremonial attire followed closely, by as far as could be ascertained, all the priests from the Palace. As they progressed through the streets it seemed that the whole of the population of Capri had gathered to watch. They stood in total silence and as the dignitaries passed by the male spectators doffed their hats and held them to their chests while the females bowed their heads and made the sign of the cross.

Nathaniel sitting on his piazza with Anna, watched as the procession reached its destination, 'It looks as if he is definitely going Anna, do you think he will be back?'

'I have no idea but I sincerely hope not, he is an arrogant bully and not fit to oversee the welfare of all these lovely people.'

'What's he doing now?' asked Nathaniel as the first two priests left the boat and joined the rest of the procession.

'He looks as if he is going to bless his flock,' said Anna. 'He's such a hypocrite. He has never done anything good for these people and now just look at him. He makes me sick.'

They watched the proceedings with interest and saying prayers for the population and after blessing their boat, the Bishop with three priests, were welcomed on board by the captain. As soon as the gangway was removed the boat cast off and sailed slowly out of the harbour under the mid-day sun.

'Is that it Nathaniel?' asked Anna.

'I would love to think so,' replied a cynical Nathaniel, 'but why do you think I am not so sure?'

Chapter 36

With the Bishop away in Rome and no indication of when or if he would ever return to the island, Nathaniel and Anna welcomed in the New Year of 1755 with a degree of optimism, but unfortunately this situation was not to last.

In early February Antonino caught a cold and was confined to his bed for several weeks and showed no signs of improvement. His lifelong career as an apothecary convinced him that he would be able to cure himself even though he had to get a local practitioner, Roberto Mancini, to mix his potions for him.

Anna was very concerned with the way Antonino was responding to his treatment and when she talked to him he said that Roberto was not following his instructions accurately.

'These medicines have been tried and tested over many years and they have always worked very well,' said a very weary Antonino, 'I don't think Roberto knows what he is doing and I am not taking any more of his cheating.'

'He is not cheating Antonino, he is doing exactly what you ask him to do and you must continue with the treatment or you will never get any better.'

That evening Anna talked to Nathaniel about Antonino's problem and asked, 'Do you think we should see what Roberto has to say on the matter darling?'

'Of course we should. We will pay him a visit in the morning and see what he has to say.'

**

'Good morning Sir Nathaniel, Mrs Canale, is all well with Mr Canale?'

'Well he doesn't seem to be making much progress at the moment and he is under the impression that you are not making the potions to his exact specifications. I am sure that is not the case but we would like to get your opinion on the matter.' said Nathaniel.

'With regard to the potions, I am making them exactly as he demands but the problem is, his remedies are years out of date and no one prescribes them these days. I have tried to get him to accept the latest methods but he is, I am afraid to say, as stubborn as a mule and flatly refuses all my efforts.'

'Do you think I should try to get him to change his mind?' asked Anna.

'If you could I am sure he would stand a much better chance of improvement. We are not making any progress at all at the moment.' replied Roberto.

'Well Roberto, thank you for your comments. I think both Mrs Canale and I will have to try to get him to change his mind.' said Nathaniel.

***

After a concerted effort and a certain amount of coercion by both Anna and Nathaniel, Antonino decided to comply with their wishes and started on a different course of potions. Gradually he showed signs of improvement and eventually by the end of March he was able to sit in a chair for most of the day and enjoy his games of chess with Giuseppe.

***

Dark clouds had rolled over the *Palazzo Englese* in mid-March. Everyone thought a new Bishop had been appointed to the island but when the new Bishop arrived amid much speculation, euphoria was replaced with extreme disappointment, Rocco was back!

The harassment started the next morning with news that Sir Nathaniel and the family were on the Bishops morning agenda once again.

Father Giuseppe continued his visits to see Antonino, the other priests kept Nathaniel informed of appropriate gossip from the palace and Rocco steadfastly refused to talk to Nathaniel.

Meanwhile Antonino's health deteriorated and eventually towards the end of May he passed away in his sleep.

***

Antonino's funeral was an extremely sad day for Nathaniel. The Bishop gave instructions to all his priests that on no account would Nathaniel be allowed into the Church for the funeral service. He was considered to be a heretic and a non-believer who had openly sinned against all that the Catholic Church stood for in that he had conducted an illicit liaison with a married member of his flock. When Father Giuseppe had told him, Nathaniel took it quite badly and vowed to get even with the Bishop.

'Don't upset yourself Nathaniel; I am sure I know a way to get around the problem.'

'I don't see how, he will have every door guarded and there will be no way anywhere near the church for the funeral.' said a visibly distressed Nathaniel.

'How would you like me to conduct the service here in your villa?' asked Giuseppe. 'All the family can attend and say their farewells and then when he has the funeral service in the Church he will be doubly blessed.'

'But you would be at grave risk of the Bishop's temper when he finds out.'

'How is he going to find out? I will not tell him and I am sure none of you will want to upset him, will you?'

'It is a brilliant idea Giuseppe and can't thank you enough for your offer. We must arrange it carefully so that no one suspects anything or it will quickly become common knowledge and the Bishop will put an abrupt stop to it before we can carry it out.'

382

***

Both services went smoothly and much to the Bishop's surprise and consternation, Nathaniel stayed at home for the duration of the church service. The fact that Nathaniel didn't try to attend the funeral puzzled Rocco for months afterwards and he regularly referred to his 'getting the better of that man' at his morning briefings with his priests.

Nathaniel, however, visited Antonino's grave as often as he could and smiled to himself as he told his old friend how he had managed to beat the Bishops ban.

Chapter 37
1756 - 1757

The Bishop decided to renew the pressure on Nathaniel and Anna a couple of days after the funeral. As far as he was concerned they were still living in sin and he realised he would never get them to part. 'They are plainly in love so maybe we can convince them to get married,' he thought, 'but I could never approve of a wedding unless both parties were of the Catholic religion.'

At the daily priests meeting Bishop Rocco announced a new plan for dealing with 'that heretic English Nobleman.'

'I want you all to treat Mrs Canale and Sir Nathaniel politely and with respect. I don't want any mention made to Sir Nathaniel on the subject of converting to Catholicism nor do I want it raised with Mrs Canale. What I *AM* telling you all to do is, at every opportunity you are to raise the subject of marriage! I am of the opinion that Mrs Canale would love to get married now that her poor cuckolded husband has passed on and with the right approach she could be persuaded to pressurise Sir Nathaniel into changing his religion. She is the only one who has any chance of succeeding in this delicate problem.'

The change in tactics was less than a day old when Nathaniel was made fully aware of the Bishop's new approach. 'It will be lovely to be treated politely and with respect, won't it darling?' he said with a wide grin. 'Though I don't know why he thinks I will ever change my mind. He still wants me to convert to Catholicism and he knows full well that it's never going to happen.'

'Well what are you going to do about it Nathaniel?' asked Anna.

'Absolutely nothing.' was his instant response.

***

By now the young Samuel was seven years old and was being educated locally by a retired priest. Progress had not been up to Nathaniel's expectation and he had thought of getting another tutor. He had also noticed on more than one occasion that Samuel had raised the subject of his mother getting married.

'I am not having that bloody Bishop getting at my son to do his dirty work for him,' he fumed 'I will teach the boy myself.'

'Do you think that is wise?' asked Anna, 'you have your business to look after and you are often away from home.'

'I have plenty of spare time and anyway, there is nothing that priest can teach him that I can't.'

'But what will he do when you are away in Naples?' she asked with genuine concern in her voice.

'He can come with me on my trips, can't he? He will learn more about business and life in general than he ever will from that old priest. Anyway, I want to improve his grasp of the English language, and he will never do that as things stand.'

'Well I agree we can't leave him under the control of the Bishop so if you think you can teach him all he needs then I am all for it. Just promise me one thing Nathaniel.'

'What's that?'

'If you ever think you are out of your depth you will find a good replacement tutor immediately.'

'Of course I will my darling. I promise.'

'Well if you think you can do it then you should start immediately. I am sure Samuel will be pleased as he is not too keen on the way that priest bosses him around.'

***

Nathaniel took to his new task with gusto and Samuel proved to be a quick learner who really enjoyed the variety of learning in a mainly practical situation. He found the random way that his father introduced topics to fit with the family and business routines was a pleasant change from the formal learning he had experienced with the priest. Lessons included topics which the old priest would have heartily disapproved particularly religious studies which were now firmly based on the teachings of the English gospel. Nathaniel completely ignored the fact that Samuel had been baptised into the Catholic Church.

The Bishop, however, was incandescent with rage and soon called the old priest to the Palace. 'What the hell do you think you have been doing?' shouted Rocco as he stomped up and down in front of the poor old cowering priest. 'You were in the perfect place to influence the child and you messed up. You knew what I required and you ignored my instructions…'

'But I…'

'Don't interrupt me I haven't finished yet! I told you to guide the boy gradually down the path of the importance of marriage and so that eventually he could see the error of his parents ways and persuade them to get married.'

'But that's exac…'

'You were in the ideal situation to influence the boy and you messed up you stupid old fool.'

'I am ver….'

'Be quiet and get out of here you snivelling idiot until I decide what to do with you. Now, GO!'

***

Nathaniel also took Samuel with him on his trips to Naples and gradually introduced him into the intricacies of running a successful business. The visits to the warehouses in Naples were exciting times for the young

385

Samuel and he occasionally spent several weeks at a time under Marco's supervision while staying with his family.

Time flew by for Nathaniel and in turn Samuel continued to be an able student and a very quick learner. He soon became fluent in English and also developed business skills that Nathaniel hadn't even thought of at his age.

The time between visits to Naples was not wasted, Nathaniel ensured his son was well read and given a grounding in the best English literature.

***

Things didn't always go smoothly however, about a year after Nathaniel had taken up the task of tutoring, a major crisis occurred. Nathaniel and Samuel had been away for a week in Naples and on their return Anna appeared to be somewhat agitated. She steadfastly denied there was a problem but eventually, when they were alone and all the children were in bed, she said, holding back tears 'We have a problem Nathaniel and I am very worried.'

'What is it darling?' he asked, wiping the emerging tears gently from her cheeks. 'Has that bloody Bishop been at it again?'

'No it's not that, it's me. I am expecting again.'

'But that's wonderful, it's not a problem at all.' he responded enthusiastically.

'But Antonino passed away two years ago so things will be totally obvious now, won't they?' she asked, 'and what's more, the Bishop will not let this chance pass without comment will he?'

'I had forgotten about that but I am sure you are right. Still there is absolutely nothing he can do about it, and it will not be obvious for a few months will it?'

'That's true.' replied Anna, 'and we don't need to tell anyone do we?'

***

Several months passed before Bishop Rocco heard that Anna was expecting another child. He had been strolling in the palace gardens and as he passed the time of day in conversation with the head gardener he asked if there had been any parties recently at the 'Pallazzo Inglese.'

I don't think so Sir,' the gardener replied, 'but I don't suppose they will be having any for a while now that Mrs Canale is expecting another baby.'

'What! Is that true? Who told you?' raged the Bishop. 'How the hell do you know?' his questions spat out as his face took on a purple shade and the veins on his neck tensed to form a series of prominent ridges ready to burst through the wrinkled skin.

'Everyone knows Sir, it's obvious.'

'I'll give them obvious,' he shouted, stamping his feet and lashing out at anything or anyone who crossed his path as he stormed off. He crossed the immaculately tended lawn bellowing instructions to anyone within hearing that all the priests were to assemble for a meeting immediately.

386

By the time all the priests had been informed of the hurriedly arranged meeting it was getting dark and Bishop Rocco was absolutely fuming. It was quite late before they were all assembled and most of them were very tired after trekking from all points of the island.

'Where the hell have you all been?' he screamed 'I called this meeting early this afternoon and it is now past my bed time!' but before he had given anyone the chance to answer he carried on with his rant about what had happened and why hadn't he been informed months ago. This went on for over an hour and by the time Rocco had finished no one had escaped his wrath and they were still no the wiser on what was expected of them.

One priest was heard to mutter, 'I think Sir Nathaniel has won this time, Rocco doesn't know what to do next.'

The next morning while Nathaniel was on his morning walk around the harbour, a very tired looking Father Giuseppe approached him and told him all about the meeting. 'I think you have got the better of him this time Sir Nathaniel, he is clueless as to what to do.'

'I doubt it Giuseppe, he will think of something soon. He is most dangerous when he is angry and he is certainly angry now.'

When Nathaniel told Anna about the Bishop's meeting she said, 'We must be extra careful now Nathaniel, you never know what he will do next. He will certainly never baptise our new baby.'

'Don't worry darling we will cross that obstacle when it arrives.'

'Of course we will,' she said giving him a quick kiss on the cheek, 'Oh by the way a packet has arrived for you. I think it is from England.'

'It's from Charles at Grantham,' said Nathaniel as he tore open the seal on the wrapping. 'I wasn't expecting anything for a few months yet. I hope it's not serious.' He sat down and read the letter which was several sheets long and when he had finished, sighed and closed his eyes.

'Is it serious darling? Anna asked.

'It's a bit of a problem but I can easily sort it out.'

'It won't mean you going back to England again will it?' asked a very concerned Anna.

'I told you I will never be going back there Anna so you have no need to worry. Charles tells me the cost of enclosing the Harmston estate is escalating and money is running very low. He urgently needs to know what I think should be done.'

'And what do you think should be done?'

'I will take my time making a decision but it will be easily solved.'

'We will not run out of money will we darling?'

'Of course not, we could live comfortably for the rest of our lives on the income from our businesses in Naples and Livorno.'

'Well that's a relief.'

Nathaniel took a cup of coffee into his study, sat at his desk and tried to think of the best way to solve the problem. Despite his outward appearance of being in control he was extremely worried about how the situation at Harmston should have deteriorated so quickly. Whilst he knew enclosure of the estate was going to cost money, it should never be a drain on the finances, certainly not enough to cause financial difficulties.

The thought briefly crossed Nathaniel's mind that he should go back to England to try to sort things out but quickly dismissed it. 'I said I was never going back and I am not changing my mind at the first signs of a problem. I don't suppose I could make any difference if I was there anyway.'

He closed his eyes and leant back in his chair, 'Let me think,' he said, 'What would I do if I was there?'

There was a light tapping on his study door and Nathaniel opened his eyes and rubbed them vigorously before saying, 'come in.'

'Are you alright darling?' Anna asked as she entered the room, 'you have been in here hours.'

'Yes I am fine I have just been thinking about Charles' letter. I can't understand why they are in financial trouble but whatever, I will have to give them some sort of guidance on what they can do'

'Have you come to any decisions then?'

'I think so. I know there are a couple of the leaseholders who want to own their own farms if they can and so we might be able to raise enough money to get the enclosures finished by selling some leases. Nevertheless I would like more information from Charles before we do anything rash.'

'What sort of information?'

'I need to know why the money is running out so quickly and why it has suddenly got so serious. I also need to know exactly how much has been completed and how much it will cost to complete the job.'

'Do you trust Charles, Nathaniel?'

'Implicitly. And I trust Kenneth Parman the estate manager at Harmston equally.'

'Well then, I think you should get a letter off to them today, if not sooner.'

'I will darling I can't afford to waste a moment.'

***

Nathaniel pondered over his letter to Charles before eventually writing it and the sun was rising over the calm blue sea before he had finally finished. Anna was still asleep when he went down to the harbour to send it on the first leg of its long journey. 'I just hope there is a boat leaving for England very soon,' he thought, 'we can't afford to waste too much time.'

About two weeks later he received another package from Charles which was accompanied by a note from Marco in Naples saying the package he had sent for England had only just managed to be despatched on the boat that brought this package. There had been no other sailings to England for weeks.

***

Nathaniel sat down and carefully opened the package and a tight roll of farm records spilled out on to the table. 'Charles must have read my thoughts,' he said as Anna sat watching him unroll the bundle. 'This seems to be exactly what I have asked him in the last note I sent.'

'Isn't there a letter?' asked Anna as Nathaniel extracted a document from the centre of the roll.

'This looks like it,' muttered Nathaniel flattening out the paper with the back of his hand.

He read through the letter as Anna sat fidgeting impatiently on the other side of the table. She couldn't contain herself and finally asked, 'Is there another problem darling?'

'Not really, he apologises for not explaining things in more detail in his last letter and has made things a lot clearer. The cost of enclosure of the estate at Harmston has far exceeded the initial forecast mainly due extra labour that had to be employed. However, the work at Harmston is now complete and he has put things on hold until he hears from me.

'What are you going to do darling, if it is so expensive, is it going to be worth carrying on elsewhere?'

'Well Charles has suggested that the costs of carrying on could probably be covered by selling the leases of two or three of the farms but he says that Kenneth Parman has reported that the benefits gained do not seem to be worth the costs incurred. He also said that the tenants who live in the area already enclosed are not very happy with what has happened.'

'Didn't you say that you told them that the workforce and the tenants were not to be upset.'

'Indeed I did and I am not too happy to hear that has happened. I know we could have never completed the task without some disruption but I will write back immediately and tell Charles to abandon the whole project. The costs are too heavy, the workforce is unhappy and the benefits gained are less than forecast so why are we doing it?'

Chapter 38
1758 – 1761

In March, after a couple of false alarms, Anna gave birth to a lovely healthy daughter who they decided to call Natale. Nathaniel was absolutely delighted and promptly told everyone he met how pleased he was to have such a lovely new daughter and how Anna had come through so well.

Bishop Rocco was, of course, livid. He had been unwell for a few months and had been unable to concentrate on his campaign to convert Nathaniel to Catholicism. Although he knew the birth was inevitable, when the news finally came he flew into a violent rage. The poor priest who was unfortunate enough to have to break the tidings, left the Chamber with blood pouring from a wound in the head caused by a brass candlestick thrown by the furious Bishop.

'Come back here!' screamed the raging Bishop as the priest, holding his injured head, started to go to the door, 'where the hell do you think you are going?'

'To get a bandage for my injured head.' replied the priest holding a cloth to his bleeding wound.

'Well get over here and help me out of bed you idle lout, and don't bleed all over my bed.' he screamed.

Eventually, after a long struggle the priest managed to get the Bishop out of bed and dressed, and then send a message to all priests ordering them to attend a meeting immediately.

'No one is excused!' was the Bishop's final instruction as the priest staggered from the room, blood still running down his forehead.

***

Once again Nathaniel heard about the meeting and its contents early the next morning, in fact by the time he was ready for lunch, three different priests had called in to brief him.

It was the same old story, Rocco had ranted and raved for over an hour but there were no new strategies to implement. The number of threats had increased and of course were largely being ignored by the priests who by now were sick of the whole affair.

Rocco was becoming increasingly isolated from his priests and this was highlighted by three priests who independently told Nathaniel they were willing to risk the wrath of the bishop by offering to baptise Natale without Rocco's knowledge.

***

By the time the year ended, Nathaniel regarded it as a successful one. Having sorted out the problems in England, managed to get Natale baptised without the Bishop knowing and young Samuel progressing extremely well with his education, the only thing that was beginning to worry Nathaniel was that as winter had approached and the weather cooled down, he was beginning to feel signs of his old problem with his joints. He had survived several years with no problems but he was now suffering a certain amount of pain in his legs and hips and it was starting to spoil his walks around the lanes. He also realised he was spending more time in his chair on the patio overlooking the sea. 'I must make an effort to get out more, 'he thought. 'If I don't keep things moving I will seize up.'

***

As Spring approached, Nathaniel realised he was beginning to feel the effects of age and although he had tried to keep active he was still having problems. He had noticed that when out walking his feet seemed as if they were flapping. It was only a minor problem but try as he might, he could do nothing about it. One day after quite a heavy shower he was out walking with Anna and he stepped into a small puddle creating quite a splash to which Anna said sharply, 'For goodness sake Nathaniel, can't you be more careful? You will ruin my dress.'

'I am sorry darling,' he replied 'but I can't help it. I have tried to explain that I am having difficulty controlling my feet these days and it is becoming a bit of a problem.'

Anna brushed her dress and said rather huffily, 'Well just be more careful in future and don't step into puddles. I don't want my lovely dresses ruined'

'Of course not my darling, I am very sorry and I will try my best in future,' was Nathaniel's trite response.

***

Over the next few years Nathaniel's health problems deteriorated. His hands began to shake and he suffered periods of extreme tiredness, but worst of all his balance was causing problems. He had to hold on to things for support and he found that if he wanted to turn quickly he was liable to fall over. He had to have a stick for support wherever he went and if he went out on his own Anna was always very concerned until he returned. Eventually she insisted that he never left the villa without a companion.

Samuel's schooling continued throughout but Nathaniel's involvement was restricted to what could be carried out without leaving the villa. He would give Samuel tasks to do or information to collect from various sources on the island and then discuss the results when he returned.

This method of learning often involved the cooperation of a priest, several of whom were very happy to help and understood Nathaniel's stance on the Catholic Church.

391

When Samuel was about twelve years old he asked his father, 'Papa, why do you dislike the Catholic Church so much?'

'You have been in the Cathedral haven't you son?'

'Yes Papa.'

'What did you think of it?'

'It was very beautiful.'

'In what way did you think it was so beautiful?'

'The paintings and all the gold decorations and the tapestries are so lovely and expensive.'

'And who paid for them?'

'The church of course.'

'And where did the Church get the money from for all that finery?'

'From the people Papa.'

'Of course and even though the people are poor, the Church squeezes every last lira form them to buy more riches and keep the Bishop in his opulent living.'

'But you and Momma have fine clothes and we live very well Papa.'

'Yes we do Samuel and every person who works for me gets paid a fair wage and is treated as a human being. Once they have been paid, they have to declare what they have earned and the Bishop and his henchmen then decide what they are going to take. It can be anything up to a half and if the Bishop so decides then they still come back for more. Do you think that is fair on the people, why even the priests get nothing except food and a bed.'

'I didn't realise that happened Papa.'

'I am not a member of the Catholic Church Samuel, but half of the money I pay in wages goes straight to the coffers of that brigand, the Bishop. He steals it from the poor, the ones who earn it and need it. Do you think that is fair Samuel?'

'No I don't. I think it's a crime Papa.'

'That's why I will never convert to the Catholic faith Samuel, no matter how long the Bishop vows I will. I will go to my grave as I am and the Bishop can go to his private hell.'

Chapter 39
1761 – 1763

Early in December 1761 Nathaniel heard from Charles who informed him that all was well on the estates but that his best friend Mo had passed away suddenly. It had been a complete surprise to everyone as, apart from his damaged leg, he had always been so fit. Fortunately Mo had recruited an able farmhand just after Nathaniel's last visit to England and had trained him to be his successor.

Mo's death weighed heavily on Nathaniel and although he never had any intentions of visiting England again he felt pangs of regret that he never had the chance to have another drink with Mo in the *'The King's Head'* or *'The Five Bells.'* 'Here's to you Mo,' he said as he raised a glass of brandy, 'to the best friend I ever had.'

***

Nathaniel's health showed no signs of improving but he still managed to get to Naples at least once a year to visit the warehouses but he had not been to Livorno for the last four years. Business was continuing to thrive and the young Samuel was spending quite long periods in the Naples warehouses. 'I think he is about ready to have a spell in Livorno, Nathaniel told Anna, 'he hasn't been there yet has he?'

'He's too young to go there on his own Nathaniel, surely you can see that.'

'Well Marco thinks Samuel is capable of running the Naples warehouses already so it would be nothing more than getting to know the place for a few weeks. Besides, being away from home for a while will do him good. After all he *is* thirteen years old and Silvio will take good care of him.'

***

Anna took some persuading to agree to Nathaniel's proposal regarding their young son's trip to Livorno but eventually she agreed, mainly because of Samuel's constant insisting he should go. 'Please let me go Mama, I am old enough and Papa says I will learn a lot if I go.' he begged, 'and Papa is too frail to go so who else is there to check on how things are going?'

After the constant barrage of complaints from Samuel and his repeated nagging, Anna finally had agreed that the young boy could go for a few weeks. However, she insisted that he should be accompanied by an adult for the trip. 'I still don't agree with it Nathaniel and I want a say in who you choose to be his companion.'

'I was already thinking of sending Massimo to Livorno to see how things work there. He has worked for Marco for a while now and has proved to be a reliable young man. I am sure it could be arranged for Samuel to go at the same time darling.

'Well, I like Massimo he is always polite and friendly when I see him and I suppose he is as good as anyone.' replied Anna 'but you know I am not happy sending young Samuel away at such a young age.'

'I know darling but I am sure he will be alright and it will be an adventure for him.' said Nathaniel promptly turning to go and give Samuel the good news.

'...and I want to talk to Massimo before they go.' called Anna as Nathaniel disappeared smartly from the room.

***

Samuel spent three months in Livorno, and to please his mother he had written a letter home every Sunday. He had stayed with Silvio and his family while Massimo had stayed with Fabio's son Roberto and his family. This arrangement had proved beneficial to all concerned both in the two visitors' grasp of the wider business and their general knowledge.

Samuel couldn't wait to tell his mother how wonderful it had been, particularly the trip on the boat. 'It was so exciting, the waves were very high and the boat bounced all over the place and we all got soaked. Massimo was sick and didn't eat for a whole day so I had some of his food but when the waves calmed down he started to eat again.'

'So you enjoyed the boat trip but what was it like at Livorno?' asked Anna.

'Oh, it was alright. Just like Naples really but smaller.'

'Well I am so pleased you are safely home Samuel, I was very worried about you and I was thinking of you all the time.'

'There was no need to worry Mamma I was perfectly alright; I was looked after very well by everyone there.'

I am sure you were Samuel, but I just can't help it.' said Anna hugging her son. It's wonderful to have you back.'

'Is Papa unwell, he looks very tired to me?' asked Samuel with concern in his voice.

'I think he is feeling the pains in his joints more than ever and he is finding it more difficult to get around. Don't for goodness sake mention it to him as he is trying to hide his problems by putting on a brave face.'

***

Later, after Nathaniel had talked to Samuel, he wondered if it had been beneficial sending the boy to Livorno as the only thing he seemed to remember was the boat trip. 'At least he has met all the people up there and he has identified a few minor differences in the way they do things.' he told Anna.

'Yes and he seems to have grown up in some ways. I think you did the right thing darling, he has returned more of a man than a boy.' replied Anna.

***

Early in the Spring of 1763 Nathaniel was pleased that the weather was gradually getting warmer. He had suffered badly with the pains in his hips and knees but was thankful that he had moved from Lincolnshire and its cold freezing winters. As he sat in his chair on the patio he mused, 'At least the warm weather here in Italy has kept the pains at bay for nearly twenty years. I am sure I would have been in my grave by now if I had stayed there.'

'Are you talking to yourself again Nathaniel,' asked Anna as she brought him a glass of wine, I thought you had a visitor.'

'No visitor darling, I was just talking aloud remembering the cold icy winters they suffer in Lincolnshire.'

'Do you ever wish you were back there?'

'Never! Everyone and everything I love is here in Capri. What sort of fool would wish otherwise?'

As they sat quietly drinking their wine and watching the sun go down over the calm, pale blue shimmering sea Anna asked, 'How are you feeling darling, you never say much but I can tell you are in pain?'

'It's just a problem that comes with old age which I am sure happens to everyone.'

'Don't be silly my love, you are not old yet.'

'I might not be old but before this year is over I will be sixty so I can't call myself a young man anymore.'

'You will always be my young man Nathaniel and I hope I will always be your young lady.' replied Anna brushing a tear from her eye.

'Talking of young ladies,' said Nathaniel, 'what are the young girls going to do? Don't you think they should be looking out for a suitable man, after all Maria is almost twenty six years old, Nancy is twenty four and Anna is twenty two. As far as I know none of them seems at all interested.

That's true darling but it is up to a suitable man to ask for their hand, not for the girls to chase the boys. Don't you remember that far back?' she replied with chuckle.

'I suppose you are right again.' replied Nathaniel as he leant back in his chair and took another sip of his wine.

Anna reached out and squeezed Nathaniel's hand and they sat quietly as the sun gradually sank over the distant horizon in a blaze of glorious reds and orange hues.

***

Nathaniel only made one trip to Naples during the year and on his return he told Anna that he didn't think he would be going again. 'I found it very painful getting on and off the boat and had to be helped nearly everywhere I went. As well as the pain I found I had great difficulty with my balance and tended to stumble regularly. I even fell over twice and both times it was on level ground.'

'Did you hurt yourself darling?'

'Not really, just my pride and a couple of bruises.'

'Did you use your stick?'

'Of course I did – most of the time.'

'Well you *WILL* use your stick here or you will be in real trouble from me.' said Anna rather forcibly.

***

'I have been thinking darling, I feel it's about time we had another party.' said Anna. 'It's been ages since we last had one.'

'What a good idea, when shall we hold it?' replied an enthusiastic Nathaniel.

'I thought it would lovely to celebrate your sixtieth birthday in November and invite all our friends and neighbours and of course all your colleagues from Naples and Livorno.'

'I agree and we have a couple of months to organise it and give every one ample notice. Let's do it, it will be a good opportunity to invite some eligible young men to keep the girls happy.'

'You are incorrigible Nathaniel, but are you sure you will be well enough to enjoy a hectic party?'

'Of course I will. Even if I stay in my bed we can put the bed in the middle of the piazza and I will enjoy it from there.'

***

Nathaniel spent the next few months organising what he hoped would be the most talked about party ever held on Capri. No expense was spared and a guest list of over two hundred people was prepared and invitations sent out. After strong objections from Anna, Bishop Rocco was included when Nathaniel explained his plans to humiliate him if he should turn up. 'Promise you will be very careful Nathaniel, you know how he holds a grudge and we don't want to make things any more difficult than they already are, do we?'

'Don't worry darling, I know what I am doing but I expect he will send a refusal well before the event.'

'You are probably right but I don't want him spoiling the party.'

'Neither do I but if he doesn't come I have another plan ready.'

396

Chapter 40

1763 – 1764

Although Nathaniel had suffered considerably with pains in his legs and hips throughout the party he was delighted with the way it was received. The Bishop failed to turn up – as expected - but he wasn't missed as only a few of the guests knew that he had been invited. Everyone went away happy and once again a party at the *Palazzo* was the talk of the island.

'Did our lovely daughters enjoy themselves?' Nathaniel asked Anna when all the guests had departed.

'Both Nancy and Anna were very excited and got on very well with Mr Desiderio's two sons and I am sure they will want you to invite them back fairly soon.'

'And what about Maria, did she meet anyone she liked?'

'I don't think so, she is always so quiet you never know what she is thinking do you?'

'No you don't, I doubt if she will ever get a man and I sometimes doubt if she is even interested.'

'Have you thought any more about what you said about the Bishop, Nathaniel?'

'Yes I have darling but I am not quite ready to sort him out just yet. I think I am ready for a good night's sleep now, aren't you?'

***

By early February Nathaniel told Anna he was ready to deal with his old adversary, Bishop Rocco and he would require some help to put his plan into operation. 'What I need to do is sow the seeds into Rocco's mind that I am ready to convert to Catholicism.'

'He will never believe you,' replied an astonished Anna, 'not in a million years.'

'I am sure he will, he has spent all his waking hours trying to get me to convert and he will not pass up the chance to think he was right all along.'

'You might be right Nathaniel but how can I help. I can't just go and tell everyone that you have changed your mind, can I?'

'No, we will have to go very carefully. I think we should drop a few hints when we know we can be overheard to suggest that I am considering conversion. Over time, if enough people overhear us it will eventually get back to Rocco.'

'What do you think he will do if he believes the rumours?'

'I think he will almost certainly invite me to the Palace.'

'So you will go there then. You know you swore you would never set foot in the place.'

'Of course I won't, he will come here when I am ready.'

'What makes you think he will come here? How are you going to get him to come, you can't force him can you?' said an exasperated Anna, puzzled by Nathaniel's argument.

'You will just have to wait, won't you?' grinned Nathaniel 'I will tell you when I am ready but I know it's an opportunity he won't be able to resist.'

***

It was nearly six weeks before one of his old friends asked Nathaniel if the rumour that he was going to convert was true. 'It's working,' he thought. 'I will soon be hearing from the Bishop.'

About ten days later one of the priests called to see Nathaniel with a request saying that the Bishop cordially invited Nathaniel to the Palace to discuss topics of mutual interest. After reading the short note he scribed a reply thanking the Bishop but politely rejecting the offer saying that he did not think there was any topic of mutual interest that he could think of and that any meeting would be a waste of both 'yours and my time.'

After the priest had gone, Anna came into the study and found Nathaniel sitting with a glass of wine in his hand and a wide grin on his face. 'He's on the hook Anna, I told you he would bite. Now I can play him like a trout on a line, so let the fun begin!'

***

Nathaniel's problems with his health did not seem to be improving and he was spending more time in his chair watching the world go by. In early June, as the rumours continued and speculation grew, Bishop Rocco sent another request asking for urgent discussions on a topic of mutual interest. Again Nathaniel politely refused and told Anna it was time to spring the trap and get the Bishop to visit the *Palazzo Inglese.*

'How are you going to lure him out of his lair Nathaniel, you know he has always refused so far?'

'He knows I am not a well man and would not be surprised if I should be confined to my bed, so that is what I am going to do.'

'You don't think that will work do you? You know he will still refuse to come.'

'You are probably right, that is why I will let it be known that I am keen to get it sorted before I pass on.'

'You are not going to pass on for ages Nathaniel, don't be so morbid.'

'I know that and you know that, but Rocco only believes what he wants to believe. He won't be able to keep away.'

'What are you going to say if he does turn up?'

'I have plans and I think you will enjoy what I have to say darling. This is going to be something old Rocco will never forget.'

***

It was the last week in June when Nathaniel welcomed a priest who brought a message from the Bishop. Nathaniel had been informed that the visit was imminent and had made sure he was in bed and looking suitably ill when the priest arrived.

Anna ushered the messenger into Nathaniel's bedchamber and said 'Sir Nathaniel is very poorly so please don't stay very long or cause him any unnecessary stress.'

'I won't be long but I hope he has a message for the Bishop,' replied the priest.

Anna approached Nathaniel's bed and gently touched his shoulder. 'Are you awake darling,' she said. 'There is a message from Bishop Rocco.'

'What the hell does he want?' Nathaniel asked in a quiet, painful voice making sure he kept his head and face out of sight under the covers.

'Bishop Rocco says he is very sorry to hear about your state of health and asks if it would be convenient to visit you this afternoon to discuss a topic of mutual interest.' replied the priest.

Still keeping his face well hidden, Nathaniel said hesitantly, 'Yes, but only if he knows he can't stay long. I get tired very quickly.'

'I am sure he understands.' said the priest, and before he could say any more Anna, led him out of the room.

***

'How do you think that went darling?' asked Nathaniel. 'The nasty old tyrant is going to get a dose of his own medicine this afternoon.'

'Just you be careful Nathaniel and don't lose your temper. Remember you are not well.' she said as she helped him out of the bed. 'Anyway, what are you going to say to him?'

'Just wait and see. I am sure you will enjoy it, and by the way would you make sure all the chairs are removed from the room as I don't want him getting too comfortable.'

***

The Bishop arrived mid-afternoon accompanied by two of his senior priests and Anna showed them into Nathaniel's room where he was asleep. Anna woke him gently and the Bishop watched in silence as Anna carefully helped him sit up and plumped his pillows to make him comfortable. 'Can you get me a glass of water please?' he asked, and Anna disappeared and after quite some time, returned with the water. She held the glass for him as he took a sip and re-arranged his pillows before Nathaniel said, 'Good afternoon Bishop, it's so nice to see you after all this time. What can I do for you?'

The Bishop was direct in his intentions; he said 'I have come here at last, to discuss your conversion to the Catholic religion.'

'Well, you will have to be patient; we will discuss that "bye and bye" as I have a few other things to say to you before we get to that subject.'

399

'What other things?'

'First, I understand you sent a letter to Rome complaining about my behaviour. Is that correct?'

'Who told you that?'

'That's a yes then. And my good friend Antonino threatened to write to Rome about your refusal to baptise young Samuel?'

'I don't know anything about that.'

'And then there is the constant harassment you have conducted against the Canale's and myself ever since we came to Capri'

At this, the Bishop started to clench his fists and his face started signs of turning a deep shade of purple. 'That's all hearsay and vicious rumours, there is no truth in it whatsoever.' he shouted.

'It seems I have touched a raw nerve doesn't it and we all know that everything I have said so far is true.'

'Its absolute rubbish and what do you think you can do about it? No one will believe you and all your lies.'

'That remains to be seen, I expect an answer from Rome any day now.'

The Bishop lost his temper exactly as Nathaniel had expected, he kicked at the bed and shouted; 'You would never write to His Holiness and tell him all that rubbish.'

'I already have and also told him a great deal more.'

'What other lies have you told him?'

'Oh, there are the clandestine visits you make to married ladies when their husbands are at work. There is the graveyard outside the Nuns quarters at the palace where babies are buried in the dead of night. The extortionate taxes you impose on every working man on this island to make sure they remain in poverty and you live in luxury. Do you want me to go on?'

A fuming Rocco had heard all he wanted to and started to leave the room. 'Just before you go Bishop, you are fully aware that I will never convert to your religion while there are men like you in positions of power. You are an arrogant, self-important, ignorant bully and now that the Pope is aware of what is going on I am sure you will be receiving a message from him in the near future.'

As the Bishop left the room he slammed the door and thumped the nearest priest as hard as he could.

'Did you really write to the Holy Father Nathaniel?'

'Of course not darling, but it won't hurt him to sweat a bit will it?

***

A week or so after the meeting, Nathaniel began to hear rumours that Rocco had requested an audience with the Pope to try to explain his actions and dispel lies which were circulating the island. This seemed to have worked when Rocco, unannounced, headed a procession to the harbour and sailed off

400

to Naples with his entourage and a cartload of baggage.

From his seat on the patio, Nathaniel called Anna to, 'Come out here and see this darling, it's true, he's off to see the Pope.'

'What do you think he will say?'

'I don't know but I would love to be there hearing all his excuses and lies, especially when he finds out the Pope has no idea what he is talking about.'

Chapter 41

August 1764

All through the latter days of July the island had experienced very high temperatures and the oppressive heat had continued into August. Nathaniel was finding great difficulty in breathing and keeping cool was impossible. He found simple tasks and even moving around was becoming impossible and eventually he had had to employ a full time personal helper. He spent most of his days in his chair on the patio either reading or sleeping and very rarely had any visitors as he found it very difficult to concentrate for long.

Anna was extremely worried about him and eventually after some very heated discussions she finally persuaded Nathaniel to agree to a visit from the apothecary, Roberto Mancini.

When Roberto arrived, Anna took him aside and told him of her concerns and said, 'I really hope you can do something Roberto, I have never seen him like this. He looks so poorly and I am really worried.'

'Don't worry yourself Mrs Canale, I am sure I can find something to help him but I must see him first.'

'Of course you must, just come with me. He is out on the patio.'

***

Nathaniel was asleep when Roberto approached and he was very surprised at how old he looked. 'Gosh, he has aged a lot since I last saw him,' thought Roberto, 'this is a lot worse than I expected.'

Anna gently woke Nathaniel by kissing him on his forehead saying, 'Nathaniel, Roberto is here to see you darling.'

Roberto had a long but difficult discussion with Nathaniel trying to get to know exactly what the problem was and eventually said, 'I am going back to my premises Nathaniel and will prepare some medicine to help you with your breathing. It will not taste very nice but you must have a spoonful when you wake in the morning, another at midday and one last thing in the evening. If you are still having problems when you have used it all, let me know and I will get you some more.' and then, 'Mrs Canale, will you make sure he takes it all as I have instructed? It will take time to work properly.'

'Of course I will Roberto, I know he can be stubborn but he *will* take it.'

***

The next few weeks were very stressful for the Canale family. Nathaniel's health showed no signs of improvement. Roberto was a regular visitor to the palazzo and Anna and the children hardly left Nathaniel's bedside.

'He's getting worse isn't he Roberto, what else can you do?' sobbed Anna.

'I have tried everything I know Mrs Canale. It is very worrying.'

'He is dying isn't he?' she said with tears flooding down her cheeks.

'I don't know, but he is incapable of swallowing anything and that is a very bad sign. I am afraid that if this continues you and your family must prepare for the worst. '

***

Anna stayed the night in a chair by Nathaniel's bed and was so worried about him that she sent a messenger to find father Giuseppe. 'You must be very careful not to let anyone know what you are doing or where you are going, we don't want to get him into trouble.'

When the messenger returned he said Father Giuseppe was on his way but he would come to the back door as he didn't want to be seen and he also said that the rumours were doing the rounds and saying that Nathaniel had already passed on.

When father Giuseppe arrived he said, 'I had great difficulty in getting here unseen, people are beginning to gather at the bottom of the drive, they believe the rumours that are already circulating.'

'Thank you for coming Giuseppe. I know Nathaniel is not of your faith but he said he would like a few words with you and I am sure he would appreciate a few words of comfort from you.'

'Of course I will,' he said as he knelt beside the bed and took Nathaniel's hand in his, 'it would be an honour to comfort my friend in his hour of need, but first I have some very important news to tell him, and you Anna.'

'What's happened Giuseppe?' asked Anna anxiously.

'When I got your message to call round, I was just getting ready to visit you. I have heard this very morning that your dear friend Rocco is no longer the Bishop of Capri. He has been replaced by Bishop Phillippe from Naples. In fact you probably met him before you came to Capri yourselves, he was Father Phillippe then.

'Did you hear that Nathaniel? Rocco's gone for ever.

Nathaniel slowly opened his eyes, smiled and said in a soft, quiet voice, 'Yes I know Phillippe, he is a good man and will be good for the island. He paused and squeezed the priests hand and said in no more than a whisper, 'Thank you for everything you have done for our family Giuseppe. You are an honourable man who has been working under a regime which is nothing more than a disgrace to the lovely people of this beautiful island.'

'Thank you for those kind words Nathaniel. Would you like me to say a small, appropriate prayer before I leave?'

It would be an honour Giuseppe, please do.'

After a short spoken prayer, Giuseppe prayed silently before releasing his friends hand and saying a final goodbye. As he left the room with tears in

403

his eyes, he said to Anna, 'He asked that you gather all the family together and come and see him now. I fear the end is near.'

***

The family were already gathered together waiting for the inevitable when Anna asked them to come with her to Nathaniel's room. Nathaniel was propped up on his pillows and his head, leaning to one side with both eyes closed and his mouth wide open, looked thin and lifeless. Two of the girls thought he had already passed on and instantly burst into floods of tears. Nathaniel gradually opened his eyes and said slowly in a pale, croaky voice, 'Calm down girls, I haven't gone yet.'

They all tried to laugh but it was obvious that their father was very close to death. When he spoke his voice was strained and showed the signs of the effort he had to make to be heard. He raised a frail hand to indicate to them to come closer and with extreme effort and many pauses to get his breath, he explained to Samuel he must promise to take on the duties of 'man of the house' and look after his mother and sisters.

Samuel clutched his father's hand and with tears streaming down his cheeks and trying his hardest not to be seen crying, promised to do his best.

'Thank you son, you are man now,' and reaching up he tousled Samuel's hair with his thin bony hand saying 'as long as you do your best that's all I can ask.'

He closed his eyes again and after what seemed an age he whispered, 'Kiss me Anna my darling. I have always loved you and you have brought me joy for these many years.'

Anna took his outstretched hand and kissed him gently on his forehead, 'I love you too my sweetheart, I always have.'

Nathaniel smiled gently, sighed heavily and closed his eyes for the very last time.

Epilogue

Nathaniel had passed away on 28ᵗʰ August 1764 and immediately after his death Anna consulted Father Giuseppe to discuss what they should do about the burial. She was very concerned that he would not be able to have a religious service nor could he be buried in consecrated ground on the island. His not being of the Catholic faith barred him from access to any such ceremony.

'What am I going to do Father Giuseppe,' she sobbed, 'is there any way you can help me?'

Giuseppe gradually eased Anna's concern by explaining that she was perfectly entitled to bury Nathaniel wherever she liked and after further discussion it was decided that a suitable place in Nathaniel's beloved vineyard would be ideal. As to the religious service Giuseppe said he would be willing to say a few words at the burial, provided that it was kept as quiet as possible and none of the local population would be at the ceremony.

To try to deflect any concern the local population might have about a burial with no religious input, the rumour was spread that a friend of Nathaniel's, an English priest from Naples would conduct the service. This ploy seemed to work and Nathaniel was buried in a very simple ceremony in a quiet corner of the vineyard overlooking the blue Mediterranean Sea.

**

A few days after the burial Anna suddenly went into a state of panic when she realised that Nathaniel had not made a will. She had a very restless night and thought the best thing she could do was to get one written, and the quicker it was done, the better. If there was no will, because she was not married to Nathaniel she would be entitled to nothing.

She summoned a clerk named Michele Pagano to do the deed and he set it out in his most elegant Italian stating that *'Sir Nathaniel, bed ridden and bodily weak, but through the grace of God, of sound mind, clear in speech and thought, and both able to understand and speak Italian.....had bidden him to make out this will by which he leaves all his worldly possessions (specified in full detail) to Anna de la Noce.'*

Unfortunately for Anna, two authentic wills were found later, one had been left with his partners in Naples for safe keeping and the other had been written on his last visit to London.

The main thrust of the wills said that Anna and her children inherited the villa on Capri and Nathaniel's share of the Italian business. However, Nathaniel himself was to be buried in the church at Harmston and that a suitable monument be erected in his honour in the above church.

All of estates in England were left to Anna's son Samuel provided that;

405

'1) Samuel shall go to England and convert to the Protestant religion.

2) On attaining the age of twenty one he shall petition Parliament to change his nationality to English enabling him to use the name Thorold.

3) On meeting these requirements he will inherit all the estates as defined in the will, from the trustees.'

***

On 20th May 1765 an order was made by the Master of the Rolls, giving authority to appoint an agent in Naples to ensure the wishes of the will were carried out. The young Samuel, still a minor, was to be placed under the legal guardianship of England's Lord Chancellor, The Lord Camden, and the agent would ensure the youth and Sir Nathaniel's remains were transported to England.

Meanwhile Anna had settled into a relaxed routine but when she heard of the imminent visit of the Lord Chancellors representative she went into a panic. She knew the young Samuel would eventually have to go and she was actually pleased for him but she hadn't expected her beloved Nathaniel being taken away.

Despite Nathaniel's statement in his will wanting to be buried at Harmston, Anna was determined that he was going to stay where he was. 'He is not going to leave here,' raged Anna, 'he always said he would never leave, so he is not going,' She hatched a plan to ensure Nathaniel would not be disturbed and put it into action immediately by instructing her gardeners to remove all the decorations from Nathaniel's grave and cover it with rubbish to disguise it from a casual observer. They were then to go to the grave on the other side of the vineyard where an old hermit was buried and, 'make it look as if was Sir Nathaniel's. We can put Sir Nathaniel's grave back when the agent has gone'

The agent duly arrived and when he asked Anna where Sir Nathaniel was buried she said she didn't know but it was, 'Somewhere in the Vineyard.'

'But surely you visit his grave, don't you?'

'I haven't been there for some time, it's too upsetting. You will have to ask the gardener to show you.'

***

As a result of these bequests, the young Samuel came to England and in due course met all the requirements of the will and claimed his inheritance.

A body was removed from Capri and it is assumed that it was taken on board a ship but there is no sign of either a grave or a monument to Sir Nathaniel in Harmston Church.

There is also no sign of Sir Nathaniel's last resting place on Capri as the vineyard was neglected for over a hundred years and has now been built on.

The Palazzo Inglese, which once had the only swimming pool on Capri, went through many changes over the years. After Nathaniel's death its name was changed to 'Palazzo Canale.' Later, on his arrival on Capri, Ferdinand IV, King of Naples, took up residence there and during the English occupation it became the residence of Hudson Lowe, the Governor of the island. From 1808 to 1815 it was the headquarters of the French and became known as the 'Maison Blanche.'

Subsequently it later changed its name back to Palazzo Canale and is now divided into apartments.

***

Nathaniel's presence in Italy made some interesting additions to the language. His introduction of the stockfish trade in Livorno resulted in "Baccala" becoming well known throughout Italy and "Baccala alla Livornese" soaked and cooked with onions is an inexpensive delicious Friday dish throughout Italy.

***

His expression 'Bye and Bye' as a delaying tactic, particularly when being pressed to convert to Catholicism is still commonly used in Capri as 'Baibai dicette u inglese.'

***

Nathaniel left the Harmston estates in relatively good financial order but over the following years things deteriorated dramatically partly due to his descendants living comfortably off the estate income and a resulting lack of investment. However, probably the main reason was the wording of the extremely complicated and numerous bequests in his wills. Family matters were still being argued in court as late as June 1859, these arguments were directly attributed to convoluted way in which the will of Sir Nathaniel was drafted almost a hundred years previously.